# Praise for *The Armagedd...*

'Full of insight into how the trading floo... surprise from a City journalist of repute,), it never lets up ior a moment. Fresh as today's headlines, it reminds the world just how close it could be to financial meltdown.' – **Geoffrey Wansell**, *Daily Mail*

'Like a digital-age John le Carré, Clem Chambers spins a gripping tale of terrorist apocalypse informed by a deep understanding of financial markets and computer technology' – **Ted Greenwald**, Senior Editor, *Wired Magazine*

'At last, a book where the words finance and thriller truly belong in the same sentence' – **Steve Eckett**, former Barings trader and co-founder of Global Investor Bookshops and Harriman House

'Hit the panic button! A spell-binding look, by a market master at what happens when professional money meets international terrorism. On the outcome of this trading hangs billions of dollars – and millions of lives.' – **Richard L. Hudson**, former Editor of *The Wall Street Journal Europe*, author of *The Misbehaviour of Markets*

'Part science-fiction, part Grisham thriller, *The Armageddon Trade* plays out its doomy prophecies with unerring skill. A real page-turner' – **Mark Campbell**, *Crime Time*

'More shocking than a squirt of lemon juice in the eye' – **Sally Nicoll**, author of the bestselling spread-betting diary, *Bets and the City*

By the same author

*The Armageddon Trade*

Coming soon

*The Excalibur Trade*

# CLEM CHAMBERS

# THE
# TWAIN
# MAXIM

*Dorset Libraries*
*Withdrawn Stock*

First Published in hardcover in 2010
This edition published in 2010 by No Exit Press,
P.O.Box 394, Harpenden, Herts, AL5 1XJ
www.noexit.co.uk

ISBN 978-1-84243-341-6

2 4 6 8 10 9 7 5 3 1

Typeset by Avocet Typeset, Chilton, Aylesbury, Bucks
Printed and bound in Great Britain by
Cox & Wyman, Reading, Berks

To my mother

with thanks to:
Ion and Annette
Hazel and Claire
Fran and Chris
And Brian for the Platinum bullet.

'A mine is a hole in the ground with a fool at the bottom and a crook at the top.'

*Mark Twain*

*March 1900*

Samuel Clemens gazed up at the Royal Exchange, its sooty face imposing and fierce. "It seems strange to me that in two years New York will house its market in a yet mightier building."

"Humbug, Mr Twain," said the publisher. "As robust as you Yankees are becoming, the power of the British Empire will remain greater."

Clemens smiled beneath his droopy white moustache.

A man in a pork-pie hat ran up to them, panting like a dog. "Mr Twain – Mr Twain! May I introduce myself? My name is Phineas Crouch. I'm a stockbroker and a great admirer of your work. I would like to offer you," he said, catching his breath, "as humble thanks," he gulped, "an opportunity to invest in a most exciting mining promotion in South Africa." He seemed almost overcome with excitement. "It's a truly remarkable opportunity and I can make it conveniently available to you."

The sun was setting behind the iron-grey clouds and the gas lights were being lit. A shabby man was shovelling horse dung into a little cart. Clemens looked at the broker and allowed himself a private smirk. "You know, son, a mine is a hole in the ground with a fool at the bottom and a crook at the top. Excuse me if I don't take you up on your kind offer."

The publisher frowned at the broker and they walked on.

"The best way to ruin a good gold mine," continued Clemens, "is to start the digging." He chuckled.

7

*April 2008*

It was cold. The air con was never bloody right. Baz's head was throbbing – he'd drunk too much whisky the night before. The woman curled up on the far side of the bed had most of the duvet. He threw back what remained over him, got up and walked slowly to a white wicker chair. His fiftyish body was in reasonable shape, considering the abuse it had received over the years. It was covered with a red-brown fuzz so he resembled an ape. He put on his Bermuda shorts and ambled to the windows.

He drew back the curtains and looked out on to a beautiful Cayman Islands morning. The world outside was chalk white and ultramarine. He pulled back the sliding door, went across the deck and down the wooden stairs to the white sand beach. He could feel the sun on his chest and the heat filling his torso. He arched his back, arms outstretched. 'Thank you, God,' he said, as he waded into the sea.

After a few minutes in the warm water he returned to the house. The tart was standing at the window, wrapped in a gauzy piece of linen. He was smiling at her as he ran up the stairs, sand falling off his feet. She passed him a towel. "Thank you, lovely," he said.

"Do you want me to stay for another week?" she asked.

"It depends," he said, trying to empty the water out of his right ear into the towel. His head cocked, he gave her a mischievous look. "On how much it's going to cost me."

"The same," she said, without a flicker of emotion.

"Baby, I'd have another week for ten thousand but not twenty."

"That's all right, darling," she said, turning slowly away.

"I understand. Perhaps another time?"

He chuckled. "Yeah, another time." He bent down and caught the hem of her wrap. "But seeing as you're here until lunch, I should make the most of you." He pulled on the sheet and she let it fall away from her. Naked, she struck a pose like Botticelli's Venus on the shell. He stepped up on to the deck and dropped his wet trunks. She took his hand and led him towards the bedroom.

*May 2008*

Baz hated the Internet. When he typed his name into Google it brought up way too much information about him and his dealings – far more than he was comfortable with. You might need to be some kind of stalker to spend days piecing the patchwork together, but if you did it wouldn't show the sort of picture he wanted.

Baz Mycock was a respected mining promoter, or so his Filipino web team had sprinkled liberally around the Net, but even that designation gave a clue as to what he did. Pop venues had promoters, and dodgy selling practices were called promotions, so at best "promoter" might be seen as a nice word for "pimp". In reality, it was a nice word for "scammer". Mining promoters, however, fulfilled a need. Just like a real pimp, they sold product to a desperate and grateful audience – the gambling fraternity who bet on volatile stocks.

An Arabian thoroughbred was designed to race not to transport, and in much the same way his promotions were meant to trade violently and not necessarily turn into mines. The stupid, greedy rich wanted their fun and he provided it.

He double-checked his BlackBerry. It listed all his contacts. He checked the DVD again; all his contacts were there too.

He ejected the DVD – didn't bother to close down the computer – then took out the power cord and mouse. He walked from the study into the bedroom and out on to the deck, then went down the stairs to the hot sand. There was only so much shagging and swimming he could bear. It was time to start the next deal. He hopped up on to the jetty and walked to the end. Notebook under his arm, he climbed down into the speedboat, cast off and drove into deep water.

The gentle waves slopped against the hull as the speedboat wallowed, powerless, the engine gurgling. Baz tossed his notebook overboard. Its LEDs flashed red and green as it spun through the air, then plopped into the water; a plastic capsule of toxic metals. He pulled the accelerator handle and turned the boat hard right. The last repository of undeniable truth about his last operation was now gone for good. Anything left was hearsay.

The water fizzed as the bow of the boat carved through it and the smell of brine filled his nostrils. "Game on," he shouted to the world.

## October 2008

"Not now, love," said Baz, shooing away the scrawny lap-dancer. "Congo, that's where I'm going. Congo's where it's at."

She sat down on the fat leather arm of Ralph's chair. "Shoo," said Ralph, smiling charmingly. "Later, my dear. Give us a few minutes."

Ralph was about Baz's age, fifty, and had been a broker in

dodgy mining stocks all his life. These days, they called people like him "corporate financiers". He had been helped along in his career by his dashing looks and even now – at a distance, in a kind light, through soft gauze – he looked pretty good and might even be mistaken for a man in his twenties. He liked to imagine himself as akin to Oscar Wilde's Dorian Gray. Baz looked like the picture in the attic, his face as worn as a Hell's Angel's leather jacket. Up close, though, Ralph's physiognomy was not that of youth: in the cold hard light of day, the lines of his face showed deep, while his nut-brown hair with its schoolboy cut sat ridiculously on the head of an older man.

"It's the right time."

"It's very flat out there for resource plays," said Ralph. "Mining's completely out of favour, as you know."

"Right," said Baz. "Good time to start winding up a new one."

"Quite," said Ralph, not really agreeing.

"It'll take me a year or so to get the project rolling."

"You'll need a nice parcel of rights this time round," said Ralph, and had a sip of his brandy.

"Right," said Baz. "Got to get something really tasty. Congo's perfect. All the minerals on God's earth are there. The place is jammed with metals. It's just a question of hooking up the right deal."

"A year, you reckon," replied Ralph, happy that Baz wasn't going to ask him to raise money in the worst stock market since 1929.

"Yeah. Right now no one wants deals so no one's doing any. It's a perfect time for me to do some with the Congolese. They're bound to be feeling the pinch. No buckshee like the old days."

"True," said Ralph. "Very true."

"By the time I've got a nice parcel of rights, things'll be picking up and I'll have a lovely mine, all ready for you to raise money for."

"So, you'll want to float the project on the London AIM market in about two years?"

"It should be ready for an IPO by then."

Floating a company on the stock market was when the real fun began. The Initial Public Offering gave anyone the chance to trade its shares. While pre-IPO money raising was the dress rehearsal, the IPO was Baz's scheme's opening night.

"Want a pre-IPO money raise?"

"Of course."

"Pre-pre-IPO money raise?

"Obviously."

"Founders' stock?' He meant the cheap shares handed out at the birth of the deal. It was a promise of free money later.

"Ker, ker, ker." Baz laughed, nodding.

"Warrants, options, convertibles, shadow stock?"

"Ker, ker, ker." Baz raised his glass.

Ralph clinked it. It was going to be another mining ramp from the master. Baz always made "the boys" money while the suckers got utterly fleeced. Every few years he would show up with a new deal. "The boys" would get a nice piece of action and the suckers would take the bait for the umpteenth time and be shafted.

Ralph turned. "Young lady," he called. The five, mainly naked, girls on the stage turned towards them. He stared at the particularly scrawny unhealthy-looking one with the badly enlarged breasts, who swung limply around the central pole. She was dressed in only a light blue spangled thong.

"Yes, you, pretty thing."

She straightened and came towards them in what might have passed for a lazy, seductive strut.

"Sounds like a runner, Baz," said Ralph. "We're in."

Baz was peering at the stage. The short blonde tart was passable. "Good news," he said to Ralph, wagging a finger at her. She caught his drift.

McCoy was a mining engineer. However, his job was not designing mines but validating potential ones. He extrapolated the findings of explorers and outlined the possibilities of deposits that had been sketchily defined by seismic tests, drilling cores and other such geological evidence. It was his rubber stamp that got many a speculative mine off the drawing board and, more often than not, he had to be wildly optimistic about the data he was provided. Optimism was well remunerated by promoters like Baz.

He lived in the middle of a thousand hectares of Canada, in a house many would consider a shack. There, the detritus of a lifetime of mining projects had built up into a clutter only its solitary parent could love.

McCoy filled his whisky glass, put the bottle down and said, "No, mate, no. We want it in Kivu, next to Nyiragongo. It's a pretty much unexplored area in Congo, right on a seismic fault with a fantastic volcano slap-bang in the middle."

Baz topped up his glass. "This volcano, is it hot?"

"Hot?" laughed McCoy. "It blows up every year or two. Big fucking ash clouds everywhere. It's perfect for the gold story."

"Hydrothermal, right?"

"Right. Gold and silver too."

"They love the hydrothermal pitch," said Baz. "'Gold dissolved in water precipitates out in veins,' I tell them, and they get all stressed out. 'Gold can't dissolve in water,' they say. 'Everyone knows *that*. You're having us on.'" He took a slug of whisky. "'Oh, no, Mr Fuckface Fund Manager. Gold dissolves in water at two hundred degrees centigrade, like bath salts in your tub, and in our volcano we have lots of seriously hot water coming from the centre of the earth carrying gold with it. Look it up on Wikipedia!'" He quaked with laughter as McCoy grinned at him. "Brilliant. Once they verify that, they believe anything I tell them."

Sensing his time was right, McCoy said, "I want three mil."

Baz was no longer laughing. "That's twice as much as last time."

"I know, but this is the last job for me. I'm getting too old for it."

Baz stared at the old drunk. He was right: he was too old for the job. "OK, three mil it is, but we've got to have more than gold."

"Copper and rare earths – lots of rare earths. Elements like indium are hundreds of dollars a pound, these days."

"Give me more."

"Diamonds."

"Gold and diamonds?" queried Baz.

"Why not? We find diamond kimberlite and then we find some gold as well. It's a copper mountain with gold veins and a network of kimberlite volcanic pipes in it."

"Like it," said Baz. "With rare earths thrown in."

14

"In the gold veins."

"Platinum?"

"That would be pushing it." McCoy sank his whisky and poured another.

"Come on."

"Cobalt, maybe."

Baz paused. "I like that. We could start with looking for cobalt and trash the share price when we don't find it. Then we come up with the kimberlite."

"And then the gold."

"It's sounding good."

McCoy picked up his pencil and ringed an area on the map where the Democratic Republic of Congo and Rwanda met.

"Up to about ten minutes ago, pretty much since Mobutu fucked off to hell in 'ninety-seven, this whole region has been at constant war. It's been a nightmare of murder, rape, depravity." He jabbed the pencil down to emphasise each word. "It's the perfect place for the hole."

"McCoy, you're a bloody genius."

"I want all the money by IPO."

Baz scowled. "A hundred thousand a year until IPO, a mil on IPO, a mil on the dump and the balance six months after completion."

"A quarter of a mil a year and it's agreed."

"Two hundred a year."

"I want three million or you can find yourself another mining engineer."

"You might be sweet but you aren't unique," said Baz, smiling as he topped up his glass.

McCoy poured himself some more whisky. "Two hundred and fifty K a year et cetera. Can you drink to that?"

"Phah," said Baz, raising his glass. "Why fucking not? You sure we can't have platinum?"

"Yes. No. Yes. No, we can't have platinum."

*February 2011*

Fuck me, thought Baz. It had cost him a hundred euros in bribes just to get through immigration at Kinshasa airport. The arrivals hall was chaos, packed with an impenetrable crowd that seemed intent on keeping the traveller hemmed in. It was as hot and humid as a Turkish bath attendant's armpit.

"Oi, Baz!" called a deep voice he recognised, above the noise of the crowd. "Over 'ere."

He caught sight of a stocky figure in white shorts and a loud Hawaiian shirt.

Thank Christ, he thought. He raised his hand in salute.

Mark Higgins had been a soldier once, a pretty good one. He was not, however, much good in Civvy Street and had found himself quickly back at work in "security". He liked to think of himself as a mercenary, but he didn't do any fighting. He wasn't comfortable with the moniker "bodyguard" – it sounded like a servant with a gun. He liked "security consultant". He consulted by looking mean for his clients in unsavoury spots around the world and by knowing his way about. He found the latter easy – he was naturally attracted to the sleazy underbelly of any city. Once he had that mapped out, the rest of the places were just tourist destinations. His impossibly wide forearms bore dark green tattoos, blurred but military-looking.

"What a shithole," said Baz, by way of greeting.

Higgins smiled, his missing right dog tooth giving the expression a frightening aspect. "What did you expect?"

"I'm getting fucking soft," said Baz. "Too much shagging on the beach."

"Come on, matey, let's vamoose. Mind how you go." Higgins grabbed his heavy case as if it was empty and shouted, "Gangway."

There was a minor explosion of guttural French from the crowd, but it parted as he pushed through.

Baz tucked in behind.

"Come on, out the way," Higgins snarled, carving his way through the chaos. "*Allez*, mate, *allez*."

"Fuck," said Baz, as the door of the Merc slammed, insulating them from the heat, noise and smell of the airport.

"We should have gone to Papua, Marky."

"Would have been a good choice," said Higgins. "Didn't want to say, mate, but when we were here last, and it was called Zaïre, it was fucked. Now it's the Democratic Republic of Congo, it's double-fucked. But you'll get used to it."

"Yeah," said Baz. "A bottle of strong grog, a packet of extra strong condoms, and it'll start to look up."

"There you go," said Higgins, as the car pulled away from what remained of the kerb and out across the uneven road surface.

The ministry building looked and smelt like some godforsaken east European orphanage.

They had been waiting for fifty minutes.

Baz was scowling. "It's always the fucking same, Marky."

"We could be here for days," said Higgins.

"On the hour we're off."

The ten minutes passed slowly. As the second hand swept into the next hour Baz picked up his briefcase and got out an envelope. He pulled a five hundred euro note from his jacket pocket and tore it in half. He put the left half in the envelope and the right half back in his pocket. He put his card in the envelope. He laid the envelope on top of the briefcase and wrote in big block capitals: "LAURENT JALBINYO". He got up, walked over to the receptionist and gave her a big smile. He took out a five thousand Congolese francs note and put it under the envelope. "*S'il vous plaît. La lettre est pour mon ami.*"

She took the envelope and looked very happy indeed. Five thousand francs was three days' pay.

"*À bientot*," he said. "*Merci.*"

The girl said something incomprehensible and Baz turned away. "Let's go," he said to Higgins.

Baz was lying by the hotel pool in the fading evening heat. They had gone on a bender the night before and Higgins hadn't reappeared. Baz was a bit surprised by the no-show but, then, Higgins had been drinking like a drowning man. He'd wait another day for contact from his connection, then start looking for a new one. He took a swig of his Primus beer. He could taste the maize in it.

His BlackBerry began to vibrate on the table in a heavy purr. He watched it for a moment, then snatched it up. No caller ID. "Baz Mycock."

"Mr Mycock…"

Bingo, thought Baz.

"…very sorry about yesterday. There was a mix-up. Oh, my God, so many problems."

"Sorry to hear that. Problems can be expensive."

"I've had a moment to read your proposals and I received your letter. I hope I can meet with you."

"I'm at the Hotel Grand, why not come over?"

"I can be there at lunchtime, if that is convenient for you."

"Fine, see you then."

"Thank you."

Baz hung up quicker than necessary. No one did him any favours by taking his money.

Jalbinyo looked as nervous as a rabbit eating too far from his warren. He was wearing a tired blue suit and his shirt collar was frayed. The flecks of curly white hair on his balding head stood out starkly against his skin. As they sat eating he seemed to be in constant motion, swaying slightly from side to side as if the joints holding him together had been loosened.

He had let Baz do all the talking, laughing, clapping and punctuating Baz's schtick with exclamations. He wasn't drinking enough for Baz's liking.

"Well," said Baz, halfway through his steak, "have you got my letter?"

Jalbinyo looked startled. "Letter?" He patted his suit jacket. "Oh, Jesus, yes."

He pulled out the envelope.

Baz took it, then put the other half of the five hundred euro note into it. He smiled. "Laurent, I need the names of the two best lawyers in town and the best accountant. I want invites to the right parties."

"No problem, my friend."

"But it's the rights I've got to get sorted, and I want to come to an understanding with you."

"I'm listening."

"I need you to look after me and I'll be very grateful if you do."

Jalbinyo nodded, clearly confused. "Very grateful?"

"Yes, very grateful – if I get my rights."

"Magnificent," said Jalbinyo. He squinted. "How do you mean, 'grateful'?"

"Well, I need you to sort out my mineral rights for me. When I have them I'll pay you a hundred thousand euros."

"Oh, Jesus, oh, God." Jalbinyo glanced around furtively. Then he looked back at Baz and smiled suddenly. He leant forwards. "There are lots of costs."

"I know," said Baz, "but none of them gets paid until I have my rights all done, dusted, signed and sealed. Then I'll send you twenty thousand euros a month and you'll take all the running costs from that."

Jalbinyo sat back, pouting reflectively. He seemed about to say something until Baz shot forwards in his chair. "Don't fucking try to negotiate with me," he spat, spraying a little chewed steak from his mouth. "There are fifty friends in fifty countries who'll take that and call me 'sir'. Don't give me any shit. Just say: 'Yes, Baz. Thank you, Baz. That's just perfect, Baz.'"

Jalbinyo sat back. "There are a lot of costs," he said again.

"I know, I know," said Baz, dismissively. "Lots and lots of costs." He paused and scowled. "Look, Laurent, as long as I get no trouble, the money will flow. The moment I get shit it stops. It's a simple relationship."

Jalbinyo clapped. "You are a funny man, Baz."

Baz grinned and nodded. He caught sight of Higgins in the doorway, shook his head and Higgins stayed back. "No,

Laurent, I'm a simple man. DRC is a big place with a capital about as far from the interior as you can get. All I want is forty square miles of useless land next to your country's most dangerous volcano. It's so far away from Kinshasa that it's nearly in Rwanda. Maybe I am funny, but what could be simpler?"

Jalbinyo scratched the right side of his face. He breathed in to speak.

"Don't tell me about costs."

Jalbinyo laughed, clapping his hands in front of his face and holding them there. "Relax, Mr Baz Mycock. I will look after you."

Baz smiled.

"But…"

"No buts."

"But it will take time."

"That's OK."

Jalbinyo held out his hand and Baz shook it.

"Now," said Baz, putting a hand into the briefcase by his seat. "Here are five thousand euros as a float. That's all you'll see from me until I get my rights delivered. I hope it'll speed things along for us."

Jalbinyo took the envelope and put it into his top pocket.

"You see?" said Baz. "I'm a reasonable man." He grinned and nodded at the shadow at the door. "Just don't ever, even for a moment, think I'm stupid."

A bulk in a Hawaiian shirt loomed up and sat down next to him.

"Oh, Jesus," squeaked Jalbinyo.

"No," said Higgins, "it's Mark." He offered his giant hand.

21

Jalbinyo took it as if he was expecting an electric shock.
They shook.
Jalbinyo smiled nervously. "*Enchanté*."
"Ker, ker, ker," cackled Baz.

# 1

Jim Evans knew he was in hospital, he knew he was pretty banged up, but he didn't give a fuck. Whatever it was they were filling him with, it was the nectar of the gods. Submerged, as he was, in sedation and pain relief, the recent past seemed like a fading nightmare, one in which a grenade had nearly torn him in half.

When he fell asleep the nightmare would return and terrify him. He was running down the tunnel in the volcano on Las Palmas, trying to save the world, and the soldiers were being blown to pieces. He saw himself shoot a man in the head, then blood cascading from the hole as more bullets struck the body.

When would someone come and see him?

Jane was the first. She looked as if someone had beaten the shit out of her. He couldn't hear much of what she said, but he'd given her the thumbs-up. Having a DIA agent as your girlfriend was like dating the angel of death, but it had its advantages. While he'd been saving the world she had saved his life.

Next up was Max Davas, who didn't look much better. He might be the smartest fund manager in the world but Jim's mentor, the father he'd never had, was old and fragile.

He couldn't remember much of what Davas had said

either, but Jim was happy to see him. Somehow he and Jane had helped him separate the dreams from reality.

John, the laconic MI6 man, showed up next. Of the three, he looked worst – one cheek was covered with a giant plaster and his left side was encased in something that meant he had to wear his jacket over his shoulders. He seemed happy enough, though. He grinned a lot and told jokes Jim didn't get.

His doctors told Jim he was a lucky man. They'd taken out about half a metre of his guts and various bits of shrapnel. It was a miracle he hadn't lost a kidney. He'd be OK, though, they said; nothing much wrong that wouldn't heal. Jim found lying in bed all but intolerable, but they'd said it might be another couple of months before he could leave: he'd picked up an antibiotic-resistant infection. He wasn't to worry about it, but it would slow the healing process.

Now Jane was on leave and visiting him every day. In his semi-frozen state he looked up at her adoringly. She was the most amazing woman in the world. If only he could drag her into his hospital bed and make love to her … That was his goal. But by the time he was able to go home, Jane was back on duty and had vanished into the ether …

# 2

The sergeant wanted to whistle at the babe in the black leathers but that would have been a very bad idea. Whistling at Colonel Jane Brown would have been like pinching the butt of a Tigron.

She pulled the dusty cover off her motorbike, stuffed it into the space where her helmet had been stowed, saddled up and switched on the Kawasaki Ninja ZX-14. It snarled into life. Good to be riding home, she thought, as she arced out of the hangar. At 160 m.p.h., she could be down this ten-mile straight in four minutes, but just as she hit the zone of perfect speed, she saw a police car pull on to the road behind her, blue lights flashing. She could have lost it, of course, but she throttled right back.

Damn, she thought. Busted.

The police car stopped shrinking in the wing mirror and began to grow.

"Pull over," came a voice from the bullhorns on its roof, and she steered to the edge of the tarmacked road, stopped and dismounted.

The officer on the passenger side got out as she lifted off her helmet, but as he approached her, the car let out a sudden 'Woot, woot.' The officer stopped and turned. 'Woot' from the squad car meant that something was up. He ambled back to the driver and looked in at the computer terminal his partner had twisted around for him. "Colonel J. Brown," it read. The gal in the leathers made a pretty strange colonel. His eyes went to "Gender". "F," it said. He gave his partner a look; his partner returned it. He glanced down at "Notes".

DIA.

He straightened, walked round the front of the car and got back into the passenger seat. His partner pulled out and, as they passed her, waved.

Jane put her helmet back on. Cool, she thought, starting her engine. Good to be back in ole Virginia.

Jim looked at the mess that ran down the right of his torso, then rubbed some ointment on to his wounds. It burned. Bastard bacteria, he thought. He took three large strips of plaster and covered them. The abscesses were slowly closing, but after six months, progress seemed glacial. His body had lost its previously honed outline, the result of dedicated running, and he suspected his fitness had gone with it.

He walked out of the bathroom into his bedroom. Jane was coming at the weekend and it was in worse shape than he was. Must do a tidy, he thought. He didn't make much of a mess, rattling around in his palatial London Docklands flat all on his own, but the agency cleaner didn't seem to do much. She came one morning a week and shuffled about, with her iPod on, to little effect.

He sat on the end of the bed to pull his socks on, trying not to yank at his injuries. For now, the grenade had put an end to his ability to stand on one leg and hop into a sock. It was a small loss to suffer from such a bad trade.

He pulled on his boxers, picked up his mobile and called Davas.

"Jim, how are you?"

"Great," he said, perking up at the sound of the old man's voice.

"You never ring, you never email. Have I upset you?"

"No, no," said Jim, "I know how busy you are. Don't want to trouble you."

"I was starting to worry."

"Don't be silly," said Jim. "I'm sorry I haven't been in touch."

"So what is new?"

"Nothing," said Jim. "It's just I need some advice."

"Fire away."

"It's sort of like I'm in a vacuum. It's stupid but I miss having to get up and go to work. It was great at the bank, being on the trading floor with the guys. There was always something kicking off to make money out of. I miss the buzz. I miss working with you," he laughed sadly, "not that I want to have to save the fucking world again or anything. It's just I've got no day job, nothing to do, but also no one to do the little stuff I need either."

"Bored?"

"Yes – and, well, kind of like ..." He trailed off.

"Lonely?"

"No," he said, "not really." He'd lied. "I've got Jane and she's over this weekend – but it can get a bit quiet when she's working."

"Why don't you come over?"

"That'd be great – I'll be with you after she's gone back."

"And get yourself a butler like Jeffries."

Jim laughed. "It's an idea, but I'm not sure it'd suit me."

"A man of your position needs staff," said Davas. "And a good butler is a top-quality manager as well as a confidant and an adviser."

Jim's mind flapped as he poured silence down the phone to Davas. A butler was the ultimate status symbol in the world of privilege to which his strange talent had taken him. Jim could predict the transit of a stock or currency chart. On his monitor, the tiny trail of pixels represented the inexorable grindings of the world economy: to be able to see just a minute ahead unlocked vast treasure that he had barely begun to plunder. It was the skill that had led him to see that global markets were to crash to zero and that for this to happen the world had to come to a sudden and catastrophic end. With his freakish ability he had helped to find the source of the threat and had ended up nearly dead. After that, everything seemed rather bland.

"Look, Jim," Davas interrupted his musing, "let me find you one. If you don't like him or her, I'll take care of it."

"You'll fire them?" said Jim.

"Sure."

"OK," he said, slumping on to the bed, head spinning. "Got to go." He hung up and took a few deep breaths. Not good, he thought, eyes closed.

His mobile bleeped with an SMS. It was from Davas. "Are you all right?"

"Fine. J Thanks," he sent back. Not quite true, he thought, but I'm not going to miss this weekend.

# 3

The garage door swung up and Jane rode inside, stopped the bike and jumped off, keys in hand. She unlocked the side door into the house and went into the den. There was a bowl of fruit on the table, a plate of cookies under cling-film and a little basket of silver-wrapped sweets. The mail was in a pile. It had been opened and annotated, with yellow Post-it notes poking out at the top, detailing what had been dealt with and what needed her attention.

She slipped off her leathers and boots and took them with her as she sprang up the stairs. She had a shower – always more refreshing in her own place – then put on her favourite pair of jeans and a white T-shirt. She noted the difference a little weight loss had made and determined to put it on again.

Downstairs, she went back to the den. Thanks, Mom, she thought, as she picked up a satsuma and the mail. She went into the kitchen, opened the door to the patio and stepped outside. A worn wooden table stood beside the pool with a few chairs. Jane sat down and peeled the fruit, popped a segment into her mouth and began to leaf through the envelopes.

"$16 overcharge," said the Post-it note on her bank statement, in a tight barely legible scrawl. "Have complained and requested refund. TBA." Jane smiled. Her mother

CLEM CHAMBERS

wouldn't let anyone get away with taking a penny from her daughter that they hadn't earned. The next note was attached to the phone bill: "Switched carriers. Better deal!" The bottom line on her savings-account statement showed $183,284.92. Her mother had ringed the balance in pink marker and noted "+$5327.48" on the yellow tag.

Jane ate another piece of satsuma and turned over the next sheet. "We're so proud," said the note. It was confirmation of a second oak leaf to her Purple Heart. She smiled again. It was a perfect afternoon.

The front-door bell chimed.

She dropped the sheaf of papers on to the table and jumped up. Friendly neighbours must have spotted her come in. Doubtless, some urgent community action needed her support – paving had to be replaced or a gate changed. Whenever she was at home they always collared her fast. They knew they had to catch her while they could.

She opened the door to a smartly dressed guy and two of the shiniest Ferraris she had ever seen.

"Jane Brown?" said the guy, smiling.

"Yes," she said, a little surprised.

"Brad Wilson. I've brought you your Ferrari Enzo." He jerked a thumb over his shoulder at the shiny red shark.

"Sorry, you've got the wrong Jane Brown."

"Pardon me, ma'am, but I don't think so. You are Ms Jane Brown and this is your address, right?" He showed her the paper on his clipboard.

"That's me," she said.

"It's a gift, I believe, from a Mr James Evans." He beckoned her to follow him. "Come and take a look."

It was an amazing-looking car. She walked towards it,

30

taking in its fabulous lines – and stopped in her tracks. "No," she said.

Brad paused mid-pace and turned. "Ma'am?"

"I don't want it."

Brad flashed white teeth. "Well, I can't say I've ever had that reaction before."

"I prefer bikes," she said. "Tell him I don't want it and give him his money back."

"We can't do that, ma'am."

"How much?"

"Five hundred and fifty thousand dollars."

"Five ..." Her voice died.

"Why don't you take it for a spin, then make up your mind?"

"I couldn't afford the gas," she barked.

Brad's partner, in the other Ferrari, was looking at her from behind dark sunglasses as Brad gently threw her the keys. She let them fall to the ground.

"Look, lady, take the car for a drive and if you don't want it then I'll buy it off you for three hundred grand tomorrow." He took out a pen and offered it to her with the clipboard. "Care to sign this?"

"No."

He scribbled in the signature box. "If you don't want it I can just take it away?" he offered, with a grin.

She bent down and picked up the keys.

"You'll love it. You won't be sorry." With that, he turned away and climbed into his partner's car.

Jim snatched up his phone. "Jane –"

"What were you thinking?" she snapped.

His heart plummeted. "What's wrong?"

31

"How could you buy me that car?"

He wanted to say, "What car?" but that would be ridiculous. "What car?"

"Don't be ridiculous."

"What's wrong with it?"

"Everything."

"Everything?"

"Everything."

"Everything?"

"Stop repeating me."

"Repeating you?"

There was an extended silence, which, eventually, Jane broke. "I'm a special agent in the employ of the American Government. I can't afford a Ferrari."

"Oh," said Jim, crestfallen.

"Five hundred and fifty thousand dollars, Jim! That's a hell of a lot of money."

"Not for me," he said indignantly.

"But it is for me," she said, exasperated

Jim sighed. "I guess." Within seconds he had gone from elated to miserable. "Stupid of me," he said. "I just wanted to buy you something nice, something to make you happy."

"That's sweet," she said, "but I can't accept it."

"What do you want to do?"

"I'll sell it and give you your money back."

"Don't let it worry you."

"It will. I'll get my mom on to it."

Jim's side was aching. "You still coming Saturday?"

"You bet. I'm about to get a last-minute deal on a flight."

"I'll send the jet."

"No, Jim."

"For pity's sake," he heard himself shout, "it's my plane! I can pick up who I want in it."

She backed off. "OK," she said, "that's really kind."

"That's settled, then. Sorry about the car. I got carried away."

"I'm sorry too, Jim," she said, "I really appreciate the gesture." She hated lying. "Got to go," she said. "Love you."

What had she just said? "Oh, crap," she muttered.

What *had* she just said? A big smile spread over Jim's face.

She had said, "Love you." He squeezed the phone. "Yes." He felt his whole body inflate. He wanted to call straight back, but he knew she'd burst his bubble

Jane's mobile signalled an incoming SMS. It was from Jim: "I love you too." She groaned. She must be losing it.


Jim looked at the foreign-exchange charts. Nothing meant anything to him. For a change, he couldn't see the coming moves. He switched off the monitor. He'd better get tidying.


"It's a lovely car, dear," said her mom. "Are you sure you want me to sell it?"

Jane gazed out of the front window. Her dad was standing by the Ferrari with the next-door neighbour, admiring it. The local kids had all cycled up to stare at it respectfully too. It was like a magnet. The journey to her parents' home had been one long, uncomfortable stare-at-Jane extravaganza. She turned away. "I'm sure," she said.

Her dad came in. "You've got yourself one hell of a guy," he said, "someone finally good enough for my little girl."

Jane scowled.

"It's not that simple," remonstrated her mom.

"Looks pretty simple to me," he said. "Anyone want a soda?"

"Beer," said Jane, flopping into an armchair that almost swallowed her.

"Ice T, please – the peach one," said her mom.

Jane heaved a despairing sigh. "How am I meant to keep up?"

"I know, sweetie, I know," her mother murmured soothingly.

"Keep up?" came a voice from the kitchen. "He doesn't want you to keep up. He just wants to make you happy."

Mrs Brown gave a girlish giggle. "But it is rather exciting, don't you think? Does he love you?"

Jane grabbed a cushion and grappled with it. "That is not the issue."

"Sure," agreed her mom.

"That is the *only* issue," called her dad.

"You keep out of this," her mom told him. "It's strictly girl-talk."

Mr Brown came in with two bottles and a beaker of Ice T. "He sounds like a keeper to me," he said, grinning. "And you both know it."

34

# 4

Baz looked at the FedEx package in the delivery man's hand. He signed for it. "Thanks." He went into the kitchen of the Mayfair maisonette and tore open the envelope by the thin red strip. "My little ducks," he said, pulling out the contracts and kissing them. "My sweet little ducks." He had the unfettered rights to explore and mine forty square miles of the Democratic Republic of Congo. It might as well be carte blanche from the British stock market to steal tens of millions of pounds from greedy speculators everywhere. He had done the difficult bit: he had created the truth on which he would build his lie. Forty square miles of mineral rights were not easy to come by, even in the arse end of the world, and they were priceless, whether or not there were any minerals to be had. Human optimism and avarice would do the rest.

Now the trawl line was set for the huge and hungry shoal of investors that lived the dream of getting rich quick. There would be a feeding frenzy for his fabulous mine and he was about to turn the greedy dreams of many into a river of gold for himself. Rather than dig treasure from the ground, he would lever it from other people's brokerage accounts and re-bury it among his invisible deposits. He had been running the same scam for twenty-five years in Australia, Canada, South Africa and London. He wasn't the only one at it –

many others were playing the same game – yet no one, except a few terminally stupid individuals, had ever been caught. Mining fraud was the perfect crime.

He laid the contracts to the mineral rights on the black slate kitchen counter. There it all was. The rest would be easy.

Jim heard the distant sound of urgent buzzing and looked round from his screen. He got up from his desk and walked towards the front door, tucking in his T-shirt. The market was too vague for him today. Nothing seemed to be trending with any predictability so he hadn't entered into any positions. It was a rare morning when nothing was cooking but sometimes the charts just didn't speak to him. He was tempted by a few boredom trades but resisted. Instead he thought about Jane.

He was faxing fewer and fewer analysis reports to his old firm, but they kept paying him his enormous retainer. The bank was a vast financial organisation, one of the "vampire squid" that had wrapped itself around the face of the world economy. It thought in billions and aimed for trillions. His fees were less than small change compared to the scale of their schemes. Some time soon they'd stop paying him, but with £100 million in the bank he didn't care. Money had lost all meaning for him. It was like water from a tap to a man who owned a vast lake. As a kid he had been as poor as a church mouse. Now he owned the church but had no idea of what to do with it.

Jim peered through the spy-hole on the front door. A rotund old man, dressed as if he was going to a wedding, stood outside. He was bald, with a strip of grey hair round the side of his head. He had a beak of a nose and an eagle-like expression. The buzzer sounded again as Jim was wondering who the man was, so he pressed the intercom. "Hold on a second." He turned the latch and opened the door.

"Good morning, sir," said the man, and stood to attention. He smiled. "I'm not sure whether you're expecting me, but your friend Mr Davas suggested I pay you a call. My name is Stafford Lees."

"Max sent you?"

"That is correct, sir," said the man.

"You've come for the butler job?"

"Yes, sir."

Crikey, thought Jim. He'd forgotten about it. "Come in."

"Thank you, sir." He walked into the hall and was immediately eyeing the place up like a burglar.

"Through here," said Jim, pointing him into the lounge.

"May I say what a wonderful view you have, sir?"

"Thank you." He smiled nervously. "And it's Jim. Please."

"Yes, sir."

"Take the weight off your feet." He gestured to the two sofas that stood at ninety degrees to the picture window, facing each other over a low coffee-table. He sat down and Stafford, with some difficulty, lowered himself into the other.

Jim noticed that the coffee-table was piled with crap. Apart from letters and magazines, there was a huge stack of fifty-pound notes. He realised, with horror, that it probably looked a bit sick. He had got the bank to run him over ten grand in cash and had plonked it there to dip into it when he needed to. There were heaps of coins, too, a couple of mobile phones, a dismantled PlayStation 3, three notebook computers, four mugs, an empty takeaway pizza box, a clear plastic bag full of random papers and a plastic rabbit. He felt rather disgusted with himself.

"These are my credentials," said Stafford, passing him a wad of paper.

"Blimey." The first page was headed "1980–2005, Royal Household" He turned the page. "That's impressive."

"Have you any questions?" asked Stafford, in a strong military voice. His eyes sparkled behind circular glasses.

A little switch flicked on in Jim's head. If he had learnt one thing it was that he had to get on the front foot. You couldn't react to a situation by letting it wash over you. He had to grab it and shake it by the collar. "Well, yes, I do," said Jim. "Why did you leave the Royal Household?"

"I had to nurse my wife, which was not compatible with the demands of my job."

"And how is she now?"

"She passed away last month."

"Oh." Jim felt awful. "I'm sorry."

"It was a blessed release."

Jim took a breath. Then he said, "Stafford, to be honest, I have no idea how this is meant to work."

"Well, first off, sir," he said quietly, "I would expect the master to address me by my surname while I will address you as 'sir'."

"Can't I call you Stafford? It sounds pretty much like a surname anyway."

The butler smiled. "You may, of course, call me whatever you wish."

"What else?" said Jim.

"Well, I take it, from the size of the house, that you have quarters for staff?"

"There's a couple of bedsits on the top floor and, like, a small flat in the basement," said Jim.

"Very good. Now, are you a gentleman who likes plenty of staff, a cook, a housekeeper, an assistant, a gardener – well, perhaps not a gardener, but you follow my general drift – or would you prefer me to look after everything?" He raised his right eyebrow and his look drilled into Jim.

Jim glanced around the sparsely furnished lounge. A cook, a housekeeper and an assistant? His home would turn into a zoo. "I'm a minimalist," he said.

"Very good, sir."

"If that's OK?"

"Leave it all to me," said Stafford, hauling himself to his feet.

"Right," agreed Jim. He got up and offered his hand, feeling rather as though he had been hired rather than the other way round.

Stafford shook it. "I'll be in contact." He smiled. "I'll let myself out, sir."

"OK," said Jim, catching sight of the pound shooting up against the dollar on his central monitor. He ran over to the screens. He hadn't seen that one coming.

The pilot had called to say Jane was on the way. Jim knew he could have gone to the airport, but with the private jets, an immigration officer met you at the bottom of the plane's steps, glanced at your passport and you were straight into a limo.

So he should have been in the limo waiting for her, he thought. Perhaps that was the kind of thing Stafford would fix up for him. He nearly jumped out of his skin when the bell rang. He ran to the door, where he took a few deep breaths. There she was on the TV screen. At last.

He threw open the door. "Da-*nah*!" he said, with a grin as wide as his face.

She dropped her kit-bag and he swept her into his arms. Immediately, he felt an agonising shooting pain in his healing wound and collapsed backwards.

"Jim!"

His face was contorted. "Ow," he said, clutching his side.

"Are you OK?"

"Yeah," he said, and raised his hand. She hauled him to his feet. He staggered, then found his balance. "Come on in," he said, limping backwards as he rubbed his watering eyes.

"You need a medic?" Jane asked.

"No," he replied. "Just got a bit carried away, that's all." He stopped, turned and kissed her slowly. "Nothing wrong with my snogging muscles."

"Let's go upstairs and have a look at that abdomen. I'm not having you dying on me."

"Now you're talking," he said, squeezing her.

"No more fun for you, mister, until I'm sure it's safe."

# 5

Jane sat bolt upright in bed. "No," she said. "Eurostar."

"Jet," Jim insisted.

"Definitely not. We go on the Eurostar."

Jim admired her back as he sat up next to her. "Jet."

"The train's more practical and infinitely cheaper."

"It's just a phone call to the pilot."

"We don't need to call anyone to get the train."

"Then a taxi to the airport."

"Which is further than a taxi to the station, right?"

"A little bit of paperwork at the airport."

"Tickets at the station," she countered.

"Fifty minutes' flight time."

"Plus fifteen minutes' taxiing and queuing at each end making it one hour twenty minutes point to point."

"Then a taxi to Paris," said Jim.

"From somewhere miles away from the city, rather than getting a cab from wham-bang in the middle of town. The train will take about the same time and cost nothing in comparison."

He slumped back on his pillows. "You're right," he said.

"And then there's the environmental impact."

"Stuff the environment."

She lay back and toyed with the long scar down his right

41

side. "I agree, stuff the environment," she said, "but it'll be more relaxed. Hey, I never get to ride a train."

"You're tickling." He wriggled.

"Great," she said. "It must have knitted up good."

They stood in the lengthy taxi queue at the Gare du Nord in Paris.

"Where, in your calculations, was waiting in line for an hour?" said Jim, grumpily.

"You should have booked a cab through the hotel," she advised him.

"Now you tell me."

"We could walk."

"You know the way?"

"Sure I do." She smiled. "By the time we get a cab we could have been there a half-hour."

He grasped her kitbag, which held all their stuff.

"Hey," she said, "I told you to cut that out. And, anyway, you'll need all your strength for later."

"Oooh," she squealed, "a steam room. This is like Vegas but with class."

The Ritz suite was a Louis XIV palace in miniature with all mod cons hidden away.

She came out of the bathroom naked and began to strip him off. "Let's see if you're fit enough for manoeuvres in an extreme environment."

Later, when they were getting ready for bed, Jane's mood seemed to have changed: she was drying her hair furiously with a towel. "So, what does this place cost?" she asked somewhat tersely, as he brushed his teeth.

He spat out toothpaste. "A bit," he said.

"Come on spill the beans."

"Six."

"Six thousand for the weekend?" She frowned.

" Per night." He put the brush down and turned. She had gone back into the bedroom. He spent a few minutes applying his dressings, then turned off the light and followed her.

She seemed to be asleep when he slipped between the cool linen sheets. "You awake?" he said hopefully, wrapping his left arm around her.

She rolled on to her back. She looked sad, and he wondered why. "Let's get some sleep," was all she said.

The next morning, after a leisurely breakfast in their room, they decided to do a little sightseeing. They started at the Louvre, where Jim discovered that most other visitors were Dan Brown fans, there to retrace parts of *The Da Vinci Code*. He could tell the Americans among them by the glaring whiteness of their trainers, and the size of their arses.

Jane spent a long time studying a Leonardo terracotta sculpture of five ragged infantrymen taking down a cavalry rider. One man was jamming two fingers up the horse's nostrils while three held the legs of the struggling beast, and the fifth man vaulted at the rider to knock him out of his saddle. "I've never seen a training manual done in sculpture," she said. "Fantastic."

"Yes," said Jim, who was bored with it.

"A cavalry officer was the tank of his day," said Jane. "All that dressage stuff with the horses prancing about, it's battlefield manoeuvres."

"Never paid attention," said Jim.

"The kicking out's meant to take out infantry guys like these – fascinating, huh?"

"I guess."

She must have caught his tone because she spun round suddenly. "OK, let's go."

As they walked on, she pointed out the Caesars who punctuated the long corridors and detailed the sticky ends to which they'd come. "While the Roman guys were real bad asses they did just great ruling the world. When they went soft it all fell apart."

"The women all have big hair," Jim commented, "but the guys don't seem to have much in the way of hair at all."

"Well, the guys were probably military."

"Thought they were Caesars. Look, that guy's got some."

"He's an Assyrian."

"So they must have had barbers. That's a seriously plaited beard."

"Very dangerous in battle," said Jane. "The Israelites shaved so the other guys couldn't grab them and get an advantage in grappling. If someone got you by the beard you were toast." She changed tack. "Look at that sword." She skipped over to a display case. "Jim, that's just amazing. It's, like, four thousand years old."

"I prefer the gold jewellery," said Jim, peering at a fat ring with a big red stone in it.

"It's pretty," she said, "but I like the bronze. When they ran out of it civilisation collapsed. The population of Europe shrank by seventy per cent. That's like the credit crunch but for human life. No bronze, no tools, no food. It wasn't till they cracked steel that humanity made a comeback. Of course, they used mainly stone in the Americas, but when we showed up with steel, we wiped them out."

Jim was pulling a face at his reflection in the glass of the cabinet.

"The history of weaponry goes claws and teeth, wood and stone, bronze, steel, plutonium, silicon, tungsten and ceramic."

He'd moved to a Greek urn – ceramic, he thought. He imagined someone getting hit over the head with it. "All this war stuff's a bit grim." A couple of earnest-looking Orientals were snapping away at the Venus de Milo, positioned further down the gallery. "At least she's 'armless."

Jane glanced at the statue and then at him. "Was that a joke?"

"Yes," he said. "From about the stone age."

They found a heaving crowd in front of the *Mona Lisa*. "What a load of hype," said Jim. He looked at Jane to gauge her reaction and as he did so Mona Lisa smiled at him. He looked back at her. She wasn't smiling. He looked at Jane and the painting smiled again. "The picture's smiling at me when I look at you, but when I look at it, it's not."

"Sure," said Jane. "The edge of your vision is more sensitive to certain things. You're seeing under the glaze to a smile that's been painted out. It's like movement – you can see it from the corner of your eye even when the same object is invisible when it's stationary."

She squeezed up by his side. "Imagine my finger's someone who's going to frag you. Now, you can't see him when he isn't moving, but suddenly he moves." She wagged her finger and Jim suddenly saw it at the edge of his range.

"So, when you see that movement, you've got a fraction of a second to respond. Cool, huh?"

"Are you saying that if Mona Lisa smiles at me again I should take her down?"

"No point," she said, laughing. "She's behind bullet-proof glass."

He looked at Mona Lisa again and then at Jane. They were both smiling.

The Hemingway bar at the Ritz was small and full. Jim's Platinum Bullet was by far the best martini he'd ever had. Jane had ordered a glass of water with a slice of cucumber in it but after a little encouragement she had a Kir Royale. The bill arrived. She tried to pick it up but Jim grabbed the silver plate.

"Let me see," she said, snatching the piece of paper. Her jaw dropped. "A hundred bucks. That's ridiculous."

"No shortage of ridiculous things in the world," said Jim.

"One hundred bucks!" she said quietly, but her face registered shock and a hint of anger.

"For fuck sake," he snapped, "we've been apart for months and you're worried about a bit of money. Can't you just enjoy us being together? Isn't that more important?"

"OK." She put the bill back on the plate. "OK." She threw her hands up apologetically. "It's your money. You've got plenty. I'll stop complaining."

"Great," said Jim. He kissed her and she put her hands on his legs and played his lips with hers. "I'm glad we've got that straight," said Jim, "because," he lowered his voice, "the restaurant in this place costs a packet."

*

46

It had been a hot, stuffy night of passion and the outside world felt good to Jim, but Jane was holding back. "Aw," she said, "I'd rather just go for a walk."

He'd suggested shopping. "Come on," he said. "We don't have to buy anything."

"Jewellery's not my thing," she protested, lagging behind him as he headed around the square. "I don't like things on my fingers or my wrists."

"How about a tiara?" he said, pointing at one in the window of Van Arpels.

"Nice," she said. "That would look good on me at work."

"Want it?"

"Not enough diamonds," she said. "It must have one the size of a goose egg."

Jim was looking at gold watches in the window of a store called Zera. There was a chronograph big enough to contain a small steam engine. "Let's go in here."

The shop was empty, but when they buzzed at the door it clicked open. They went in.

Jim realised he might look a little scruffy but the assistants greeted them cheerfully. He glanced at his wrist and, sure enough, his gold Rolex Cosmonaut was poking out from beneath his leather jacket.

Jane was clearly uncomfortable – her nose wrinkled as if there was a bad smell under it.

"Let me choose something for you," he said.

"No way," she said, and added to a man who appeared to be the manager, "How much is that?" She gestured at a necklace, displayed around a black marble neck.

"Five million euros," he said, with a little bow.

"Do you want it?" said Jim.

She glared at him. "Don't you dare."

"Let's sit down and look at a few things, then."

"I don't want anything." She flushed bright red and her short black hair seemed to bristle.

"It's OK! We don't have to buy anything."

"I don't want anything," she repeated.

"That'll be cheap, then," he said, and sat in front of a display case. He pulled a funny face at Jane.

Reluctantly, Jane took the seat beside him.

"What would you like to see?" said the manager, in refined and slightly formal tones.

"Ladies' watches."

"Certainly, sir."

"What's your name?" Jim wanted to know.

"Henri."

"I don't need a watch," Jane insisted.

She was starting to wind Jim up.

The manager came back with a tray of variously coloured gold watches.

Jane seemed only interested in their weight and price. "That's like fifty thousand bucks," she commented on the first.

"Would you like to try it on?" asked the manager.

"No thanks, Henri," said Jane. "Forty K," she said, when the next was dangled before her. "Ha!"

"Got anything more expensive?" said Jim, with more than a hint of irritation.

"Not in plain ladies' watches. Gentlemen's, yes, and in gem-encrusted ladies' timepieces we have much more expensive items."

"No, thanks," said Jane. "Bling's a bit *passé*."

Henri smiled. "Let me bring you a few interesting things."

Jim was looking disgruntled and Jane's expression matched his. "Can't we just have some fun?" he said.

"Sure," she said. "Outside."

Jim was just about to say, "What's wrong with having fun here?" when Henri was suddenly behind the counter with a tray of sparkling baubles. He placed it in front of them. Among the golden bangles lay a huge diamond solitaire ring.

Jane's hand went out and she picked up the massive rock. Yellow flashes sparkled in her eyes and a spark of joy ignited in her face.

"You like that," said Jim.

The magic evaporated. She looked at him as if he was some kind of idiot. "That's an engagement ring."

As Jim said, "Ah, right," the buzzer sounded. There was a click as Henri released the door and it opened. Suddenly four figures were in the shop and there was a burst of shouting.

"Shit!" cried Jim, rocking back in his seat.

"Stay calm," said Henri, stiffening. "These things take moments."

A short man in his mid-twenties ran up to them, screaming in French and brandishing an automatic pistol. He was wearing a black nylon bomber jacket and jeans, with clear tape across his face that pulled his features out of synch.

Another man was shoving a bag in the face of the shop assistant, while the two accomplices moved quickly to the display cases embedded in the walls. One pulled out a device from under his coat and placed it against the thick glass protecting the multi-million-dollar necklace. It cracked open.

Jane was glaring at the robber as he watched the manager

fill his bag from the display case in front of them. The robber caught the contempt in her eyes and fumbled with his pocket. With a triumphant smile he took out a grenade.

Jim's eyes were trying to tell her 'no' but she was looking at the grenade.

The robber waved it under her nose, grinning.

"Oh, no," she whimpered.

Jim hadn't expected to hear fear in her voice. It shocked and relieved him. At least she wasn't going to do something stupid.

Then she did.

She grabbed the grenade out of the man's hand in a stiff yank and pulled out the pin. She stuffed her hand, with the grenade, into the robber's trouser pocket. "Now what you going to do?" she spat.

The three other men froze – then turned on them. The first man was screaming in terror as Jane yanked the pistol out of his hand, tossed it, and caught the butt. By now a second man was aiming at Jim. Jane turned the gun on him and, without a moment's hesitation, shot him. The robber with the gadget ran for the door and the third stared at Jane in horror. He dropped his aim but not his gun.

Jim vaulted over the counter, almost landing on the manager, who was hiding behind it. Jane was aiming at the third robber now, a deadly bead, one eye on him and one on Jim.

Jim picked up the dead man's pistol and pointed it at the third. "Drop the fucking gun," he shouted.

The robber with the gadget had found the release button for the front door and slung it open, while the third was backed away towards freedom. He kept his pistol pointing at the floor and began to smile. "It's OK," he said, in English, "I'm going. No problems. No problems," and ran out after his colleague. Jim sprang to the door and watched him jump into a waiting car, which set off with a screech.

Jane pulled the grenade out of the first robber's pocket and smashed him across the back of the head with the butt of the pistol. He fell with a grunt on to one knee. She administered a second brutal blow, and he fell, limp, to the floor. She uncocked the pistol and put it on the glass counter.

The manager stood up and looked at the pistol, then at Jane. "*Formidable*." Then, "If I may." He took the pistol by the barrel and put it out of sight.

Jim ran over to them. "Fuck," he stated.

"If I may take the gun," said Henri, "the police will be here shortly and I wouldn't want them to misunderstand."

"My pleasure," said Jim. He slammed the gun down, hitting the jewellery tray. The engagement ring shot into the air and fell behind the counter.

"I'll pick it up later," said Henri, with some urgency. He took the gun and put it away.

Jane sat down. "Have you, like, got a pin or something?" she said, holding up the grenade. She glanced at Jim strangely.

"One moment." Henri looked around. "Albert."

His assistant was crouching, transfixed, over the dead robber. He straightened up stiffly. Henri gabbled at him, and Albert pushed at the wall behind him. A drawer floated open. He took out several items and instinctively put them on a tray, which he carried over to them.

Jane rolled the hairpins around with her free hand. "Gold might shear." She picked one out. "What metal is this?"

"Platinum, Madame."

It had a ruby on the end. "How much is it?"

"A hundred thousand euros."

"Fine," she said. "It should work."

She threaded the hard platinum pin though the grenade's handle and loosened her grip. The firing lever moved a little and the hairpin twitched, but it held.

"No problem," she said. She took the handle in one hand and the base in the other, then, with a little grunt, twisted the top. Something gave and she unscrewed the base. She put the green bulb on the tray. "That's a little bit safer."

"Henri, where are the police?" asked Jim.

"Probably outside," said Jane.

A hidden door opened in the far wall and a very tall old man walked slowly out. "Is everybody all right?" he enquired, drifting towards them. He looked down in silence at the body. Three armoured gendarmes stood outside the window. Henri pressed the button and the door buzzed open.

A moment passed, and a senior policeman walked in ahead of his armed troop. "*Ça va*, Monsieur Zera?"

"*Oui*," said the old man, slowly. "*Ça va bien.*"

The inspector looked at the mess, an eyebrow raised. He passed a few remarks with Zera and then regarded the two young customers. "*Bonjour*," he said.

"*Bonjour*," Jane said politely, and shook his hand.

"Hi," said Jim.

"I am very sorry about this," said the inspector.

"Don't be," said Jane. "It's proved a lucky escape."

Jim wasn't quite sure what she meant.

# 6

"Good grief," exclaimed Max Davas. "What *is* it with you?"

"I don't know," said Jim, into his phone. He was slumped in the back seat of a Mercedes limo. "I seem to have turned into a disaster magnet."

"Are you sure you're all right?"

"Just a bit shaken up," said Jim, "but I'm getting used to that."

"And Jane?"

"She's had to go back to the US embassy, and when they've finished with her she's got to go straight home."

"I take it she's unhurt," said Davas.

"Oh, yes," said Jim. "Just another day at the office."

"At least you are both well."

"I suppose," said Jim, after a pause.

"You're quite a couple," said Davas

"I suppose," said Jim again. They chatted a little more, then said goodbye and hung up. Jim's jet was waiting at Orly. It might take longer to get home than it would by train and it might cost a fortune, but he was going to fly in his own plane, dammit. His side was aching – vaulting over that counter hadn't been such a brilliant idea.

\*

Much later, he was standing by his front door, searching his pockets for his keys, when it opened unexpectedly. He started. "Stafford!" he exclaimed.

"Welcome back, sir."

"Thank you," he said, as Stafford took his bag from him. "What are you doing here?"

"As agreed, sir, I have started in your employ."

Jim racked his brain, "Yes, I suppose we did agree – but how did you get in?"

"I arrived yesterday, and as you were not about I let myself in."

"I guessed that, but how?"

"There was a key under the mat. I took it that you left it for me."

"I didn't leave a key under the mat."

"Very good, sir."

"There was a key under the mat?"

"Yes, sir. The previous owners must have left it there."

He was about to ask why they'd have done such a thing, but found himself observing, "Weird."

"Yes, sir. Would you like a pot of tea or coffee?"

Jim went into the lounge and dropped down on to a sofa. "Sounds great, but just a mug of builder's tea."

"Would that be strong, three sugars and full cream milk, sir?"

"Yes, please," said Jim, stretching. His side ached, but not too badly. He got up and switched on his computer. His desktop opened up and his picture of Jane crawling under a tangle of barbed wire confronted him. She was covered with mud and smiling like a model.

What a crazy girl she was.

A ton of email shot down into his Outlook as his OC24 1 gigabyte connection sucked it from the Net like a black hole draws in space. At the top he found one from Jane, headed "*Adios muchacho.*"

Jim,
I'm sorry but I've got to call time on our relationship. We've got to face up to the fact we're not compatible, me with my crazy life and you with yours, so I need to say goodbye. Thanks for the moments. Wish you better.
Jane

He clicked reply.

Jane,
What the hell has got into you?

"Tea, sir," said his butler, placing a small tray beside him.

Jim rolled the chair back. "I've just been dumped by my girlfriend," he said, incredulous.

"I'm sorry to hear that, sir."

Jim rubbed his forehead and looked back at the screen. He deleted what he'd typed and started again.

Dear Jane,
I

He deleted 'I'. He groaned and turned round. Stafford was gone. 'I,' he typed again. He took a mouthful of perfect tea. He looked at his first person singular and couldn't think of anything to add. He felt a rush of acid to his stomach, which sent his hand across the table to a half-empty sachet of Rennies. As a trader, antacid tablets were his staple diet.

He opened a chart of 'cable', the US dollar versus British sterling price, pushed out a tablet and popped it into his mouth. With the chalky crunch, he tasted peppermint. The price of the pound was going to drop about one per cent in the next two hours, a pretty big move for that Forex pair. His eyes narrowed as his trading front-end loaded. The software came up slowly. He told the robot to sell a hundred million pounds of the cable contract, short, and watched his orders melt into the ocean of the foreign-exchange trades that flood back and forth across the world.

Trillions fluttered every day between computers at the nodes of laser-driven fibres. The wealth of nations flew around the globe while not one atom shifted a nanometre from one quantum of space to another. Almost all of the money in the world was just electric charge on the spinning platters of innumerable computer drives. If money was power and power corrupted, the computer drives remained unscathed, while on their impossibly delicate surfaces lived the sum total record of mankind's assets. And Jim was doing just great, he thought, imagining Jane lecturing him at the Louvre, until he went soft and his empire turned to dust.

He had £50 million at the bank in his trading account and they had given him a hundred times leverage on Forex. It meant, theoretically, that he could trade with £5 billion.

Fuck it, he thought, and set his robot off to sell another £900 million of the cable contract.

The chart of the day ahead was as clear in his mind as if it was printed on paper. Why had he been pissing around with small trades for so long? It was time to cane the market. It was time to make the big money.

He was a billion short of the British pound against the dollar and his finger was itching to drop another billion on it. He let the mouse go and watched the chart wriggle. There was no rush. As he stared at it, the chart's final pixel, representing the actual price in the here and now, seemed to move in time with his heartbeat. "Fuck the pound," he muttered.

There were 3.5 billion women in the world so the world's richest man would have a pretty good chance of finding a replacement for Jane – perhaps even someone who couldn't beat the shit out of him with her little finger.

He dropped another billion on the pound: one per cent of £2 billion was £20 million. That would be a nice start.

Why had he held back his trading for all this time? He knew what the charts were going to do, and that everyone knew he knew what they'd do, but somehow it had never occurred to him to take his trading to the logical extreme that his abilities allowed. Risk management was for banks that knew shit about what would happen next. Even with departments of mathematicians and compliance officers, they still blew themselves up with stupid trades and clueless traders.

The theory went that you had to be careful when you took a risk because one piece of bad luck could jump up and tear you apart. And bad luck could be so huge that only small risks chasing small profits could survive an onslaught of titanic misfortune. The bank traders played blind man's bluff and they kept as far away from the cliff edge as they could. Jim, though, could see not only the cliff but had a map of the countryside and a safety harness attached to a tree. He could play right at the edge and never have to worry. He could smack the markets about at will.

The equity indices were going to be very volatile over the next week, as were the foreign currencies, and that suited him perfectly: he would dig into the market like a bulldozer into sand.

He was already up £3 million.

Fuck the pound and fuck the yen too, he thought, dropping a billion pounds' worth of dollars on to the yen. £3 billion in Forex was enough for now.

Nothing was bigger or more explosive than currency trading. The hundred-times leverage made it the crack cocaine of trading. Ten thousand pounds in an account bought £1 million in firepower and every one per cent in market moves meant 100 per cent profit and vice versa. If you could call a one per cent move, you could double your money – or be wiped out. It was like roulette without the green and double zeros.

He dropped another billion on to the yen, which sagged a little. He was up £10 million and that gave him another £1 billion in leverage.

His mug was empty. "Stafford," he called, and straight away the butler was beside him. "Got another tea and maybe some sandwiches?"

"Certainly, sir. I have in some fine Cheddar."

"Great," said Jim, watching the chart flitter.

The butler cast an eye over Jim's big screens and at the charts that formed outline mountain ranges. "Very good, sir."

*

Jim could hardly keep his eyes open. "£99,872,312," said the profit line, as the last six digits spun back and forth. It was three a.m. and he wasn't going to close until he saw 100 in the millions column. The dollar-pound-yen trio had grown increasingly volatile over the hours he had been playing it and he had been forced to jump in and out of the market like a tap-dancing giant. "£99,9" said the first three digits. He started to unload as the number grew to £103 million, then began to fall back. His closing was pushing the market against him, but it looked as though he'd get out before the total went below 100. His positions were shrinking as his profits were slipping. "Come on," he growled at the screen, "you can do it."

Suddenly the market changed direction and he closed his positions as they chewed through his remaining orders. He was flat – and a £101 million richer. "Pretty fucking cool," he muttered, as he staggered to his feet. This was the way to go. If some lucky bugger could win £100 million with a single lottery ticket, why couldn't the freak trader with two heads do a thousand times better by draining off a small part of the flow of the world's financial Amazon?

In his bedroom, a new pair of silk pyjamas lay on his pillow, a present from Davas. In moments like this he liked to trace the chart of his life in the air with an index finger, but he was knackered. He flopped on to the duvet and fell asleep.

At eight a.m. Jim was back at his computer, feeling a little groggy. He'd been dreaming about Jane all night. The image of her gunning down the robber had stuck in his consciousness and replayed in his dreams, as had the way she had knocked the other robber down with the pistol. Fuck me, he thought. Sterling was about to zoom against the yen, dollar and euro. He loaded the robots with £3 billion for each pair and set them off buying. The sterling juddered across all the foreign-exchange markets and spiked up a tenth of one per cent. He grunted. He'd better tune down the robots' aggression next time.

His mobile rang. Caller ID said, "Withheld."

Someone in the States perhaps?

He snatched it up. "Hello."

"Mr Evans?"

"Yes," he said, disappointed and instantly irritable. "What? Who is this?"

"It's Dale Watkins. I'm in Risk at the bank."

"So?"

"I've been asked to call about your trading."

"What about it?"

"It's a bit erratic?"

"How so? Do you mean it's a bit too big for you?"

"Well, yes, actually."

"Talk to Wolfsberg and don't bother me again."

He hung up.

The phone rang again. "I'm sorry," said Dale, "but the line went dead."

"It didn't. I hung up on you."

"Oh," he said. "Well, I can't call the CEO, as you probably know."

The huge trades were going Jim's way, as he'd expected. "OK, then, I will. I'll expect your call in fifteen minutes if I don't get through to him."

*

60

Wolfsberg's PA connected Jim immediately.

"Al," said Jim, "I need your help."

"I see," said Wolfsberg. "I'm looking at your problem – you're tripping all the rogue-trader alarms. What do you want to do?"

"There's some serious action on the way and I want to hit it hard."

"Looks like you're pulling a Martingale, Jim."

"I am."

"If you keep doubling up on your winnings and then going all in, you'll get fucked pretty quick."

"Maybe."

"Maybe, huh?" clucked Wolfsberg.

"I want two hundred times leverage."

Wolfsberg laughed. "Not on my balance sheet."

"Come on," said Jim. "What harm can it do?"

"Plenty." The banker laughed again. Wolfsberg knew there were several reasons why he was the most successful banker in Europe, and at least three of them were Jim. "OK, Jim, you can keep your hundred-times leverage and Martingale your face off, but your old friends on the floor are going to coat-tail you while you're at it. OK?"

"Is that like enhanced commission?" asked Jim.

"You can call it that if you like. I'll call it a cat-insurance premium."

Banks and other companies needed protection from the financial risks associated with hurricanes and earthquakes so they bought derivatives contracts that could be traded like a physical commodity, such as copper or wheat. Following Jim's trades, perhaps mirroring them, was like buying an insurance policy for a hurricane they knew was coming.

"We've done catastrophes, Al. This is just a few sweaty days racking up jumbo profits."

"From your mouth to God's ear," said Wolfsberg. "You're dealt."

"Before I go, I want a hundred-times leverage on indices. Currently I've only got fifty."

"OK, Jim, we're all done."

He smiled as he hung up. He could almost smell the fun he was going to have.

Jim felt a touch on his shoulder. Fuck, he'd fallen asleep. Did he have any positions?

"Hold on," he muttered, and squinted at the form on the screen listing his positions.

He let out a sigh of relief. He had nothing open.

"If you'll forgive me, sir, I thought you'd perhaps forgotten it was four in the morning and might appreciate a reminder." Stafford's eyes flickered over the screens.

"Thanks," said Jim. "That's good of you." In the light of the monitor his butler looked like an owl, peering at Jim with a calculating but faintly confused expression. "Don't let my crazy stuff get you out of bed again."

"Very good, sir."

# 7

Baz was a stylish geezer, thought Higgins, as he rose in the lift past the giant fish tanks of the Burj al-Arab Hotel. Not only was he prepared to meet him halfway, in Dubai, he did it in style.

Higgins lived in the Philippines with his wife and five kids. He did what he did because he had to, for them. He had never thought much of women, except his mum. "Mum," was his first tattoo on his forearm. She was unique, saintly, but all the others had been whores to be used on his way around the world. Until one day, on leave in Hong Kong, he had been walking through a park among the Filipina au pairs, sitting on their blankets on their given day off to meet and gossip, when a little lady had looked up at him and knocked him off his perch.

He had sat down next to her and she had laughed at him – what a beautiful laugh it was. To anyone else she might have seemed plain – he'd probably glimpsed a million girls like her and never registered their faces – but for Higgins she was like a puff of cyanide that went up his nose and topped his bitter, carbonised spirit. That day, his old self had died and he was reborn, hopelessly in love with a little Filipina who loved him back.

There's a fucking frogman cleaning the tank, he thought,

watching a black creature with big mask eyes rubbing algae off the immense glass wall.

Britain was too cold and depressing for his little Rose so they had gone back to Manila, where he'd bought her a bleeding palace. But love didn't mean money fell from the trees, so it was back to work in his nasty line of business: security in the infected shitholes of the world.

"How'd you like to make an extra fifty grand?" said Baz, from behind his desk in the gaudy but luxurious suite.

"Sure," said Higgins. "So long as it's not a hit."

"No, no," said Baz, "that's not my style. Do I look like a Russkie to you?" He uttered his trademark cackle. "Ker, ker, ker."

"What do you need?" Higgins knew Baz was going to pull something out of his inside top pocket. Baz always did. Whatever it was, the job would be tricky, lucrative and definitely bent.

Baz pulled out a map of the Democratic Republic of Congo and flattened it on the table. There was a big ring on the map up by the Rwandan border. "I want you to get me some rough diamonds from here. Nice ones, nothing too big or too small. All from the same deposit but it must be a wacky mine, nothing official – a local-talent dig. Don't care if they're blood diamonds, whatever, just not out of any commercial mine."

Higgins nodded. "OK."

"Also, I want gold, four or five ounces, two or three minimum. Must be from the same area or thereabouts. Not the same hole but from the general region. No grinding up old wedding rings, it must be out of the ground here." He stabbed the ringed area on the map. "And copper ore, if you can get it – but that's a bonus, not a must-have. Likewise, if there's any funky-looking rocks offered you by the locals, grab them for a few bucks. Pick up anything that looks like a chunk of ore."

"Sure," said Higgins. "I'll take about a month."

"Fine," said Baz. "But no longer, mind."

"That's plenty of time – no way I want to hang around out there."

"Ker, ker, ker."

"You know, Baz, that's a mighty fucked-up location to find a mine."

"As luck would have it," Baz rejoined. "Now, I'm wiring you twenty thousand euros to buy the stuff with. You can keep the change but don't be greedy."

"Don't worry, boss, I learnt my rough diamonds the hard way. I'll get you value for money."

Baz looked over the sea towards Iran. "Fancy a drink?"

"Do pigs shit in the woods?" said Higgins.

Baz hesitated. "No, mate, pigs don't. Bears shit in the woods but pigs are different. Pigs like shit."

Briefly Higgins was perplexed. "Yeah, you're right. Bears shit and pigs fly."

"And like shit," added Baz.

Baz was one sharp bastard and her-indoors would love this news of the job. Fifty grand would go down a storm. "Yeah," he mused, "I could murder a drink."

Sebastian Fuch-Smith rolled the shard of broken windscreen in his palm. It was a funny square pyramid shape, about the size of a large grain of sugar. He'd never held a rough diamond before.

CLEM CHAMBERS

"Keep it," said Baz. "We've got a load of them the locals stumbled on, panned straight out of the stream."

"Really?" said Sebastian. "Thank you. May I ask you a rude question?"

Baz's broker sat impassively at his side, practically asleep. He said nothing.

"Of course," said Baz. "Go ahead."

"If this stuff's just lying around, why don't you dig it up and fund the mine that way?"

"Good question," said Baz. "I wish more people would ask it. You see, the play for us is to map it out, then flog the property to a major mining company. That way we don't spoil the picture. If we start digging it up big-time, the world and his wife will show up and make life bloody difficult. This way we keep the lid on what we've got and when we get all the data sorted we sell the hole and pocket a couple of billion with no mess and no hassle. If we start spitting out tens of millions of dollars in rocks, it'll get hairy."

"Right," said Sebastian. "How do we keep a lid on it?"

Baz smiled. The guy had said "we". What a greedy shit-for-brains he was. He was already imagining he'd bought into the mine. "We park a couple of hundred Congolese soldiers on the land. That's already sorted. It keeps the freelancers off and lets us get on with drilling. Drills are boring, soldiers are scary. Always does the trick."

"How much are you raising?" asked Sebastian.

"Just a mil, pre, pre." The broker had woken up.

"I'll take half," said Sebastian.

"No, no, mate," said Baz, "there's not a half to be had. You can have ..." He looked at the broker.

"A hundred," said the broker.

"A hundred thousand pounds!" exclaimed Sebastian. "That's hardly worth me coming out to this meeting."

Baz shrugged. "If a quarter of a million profit at pre-IPO isn't enough for you, I'm sorry we wasted your time."

Sebastian blushed. "Well, I'm rather disappointed."

The broker sat up a bit. "If you want to roll the quarter into the pre-IPO there'll be a hundred per cent uplift at that point."

"Righty-ho, then," said Sebastian. "I'll play."

"We'll hold your pre-pre-certificates in that case," said the broker. "We do like to control the stock, you understand."

Sebastian nodded. If they held the stock certificates, the promoters could ramp the stock to the sky without the risk of early investors betraying them by selling for a quick turn. He'd be able to sell out but only when they said he could. That was the quid pro quo of being invited to the party early: the risk of powerlessness and complete loss was counterbalanced by a thumping great up-side. He was prepared to take the risk because he'd heard that Baz Mycock was the Elvis Presley of mining promotion. Here was a man with enough balls to float a resources company called Barron Mining and have no one spot the irony of the name. He always made the boys a mint so Sebastian wasn't going to look a gift horse in the mouth – even if it might be a Trojan one.

# 8

Jim scratched at his stubble. He had certainly picked a good time to hammer the markets. They had hit a period of turbulence and the value of stocks and currencies were swinging about with increasing volatility. Something must be going on in the world economy, bad news filtering out and coming to the attention of the big money players. He had made a billion dollars in a week and the total would be a billion pounds by the end of the day.

Stafford had been a brilliant idea on Davas's part: the butler pampered Jim with drinks and snacks, as if he was a giant baby, fuelling him to plunder the world's twenty-four-hour markets. A computer, the Internet and food were all he required to stack up his colossal winnings. He just needed to get up in the morning, sit in front of his screen and be right.

There was no gatekeeper or umpire, no judge and jury except the market. He could sit at his screens stark naked if he liked. Trading was a game Jim didn't lose. He looked at the charts and saw what would happen next – and it did, just as thousands of books on trading promised anyone could do if they read and understood them.

They always said that the patterns were there to be seen: all you had to do was follow the program and you'd make money. The smart investors knew this must be crap because, with a winning formula, any greedy trader could simply grow their trading in scale and soon, like an expanding blob from some 1950s horror movie, all the money in the world would be sucked into the scheme's exponentially expanding ectoplasm.

But a system like that could only work if it was known to just one person: two people equally matched in a game would cancel out each other's advantage. In any event, no system could ever work for long and the Nobel Prize theorists said no system could ever work at all.

The books on reading charts came out in their hundreds every year and the hopeful dutifully bought them, searching for the key to riches, but no one had yet found the system that worked, not even Jim. He just saw where the chart would go next: there was no technical trick beyond that. The charts of stocks, commodities and Forex moved as the natural flow of events, Jim believed, which suggested what would kick off next. To him it was all obvious, like the next note in a simple tune or the fate of the cute dog in this summer's Hollywood blockbuster. It wasn't often that the dog snuffed it and it was equally rare for Jim to find himself in a losing trade. Sometimes the charts didn't make sense, but when they did he might as well have drawn them himself.

Trading stopped him thinking about Jane, which was more important to him than the money that was pelting down on him in a cash monsoon. The trading software blotted out her smiling muddy face.

# 9

Sebastian got up and walked out of the meeting, his phone pressed tightly to his ear. He was speaking to Ralph, Barron's broker.

"Would you like to cash out now?" said the broker. "The pre-IPO money-raising kicks off today. It's at two hundred and fifty per cent of the pre-pre-IPO price and we can bid you a two hundred per cent profit in cash for your holding."

A two-hundred-thousand-pound profit was a nice hit, he thought, but from the serious face he was pulling, he looked as though he was receiving bad news. "What's the IPO price going to be?"

"A fifty to a hundred per cent uplift," said the broker.

"So if I hold on I'm up for between three hundred and seventy-five and half a million pounds," he said.

"No guarantees," said the voice. "We're happy to let you out here."

Sure, thought Sebastian. You bastards want it all for yourselves. Coming out with half a million pounds from an investment of a hundred thousand would be a tidy result. Now that Jim wasn't on-side any more, pickings from the bank would be a lot thinner. His bonanza was coming quickly to an end and he had to make up the slack elsewhere. He had taken on an enormous bank loan and bought back the family

70

estate, paying way over the odds for it, from the money-grubbing farmers who had blighted the land like environmental vandals. But when he had done it, the end of the world had been nigh and his bonus, thanks to Jim's supernatural trading, obscene. Even so, the upkeep of the newly renovated historic pile, as his forebears had found out, was stratospheric. Keeping the thing up to muster required riches, rather than wealth, and his million-pound salary didn't stretch that far.

But he had ways and means of stretching his incomings, this being one. He had a bit of capital to play with and, for now, a whole lot of credit, thanks to his employer. He was a bright boy and he had the strategy worked out.

"Roll my position into the pre-IPO."

"You could," said the broker, "but we're looking for more money and if you want to be on-side you'll need to toss in another couple of hundred thousand."

"Really?" he said. "That's a little unexpected."

"You know how it works," said the broker, condescending.

Sebastian didn't. He'd never done a mining stock before and this had been a recommendation from an Old Etonian friend. Sebastian was a bulge-bracket banker, not some spivvy small-cap brokerage man. A further 50 to 100 per cent profit on a bigger stake would see his investment grow to between seven hundred thousand and a million pounds. That would be quite a killing.

And Mycock was a legend. He'd heard the stories. He'd met the man.

"OK, put me down for another two hundred grand."

"Right you are," said the broker.

*

Baz looked happy sitting in the chair by the hotel window, the Manila sunset behind him. Normally he wouldn't have answered the phone but it was his broker. He was in the final stretch of part one of the project: the flotation of his mining fiction. Once the pre-IPO was complete, the company would float on the London AIM market and the first slug of the big money would pour in. Ostensibly the initial money raised was to develop the mine, but in fact it would go into his bank account via a series of fictitious mining-services suppliers. They would drill, survey and assay to a choreographed timetable that would see the share price rise and fall as he insider-traded it, both long and short.

At the end of the process all that would have been generated were some funky maps, disks of fictitious data, some drill holes and acres of media carefully orchestrated through the financial grapevine. There would be no evidence to probe, even if anyone could be bothered, only drill holes in the jungle of a war zone in a faraway fetid cesspit. An empty drill hole was an empty drill hole, and whether it went down ten thousand feet or a hundred – or even whether it was there at all – no one would ever know. In the old days when someone might have checked up, he'd had concrete poured down the holes for "environmental reasons". But his final gambit probably wouldn't need such care. Things would go pear-shaped rather more cleverly than merely not finding anything. This time his man on the inside would make sure that the licence to the mine was pulled just as they were about to hit it big. Bloody tin-pot countries had no rule of law, no land rights or tenure. Everyone would believe that venal, greedy, kleptomaniac politicians had seized his Eldorado at gunpoint. That would be his exit.

It wasn't uncommon for amazing mineral deposits to be indefinitely mired in third-world politics, and he'd use that as the *coup de grâce* when all possibility of sucking more money out of gullible investors had been exhausted. There would be one last ramp, then goodbye.

"How's it going?" he said, distracted.

"We're done."

"That was quick."

"They lapped it up," said the broker.

Baz looked down at the pretty little tart performing on him. He ran his fingers through her hair. "I thought they would," he said, and hung up. "Life is good," he said, to the naked girl kneeling before him. People would risk all forms of danger and humiliation for money. The only question was: were they the fuckee or the fuckor?

# 10

Jane rolled through the recent email on her phone. It had
been three weeks since she had broken up with Jim and she
hadn't had a word from him. The jerk, she thought.

Jane rolled through the recent email on her phone. It had
been three weeks since she had broken up with Jim and she
hadn't had a word from him. The jerk, she thought.

John Smith was regarding her with a toothy sarcastic
smile. "You're not being very forthcoming."

"Is this an interrogation?" she said. "Because if it is,
you've come to the wrong country to do it."

"No, no," said Smith. "I'm just concerned."

"So you flew over to see me on your government's tab to
find out how your old co-worker was shaping up."

"Well, not exactly."

"So why did they send you?"

"It's not often that two important people end up offing two
members of the Black Hand in a Paris boutique."

"One member."

"Two."

She didn't respond.

"The gentleman with the sore head? His troubles are at an
end."

"Really?" she said. "Good." John was waiting for her to
say something more. "Well, you can take it from me I didn't
know that there still was a Black Hand."

"Neither did I," said John, "but my co-workers," he

74

grinned, "just want a report on what happened."

"Simple. We go shopping across the street from where we're staying, we get into a situation and it's resolved quickly. The end."

"And how's Jim?"

"I don't know. We're not together any more."

"Why?"

"That's a personal matter,"

"Come on," said Smith, "you can say, you're with a friend now."

She rolled the pearl on her BlackBerry. "At this rate you might not be a friend for much longer. Work it out for yourself."

"I'll ask Jim."

"You do that."

The markets were getting wilder. The indices were thrashing around three and four per cent a day and the Forex markets were gyrating like an Internet dancing parrot listening to Gabba.

Jim rammed his buying and selling into every twist and turn in the markets with his multi-billion-pound positions. By the end of the month he would hit the ten billion, and on he would go to a hundred billion and continue until he was the first trillionaire in the history of the world.

The moustache was good: he looked like a serious fellow. He had scraped the beard off the week before.

Every now and again he would minimise his trading software and look at the wallpaper on his desktop. He thought about resetting the default, but instead he stared at the picture of Jane. He wanted to call her, but how could he?

She had said it all in her email. He wasn't the guy for her. Of course he wasn't. He was no brick–shithouse special–forces officer, with a chiselled chin and muscles on his muscles. He was no martial artist, PhD genius superhero. He was just a common bloke with some freaky crystal–ball–reading skill. Princesses didn't marry milkmen, goddesses didn't fall for mortals, and money didn't buy love. In fact, it poisoned it.

He was trading so big now that he could tell the market knew he was there. When he went long the market rose, and when he went short it fell. He was becoming part of the market itself. That was strangely gratifying. He was bullying the world.

The phone rang. He brought up his trading software to cover the picture of Jane.

It was Davas. "Jim, what are you doing?"

"What do you mean?"

"You know what I mean."

"I'm trading."

"I can see that."

"I know. So what?"

"What do you think you're doing?"

"Making money."

"You're making too much. You're bending the markets."

"So?"

"If you keep bending them, they'll break."

"Oh, really?"

"Yes, really. How much have you made? Four, five billion?"

"Eight."

"Eight." Max paused. "And where do you think all this money's coming from?"

"You?"

"No, not me. From everyone else."

"So?"

"It's too fast, Jim. If you're doing what I think you're doing, you'll break the bank."

"There is no bank."

"Of course there is. It's the Bank of Everybody."

"Why should I care?"

"Because you'll end up hurting people, so many, many people. You're producing an inefficient market that will choke and die. Without the market we all perish."

"You're exaggerating."

"What are you going to do with all this money? Don't you already have enough?"

"That's fine coming from you, Max. You have more than Bill Gates."

"Yes, Jim, but it's the gains of a lifetime of work, not treasure plundered in a few weeks."

"I'm not plundering – you sound like Jane."

There was a short silence. "Jim, you have to stop. If you go on there'll be untold suffering. You've already driven the markets into panic."

"Me?" said Jim. "What are you talking about? I'm just surfing this."

"You're not. You're causing it. Can't you tell?"

"You're not serious, right?"

"I'm very serious, Jim."

He began to laugh. "Have I cracked the game?"

"Yes."

"Is that what the models say?"

"Yes."

"I knew I could," he said. "I just knew it."

"You know you must stop, then, don't you?"

Jim's mouse hand was aching. He flexed his fingers. "Tell me again, Max – tell me I've beaten the market."

"You've won, Jim. The moment I realised what you could do, I knew it was a risk you'd try and then might not stop."

"And did you win the game, too, Max?"

"Yes, my friend, and I, too, had to stop. You know my game is different now."

"Yes," said Jim. "Ten billion would be nice, though."

"Jim, you can always revisit it. Take it slowly. Put it in my treasuries and it will be ten billion soon enough."

"A hundred billion would be nicer still."

"Would you want the attention that would bring? I think not. What you have now will be hard enough to keep secret, and if it becomes known, your life will be spoilt. Trust me on that."

"What am I going to do?" said Jim. "This is the only game I can play."

"It's a cosmic joke, Jim – you, the richest man in the world with no job and no girlfriend."

"Oh," said Jim, "you know about that."

"Yes," said Davas.

Jim was rather annoyed now. "Do you know everything?"

"Pretty much," said Davas.

Jim minimised his trading software and looked at the picture of Jane. "OK, Max," he said sadly, suddenly feeling extremely tired, "I've stopped. Hell, it was an amazing run."

"Yes, and thank you. You're a good, wise and smart man – thank God for that."

# 11

Sebastian's eyes glazed over as he watched his motionless screen. He was about as low as he could get. It was two days since Jim had stopped trading and his team no longer had anything to mirror. Using Jim's trades as their guide was legal and extremely lucrative, but the gravy train had stopped on the tracks.

By the time they had got clearance from the risk managers to coat-tail him, big-time, Jim's stunning campaign had been practically over. The team's profits would turn into a reasonable addition to Sebastian's bonus, but nothing like the bonanza it might have been if Jim had carried on for a few more weeks. Jim had kept up a pitched battle for eighteen hours a day in an orgy of indiscriminate trading. Some of his traders, Jim's old compadres on the floor at the bank, thought he must have developed some kind of robot that had found a magic trading algorithm, but the IT department had confirmed their software, operated manually, was doing the work. Everyone knew Jim was out there and, once again, he had proved what a bunch of tossers they all were, scratching about for scraps in the dirt.

Now Jim had just made an obscene amount of money while Sebastian had snagged just a tiny part of it. That was very depressing indeed.

Why had the bastard stopped like that?

At that moment life seemed an impenetrable but painful mystery to Sebastian. Now he understood why his great-great-grandfather had hanged himself in one of the stables. Sometimes when things were good, they just weren't good enough.

"Hi, Al," said Jim, "nice to hear from you."

"That was an outstanding set of trading, Jim. Everyone's talking about it."

"Really?" said Jim. "I hope you guys can keep it under your hats."

"Sure," said Wolfsberg. "What's up next?"

Jim's eyes narrowed. For Wolfsberg to call him, they must have made a packet off his back. Of course they had. Now they wanted more. "Don't know," he said. "Have another break, probably."

"You should take a stake in the bank," said Wolfsberg. "With your sort of money you could have quite a piece and be on the board."

"Not a bad idea," said Jim. "I'll do that next year when the stock price is back at five bucks again." It was now at forty dollars.

"It's going to five bucks?" whimpered Wolfsberg, horror-stricken. "You're kidding me."

"Yes, I am," said Jim.

"Ha," grunted Wolfsberg. "You had me there. Where's it going?"

"Don't know," said Jim. "I've got to be careful with my predictions."

"You're probably right," said Wolfsberg. "So, now you're

80

among the super-rich do you want to put your name to a university or something? I'm fixed up with the philanthropist networks so I can hook you up."

"Thanks," said Jim. "I'll let you know." He hung up on him, as he used to do with the junior muppets who called him when he was on the trading floor.

Jim was watching the market ticking. Davas had been right. Now he wasn't yanking the Forex pairs and the international stock indices, the volatility had drained away. He had made the world economy writhe with pain as he had hit the same sensitive spot time and again with his huge trades.

Stafford put a tray with tea and toast next to him. "May I make a suggestion, sir?"

"Go ahead."

"Perhaps you might consider going out. It's been approximately three weeks since you left the apartment."

"Yeah," said Jim. "That's quite a long time, isn't it?" He felt a little told off. "But I did just make eight billion pounds."

"Eight billion pounds?" The butler's grey eyebrows rose. "That's an awful lot of money."

"Yes," Jim said, smiling to himself. "It's a fuck of a lot, isn't it?"

An SMS buzzed on his phone. It was Smith. "Curry?"

"Bingo," said Jim. "I've got a date."

"Very good, sir," said Stafford. "On another subject, sir, if I may, I'd like to invite my two godchildren over to see me."

"Of course," said Jim, and picked up his phone to call Smith. Stafford left as he listened for the dial tone.

"Jimbo," said Smith, by way of greeting.

"Agent Smith," said Jim, knowing it would be equally annoying to Smith. "What's up, doc?"

"Well, I could say that I find myself at a loose end, but that would sound like I'm a Billy-no-mates, so instead I'll imply that I need to see you on a matter of some urgency."

"Do you?"

"No," said Smith, "none whatsoever. Just a catch-up."

"When have you got in mind?"

"Tonight's a goer but next week's looking chaotic."

"Tonight," said Jim.

Jim looked sceptically at Smith's *phal*. It was allegedly four times hotter than the wickedest vindaloo and had been responsible for people keeling over dead of a heart attack.

"I don't normally eat this particular delicacy in company," said Smith, "but seeing as it's you ... Did Jane tell you about the Black Hand?" He spooned curry on to his rice.

"Jane? The Black Hand? No," he said. "We're not together any more."

"That's what she said, and that's why I wanted to meet."

"Who are the Black Hand, and why should I need to know about them?" said Jim, thinking of how much he missed Jane.

"They were the robbers you bumped into – or, rather, bumped off – in Paris. The Black Hand is a smallish Serbian terror organisation. They started the First World War."

"Bloody hell," said Jim. "They're a bit old, aren't they?"

Smith nodded and took his first forkful. As he savoured the moment, tiny beads of perspiration appeared on his forehead. "They are indeed, but that's Balkan politics for you."

"So what does that mean for me?"

"Well, you should avoid any trips to Serbia for a start."

"OK," said Jim. "That should be easy."

"Otherwise, I just thought you should be aware – you know, friend to friend."

"How's Jane?" said Jim, trying for nonchalance.

"I wouldn't know," said Smith. "All women are a complete and utter mystery to me. When they look happy, they're sad, and they cry when they should be laughing with joy. You buy them flowers and they think you've done something wrong. I've long since given up trying to read them."

"Did she talk about me?"

"No," said Smith. "Not in any meaningful way."

Jim looked at Smith's *phal* and determined to commit suicide. "Can I have a mouthful of that?"

"Are you sure, Jimbo?"

"Yes," he said, his fork poised over the dish.

"Gently does it," said Smith.

Jim forked some into his mouth. Someone had poured molten metal on his tongue. He went bright red. His mouth puffed out and his eyes bulged. "Faaarkin' 'ell," he spluttered, reaching for his lager.

Smith was catching the eye of the waiter.

The lager extinguished the pain for as long as it was in his mouth. When he'd swallowed it, the heat came back with a vengeance. He was panting and glaring at Smith.

"I did say."

Jim emptied his glass. The pain was still fierce.

"*Raitha*," Smith told the waiter, "and pronto." The man smiled and scooted off. "Help is on its way."

Jim eyed Smith's beer.

"Beer's no good," said Smith. "The active ingredient of chilli is only fat soluble and right now it's glued to your tongue. Only fat'll get rid of it."

Jim nodded, mute.

"Hence my order of yogurt" said John. "Shortly the antidote will be on hand."

Much to Jim's relief, after two small dishes of cucumber yogurt the sensation had all but gone.

"Chillies are poison to birds," said Smith, "which is why the bird-eating spider, usually called the tarantula, has venom made of the active ingredient in chilli. It's the only poison common to plant and animal."

"That's good to know," said Jim, through a mouthful of his own curry. "I won't eat tarantula curry and I won't go to Belgrade."

Next morning Jim found himself watching the markets. He wanted to trade but it was pointless. Instead he surfed the Net and looked up the Black Hand. He found nothing that referred to any event later than the 1920s. He listened to music and started to buy hundreds of tracks from iTunes.

He was becoming a little bored when Stafford came in with two gorgeous girls. Jim was immediately on his feet.

"These are my two godchildren," his butler informed him. "Lavender and Tulip. Lavender and Tulip, this is Mr James Evans."

"Jim," he said, shifting from one foot to the other. "Nice to meet you."

"Come now, girls," Stafford said, "we shouldn't waste any more of Mr Evans's precious time."

"Don't worry, that's fine," said Jim.

Tulip gave him a cheeky look as they left the room.

Jim felt suddenly invigorated. Blimey, he thought. He sat down and closed his browser. He looked at the desktop wallpaper of Jane and her lovely muddy smile. It had to go.

Later that day he was staring out at the river. He should buy himself a boat and park it outside his window, he mused. Maybe he should extend the basement and build a submarine pen so he could pull out in secret at full tide. How cool would that be? And maybe he'd buy a mansion and fill it with cool toys. He could afford anything and everything. How great was that? Even things that weren't possible now, he could fund and make happen. But what would bring him the most happiness? He'd never really had much fun. Happiness and pleasure had been in short supply all his life. His training for happiness had been pretty much limited to an unexpected ice-cream, a hoped-for present on his birthday or at Christmas or a quick kiss in the corridor at school. And his adult life had been one of ever-increasing drama and stress. Happiness and pleasure were pretty much strangers to him. He needed some kind of guide, he realised.

Tulip came into the room and headed for his screens. She picked up his phone and dialled a number into it. A phone somewhere on her person rang and she hung up. She smiled cheekily at him and walked out.

Something was wriggling in his guts – and it probably wasn't last night's curry.

# 12

The flotation paperwork was about ten feet thick and the whole process had cost Baz around seven hundred and fifty thousand pounds. It was all legal cut-and-paste work, put together by well-paid but clueless junior lawyers and accountants' minions for the fat cats who ran firms that floated companies on the stock market. The firms he used specialised in mining explorers – or mining promotions, as they'd referred to them when they called a spade a spade rather than "environmentally friendly mineral extraction equipment".

The right fees ensured that his engineering reports were perfectly prepared. Very shortly he would be selling Barron's story to the institutions. As Higgins had said, it was like shooting ducks in a barrel. The market wanted speculative mines and, by God, it got them. Did they ever turn into billion-dollar mines? It happened occasionally, just as a racing punter got the odd winner in the Grand National.

Still, the City needed speculative mines because the audience loved them, and fund managers, who couldn't outperform the index if their lives depended on it, relied on mining stocks to give them a shot at a freak win.

There was no perfect market, no random walk: the financial world was just an encrustation of fools, crooks and functionaries driven by fear and greed. Baz fed the greed and the City paid him for it.

Barron was going to be a hell of a ride. Even those who knew what he was up to, and that included many around the table at the completion meeting to finalise the flotation, still thought they could ride along to their advantage. They could own the share on the ride up and drop it on to a greater fool before it turned to shit.

The wild journey might last three years – he never knew how long a story would hold. What he did know was that he would make another fortune and get away with it. In the thirty years he had spent taking the piss, no one had even come close to collaring him. It was *caveat* fucking *emptor*.

Everything was ready to go into phase two and he felt as bullish as hell.

He was going to place 49 per cent of the business for £30 million ostensibly to fund the mine and he would start sucking that money out of the business almost immediately. Then he would ramp the stock price higher with exciting but bogus news, secretly selling shares as it rose. Then the bad news that the mine had chewed through the money raised in the float would collapse the price. He would buy back the stock he had sold, closing his short for a massive profit, and the cycle would continue until the market tired of the Barron story and it was time for Baz to lie low and drop his notebook into the lagoon.

# 13

I don't fucking need this, thought Baz, as the DC-9 started its approach to Goma international airport with a tight, bumpy swerve. None of the planes that flew into Goma were allowed to fly anywhere other than domestically – the EU listed them as too dangerous to fly at all but, as usual, standards were different in the Democratic Republic of Congo. It would be ironic if, after all his hard work, a dodgy junk aircraft was his undoing.

The millions were raised and now it was just a matter of siphoning the money away without leaving any obvious clues that it was all one big con. In theory the location was perfect. The forty square miles of prospect were north of Goma and between a set of volcanoes. It really was the arse end of the world. Not only had it been a war zone until recently, but the two volcanoes went off as regularly as clockwork. No one in their right mind would go there and he was suddenly regretting being quite so thorough in his selection of a site that no one would check up on.

He was going to stay in Goma and make arrangements for his expatriate construction party. They would fly in and put up the mining compound. Then he would ship in the putative drillers and appear to be prospecting. He had to get the ball rolling: soon enough people would be enquiring about progress and he'd need photos of how things were going to keep them happy.

The plane was shaking as if it was about to fall apart. He took a slug from a miniature of vodka and gritted his teeth. He could see Nyiragongo through the window.

Fuck me, he thought. That really is a mean-looking bastard. McCoy was a fucking idiot: this certainly was the place where the devil would put the pipe in to give the world an enema. Lava had flowed across much of the city and had even swept over the end of the runway. Perhaps the enema had already happened.

When the two men met in the airport building, Higgins looked happy enough. He was worth every cent Baz paid him. But Baz was either getting softer or the world was getting harder: whichever it was, he promised himself that this would be his last ramp. He'd have enough from this job to last him for all time. Once it was over he'd sit on his beach and screw and drink himself to death.

"Good news and bad," said Higgins, as he slammed the jeep's door.

"Tell me the good news first," said Baz. "I could use some after that flight."

"Well, we've got a nice hotel on the lake. Good grub, clean, friendly and a pretty view over the water."

"And the bad news?"

"If there's an earthquake we'll get gassed."

"Gassed?"

"Yeah, the lake's full of carbon dioxide from the volcano, and if there's the wrong kind of seismic activity, up it comes and goodbye, Vienna. Everyone around the fucking lake dies."

"Ah, choice," said Baz. "Ker, ker, ker, ker, ker, ker." The jeep was bouncing over potholes. "This is going to be a riot. Anything else I need to know?"

"Oh, nothing much," said Higgins. "The civil war's about to break out again and there's still genocidal militias rampaging around the area."

"Anything else?"

"We're a bit too close to the gorillas for comfort."

"Can we buy them off?"

"No," said Higgins. "Or not without tonnes of bananas at any rate."

"*What?*"

"Not guerrillas. The animals. We're on the edge of a reserve. We might attract a bit of tree-hugger attention if we're not careful."

"Christ, that's all we need."

"And there's a pygmy problem. They're swarming all over our forty square miles."

"And what are they doing that's a problem?"

"Just being there. Some of the locals are scared of them. They're, like, magical."

"*Magical?*"

"Yeah."

"We've got magical pygmies?"

"That's right."

The jeep took a particularly big jolt.

"And this is a problem?"

"Yeah, because it could prove hard to hire local people and stuff."

"I see," said Baz. "Anything else?"

"That's about it."

90

"Are you sure?"

"Well, there's ..."

"Shut up, Mark!" Baz was laughing again. "Just don't tell me about the cannibals."

"Funny you should say that ..."

"No shut up, will you? Just shut up."

The volcano had what looked like a cloud of steam perched over it, and now he could see the lava that had flowed through the city in tar-like solid rivers. He marvelled at how two million people could place themselves, their families and their worldly goods in the lap of disaster. All you had to do was leave and go somewhere else. Anywhere would do, so long as it wasn't beside an exploding mountain. How hard could it be?

As long as the mountain didn't go bang in the short term he and his plans would be fine. But the benighted citizens of Goma had ended up and would spend their whole lives in this perverse location. It seemed like a basic form of self-preservation to leave. But if a smoking mountain and streets full of lava couldn't convince you to get on your bike then nothing would.

Hotel Ihusi would be their base, and Baz would marshal his forces from the side of Lake Kivu. Then, when everything was in place, he might venture out to see the property. Or maybe not this time. Once they had the compound sorted, he would helicopter in and cut out all the nonsense of driving a hundred kilometres over barely passable roads.

Once the compound was in place things would be a lot easier, Baz thought. Higgins had signed up as his on-site manager and was turning up trumps. Settling down had done the old bruiser no end of good, it appeared. After years of proving otherwise, he had now made plain that he could, in fact, operate his brain, which would be convenient for both of them.

# 14

Barron Mining was due to go public any day and Sebastian was nervous. He hadn't received a call about it and he was expecting one. He saw on his Bloomberg that a ten-day notice had been released and therefore that the company was in the final days of its flotation but calls to the broker were going unanswered. Something was up and he decided to write a stinky email.

"Ralph, I need to speak to you about Barron. I still haven't got my share certs and I'm awaiting a call from you about the float. I'm interested in participating and concerned to get my existing shares into my account. If I can't speak to you shortly I'll have to resort to my bank's analysts and ask them to go digging. Seb"

That should get their attention, he thought. He didn't think they'd appreciate his bank's team of red-hot financial gurus let loose on them. A bad note from them and the whole issue might be scuppered. It was a threat of mutually assured destruction.

Sure enough, his BlackBerry rang.

"Sebastian, I've been meaning to call you for days. Very busy, you understand."

"Of course. What uplift is the IPO coming in at?"

"A hundred per cent of the pre-IPO."

"Excellent."

"Would you like to be taken out?" asked the broker.

If they took the stock he'd bought he'd make a very tidy sum but, as they clearly wanted it, the share price was obviously about to ride high after the float. "How much is the float raising?"

"Thirty million pounds."

"Is anyone else coming out?"

"Plenty," said the broker.

That sounded like no one to Sebastian. "I'd like an allocation in the IPO," he said.

There was a note of hesitation at the other end. "I'm not sure," said Ralph. "This is institutional placing, not a PA round. How much were you looking for?"

"Two million," he said, rather rashly. He'd have to borrow it from the firm's credit line to him.

"All right. I'll put you down for two million but there will be a scale back, so you won't get the full amount. I'll know more nearer the time."

Sebastian felt relieved. Going in for another two million was madness. If he was sensible he'd cash his pre-IPO position now and take the fat profit. "Let me know," he said.

He had dreamt every night about the mine in Congo: sometimes the dream was pleasant, but at others it was a nightmare.

On Monday morning his phone rang again. "The offer's closed," said Ralph. "It was fifty times oversubscribed but I managed to get you another hundred K."

"That's pathetic," Sebastian protested.

"A lot of people got nothing, but, as you were in from day one, I called in a favour."

"Can't you manage some more?"

"Sorry. It was hard enough to get you this many."

"When's the first day of trading?"

"Next Monday."

"Is it going to pop?"

"Oh, yes," said Ralph, "and if you want to sell, just give me the nod and I'll get you out right away."

"Thanks. I'll be in touch" He slammed the phone down, his pale skin flushing red. Bloody hell! He'd missed out on a huge amount of money again.

Now all his dreams were nightmares. In the worst, Jemima had run off with Jim, his old junior, now a zillionaire. They were dismantling his home brick by brick and auctioning it off on eBay. He hadn't made a fortune and that was exactly the same as losing one.

He was going to buy in the market on the first day. He was sure the Barron Mining deposit in Congo was a huge one, that 'the boys' knew it and wanted it all for themselves.

At eight a.m. on Monday morning Barron Mining opened for trading. Sebastian had typed its ticker into his screen and watched the market-makers open their prices. The Barron Mining stock ticker was "BOM" and people would use these three letters to look up its share price from now on. On the chat sites they were calling the company Barmin and the posters seemed to know a lot of stuff he hadn't heard about. Apart from the cobalt there were unannounced kimberlitic structures on the land. Amazing, thought Sebastian. And then it all made sense. That was why they'd been so keen to buy back his stock at every stage of the flotation process. The diamonds Baz had shown him weren't a sideshow but the real deal. Everyone knew the area was riddled with them. The reason the place had been a war zone was because it had so many. After all, the site was right next to several volcanoes and that was where diamonds came from. All the pieces fell into place.

He bought in the market as it opened 60 per cent up from the IPO price. He chased the price as the share zoomed up, and, by the time he had spent his borrowed two million, the price was two pounds. He felt strong and powerful. He had sussed their little game.

Barron was 200p and sooner or later it would be a fiver – maybe even a tenner.

The price ticked down and started to drift off. Who was selling?

By the close of play the share price was 155p. Sebastian had lost nigh on three-quarters of a million pounds and a lot of his initial profits had been eaten away. At the flotation price he could have taken a six hundred thousand pounds' profit.

Within minutes of the opening, if he hadn't bought more, he would have been sitting on a £1.2 million win.

At two quid he would have been more than one and a half million ahead, but he had gone "all in", and after the last-minute faint in the price he was back profit-wise to roughly where he would have been if he'd let them sell his initial stake at the float price. The trouble was, the stakes were now so very much higher.

That night the nightmares came again. What the blazes had he done?

In the morning the share price opened up 5p. His frown

turned immediately into a smile. The first days of trading were going to be volatile. He should switch off his screen and look at it again in a week. It would save him a lot of trouble. Instead he fixated on Barron's progress. Every tick up was delicious, every tick down a smack in the face. But it was ticking up slowly and, as the days passed, its rise accelerated.

Barron was the talk of the Internet. On the ADVFN website, posters were singing the stock to the skies. Small investors riding the wave were cheering it on like football fans.

To Sebastian, they seemed well informed, while the "de-rampers", who suggested it was just another swindle, were clearly evil shorters, trying to ruin a perfectly good mine.

The only people posting who really knew any more than was in the share prospectus were Baz's Filipino team of rampers, employed to spread the word, or at least Baz's version of it, around the grapevine of the web. It was they who kept a flame under the wild talk that spewed out of the speculators. This was a world that Sebastian didn't know existed. While his bank might float a company for a few billion, he had no idea how the small-cap market worked.

Any company worth below two hundred and fifty million was considered a minnow and ignored as irrelevant. A company of Barron's size was too tiny to warrant anyone's time at his bank so he had never been involved at that end of the market. He was ignorant of the situation in which he now found himself.

Barron pulled back from 198p a share. He told himself it was profit-taking at the 200p level and that soon enough it would break new ground. In a fit of excitement he bought another half-million, trying to push it over the 200p price line. He managed it but it immediately fell back. He had now bought nearly £3 million of the stock and found himself having to announce a significant interest in the company to the stock exchange. That was a little embarrassing. A compliance officer turned up and asked him lots of loaded questions.

He hadn't done anything wrong, though, so unless they wanted shot of him, nothing would follow.

The share price popped up on the announcement. The bulletin boards were singing that a big wheel in a big bank held a huge stake, proof enough that Barron would be a billion-pound company by Christmas. Sebastian smiled to himself. That was flattering. The price hit 220p.

Then it slipped again.

Jim looked out on to the foreshore as the tide dropped to its lowest point. On the other side of the river, someone was walking along the bank searching among the stones and rubble. He got up and opened the window. There was a ladder just below the sill, leading down to the grey, pebbly beach. He climbed down it and began to search between the stones. Apart from broken bricks and slates, there was lots of smashed pottery, much of it ancient, lumps of iron, nails, screws and bolts. On a chalk bed he spotted a dull silver disc, picked it up and peered at it. There didn't appear to be anything on its surface. He walked on.

The City looked different from down there, a view he had never had of it before. His nan had always warned him to keep away from the river. "Sinking mud," she would say, "will suck you down and drown you." Now he could see that was nonsense. It was just a stony riverbank littered with the rubbish of a thousand years.

# 15

Barron Mining had been slipping every day. Sebastian's profits were gone and now, as the share price hit 100p, he was looking at a nasty loss, a six-hundred-thousand-pound loss, equivalent to more than half of his annual salary in one horrific investment, rather than the fat profit he had started with. The brokers who had sold him the deal in the first place always made reassuring noises when he called them – the project was going well, they declared, and there were buyers in the wings.

According to the mining reports, Barron was an amazing resource. It had untold quantities of cobalt, which was in huge demand for hardened steel. Every now and then the price would spike upwards and he would be sure it was about to take off again – until it then slipped off and headed south. Sebastian contacted his own broker and looked into selling.

"What?" he had found himself shouting. "What do you mean I can only get ten thousand pounds away without hitting the price?"

"Eh, eh," his broker had replied. "This is a market-maker stock and that's all they'll take at a go."

"I didn't seem to have that problem buying," he said. "And I've got three million pounds of stock I might want to sell." In fact, he hadn't got three million pounds of stock any more, but he held so much that he couldn't get out – at least not quickly. It might take months to unload a position of that size *and* at a whopping discount. If he tried to withdraw slowly and got lucky, he might get out over weeks or months and then, unless something unexpectedly good turned up, he'd have nailed the price indefinitely at the current level. Most likely, though, he'd drive the share price into the ground – he might halve it if he tried to get out quickly.

"These microcaps are tricky," said the broker finally. "I can leave an order with the market-maker."

"You mean you'll tell them I'm a seller of a huge block of stock?"

"That's how it works."

Sebastian looked at the screen showing the market-makers in BOM: they would buy a maximum lot of 10,000 shares at a time. He was stuck in his multi-million share position, unable to sell enough to get out for weeks. He was in big trouble. At least the price was holding above 100p.

Sebastian's BlackBerry buzzed. It was seven forty. An alert about Barron, an RNS stock-market news release, had been emailed to him on the phone's screen. He was in the middle of telling the traders that the month had been a fair one and to keep at it. They didn't pay him much attention when he gave them a bollocking or a pep talk: they were the masters of the universe who saved or broke markets. At least, they had been when Jim had been there. Now they were living off the legend.

Sebastian stopped talking and picked up the phone. He opened the email and practically dropped the BlackBerry. He let out a little cry. Barron had problems, and the price was going to crash at the open. He collected himself. "Thanks, guys," he said, his face white and speckled red, then stumbled to the door and out of the room. He was going to vomit for sure.

"Thanks, apropos fucking nothing, to you too," said Dirk, the options specialist, a little startled by his boss's abrupt departure. "What's got into him?"

"Irritable bowel," said Fat Joe, and took a big swig of his latte.

The traders scowled at each other and got up to leave.

Sebastian was sitting miserably on the toilet waiting for two things to happen: the danger of puking to subside, and the market to open in six minutes. In the cubicle, though, with just a web page for company, it was hard to tell what was going on. At his terminal he would be able to see the FTSE futures trading, suggesting either strength or weakness in the market. The market-makers would be coming online with their orders before kick-off and this would give him an idea of what would happen when trading started. But he was caught in a China limbo and, with his tiny screen, all he could do was refresh the page with yesterday's price on it while he waited for the market to open.

The drilling rig for Barron's initial exploration programme had been seized in Customs at the Rwandan border and had been impounded. The project was going to be delayed. It wasn't the end of the world by any means but it was sure to smash the price. The final seconds ticked down unbearably slowly. Then, at last, it was 8:00:01.

He hit the page refresh: 38 per cent down. He blinked in the hope that he had misread it. He refreshed again – 42 per cent down

Suddenly he was calm. He'd had it. He was well and truly scuppered. He got up, flushed the toilet to complete the fiction, and left the stall. He was powerless. He was like an ant scooped up in a spoon of sugar and about to be dropped into a cup of boiling tea.

By the time he reached his screen the price was down only 25 per cent His whole body reacted in a moment of pure relief. Maybe it would zoom ahead now.

His life was hanging by a thread and the market makers, the stock market's middle men who mediated the price swings of shares, seemed to be pulling him upwards to safety. Now it was only 15 per cent down. Maybe it had been falling because the insiders had known this bad news was coming and were getting out. Now the price would recover as they bought back in. Why the hell wasn't he an insider on this?

The price suddenly dropped 10 per cent. He closed the screen and opened his email. He had to find a way out of this mess.

He called Ralph, the stinking broker who had sold him the stock, but he wasn't in.

"Nine o'clock!" he heard himself protest. "The market opens at eight."

"Not around here," said the junior sheepishly.

By the time Ralph called the price was at 90p. "Don't worry," he said. "It'll come good, but you'll have to take the rough with the smooth on this one. The DRC is a bit difficult."

"Can you place my stock?"

"In what way?"

"Well, take it off me at a pound."

"Well, the share's at 90p at the minute."

"I can see that, but when it gets back there."

"Perhaps. The market's a bit thin right now, but we should be able to do something when the next good news comes out."

"When will that be?"

"That's tricky. Is your line recorded?"

"No – I'm on the mobile."

"Good. Have to be careful, you know."

"Of course."

"Well, there are reports from the kimberlites." Sebastian remembered the tiny diamond – he still had it somewhere. "My analysts think they're important. We have some satellite photos showing a very interesting cluster of kimberlitic structures on the property. Most stones in the region come out of local hand-dug pits only a few metres deep, but the potential for proper exploitation is colossal – and there's the Eye of Kivu, a five hundred carat stone that showed up in Goma only last month. It's all very promising."

"When do you think all this will come out?"

"Can't be sure. Things always take a little longer than you expect, but it's a strong management team."

BOM was falling again, ticking down to 85p.

Sebastian had a good mind to buy some more, but he was in way too deep. The price ticked up again as he hung up. He scrunched his eyes up to peer at the Barron chart and tried to make sense of it. He wanted to draw lines on it but there was so little to go on. Then he had a good idea.

The riverbank was full of fascinating old bits and pieces. Wherever Jim looked his eyes picked out strange shapes that turned into old coins or broken cutlery. He could spot even the slightest edge of something interesting and on the banks outside his flat there seemed no end of junk.

Stafford seemed to know what it all was. "The corner of a seventeenth-century pewter shoe buckle," he might say. "A James the Second tin farthing in very poor condition. An early twentieth-century penknife I should think. A decorated clay-pipe bowl, from the mid-seventeenth century." He claimed he was no authority, but Jim was impressed, amused and pleased. When he found the pewter end of a Stuart scabbard, which felt like treasure, he was totally hooked.

Stafford had sourced a large glass display case and Jim was filling it with his precious finds. There were two tides a day and only one usually in daylight. Each one was different as every tide had a different rise and fall, and there were miles of foreshore for him to visit.

He had found a passion, if not a purpose.

As he climbed back through the window Stafford was waiting for him. He stepped out of his boots on the large mat that had appeared one day out of the blue. Jim sat on the sofa and emptied his pockets on to a cloth that Stafford produced. "I have tidings, so to speak," said the butler, plucking a small piece of copper whatnot from the dirty pile. "Anglo-Saxon strap end. Very nice."

"Really?" said Jim, taking it back. "Really?"

"I should think so."

"Wow."

Stafford picked up a tiny slice of what had been a disc. "A quarter-cut penny, thirteenth to fifteenth century. My word you have a sharp eye."

Jim took the tiny piece of stamped metal. "Wow," he said again.

There was a pair of ship's dividers, corroded solid but open. Stafford picked them up and examined them very closely. "Very, very interesting," he said, lost for a moment in thought.

"Really?"

Stafford looked at Jim queerly. "It depends," he said mysteriously. He put them down. "Anyway, there's someone I'd like you to meet, seeing how much you enjoy the ancient. The lady in question is currently excavating Mearde Street in the City. A huge development's going up and they're on a site picking over the Roman layer. Would you like to see?"

"Bloody right!"

Stafford picked up a grey piece of twisted metal with a blob on one end. "A sixteenth-century spoon handle."

Although it didn't look like it, Baz owned 53 per cent of Barron Mining through a series of front companies spread around all the tax havens of the world. The arrangement wasn't too elaborate but was complicated enough to confuse and stymie any investigation into who really owned the company. Once his holdings were anonymous he was free to do as he liked with the stock, so he lent it to himself in the guise of yet another company and sold it. When his good news was made public, he would sell into the buying, and when the bad news arrived he'd buy it back after the fall. In due course he would sell the stock into the ground and buy it back when the company had to raise more money to fund the expensive dig that wasn't happening. The cash needed to pay the bogus costs went to him.

The combination of his fabricated news, his rumour mill and the happy gambling muppets who punted his share was like the key to the back door of a bank vault. He was going to shovel money out of it and into his waiting van for as long as it was prudent to do so. His campaign had started well: the millions were already piling up.

He had been doing broker presentations to institutions. They liked the story, and as the stock was cheap, they were happy to snap it up in the market. As they bought, he sold. The price might rise but soon enough it would fall again. He could sell it down to zero if he wanted to, and he could crash the price by releasing a news story or two. He was lining up to do just that.


Jim gazed down at the door lying on the black mud. The archaeologist was squatting on her haunches. She waved her trowel in a large arc. "Isn't that wonderful?" she said.

"And it's Roman?"

"Yes," she said, surreptitiously chewing Nicorette gum, "preserved in the mud. It's basically waterlogged at this level."

"And why is it lying there like that?"

"Good question."

"Is there like a Roman basement down there?"

"Probably not. We think it's symbolic."

"Symbolic of what?"

"The door to the underworld."

"Hell?"

"Not quite. Hades wasn't considered hell, just a kind of heaven, an afterlife."

"And under the door is a staircase to hell?"

"We'll find out shortly, because we aren't going to leave it behind."

"I'd love to be there when you open it."

"I think we'll be more lifting it than opening it," she said, a faint smile on her lips.

"If I may," said Stafford, stepping forwards, "I wondered, Jill, what your next project will be."

She stood up and looked rather sad. "I don't know," she said. "It depends on funding. There's not much going around at the moment."

"Funding?" said Jim. "What does a dig like this cost?"

"Oh, a lot," she said, "hundreds of thousands."

"Is that all?" He laughed.

No one joined in.

Jim decided to press on with the thought. "Maybe we could organise a dig in my back garden."

"Your back garden?" Jill said, throwing Stafford a look.

"The Thames, my dear," he said. "I'm sure Mr Evans will be very happy to cover the costs."

"Wapping," said Jim. "I'm bloody sure all the good stuff's down deep. We could put a dam in and dredge it."

"That would cost a fortune."

"No worries."

Jill turned to Stafford for confirmation. He smiled reassuringly.

"Planning will be tricky but I can sort that." She rested her chin on the handle of her trowel. "A ten-by-ten-metre dam excavation could come in at over a million."

"Can you make it bigger?" asked Jim.

"Probably," she said. "Things can usually be done bigger."

"Can I touch it?" said Jim, pointing at the door.

"Yes," she said, "but gently."

Jim hunkered down and ran his finger over the rough wet wood. "Now I can say I've touched the door to hell itself," he said.

"Again," said Stafford.

Jim was about to query this but Jill clapped her hands. "I'm getting excited now," she said. "I've always wanted to strip a piece of the river back to the beginning. It's never really been done. Imagine what we might find."

Jim could see it now, right outside his window. It would be awesome, he marvelled. His thoughts were interrupted by his phone. He took it out of his pocket and looked at the caller ID on the screen

It was Sebastian Fuch-Smith.

# 16

Sebastian rang the doorbell on the dot of one o'clock. Jim was sitting on the sofa, mournfully watching the tide go down. He could have been out there a full hour ago and now, in another hour, it would be low tide. By the time he'd finished with his old friend it would be coming up again. Not that there wouldn't be another tomorrow, but this was a particularly low tide and a large stretch of river would be exposed that he hadn't yet had the opportunity to explore. It was like missing an important football match.

"Love the butler," said Sebastian, as soon as Stafford was out of earshot. He got straight to the point. "I need your advice." He took some charts out of a leather portfolio.

"I don't do that kind of thing any more."

"No, mate, just look at these."

Jim could see it was some crazy-arsed stock.

"I've got myself into a bit of a mess, old chap, and I desperately need some guidance."

Jim got up. "Let me see," he said, going to his screens. "What's the ticker?"

"BOM," said Sebastian.

"Bum?"

"No BOM."

"Ah, right."

Jim pulled up the chart. "Ugh," he said. "This one's all over the place,"

"Is it going up over a hundred and thirty?"

"Oh, yeah," said Jim.

"Thank God for that." Sebastian sighed.

"But it's going all over the place by the look of it. It might go via 20p."

"Oh, God, don't say that."

"It'll probably go to the moon too but, like I say, it's all over the place. This is totally fucking chaotic." Jim pulled the chart around.

"How far is the moon?"

"Don't know, mate. This thing's just too crazy." He looked at Sebastian, whose face was ashen. "What's up mate?" he asked, suddenly worried for him.

"I've bet the bloody farm on it, Jim. I've borrowed from the firm an absolute tonne and I can't get out. My balls are in a vice on this one and I don't know what to do." Sebastian was clearly on the edge of tears.

"It's going to zoom, mate. Don't worry yourself – it'll go well over a hundred and thirty."

"I can't sleep, mate, and my fucking hair's falling out. Jemima's wondering what's got into me. Are you sure it's going over the hundred and thirty?"

"How much of it have you got?"

"At one thirty, at break-even ... about three point five bar."

"Three and a half million? Ouch, so you're down about a mil."

"Yup, and I'm worried it'll cliff and hit, you know."

"Twenty p."

"Yup, you've got it. That would be curtains."

Jim looked at the chart. It could certainly go there in a hurry but it might also go to five quid. Which happened first was anyone's guess.

His tide was sinking fast. "Tell you what," he said. "I'll sell you a put call. You give me 10p a share and I'll give you a twelve-month put at a hundred and forty. Meanwhile you give me a free call at a hundred and fifty." He should have made it 140p, but the higher call gave his friend an extra 10p profit, if Jim could be bothered to take his shares off him when it rocketed. It meant his friend could compulsorily sell the stock to him at 140p a share at any time in the next twelve months, and Jim could compulsorily buy it off him in the same period at 150p. When, and if, the price rocketed he could buy Sebastian's shares off him and sell them for a tidy profit, while Sebastian was covered for all his losses if he chose at any time to unload them on Jim. He had offered his mate a parachute halfway down a nosedive from ten thousand feet.

"Christ, would you?" gasped Sebastian. "Would you really do that?"

"Sure," said Jim. "I'm going to make a packet." He looked at the chart. "Maybe." He laughed. "What is this fucking thing?"

"It's a mine in DRC. Well, it will be a mine."

"DRC?"

"Congo – you know, Zaïre."

"Right," said Jim. "That's, like, Africa, right?" He grinned at the unconcealed relief on his mate's face.

"Yes, old chap, Africa."

"And what the fuck are you doing buying this kind of shit?"

111

"It's a long story, mate, and I'm not exactly proud of myself."

Even for Jim the chart's trail was hard to read. In comparison with the big-cap stocks, currencies and commodities he traded, it was like a Bugs Bunny cartoon. And the rabbit was grinning cheekily at him with outsize incisors. He might as well have thrown three of his eight thousand million down the toilet. "Get the paperwork over to me as soon as you can," Jim said, getting up. "I'm out the window."

"I'm sure it'll come good for you." Sebastian was about to make a fast exit. You've thrown your money out of it for sure, and God bless you, he thought. He'd get the paperwork sorted that afternoon. The ten-pence option price he'd have to pay, equivalent to £250,000, was a small price for the certainty of escape from impending ruin. At the first tick down of the share, he'd drop the lot on Jim . He'd even make a small profit. If only he could just get ink on the dotted line before Jim changed his mind.

Surprisingly, Jim was actually climbing out of the window. Sebastian didn't want to ask why so he headed for the door.

Higgins surveyed the camp. It was set on a lush green plateau at the foot of a mountain jungle that led up to a volcanic range and Nyamuragira. Behind them he could see the snaggle-toothed Mount Kikeno, and to the right the giant cone of Nyiragongo. Some Congolese soldiers, a shambolic crowd if ever there was one, were quartered in a separate compound. The fifty men were a ragtag group with no discipline and an unfathomable structure that somehow contained as many officers as other ranks. They seemed very miserable to be posted in the middle of nowhere – and in a zone that had recently been a killing ground. They were a very unsatisfactory guard indeed.

Once he had got the electrified fence up around the helipad he felt a lot happier. He could fuck off out of there in five minutes and make for Goma, Rwanda or Uganda. The whole region made him nervous. If it wasn't the area's dodgy past and present, it was the smoking mountains. The locals were pleasant enough, but he got the distinct feeling that, given half a chance, they'd recommend a swim in the lake with the friendly crocs and hippos.

The staff lodgings were hardly five-star but they were functional. The building crew and support team were Chinese, and they had thrown up the construction with breathtaking speed. There was little in the way of luxury, not that he cared. Now the base camp was sorted, he had everything and nothing to worry about.

Tulip was turning Jim's insides to jelly and, regardless of her SMS, she clearly hadn't come for a coffee. He felt himself slip into a different mode of operation. The trading nerd was morphing into a happy, laughing horny animal. He felt great. This girl was like a ripe peach and he wanted a bite. When he brushed her arm, her skin felt hot and she reacted as if he'd done her a favour.

She was smiling at him as if he was the handsomest, smartest guy in the world.

Perhaps he was.

As they bundled down New Bond Street he caught her arm and kissed her. There was no shock or embarrassment, just a passionate welcome. That look she was wearing meant only one thing – but it was all too obvious and too fast for him, Jim thought.

No, it wasn't.

They turned and ran hand-in-hand towards the Ritz. He knew London wasn't going to be like Paris.

When he woke up, it was nine a.m. She had disappeared, but there was a note on her pillow.

"Gone for a hairdo, back in a mo."

He went back to sleep to be woken again by the door opening. Her hair was done up in the old-fashioned Hollywood style of waves and curls. "Nice," he said blearily.

She had something sparkly on her wrist. "What do you think?" she said, holding it out.

"Nice," he said again. "Where did you get it?"

"Downstairs. It's on kind of approval." She sat down next to him and batted her eyelids. "Do you like it?"

"Yes," he said. "It looks good on you."

"I thought so," she said seriously. She fluttered her long eyelashes.

The heat of her body rolled over him in a wave. "Would you like it?" he asked.

"Oh, yes, please." She was smiling. "Are you sure?" she said. "It's very expensive, but it's so lovely." She lifted her hand up to admire the bracelet.

"Of course," he said.

She jumped on him and started kissing him. "You're so marvellous to me," she said, "so very marvellous."

She made him feel marvellous too.

*

St George, head of wealth management at the bank and his friendly financial handler, had called and Jim had missed him. Now he was sitting in a cab. Tulip had gone on her delicious way and left him feeling like a well-scratched tabby cat. He returned the call.

"Jim," said St George, "good of you to ring. I just want to confirm that you'd like us to look after the money in your trading account. The boys in broking don't want to let it go. They're making a fortune on interest from it, but it's not doing you much good just having it sit about doing nothing."

"Good point, Jules," said Jim. "Yes, please, get it working."

"Very good. I'm sorry to ask but they dug their heels in, greedy blighters."

"Go ahead whenever you like."

"As a matter of housekeeping, you appear to have bought a fair chunk of a scrappy mine in the back of beyond – off, if I may add, a rather unusual option agreement. We'll have to make an announcement to the exchange."

"Blimey," said Jim. "OK." Sebastian had bottled it. He wondered what the price of the stock was. Sod it: it was only about three days' interest.


Baz sat forwards in his chair. "What the fuck's that?" he muttered. Someone had bought about four per cent of the company at three times the current price. He checked the share register. It had to be the stake of the prat who'd got greedy in the pre-IPO; it was the only block of stock that fitted the size traded. What the fuck was going on?

He'd been expecting to pick the stock up at 40p to cover some of his shorts and some idiot had bought the shares at a ridiculous price, impossibly far above the current bid offer. It didn't make sense. Ralph knew a ramp was coming up but he wouldn't be so stupid as to fuck around like that.

"I've seen it," Ralph said, when he called and before Baz had said a word. "I've got someone digging under the nominees to find out who it is. Maybe it's just a paperwork shuffle."

"That would be news to me," said Baz.

"Me too," said Ralph, "but these big bank people are always up to tricks."

"I don't like it, Ralph. I don't like it one penny piece."

# 17

Jim had a hell of a time remembering the name of the stock Sebastian had dumped on him. He didn't want to call either him or St George to find out what it was – either conversation would be embarrassing. Finally he remembered the ticker: BOM.

News had come in that drilling results would be delayed as, having finally got the rig in from Rwanda, it had fallen down the mountainside and been wrecked. Another was apparently being sourced. The share price had touched 30p. He felt less annoyed with Sebastian when he saw the price: he'd saved his mate's skin as, in a way, Sebastian had saved his only a year or so ago in Venice.

He chuckled at the chart. It was the weirdest thing he'd ever seen, and pretty soon it was going to take off vertically. He called up his broker, Kitson. "I want you to pick up as much of Barron as you can, please," he said.

"Of course. Cobalt in the Congo, if I recall. It's a thin market. Hold on." Kitson pulled up a screen. "It's forty to forty-five p in ten thousand shares."

"Buy it up to a pound a share and try to get me, say, ten per cent of the company."

"This is a bit of an illiquid one, Jim," said Kitson. "It'll be hellish to get you out."

"Don't worry," said Jim. "It'll give me something to do."

"Right you are," said Kitson. "I'll winkle out as much stock as possible without moving the price, but it'll take time."

"Get as much as you can over the next two weeks. It could blow up pretty fast."

"I think I should perhaps pay the mine a visit," said Kitson. "I know you'll probably scoff but it's always a good idea to see these things."

"OK," said Jim, "but first get the stock."

"I'll start right away."

Baz didn't like the price of his stock to start misbehaving. It had to go up and down when and if he decided it should. When he made it go up with his news announcements he sold through his fronts, and when it went down, he bought the shares back. It was a slow rollercoaster ride, which he controlled, that pumped his accounts full of money.

Greedy speculators were compulsive gamblers hooked on blowing their hard-earned wealth on the search for a get-rich-quick scheme that usually ended in the reverse. But there was no putting them off. With all the advice against it, and often years of painful experience in getting skinned alive on similar exploits, they kept coming back for more. Like all abusive relationships, the story was powered by an unfathomable love of pain and misery.

Baz was the master of this financial S&M scene and he didn't like it when something gatecrashed his private dungeon.

Ralph was on the phone: the market-makers – who were essentially share wholesalers – had been on to him looking for a supply of Barron stock. Baz was in a quandary: he had hoped to hoover up a lot of stock at these levels, having sold a bundle of them when the share price had rocketed at flotation, but now someone else was wielding the vacuum-cleaner. He didn't want any big shareholders in the picture: they might end up being awkward. They might even be able to set the dogs on him.

He could let the buyer run the price up or lose interest, or he could drop stock on him, knowing that in any event the price would be zero sooner or later. It was a question of a bird in the hand being worth two in the bush. It looked as if this buyer was interested in at least a million or two, and if he sold them to him through one of his fronts he'd be that much better off, come what may. "Tell them I can find shares at the float price," said Baz.

"OK," said Ralph. He understood that Baz would sell high and buy low, not the other way around. Whoever was buying would be shaken out soon enough, and when he was he'd dump his stock cheap and Baz would buy it. Then when the stock shot up Baz would sell it again.

Kitson had the bank's market-maker sit on the bid – they made it known that they wanted stock, and as the days passed, they pushed the price around to entice owners to come out and sell to them. In fits and starts the price rose, punctuated with sharp falls when the bank's market-maker fell away, as if their order had been satisfied. This was the kind of game they played when they were trying to fill big orders and it was the kind of action Baz got up to himself when he was ramping or crashing the price. Nothing made people want to buy a stock more than a rising price, and nothing made them want to sell it more than when it fell, so as the price ran up the speculators piled in, only to pile out as the price fell. Speculators were financially suicidal, and the professionals took advantage of that.

The price jumped from 60p to 75p and the stock exchange was on to Ralph. He had to get hold of Baz to ask whether something was happening with Barron.

Baz laughed. "Well, we'll have to make an announcement that the company knows of no reason for the share-price rise. Funny how the exchange never calls when it falls." He laughed again. "It tells you all you need to know about what they think is normal and what they think is strange."

"OK," said Ralph. "We'll get that done."

The announcement caused disappointment among the speculators. The price dipped and the disillusioned sold. Then it picked up again. At 90p there was a sudden spike of selling. A lot of the pre- and pre-pre-IPO investors decided it was time to book some profit after their hair-raising ride: they knew that, at 100p, a lot of buyers at the IPO price would sell out on the basis that they had made their losses back. At 95p Kitson had got Jim up to his 10 per cent shareholding. The broker had had fun. It wasn't often he was called on to buy at the small-cap end of the market and it reminded him of his young days when shares were still traded on the floor by men with top hats. The small-cap market was still delightfully archaic and occasionally he hankered for the old ways, with real people gossiping in a colourful financial bazaar with "blue buttons", "jobbers" and "commission" men running around. The computer had done for all that.

*

*Leviathan* was a 410-foot yacht with a helipad and enough telemetry on the bridge roof to keep a destroyer informed across most of the electromagnetic spectrum. When Jim had asked Stafford to charter him a yacht for a couple of weeks, he hadn't expected him to book the biggest on the planet. He didn't want to query it, though, because he was going to take his butler's goddaughter away for two weeks of wild abandon. The thought of spending £100,000 a day on a boat that looked more like a cruise liner than a pleasure boat had made him want to laugh. Money meant nothing to him any more. "Why not? Don't they make a bigger one?"

"I'm sure one could be built for you, sir," observed Stafford.

For a split second Jim had been tempted.

Tulip looked the part. She was a beautiful mermaid in black sunglasses, and was quite at home on the giant ship. She might have been a princess with several of her own.

He sat under a canopy on the top deck with a beer in one hand and a mouse in the other. He was bored out of his skull. Tulip, however, seemed to be intensely occupied, lying naked in the sun for hours, baking herself.

There was a certain amount of fun to be had from being gawped at when he was pulling into harbour or anchoring in a bay, but Jim soon decided it was much less fun than staying in a hotel. But Tulip seemed to be having a great time and that was reason enough to sit, at vast expense, on an empty boat doing nothing for a couple of weeks except having wanton sex. Life had certainly treated him worse.

Thank God, he thought, when the phone rang.

It was Kitson. "We have your ten per cent," he said, as if he had apprehended a dangerous criminal.

"Good work," said Jim.

"It was on the expensive side, at an average 82p."

"That's OK," said Jim. "If you see 400p, get on to me about selling."

"I most certainly will. There's one thing I'd like to add. I really do think I should visit the mine now, first, so I can find out more for you, and second, so that I can potentially recommend it to some of my other clients. I shall take the cost from my commission."

"That's fine by me," said Jim. "Where is it?"

"In the western Congo basin, out by Rwanda."

"Right," said Jim. "Sounds nice."

"Well, it's not known for that but I'm sure it'll be fascinating. There'll be an announcement tomorrow about your holding at the stock exchange."

"Whatever. When are you off?"

"I'll get in touch with the firm and then we'll see."

Jim had an idea. "Why don't you fly the management down to see me here? I'm on a boat off Sardinia. It's only a hop and a skip on my jet. I'll send it for you."

"What an appealing idea," said Kitson. "I'll revert."

On the yacht, if it could have been made with cloth it was done in leather. If it should have been made of leather it was silk. If it might have been chipboard, it was mahogany. Steel was brass, and brass was gold.

Jim tried to come to terms with why you would dip so much money in brine but had to admit to himself that if you had big money, as he did, and you planned to spend it, this was the route you had to take. If someone with a net worth of half a million would happily buy a £50,000 car, then a £30–40 million boat was about right for a man with a billion or two.

In fact, it was a trifle, because after the first few millions the rest of the money was effectively disposable.

He was determined to seek Davas's advice when he got home. Without material worries he felt disembodied somehow, a ghost in the real world.

Tulip was lying face down on the white silk sheet, reading. The light gave her skin a reddish hue. He ran a finger up her back and she rolled from side to side letting out little squeals. "Do you think this is the biggest yacht there is?" she wondered.

"I don't know," said Jim. "Normally you can be sure that, however big something is, there's always a bigger one."

"Think of the fun you could have on the world's biggest yacht." Her hand was resting on her curvaceous hip, her arm like a giant shark's fin.

"We're going to need a bigger boat," he said. Where had he heard that line before?

"Fuck me, that's a big boat," said Baz, to Ralph and Kitson, as the helicopter swung round to land on *Leviathan*.

"Rather nice," said Kitson.

"So, our new shareholder is seriously minted – I mean not just jet minted but super-yacht minted."

Kitson didn't reply, he just smiled and nodded.

Fuck, thought Baz, that's not good. He looked at Ralph, who was sweating with the motion sickness the helicopter was causing. "His real name's not Evanovich, is it?" He laughed, but inside he was hoping someone nasty wasn't lying in wait behind the scenes.

Kitson smiled and didn't reply.

Ralph was thinking there were two sorts of super-rich people: those who would skin you for a penny and those who didn't give a damn about losing the odd million. It would be inconvenient if Evans was of the former persuasion.

"Bit of a mystery man," said Baz, for the umpteenth time.

Kitson nodded again as they swung into land.

Fucking bulge bracket banks, thought Baz, so fucking smug.

Ralph looked as if he was going to throw up if the pilot didn't land soon on the pad at the prow of the boat.

Jim had decided to play it cool, like a Bond villain, and waited on the upper sun deck under a canopy, surfing the markets on his Alienware notebook.

The chief steward met the party at the helipad and took them along the side of the ship, then brought his guests up to him.

"Welcome, gentlemen," said Jim, continuing to stare at his screen. "I've been expecting you."

The steward stepped in. "Can I fetch you something to drink?"

"I'll have a beer," said Baz.

"Glass of white wine," said Kitson.

"Me too," said Ralph.

"A martini for me," said Jim.

The steward vanished.

Kitson introduced Baz and Ralph, and as he did so, Tulip walked past them, dressed in a silk wrap. She ruffled Jim's hair but didn't say a word.

Kitson's mouth was still open although he'd finished speaking some time ago.

Baz was looking at Jim keenly. With his Cockney voice he was way too young to have this kind of money. If he had sounded like a scion of some big family fortune, Baz would have understood that some waster was blowing the family silver. This kid was not only a complete unknown but also an aberration.

The moment Baz had seen the stock-exchange announcement that a James Evans had bought more than three per cent of Barron at a stupid price, he had put a firm of top-notch investigators on his trail. They had come up with nothing. It didn't help that James Evans was hardly an uncommon name, but even so, someone with this kind of cash should have come out in highlighter. Instead there was a plethora of James Evanses and not one that fitted the picture. He wished he had the dossier in front of him now so he could check it again.

"Lovely ship," he said.

"Yeah," agreed Jim.

"If you don't mind," said Baz, "how much does one of these cost?"

"Don't know," said Jim. "I'm just chartering it for a couple of weeks."

"If it flies, floats or fucks, rent it, eh?" said Baz.

Ralph winced.

"One out of three anyway," said Jim.

"Like your thinking," Baz responded.

The steward laid out the drinks. Baz picked up his beer. "Welcome on board, if you will, the good ship Barron Mining." They clinked glasses. "You've made a very shrewd investment. Can I ask you what got you interested?"

"Technicals," said Jim. "I like the chart."

"Really?" said Baz. "I didn't think we had much of a chart. We've only been listed for a few weeks."

"Looks pretty good to me," said Jim.

"Well, great," said Baz, "and now you'd like to know more."

Kitson broke in, "Yes I certainly would." He was worried that Jim would say no, in his technical-trader arrogance.

"Well," said Baz, "as long as you can't remember what I'm about to tell you, you can't be an insider."

"I don't want to be inside," said Jim.

"Don't worry," said Kitson, screwing up his eyes and smiling. "Baz won't make you inside. Will you?"

"No, mate," said Baz, "couldn't possibly."

Ralph drank some of his wine.

"OK," continued Baz, "there's good news and bad news."

"What's the bad?" said Kitson.

Baz clucked. "The drilling for cobalt's not going well. It's slower than we'd like and it's not turning up trumps as we hoped. We might be a busted flush on the cobalt data."

With a bit of luck Evans would be bailing out of the stock he'd bought as soon as they took off from the helipad. "There's cobalt there, all right, but the deposit is shallow, and at a lot lower grade than we had expected. It's not looking commercial. On top of that, we've blown a lot of our money drilling the bores. Pretty much everything that could go wrong has."

Jim nodded. "What's the good news?"

"We've come up with some kimberlites, three to be exact. They might be diamond bearing.'

"Only about one in a hundred kimberlites contains diamonds," said Kitson.

Ralph nodded. "Yes," he said, "but this is a very fruitful area for diamonds so we're hopeful."

"And that's why your price crashed, right" said Jim.

"Maybe," said Baz, "but we haven't announced the cobalt news yet. It's still not certain that we're bombed out on cobalt. We're going to exhaust all possibilities. You never know."

"How did the news get out?" asked Jim.

"Fucking drillers," said Baz, looking mournful for about two seconds.

"So what you're saying," interjected Kitson, "is that your mine is dry and there's a tiny chance you may have diamonds."

"Yeah," said Baz, "that's about it. But we've got forty square miles of property in some of the richest mineral land on earth so something might still turn up."

"Sounds pretty hopeless," said Kitson.

Baz looked down at the table. "We'll come up with something," he said, "you mark my words. We're still very hopeful." The price of Barron would be 30p within days, he thought, and he'd buy back all the stock at the price he'd planned all along.

"Good," said Jim. "I'm sure you're right."

"Thanks," said Baz, suddenly confused.

"I'm tempted to buy some more," said Jim. "Do you know anyone who wants to sell?"

"No," said Baz, rather too sharply. "We don't keep track of the stock that closely."

"What about you Ralph? You're the broker."

Ralph grimaced. "I can look into it."

Jim caught the eye of the steward, who was standing well back. "Another round, please."

"I'd like to visit the property," interjected Kitson.

"Really?" said Baz, squirming. "It really is in the arse of nowhere, mate."

"I know," said Kitson. "I used to know Zaïre well under Mobutu."

"Oh, right," said Baz. He laughed. "Well, sure, come on down." Shit.

"Changing the subject a bit," he went on, "can I ask you a personal question, Jim?"

"Go ahead," said Jim.

"What kind of business is it that allows a young guy like you to afford all this?"

Jim wanted to say, "Drugs and guns," so he did.

Baz went red and Ralph went white.

Jim laughed. "Only joking."

"Ker, ker, ker," laughed Baz, "good one." He fixed Jim with a stare. "So, go on, what do you do?"

"I'm a trader."

"What do you trade?"

"Anything that moves."

# 18

Four hours later Kitson was on the phone to Jim from London. "Jim, I'm afraid, in my opinion, you've bought a lot of valueless stock."

"Could be," said Jim, his *flambé* cherries getting cold, "but the chart says it'll go to a fiver maybe even thirty quid."

"That's insane," said Kitson, his voice in a higher register than normal, "and I mean that, with due respect."

"I can afford the mistake,"

"I know," said Kitson, "and I don't doubt your abilities to read the charts but, even so, this is such a simple example of a dud mining promotion I can't entertain anything but the gravest of doubts."

"Don't bother yourself," said Jim. "It's OK. If it goes to a fiver sell it, if it goes tits up forget it."

"Well, I'm going to take a look. If it's as good as you think, I'd be a fool not to fill my own and my clients' boots. So I'm going to take a look for both of us."

"Cool," said Jim. "I might come along."

"I shouldn't," said Kitson. "There really isn't much to recommend it unless you like boiling heat, hundred per cent humidity, terrible food and no amenities. If it was, say, Mozambique I'd encourage you, but in this instance I positively recommend against it."

"OK," said Jim. "Keep me posted."

Baz lay awake, thinking. It was one a.m. and it was only a very rare problem that stopped him sleeping. He had hoped the selling would start the moment they took off from the yacht, but nothing had happened.

A lot of so-called rich men would panic at the thought of losing the smallest amount of money, and even a man on a fifty-million-dollar yacht would sweat over a $20 million position in a busted mine. Yet the kid didn't seem to give a monkey's and that was too weird. How much money did you need to have to not give a fuck about twenty million dollars? And if you were that rich, surely you'd be famous. But Evans was a nobody.

Someone was trying to con him, but who? Not only who, but why? He didn't know anyone with the money or the balls to play that kind of game and he couldn't imagine why they would, even if they did.

Something was very wrong but he had no idea what it could be. He was going to have to spend some real cash to find out who this joker was.

To make things worse, the irritating broker, Kitson, was going to visit the mine next week, with or without Baz going along. He'd have to drop everything and go too, to make sure Kitson got the right handling. Fortunately brokers never knew the slightest thing about mining so it was easy to bamboozle them. A little sightseeing, some drinking with the ladies, a spot of entertaining storytelling and they were always satisfied.

It had all been going so well. Yet now he was just going to have to get it back on track, using the old magic he had conjured up so many times before.

Perhaps tomorrow would be the day Evans would start to dump his Barron stock. If he did, the problem would evaporate, like most of Baz's problems did. Then he'd be a much happier man. If Evans didn't, he'd have to come up with another plan. At some point he'd have to ramp the price to dump his stock, so whatever happened he needed to keep the diamonds-and-gold story in place.

Baz was waiting for Kitson at the check-in desk. The broker was late, but that was OK because Baz was on a call he didn't want him to overhear.

"No, that can't be right," he said, pacing up and down. "You can't be telling me you've found nothing at all on this guy?"

"That's right," said the voice at the other end. "There are two thousand James Evanses in the London area alone and we've gone through every one. None fits your description."

"OK," said Baz, "but he's on my company register. What did you find out from his broker?"

"Nothing. They have twelve James Evanses on their books but not one is under thirty."

"But the Kitson guy checks out."

"Yes."

"That can't be right. Can it? The banks can't have mystery customers, not in this day and age."

"I'm sorry, Mr Mycock, but we've drawn a complete blank."

"I've paid you a hundred grand for this. What kind of service are you offering?"

"We'll refund you in the circumstances."

"Don't refund me," he exploded. "Just find out about him

131

for me. For God's sake, you're meant to be the best."

"We do come up blank from time to time," said the voice. "We are human, after all."

"Look," said Baz, "I'm out of town for two weeks. You've got until then to turn up the goods or I'll have my money back. OK?"

"All right. We'll continue to do our best."

"How hard can it be to trace a guy who takes holidays on a fucking huge yacht called *Leviathan*?"

"In this case, Mr Mycock, very difficult indeed."

Baz caught sight of Kitson coming his way. "Got to go," he said, and hung up. He walked towards Kitson and smiled. "I was starting to worry, mate. It's a fucking nightmare getting through security, and we're cutting it a bit fine."

# 19

The tide was high outside his lounge window. It would be hours before it was low enough for him to jump out and go searching along the foreshore. He was happy to be home – glad to be looking at the grey river rolling by.

John Smith had called him to say he'd drop by for a quick chat. That had sounded ominous but, then, Smith's voice always was in a gallows-humour sort of way.

When he'd rung the doorbell and Stafford answered, Smith's brow furrowed. "Bertie?" he was about to say.

Stafford pointed his index finger straight at him, then put it to his lips.

Smith's mouth stayed closed. He gave Stafford a glare of frustration.

Stafford pursed his lips and glared back. "Come in, sir."

Smith peered at Stafford hard.

"Please come this way."

Smith's habitual deadpan expression clicked back into place and he followed Stafford to Jim.

His friend greeted him, and Smith flopped on to the sofa, then sat up straight. "Someone's making enquiries about you."

"Really?" said Jim. "Not the Serbs, I hope."

"No, some mining fellow."

"Do you want a drink?"

"I'm tempted," said Smith, throwing a look at Stafford, "but I can't stay. Just thought you needed to know."

Stafford took the hint and left the room.

"Would that have been Baz Mycock by any chance?"

"It would indeed. Happily, he asked the wrong people and they knew to pass it on to us."

"Oh, right," said Jim. "That's good." He shifted uncomfortably in his chair. "Thanks for the favour."

"My pleasure."

"What did he want to know?"

"Just who the hell you are." Smith grinned. "I take it that's because you've bought a big chunk of his company."

Jim shrugged. "I guess that would make sense."

"My people think your Mr Mycock is a wrong 'un, so you should proceed with caution."

"My broker's in the Congo with him right now, up at the mine."

"Good luck to him. That area's well dodgy, if you ask me."

"The mine's showing a great chart," said Jim, "unless I've got it completely wrong."

"That might be true, but it's sited in the last place on earth you'll find me visiting."

"Hmm," said Jim. "I think you can rest easy on that one."

Smith got up. "Go carefully, Jim," he said.

"Have you heard anything from …" Jim trailed off.

"Jane?" said Smith. "No, not a dickybird."

"Right."

# 20

Kitson always felt strangely happy going to sleep in a rough bed in a rough billet somewhere in the middle of nowhere. It was on such rare occasions that he felt the line between himself and his environment was at its most sharply defined. In what he deemed civilisation, he was separated from the rest by tiny gradings in subtleties such as taste and manners. In a desert or a jungle the line was much clearer. Right and wrong were clearly delineated by life and death.

While he might appear a duffer in the modern landscape, he was revealed as anything but in a world stripped of decadence. The fops back at the bank would quiver at the prospect of visiting such a place, but Kitson was entirely at ease.

For some reason mines seemed to favour such remote crucibles and visiting them filled him with a sense of purpose and excitement. Bedding down, he felt as if he'd regressed to his thirties. The creatures of the night were making their soothing noises, and in the faint light of a bedside lamp he could see through the mosquito net a small lizard climb up the far wall. He turned off the light and fell asleep to the sounds of the jungle.

Jim looked out of his bedroom window at the low tide glittering in the light of the full moon. If only he could see in the dark he could be searching during the lowest tides, which always happened at night. He was tying his tie, which Tulip would probably pull off again in approximately an hour. Somehow he had made it impossible to have sex with his girlfriend in his own home.

His life had truly gone mad.

Higgins was looking out over the base camp towards the soldiers' barracks. He kept a constant eye on it for signs of trouble. They were a useless crowd but, armed with serviceable weapons, even the most ragtag collection of men could be dangerous. Now, though, only their itinerant servant, a young guy called Man Bites Dog, appeared to be up and about. He watched him carrying a crate of beer from the stores to the mess. He didn't like the kid's name. War names smacked of trouble.

Baz joined him. "Another beautiful day, ker, ker, ker," he croaked. "It'll be as hot as hell I suppose in about two hours."

"Hotter," said Higgins.

Kitson, they noticed, was walking towards them. "Good morning," he said.

"Morning," said Higgins.

"How are you feeling?" enquired Baz.

"Very well, actually," said Kitson. "I had an excellent night."

"Shall we get going?" said Higgins.

"Why not?" said Baz

"It's very reassuring that you're flying," said Kitson to Higgins, as he regarded the old Bell Huey helicopter. "The amount of times I've flown in one of these things with a drunken pilot ..."

Higgins was a little bleary-eyed. "You probably need to be drunk to fly in half the aircraft in Africa," he said. He didn't seem to be joking.

"Quite. Is the helicopter a recent model?"

"Recent enough for me to fly the thing two or three times a week," said Higgins.

"I fucking hate choppers," said Baz, grinning. "I don't like flying without wings. Seems a bit too trusting."

The helicopter was in a protected compound about a hundred metres square, the central area roughly concreted. The landing pad was in the middle, marked in white paint with a giant H. There was an open building at the far end of the compound, a roof on stilts to protect barrels of aviation fuel from the direct glare of the sun.

Higgins unlocked the armoured door in the high perimeter fence. Coils of razor wire inside the enclosure created a twenty-foot buffer of assured agony for anyone who wanted to take an unauthorised look or flight. They walked into the compound and Higgins locked the gate behind them. There was meant to be at least one guard on duty twenty-four hours a day, but attempting to get the government soldiers to do anything was a waste of effort.

Baz and Kitson sat in the Huey's rear jump seats. Kitson's gave him a good view through the door's window and, past Higgins, the large windscreen. He noted that the passenger area, which was actually the cargo bay, was almost pristine. If it had been carrying bulky loads it would have shown plenty of wear and tear. Instead, what damage there was had been repaired, perhaps by the aircraft's previous owners – it seemed unlikely that there would be anyone in the camp who

137

could touch up the interior of a helicopter. Odd, thought Kitson.

"Do you use this to run supplies to the drillers?"

"All the time," said Baz. "It's a workhorse."

"Right," said Kitson.

"Let's go see a kimberlite first."

Higgins started the engine, which whistled and screamed, and they were soon in the air.

Kitson watched the vibrant landscape pass below. He felt an excitement he never experienced at home. He took out a packet of Marlboro Lights and motioned to Baz.

"OK to smoke?" he shouted.

"Sure! This is fucking Congo, for Christ's sake."

Higgins smelt the smoke and glanced around. He didn't approve, but what the hell?

The kimberlite was a ten-minute flight into the jungle. It had once been a volcanic vent through which all manner of minerals had been blown from below the earth's mantle. Time had worn away the cone it had once formed and now there was just a large circular scar. There was no soil on the kimberlite, just the barren rock that had spewed up and solidified. No trees grew there so the Huey could land right on top of it.

Kitson and Baz gazed down at what resembled a circular clay-surfaced tennis court as they dropped towards the ground. It looked impressive, poking out of the hillside like an artificial construction, a semicircular ledge of about two hectares set into the jungle hillside. Baz nodded at the other man. At least they'd found a few kimberlites to put on a show. Kitson was asking lots of stupid questions over the clatter of the rotor blades and writing the answers on a notepad he'd got out of a beaten-up briefcase. Now he was consulting a GPS and noting down the grid reference.

Baz didn't like his attention to detail. The whole point of siting the mine somewhere awful was that no one who knew what they were talking about would want to visit.

In the past Baz had taken investors to places not actually on the ground that was in his parcel of rights. This was not such an occasion, but the more questions Kitson asked, and the more people who visited, the greater the chance of exposure. Kitson was demanding the sort of due diligence Baz hated. He wasn't used to it. Tonight he'd make sure Kitson got the worst case of food poisoning ever. The kid who had latched on to the soldiers did the cooking for the camp, spoke English and was quick on the uptake when there was money in it for him. He'd do the honours for a few thousand Congolese francs. A dose of dysentery would send the nosy broker packing.

The landing shook Baz out of his plans. They waited for the rotors to stop and for the dust to settle. Eventually he leant over Kitson and opened the door. Kitson jumped out. The morning sun was rising and the temperature was picking up. The kimberlite was about fifteen hundred feet up the mountainside from the plateau where they were standing. It afforded clear views to the valley and the camp below.

Higgins joined them, carrying a Tavor-21 assault rifle. "We've got to be careful," he said, noticing Kitson's reaction. "Pygmies."

"What about them?" asked Kitson.

"Not happy bunnies," said Baz. "They don't trust anyone around here and they can put an arrow in you as easy as look at you."

139

"They're all over the mountain," said Higgins, "and since the last war, some of them have gone nasty."

"How does that affect the drilling?"

"It doesn't make it any easier," said Baz, "but so far so good."

Kitson was gazing down the mountain to the camp, which was just a dot in the distance. "What a stunning place," he breathed. He turned and looked towards the cone of the volcano a mile behind them. A plume of smoke rose lazily above it.

"Yeah," said Baz, "and we may just be standing on a king's ransom."

"Have you had the rock tested for microdiamonds?" asked Kitson, peering at the eroded, porous surface of the ground.

"Sure," said Baz. "Ker, ker, ker."

"And?" said Kitson, lighting another Marlboro.

"Well, without giving too much away, it's bloody promising."

Kitson took a puff of his cigarette, his eyes screwed up. There was nothing in the way of workings to show that any drilling or digging had gone on there. There was not one piece of rubbish he'd have expected a team to leave behind. He put a hand into his pocket and took out a small hammer, chipped at the ground with the sharp end of the head and put a useful chunk of rock into his pocket.

Baz smiled. What use would a rock be to Kitson? "You collect rocks," he observed.

"I've got an old friend in Canada who's a whiz at kimberlites – he found the Silver Fox deposit. I thought he might be persuaded to take a look."

140

"Right," said Baz, "good one."

"Pygmies," mused Kitson, as he walked towards the jungle that ringed the back end of the kimberlite. "I thought they were peaceful people."

Higgins was at his side. "Maybe they were. They probably just got fed up with getting killed."

"Really?" said Kitson.

"It's not been too clever around here for years and they get a pretty raw deal."

"I see." Kitson stared longingly at the jungle. "Do you think we could meet some?"

"No!" Baz laughed, sounding nervous. "I don't think we can."

"Man Bites Dog goes in there. He speaks English – you might get him to take you."

"No, mate, that wouldn't be sensible," said Baz

"Man Bites Dog?" asked Kitson.

"He's a local lad, does for the soldiers. He gets them bush meat now and again."

"Ah, interesting," said Kitson. "That sounds like a fine idea."

As Kitson continued to gaze at the jungle, Higgins cast a glance at Baz, his eyebrows raised. His fixed smile suggested that Baz should shut up and think.

Baz's answering expression said, "You dickhead." Then it changed. Maybe instead of giving Kitson the runs he could let the kid take him on safari in the jungle. By the time the pair got back to camp, the broker would be good and ready for a quick flight home.

"OK," said Baz. "I'll fix it up if you like."

"Would you?" said Kitson, lighting yet another cigarette.

141

"That's very good of you." He pointed at the jungle ahead. "But perhaps we could take just a quick look now?"

Baz thought about the pad in Kitson's briefcase. "Why not?" he said. "Go on, Mark, take Terence for a recce – no more than an hour, mind you."

Higgins frowned. "OK – but first sign of life and we're coming straight out."

"Fine," said Kitson.

Kitson's briefcase wasn't locked – and even if it had been a school kid could have picked it open. The thin spidery handwriting was hard to decipher and what characters he could pick out seemed to form some kind of shorthand. Every four or five lines Kitson had written "MACS" among a few random doodles. It stood for mining air-conditioning systems, but Baz had no idea why Kitson had noted it so many times. Certainly it was hot but that was irrelevant: the requirement to cool a deep mine was years away from the exploration stage they were at.

Baz grunted and replaced the pad, none the wiser. He repositioned the case so that he left it exactly as he had found it. Now he had to wait the best part of three-quarters of an hour in the rising heat for the other two to get back. "That wasn't one of your best ideas," he reproved himself.

It was raining almost constantly somewhere on the mountain so the jungle was a network of streams and small rivers working their way down the mountainside to the valleys below. The tall trees, many of which were more than a hundred feet high, blanked out the sun from the ground, starving much of the undergrowth of light. This meant that the way wasn't as difficult as it had appeared, although the path was steep. Higgins checked both GPS every few minutes to make sure they tallied and kept his eye on a compass he had tied to his belt as well.

Despite the heat and humidity, Kitson was fascinated. His head swivelled as he walked. Butterflies danced in fluttering circles, illuminated by shafts of light. Hanging lianas fell from the high canopy, and distant birds chirped and squawked over a cacophony of buzzing and burbling. Yet no sound was louder than the thud of his feet on the soft wet ground or the breath in his lungs. He stood to watch a troop of ants ascend a tall tree, Higgins beside him. He wondered where they were going – their nest, perhaps, or some succulent spray of fruit.

Eventually Higgins turned away and they began to retrace their footsteps.

"Tomorrow should be fun," Kitson said, navigating down the incline.

"The pleasure's all yours, mate," said Higgins.

"I can't see the rig," shouted Kitson, above the rotors.

"It's down there somewhere," Baz yelled back.

Higgins was flying in circles over the grid reference they had identified in the mining report as a location to drill for cobalt.

"Well, I can't see a thing."

"It's under the trees," roared Baz.

"Surely there'd be a clearing?"

"What?"

"Clearing! There should be a clearing." Kitson leant forwards against his seatbelt.

Baz shrugged. "It's bloody well down there somewhere."

Kitson sat back. "Let's move on to the next point, then, and the second drilling team."

"Right," said Baz, and spoke into the microphone that broadcast into Higgins's headset. The helicopter headed off on a new course.

Kitson scribbled on his pad. To Baz, it looked like "MACS" again.

They circled the second grid reference.

"Still can't see the bloody rig," shouted Kitson.

"We're environmentally sensitive," shouted Baz.

"What?"

"En–viro–men–tal–ly sen–si–tive," Baz howled. So much so that we don't bother drilling at all, he added to himself.

"Quite," hollered Kitson, writing again. "Last rig?"

"OK." Baz passed on the command. "MACS" was bugging the hell out of him. Shit! he thought. They were heading towards open country – Kitson would know it was a scam...he shook his head. MACS was "scam" spelt backwards.

He turned in his seat and punched Kitson on the temple with all his might. Kitson sagged, then slumped into his lap. Baz punched him again in the side of the head and rabbit-punched him in the back of the neck. Then he released his own seatbelt and jumped up. Higgins was shouting something, but he wasn't listening. He pushed Kitson upright, unclipped his seatbelt and opened the helicopter door.

Higgins was yelling at him now but he shoved Kitson towards the door. The wind force was stopping it swinging open, but he continued to push the man until a gap appeared and soon Kitson was half out of the aircraft. Baz sat on the

144

floor and used his feet to gain leverage. With a final huge effort the door flew wide and Kitson was gone.

Higgins hauled the Huey to a hover. "You fucking bastard!" he screamed.

"He was on to us," shouted Baz.

The helicopter was swinging around crazily. "You fucking murderer!" Higgins was clearly beside himself. "I didn't fucking sign up for that!"

Baz struggled back to his seat and as he buckled himself in he glimpsed a beige patch in the canopy of a tall tree. It might have been a body.

Higgins landed the Huey heavily on the pad and waited for the blades to slow. Then he and Baz got out.

"I'm really sorry," said Baz.

Higgins decked him.

Baz groaned. "I deserved that."

"You deserve a lot worse," said Higgins, and stormed off to the gate.

Baz hauled himself up and followed. "Look," he said, "he'd written 'Scam' all over his notebook – he was going to bury us."

Higgins looked at him but said nothing and unlocked the gate.

Baz thought again about Kitson. If that had been him caught in the tree and he was still alive, he'd never climb down a hundred and fifty feet to the ground. Even if he did, he'd never make it back across country. And how likely was it, really, that it had been Kitson in the tree? There was no chance.

He'd have to bung Higgins a big pile of cash to keep him on side. He wondered how much.

# 21

It was low tide and parts of the foreshore were uncovered that Jim had never seen before. Where the gravel met the mud and where the mud met the shingle lower down, all sorts of tiny pieces of metal collected. He picked them up and put them into his pocket. Briefly he examined a little copper disc, a coin, but he had no idea of what period. He didn't stop to wonder: in five or ten minutes the tide would turn and within a few moments the patch of goodies would be gone until another low tide took the water that far down.

The houses were far above him now, up a steep bank. Modern London seemed to have dissolved and had been replaced by an eighteenth-century shoreline where sailing ships had just departed for the high seas.

His phone rang. Bugger, he thought. He should have switched it off. Now he felt obliged to answer it. Why was Jules St John calling him at seven in the morning? "Hello," he said.

"Jim," said St George. His voice told Jim immediately that something was wrong. "Bad news, I'm afraid. Terence has had an accident at Barron. He's fallen from a helicopter into the jungle. They don't hold out any hope for him."

"Oh, shit."

"It's on RNS for Barron and I've just got off the phone from them."

146

Jim hadn't seen that in the chart. He closed his eyes and tried to imagine it. "What are we doing about finding Terry?"

"Well, Barron's doing everything it can, but they were five hundred feet up when it happened so there isn't much hope of finding him alive – or finding him at all, for that matter."

"Fuck them, what are we doing?"

"Well, there's not much we can do. We simply don't have any way to react fast enough. It would be weeks before we could do anything meaningful."

Jim spotted a .22 round gleaming in the mud and bent down to pick it up. "How the hell do you fall out of a helicopter?" he said, looking at the pond-still river at its neap.

"I don't know," said St George. "Apparently he was leaning on the door trying to get a good look at something."

"OK, Jules. I'm going back home to look at the chart – it might tell me something. I mean, the price'll bomb, right?"

"I don't know," said St George. "Predicting markets isn't my speciality."

"Well, if he's found alive in the next few days the price'll rally, so I need to take a look." Jim started to walk up the foreshore. There was a rustle from the river as the tide turned and a ripple ran upstream. He sighed. This was his fault. Things had been going too well, and something awful had had to happen to compensate for his immense good fortune. Now it had. And it was likely to be just the start.

He stared at Barron's chart. Nothing about it said it was going to crash and bounce back. Nothing said it was going to plunge from the 87p at which it currently sat. It was only five minutes to market open and the market-makers were set up to halve the share price on the get-go. He projected the line down and stared at the mine's chart since its first days of trading. It still looked set to explode skywards.

He called St George. "Sit on the bid and take all comers. Don't get off it until 87p."

"If you go over twenty-nine per cent you'll have to make a bid."

"I'm up on the rules, Jules, don't worry."

"Why are you doing this?"

"I don't know," said Jim. "Maybe so I can go down there myself and look." He hadn't meant to say that but it felt right.

"Very well," said St George. "I'll get one of the market-makers to give you a call right away."

Jim watched as the market opened. Selling was slamming into the price and in moments Barron had dropped to 39p.

His mobile rang. He answered it. "This is Jim."

"Hi, Jim, this is Denny on the desk. You want to take all comers on Barron?"

"Yeah."

"Do you want volume or do you want to support the price?"

"I want you to suck it up. Buy the fucking company if you can."

"Right," said Denny. "In that case I'll just shake it like a Polaroid. If I slam it up to support it, the selling might stop. You know how it goes."

"Yeah," said Jim. "If the price is too strong, the sellers'll change their minds and stop selling."

"It's an honour to trade for you, mate."

"Thanks." Jim hung up, a smile twitching at his face. He returned to the chart. What the fuck was the story with Barron? Something was way out of whack.

Denny was creating mayhem in the already wrecked market for the stock. He was pulling the price around like a pit bull savaging a rag doll.

Baz was outside as the morning heat gathered. It was ten thirty. The aerial of his sat phone was pointing into the sky. "Sorry, Ralph," he said, "I don't understand you. The price has crashed and you still can't buy stock. That doesn't make any sense."

"Sorry, Baz, but our orders aren't getting filled. Wherever we put them we get leapfrogged. It's a big market-maker with some kind of flash technology that's simply gazumping us."

"How can that be?"

"We're not geared up for this kind of thing. It doesn't happen in small caps, only in big-company trading. I've never seen this before."

"It's Evans, isn't it?" said Baz. "It's got to be. You'd have to be fucking bonkers to buy now. Who else could it possibly be?"

"I don't know, but it's all a bit worrying, if you ask me. I'm not sure the boys are going to like this. People having nasty accidents isn't good."

"They've made a bob or two, haven't they? It'll be their stupid fault if they bail now."

"I know," said Ralph, "but when they make a profit it's because of their brilliance, and when they don't, it's all my doing. There's a hell of a lot of selling out there but we aren't getting it."

149

Baz grunted. "Try harder."

"Where's your limit?"

"Fifty p. Buy it up to fifty p."

"Right," said Ralph. "I'll call you back in an hour."

Baz hung up and went into his bungalow. The left side of his face was swollen and his lip split. He was reminded of his young days as a prospector in Australia. He had stopped a few punches in those days. A guy could look good with the right kind of bruises. An hour was going to be a long wait.

"It's sitting at fifty-one p pretty solidly," said Ralph. "The buyer goes off for short periods, then comes right back and keeps hoovering it up. We've got about one per cent, but there's about eight per cent gone through. I think about fifteen per cent of the company will have traded by the end of the day."

Baz stared across the compound to the soldiers. In the blistering heat they were kicking a football made of tied-up plastic bags. They looked too happy. "I'll figure something out," he said. "Just sit there at fifty p, and if the buyer goes away, fall back as much as you can."

"OK," said Ralph.

Baz cut off the sat phone. His bad news was costing him fifteen dollars a minute to receive it. Yet more salt in the wound.

Jim called Baz Mycock's mobile but it went straight to voicemail. He called Mycock's broker. The phone rang out, but rather than leave a message, he sent an SMS: "Call me. Jim Evans."

Seconds later his mobile rang.

"Hello, Jim, how can I help you?"

"Well, you know my friend Terry just had an accident at Barron? I want to go to the mine and look for him."

"All right," said Ralph. "I'll pass that on to Mycock. He's at the mine right now, though I think he's coming back to report to the board."

"Who's looking for Terry?"

"I'm sure they've got everyone they can lay hands on involved in the search. There's not much Baz himself can add to that."

"Well, tell him to hang on because I'm heading over there as soon as I can get my things together."

"I'll pass the message on."

"Tell him I want a seat on the board too."

"I certainly will."

"I knew it was him," said Baz. "It was bloody obvious."

"So what do you want me to do?"

"First off, kill our order. Let him have as much as he likes. Send out the 'no cobalt' announcement."

"You think that'll scare him off?"

"I doubt it."

"But he'll end up owning pretty much all the free float."

"That's OK," said Baz. "Let him have it – in fact, sell him a load from one of our friendly holders." He was referring to his secret accounts.

"Oh," said Ralph. "Really?"

"Yeah," said Baz. "Let him get up to, say, thirty-five per cent, if he's prepared to trigger a bid."

Ralph was feeling uncomfortable. "OK."

"There you go. All sorted," said Baz, and hung up. When

it was announced that someone had taken their stake to the brink of a takeover, the speculators would pile in and the price would rocket. He would sell into that and then, if Evans was to meet with a nasty accident, the price would crater, Baz would cover his position and that would be that. Perhaps the diamonds-and-gold story wouldn't be necessary. He'd have to lie very low afterwards, but that wouldn't be hard – he'd done it so many times before.

"No," said Higgins. "Not for two million dollars, not for three million dollars, not for five, ten, twenty, a hundred. Doesn't your fat lip tell you all you've got to know? I don't kill innocent people for money. I'm not a hitman."

Baz poured himself another whisky. "But you don't mind standing by."

"No, I don't," said Higgins. "I'm not a policeman. I'm not a righter of wrongs. I do a job and I look after myself and that's it." He took the bottle and refilled his glass. "Now get off the subject before I have to punch you again."

"Phah," said Baz. "This could set you up for life."

"No, Baz. Don't you realise that this kind of situation is just the thing that ends your life? You cross that line and there's no way back. You ruin everything. The moment you become a killer, you're a dead man."

"I don't see that," said Baz.

"Then you're a stupid fuck. Mining stock scamming is one thing, murder is another." He chugged his whisky. "You should be thinking about closing this whole thing down right now. You certainly shouldn't be thinking about offing Evans – that's just fucking crazy."

Baz took the bottle and topped up Higgins's glass again.

"Yeah, well," he said, "you're probably right. I'll think about closing up – it's an option – but I'd like to knock Evans off his perch. Then we'd be in the big money."

"No. You're. Wrong," Higgins said. "If you do that, you'll be up to your neck in shite and you'll never escape it. I've seen it so many times before. Trust me, mate. Cut your losses before it's too late."

Baz nodded. "Let me think on it. I can make a fair amount running the company down. There's no need to get in any deeper." He drank a slug of whisky. No way, he thought. No way am I going to let some young twat fuck up my brilliant scheme.

# 22

"Don't be silly," said Tulip. "I'm not going to let you go."
She was playing with the hairs on his chest. "You're not well
enough to travel. You can't go to places like that with those
sores on your side." She stroked the three small plasters that
covered the unhealed but slowly shrinking wounds.

"I've got to go," he said. "I don't trust those people to look
for Terence – they don't impress me one little bit. And if I
don't I'll hate myself. My scabs have almost gone now, so I'll
be OK."

"You can't just go charging off to Congo," she said,
tugging on the hairs. He winced.

"I can," he said, and swatted away her manicured hand.
"As soon as the satellite phone gets here in the morning I'm
on the jet. It's the least I can do."

"You don't have to do anything. It's not your responsibility."

"I think it is. I want to make sure everything's being done.
Until they find a body there's hope."

"It's very brave of you, but it's not sensible."

"I don't think sensible applies to me," he said, sitting up
and reaching for his half-empty glass of champagne.
"Nothing in my life is sensible. Anyway, Mycock and his
people are meeting me at the airport, so it's hardly going to
be an adventure."

"Well, I'm not happy about it," she said sulkily.

In his eyes her stock was dropping fast. Maybe dealing with women was like trading shares: you bought in when there was a bit of excitement and when it ended you dumped them. He considered that for a second. It had a certain logic.

He climbed out of bed. "Let's go and eat," he said, walking to the suite's bathroom. He liked the Ritz. It was seven thirty.

"Where?" She sighed.

"Nobu?"

"OK." She picked up her mobile from the bedside table and dialled.

Jim stepped into the shower. As he switched it on, he heard her shout, "Booked." The three raw blisters on his side still looked nasty but they'd shrunk over the months to the size of a fingernail. He was still prone to weakness on that side and his head still spun once in a while, but it was no big deal. Feeling a little dodgy was no excuse to do nothing when someone's life was at stake, he told himself.

The next morning Tulip kissed him goodbye outside the Ritz. "I think you should change your mind," she said.

"Don't worry," he said, "I'll only be gone for a couple of days." He gave her a final full-on kiss. She was like a ripe pear: fragrantly succulent. The porter was loading his case into the boot of the black Mercedes. He shifted the sat-phone box under his arm. "See you at the weekend," he said, as he turned to step into the car.

She waved without saying anything, as if her mind had just changed the subject and was tying off the loose ends.

He gave a fiver to the porter who had held the door open

for him and blew Tulip a kiss. The car moved off as she disappeared into the hotel.

He turned his attention to the sat phone. The box had already been opened, and as he slipped out the polystyrene packaging, the charger and manual fell into his lap. He pulled open the white plastic padding and took the phone in its protective plastic bag. It was pretty much the same as a normal one except for its chunky aerial.

As he was in the car he couldn't test it. To use it he had to be outside in line of sight to the satellite with nothing in the way to stop the signal. It was just about feasible to get a signal indoors, but it meant standing by a window or on the top floor. He looked at the chunky antenna. Somehow the phone had to pump out a signal that could reach a spacecraft 22,000 miles above by sending out enough electromagnetic radiation to get there while not cooking the neurons in his brain.

It was a sobering thought, but Jim had already moved on: he was taking the back off his regular phone to upload his contact list into the new one – no point having his new toy with him in the jungle if he couldn't remember anyone's number. He swapped the sat phone's sim card with his own and started trying to follow the inscrutable manual.

"Bloody hell!" he exclaimed. His contact list was in the phone's memory. Amazingly, he had followed the instructions in the booklet and it had worked first time. That's a miracle he thought. He went back to the booklet and discovered he could use his new phone as a modem for his computer, albeit a slow one, to grab email and even trade – although maybe his trading software wouldn't operate at such a slow connection rate. He reassembled both phones. As he switched on his iPhone, it rang.

It was Max Davas.

"Thanks for getting back to me," Jim said. "What have you got?"

"It's pretty sketchy," said Max, "but your Mycock fellow's some kind of low-level pump-and-dump specialist."

"Pump and dump,"

"Stock promoter. He comes up with speculative mines, promotes them to the sky but they don't go anywhere. He did a dotcom back in 2000 and he's involved in a few 'green-tech' plays, but he mainly does small-resource stocks. All pretty shifty but nothing big, just eight- or nine-figure ventures, nothing in the billions. He's under the radar – plenty of civil legal actions in his past but nothing criminal. It looks mainly like shady mining deals."

"Thanks."

"But there's something strange about the mining claim. I'm not getting much guidance about it on the geological side. Normally there'd be plenty. On the political side there's reams of information – the place is a full-scale horror show. Half of Africa's been fighting over it in recent years for as many reasons as you can imagine. The Rwandan genocide spilled over into the region, and the Congolese civil war has only just ended. It's been filled with soldiers mining various deposits for years. It's an awful mess, and if that's not bad enough, a volcanic eruption almost wiped out the capital city a few years ago. In fact, the lava ran over half of it."

"Blimey," said Jim.

"But you'll be OK. It's a lot quieter now than it has been. If you'd been able to wait a few days I could have arranged for some friends to escort you, but I think your colourful Mr

Mycock should do a good enough job. Did you get all the right inoculations?"

"Yesterday," said Jim, touching his sore arm.

"Look after your health," said Max, "and if you need anything call me straight away."

"Sure," said Jim. "Thanks."

"Are you flying into Cairo to refuel?"

"Don't know – I think the G5 can get the whole way and refuel there."

"Fly to Cairo, top up there, and again on the way back. It's a pain, but you don't want to end up halfway back running on the water they might put in your tank in the DRC."

# 23

Although he hardly used it, the jet filled him with pride. Most of the things he'd achieved – his meteoric rise, the massive trading profits, saving the world – now seemed dreamlike and unreal. If someone had told him it had all been a fantasy and now he had to go back to his old life, he would have accepted it. Since he'd joined the bank – straight out of school – his entire life had seemed like a gigantic hallucination, his memories of the recent past the crazed visions of a maniac.

Yet the Gulfstream was shining proof that everything he thought had happened really had, and that he actually was sitting on top of the world, the winner of a bizarre lottery.

His ability to read a stock chart had catapulted him into a new universe in which none of the old rules applied. From the outside he might seem the richest, smartest guy around, but inside he felt as clueless as a toddler playing ball beside a motorway.

Jim didn't have to put anyone right about the route: they were going via Cairo. "Do you have any spare US dollars?" the captain asked. He'd been an RAF fighter pilot in the early nineties but had since flown commercial airliners, then private jets. His face looked as if it had baked in the sun for decades, but he had a wide mischievous smile. He was a consummate professional, flying the plane with the precision of a surgeon reshaping a film star's nose.

Jim opened the top compartment of a rucksack that was waiting for him by the small dining-table. He found nothing so he rummaged in the side pockets and pulled out an envelope with a thick bundle of US dollar bills. "How much do you need?"

"A hundred dollars should do it. They'll clear us in Goma and it'd be better if we included this paperwork with the other forms."

Jim stripped out a handful of notes and handed them over. He stuck the rest in his pocket. "OK, Ewan, let's rock," he said, sitting back.

"Yes, sir."

He sighed, exasperated, then grinned. "It's Jim."

He sat on the leather sofa that ran down the length of the right mid-section of the cabin. Stafford had packed the rucksack. He had no idea what was in it, but there was meant to be enough to last him a long time in the jungle. How Stafford would know about such things he couldn't guess, and he was a little concerned that perhaps his butler actually didn't have any idea. The blind might be leading the blind. Jim knew as much about jungle survival as he did deep-sea diving.

There was an inventory in the top flap of the rucksack – a good place to start exploring the contents. The last page was a map of the packing. There was a list of clothes, all linen, $10,000 in cash, a tent, apparently in a flat pack down the right side of the rucksack, a jungle knife, small binoculars, mosquito net, all-weather blanket, fire-making equipment, sanitary wipes, rations for five days, lifesaver water-purification bottle, night-vision goggles, lures and a snare kit, a GPS, copious medical supplies, a survival guide, maps, flashlight, pocket knife and sharpening stone, batteries, pocket tools, tape, vitamins, inflatable mattress ... the list went on. He lifted the rucksack. It seemed too light for all this stuff. He folded the inventory and put it back into the top pocket.

His computer and more clothes were in a flight case at the back of the cabin.

The items in the rucksack were a little intimidating. Suddenly Tulip's advice seemed a lot more sensible.

The inside of the plane wasn't so small that it was cramped, like the smaller jets, but it wasn't a large space either. The Gulfstream was like a small flying hotel suite. Jim didn't employ a steward: even though it wouldn't have cost much in comparison with the machine itself, maintenance, two highly qualified pilots and fuel, but it seemed silly to Jim to pay someone to serve you a drink when you could pour it yourself. He could have asked Stafford to come, but Jim was appalled by the idea of travelling with a retinue. There was a platter of sandwiches in the forward galley area and that was enough for him. He had leased the plane for three years simply because he could and because he had practically nothing to spend his money on. He had given the bank's wealth management group, who looked after his affairs, £20 million to take care of him if he needed it. The rest he could spend. If only he knew how to.

When you had a certain amount of cash, you needed to develop vices to use it. Gambling and women could eat through fortunes, as could drugs, expensive toys and the wrong kind of friends. For Jim gambling was pointless: he could play the markets and win pretty much every time.

Drugs scared the hell out of him, and he'd never hooked up with the wrong kind of friends – although Sebastian Fuch-Smith had demonstrated just how expensive even good friends could be.

And now he had an expensive girl but even she wasn't a threat to the ocean of cash he had just torn out of the global forex markets.

Spending his money was a puzzle to be solved later.

In his way, Kitson was a successful man. He had a good life and a fine healthy family. Everything had been great in his world until he'd fallen out of a helicopter. He'd been well set up for the rest of his life but had still lost everything.

If Sebastian hadn't got himself suckered into a stock punt on a ridiculous mine in a godforsaken country, this chain of events would have never kicked off. A few electrons flickering on his friend's screen had fired a few greedy neurons in his brain and now Jim was flying across the globe at 80 per cent of the speed of sound to find a decomposing body in a jungle at the foot of a volcano that had nearly wiped out a city with a population of 200,000.

Tulip was rising again in Jim's estimation. He could turn the bloody plane around – but he knew he had to go through with it: it was the right thing to do.

The smoked-salmon-and-cream-cheese sandwiches were good. There was enough for about six people so he took some up to the captain and co-pilot, who were happy enough to see him. He looked out of the cockpit across the plane's short nose at the vertiginous view to the sea below and found himself trying to remember the name of the Greek kid who had stuck feathers to himself with wax and fallen out of the sky when he flew too close to the sun. He'd had a tough

162

break. He'd never understood why they had taught such a stupid story at school but now he understood what it meant. What a bunch of miserable fuckers the ancient Greeks were, he thought.

He went back into the cabin and checked his jacket for stomach settlers. He'd remembered to bring some and he wondered if there were more in the medical kit.

Even if there were, he wouldn't be carrying enough to last him on this trip. Sitting down, he thought of how Jane would love this adventure, all kitted up for a leap into the unknown… He tried to make himself think of something else but the picture of her in the muddy bog kept flashing into his mind. Her smile grabbed his inner eye and held it.

He missed her.

# 24

Goma airport was a large green tongue edged on two sides by the city, scarred by a battered black landing strip down the middle. It was truncated by a field of congealed lava.

If Jim could have seen what the pilots saw he would have freaked out.

The airstrip looked like some giant abused cricket wicket, long since abandoned and covered at one end with volcanic pumice. At the far end, near the lava flow, there were some planes, one parked like a stranded boat and apparently used as offices. Jim was still getting over the awesome sight of the Nyiragongo volcano and a glimpse of the airport would have been one view too many. Nyiragongo wasn't some long-dormant mountain with a hole in the top: it was the sort of volcano Hollywood whipped up to destroy the world.

Under dark clouds, heavy with rain, the massive caldera was spewing out white fog as if it were the devil's own chimney. It was the most evil-looking thing he'd ever seen – like an enormous bomb about to detonate. The Barron property was somewhere to the north of it. Whatever the chart had told him about the future stock price he certainly didn't feel like believing it now.

Jim looked at the shanties that surrounded the airport as the captain put the plane down lightly. A dozen or more aircraft sat reassuringly to the right of the runway, and as they taxied along he saw the terminal ahead, a rudimentary but functional 1960s building.

"We're going to drop you off and turn her straight round, Jim," said the captain, over the intercom. "If your party isn't here to meet you I suggest you stay with us and we come back tomorrow."

There wasn't any point in replying as he couldn't talk to the cockpit, but he said, "I'll be OK."

The plane pulled to a halt beside the terminal. The co-pilot opened the door and moved out on to the steps. Jim spotted a large European in a lurid Hawaiian shirt standing next to an official. The co-pilot greeted them and there was an exchange of papers. The man in the Hawaiian shirt seemed to be in charge and the official was all smiles and efficiency.

Jim perked up and went to collect his bags.

The co-pilot climbed back in. "All sorted," he said.

"Thanks, Dave," said Jim.

The co-pilot offered to help him with his stuff but Jim shook his head – only to regret it as he tried to negotiate the door with the two awkward bundles. The stifling heat struck him immediately and he tottered down the steps. The man in the Hawaiian shirt stepped up to him. "Let me have that," he said, and relieved Jim of his flight case. "Mark Higgins," he added.

"Jim Evans – good to meet you."

"We've got to move it," said Higgins. "The sun'll be going down soon and I'm not a big fan of flying in the dark." He pointed to the collection of planes, now two hundred metres away. "If we go immediately, we might get down before it's pitch black. We're only about thirty minutes away if we put our foot down."

"Sounds good," said Jim. He shook the captain's hand. "Thanks, Ewan, good trip back," he said. He shook the co-pilot's hand. "Cheers, Dave." He shook the official's hand for good measure. "See you later, guys. I'll call you." He turned to Higgins. "OK, Mark. Lead on."

Higgins was practically marching towards the planes. "That's our Huey," he said, pointing at the white liveried helicopter. He stowed Jim's luggage in the back, and they got into the cockpit. Higgins gave Jim a headset, which he put on, then fired up the aircraft and was talking to Air-traffic Control as he did his in-flight checks. Clearance for takeoff came a few seconds later and then they were lifting off. On the ground Jim could see the door closing on the G5 and the stairs being dragged away. The Huey rose into the sky, away from the airport and over the shanties.

Jim gazed at the lava field that covered the end of the runway and for miles around. It was a black inky scab that had come from the volcano. The helicopter wheeled and headed straight for it. "That's fucking impressive," said Jim into his mic.

"Nyiragongo?"

Jim laughed. "Yeah."

"It's a big scary bastard. We're on the other side of it, between it and the other big fucker, Nyamuragira. Basically, if you think of the Nyamuragira volcano as the middle of the property, we have mineral rights in forty miles of the surrounding country. But you probably knew that already, seeing how much of the company you bought."

"Well..." Jim hesitated "...sure."

They were coming up on Nyiragongo fast and Higgins was taking them around the west side, away from the smoke cloud that was being pushed to the east by the prevailing wind. "That Gulfstream must have cost a pretty penny to charter down here," Higgins remarked.

"It's mine," said Jim, mesmerised by the smoking cone of the volcano, which they were passing.

"Really?" said Higgins, clearly so surprised that Jim regretted opening his big mouth. "Very smart."

The light was failing fast as the sun fell quickly to the horizon. "I'd take you up to see the lava lake," said Higgins, "but maybe another day. It's basically about as high as this chopper will fly. Twelve thousand feet is about the limit for this thing, but it's worth the view, if you like that kind of thing."

"Thanks," said Jim, "if we have time."

Higgins nodded. "I think we'll make it before dark, and that's great. Daylight's my friend."

Mine too, Jim thought.

Higgins was flying with the determination of someone who knew exactly where he was going. They were heading for the left flank of the Nyamuragira volcano, speeding across more lava fields. "We'll be down in a couple of minutes."

Jim looked ahead but couldn't see any significant structures to signify that the mine lay below.

"Here we go," said Higgins, as if some hidden display panel showed him their destination.

Jim searched the ground in front: a mixture of forest and grassland speckled with trees and an occasional scrappy field. Then a collection of low buildings came into sight and a flat area just before the forested slopes of the volcano. It was a little bigger than a farm complex: three sets of buildings separated by rough space. The lights of the landing pad caught his eye, its large white H reassuring. The helicopter was throwing a spotlight beam on it.

Jim smiled. Night was falling faster than he'd ever experienced.

The Huey touched down and Higgins pulled off his headset as he threw various switches on the control panels. "Great timing," he said, as the noise faded. He was clearly relieved to have got down in one piece.

The compound was lit and Jim noted the cordon of razor wire that protected it. The fence was high and wickedly topped with more razor. No one would get in without a lot of effort.

They climbed out of the chopper and collected Jim's luggage. Jim looked into the cargo hold. Somehow Kitson had opened the door and fallen out. What exactly had happened? He wanted to ask but decided to leave it – maybe it would come out naturally.

Baz Mycock was walking towards them across the landing pad. "Wotcher, mate," he said. "Have a good trip?"

"Not bad," said Jim.

"He flew here in his Gulfstream," said Higgins, smiling and nodding.

"Nice," laughed Baz, shaking Jim's hand. "You're a stylish fella. And apparently you own twenty-eight per cent of Barron now." Baz's eyes twinkled in the landing pad's lights.

"Really?" said Jim. "That didn't take long."

"Maybe I should call you '*bwana*'." Baz let out a quacking laugh. "Ker, ker, ker."

"If you like," said Jim. He swung his rucksack on to his shoulder and sagged a little.

"Anyway, you kept the price up nicely, thank you very much." Baz managed a perfectly grateful smile, even though it was exactly opposite to how he felt. If only he could convince Higgins to let him push this one out of the chopper too, he'd be a happy man. "Let me take that," he said, lifting the load off Jim's shoulder in an easy sweep.

"Thanks," said Jim. "Had a bit of a rib removed."

"Nasty," said Baz, as they turned for the gate. "Accident?"

"Kind of," said Jim.

"You'll have to lighten that up if you're going trekking," said Higgins.

"I'll be all right," said Jim. "I just picked it up wrong."

"You can always ditch stuff," said Baz, opening the gate. "No litter police up there," he said, jerking a thumb in the direction of the volcanoes.

They walked to a small bungalow among the low buildings.

"It's only cold water in the shower," said Baz, putting down the rucksack, "and it's not really cold but you get the idea. Electricity comes on at ten or eleven and stays on till midnight. Getting diesel up here's a pain in the arse so we eke it out."

Higgins stood Jim's flight case next to the rucksack. "Come outside and I'll show you the lie of the land."

They went out to an open area in the centre of the camp. A road appeared to lead up to the far left end from the valley below.

"In front of you to the left are the soldiers' quarters." Higgins pointed to some buildings that, now Jim studied them, looked like basic barracks. "I wouldn't go down too close – they're a rough lot. We pay the government a shit load for them but I doubt they see any of it. We bung them some

169

extra, but let's just say they aren't the happiest bunnies ever to hop across the face of the earth. Over there on the right is where we house the Chinese crews. We've got just three looking after the camp at the moment – the rest are up country doing their thing. But you're not interested in that, are you? You're here for Terry, right?"

"Yeah," said Jim.

"Right," said Baz. "Anyway, the big bungalow next to this," he pointed behind them, "is mine and Mark's, and the one up top is like an office. It's neat and tidy but nothing splendid."

Jim glanced at the barracks again. They were lit but seemed deserted. "I think I've got all that."

"When you're sorted," said Higgins, "come to our hut and we'll have something to eat."

Jim opened his flight case and took out the satphone. He walked outside as he switched it on. It was still very hot and humid, but without the sun, it was significantly cooler than it had been earlier. There was a strong signal so he dialled home. Stafford replied.

"I'm here," Jim told him.

"Very good," said Stafford.

"Obviously the phone works fine. Anything for me?"

"No calls," said Stafford. "All quiet on the home front."

"Great," said Jim, "I'll be in touch." He looked at the handset, or "terminal", as the manual called it. It was rather like his indoor wireless phone, oversized, clunky, with a fat, stubby antenna jutting from the top. Even so, however unfashionable it looked, he was very happy that it worked. It was his lifeline.

Back inside, he stripped off and went into the bathroom, which smelt of disinfectant. He ran the shower – thankfully the water was only tepid – washed quickly, and then dried himself on the towels provided. The bungalow was pretty basic but it covered the basics and met the case: the air-con was blowing cold, the bed against the wall was enclosed in a white gauzy mosquito net and there was a low table at the foot. He put his flight case on the low table and opened it, took out fresh clothes and got dressed. Stafford had done well – the linen felt good against his skin in the humidity, seeming to absorb the moisture like blotting-paper. He turned reluctantly to the rucksack, picked it up and slung it on to his shoulders. He paced around the room, flexing his muscles. It didn't feel too bad now but what about when he'd had it on for an hour or two? Perhaps he could strip out some of the contents. For a start he wasn't going to need ten days' rations. He dropped it back on to the floor, slipped the sat phone into his pocket and went out.

The door to Baz and Higgins's bungalow stood open, although the insect screen was closed. He pushed it and went in. He found himself in a large lounge with a kitchen table plonked in the middle and four mouldering armchairs. The floor was made of unglazed red brick. There was a little bar with a stock of bottles and glasses in the far corner and a large map of Congo on the end wall, roughly framed with unvarnished wood.

Higgins was sitting at the table with a beer. "You set?" he said, as Jim came in.

"All sorted."

"Good."

Baz sauntered in. "There you are, *bwana*," he said, then

shouted over his shoulder, "Oi, MBD, how's it coming?"

"Soon," an African voice responded.

"Food'll be up shortly," said Baz. "Beer?"

"Thanks," said Jim.

Baz went to the bar and opened a fridge, took out two bottles of Primus beer and opened them. He walked over to the table and handed one to Jim. "Here's to Barron," he said, clicking his bottle against Jim's.

Higgins waved his by the neck in a token gesture.

"Cheers," said Jim, and sat down.

"We've got a bit of a problem with your journey into the hinterland looking for Terry," Baz began.

"What is it?"

"Well... how can I put it?" He coughed. "I'm not going with you and neither is Mark."

"OK," said Jim.

"And the Chinese won't take you, not that I can spare them even if they wanted to. Then there's the soldiers and, trust me, you wouldn't want to go with them – even if they were falling over themselves at the prospect. So, it's ticklish."

"What about the drilling crews?" asked Jim.

"They're up country and they aren't breaking off for anyone. They're contractors, paid by the day and by the hole."

"What's your solution?"

"My solution?" Baz laughed. "It wasn't my idea for you to come out and start wandering around in the jungle, mate."

"You're right," said Jim, putting his beer down. 'I should have held off for a couple of days and got a dozen ex-SAS down here." He pulled out the sat phone and got up. "I'll get on to it."

"Wait," said Baz – a bit terse, Jim thought. "That'll cost a fucking fortune."

"Not really," said Jim. "A couple of mil maybe. But the wait for them to arrive might cost Terence his life."

Higgins was giving Baz the hairy eyeball.

"Hold on a minute, let me think," said Baz. "MBD!" he called. "Come in here."

A Congolese boy of about fifteen came into the room, dressed incongruously in a green pinafore. He scanned the room, bug-eyed. "Yes?" he said. His voice was guttural, but with a French intonation.

"MBD, I might have a job for you." Baz looked at Jim. "This kid practically runs the place. He's in and out of the fucking jungle every day, bringing bush meat for us and the soldiers. He's our Mr Fix-it. If you want to go walkies, he's as good a guide as anyone."

"Is his name really MBD?" asked Jim.

"Yes," said Higgins.

"No," said the boy. "it's Man Bites Dog."

Jim saw Higgins wince.

"So we call him MBD," said Baz.

"Hi, Man Bites Dog, I'm Jim. Can you take me into the jungle to look for my friend?"

"You want to look for the man that fell?" said Man Bites Dog. "Forget it – he's dead."

"I'd like to try to find him. Recovering his body would mean something."

The boy's eyes swivelled to Baz and Higgins. "I'll take you, but we will find nothing."

"Thanks," said Jim.

"Must look to the food." Man Bites Dog's eyes swept the

room and he bounded out.

"'Man Bites Dog'?" said Jim to Baz and Higgins.

"Filthy war name," said Higgins.

"The kids picked them up during the Mai–Mai conflicts so that if they ever get to go home they can revert to their old ones and no one will know what they've done."

"Is he a soldier?"

"Around here everyone's been a soldier," said Higgins. "Every village and tribe broke up into little armed groups. If you want to know what 'anarchy' really means, this place has had it taped."

"Now he's just a camp follower," said Baz. "Poor kid's probably got nothing to go back to."

"But he's solid," said Higgins, "worth more than our entire flea-bitten platoon put together."

Baz agreed: "Yup, he's a good boy, which is why we don't call him by his war name."

"He needs to drop it," said Higgins.

"Right," said Jim. "Well, I'll go with him. If there's a chance that Terry's still alive it must be shrinking fast. We'll need to set off tomorrow."

"He can't be alive," said Baz. "You can't fall a thousand feet from a helicopter and live." An image of the chopper, maybe only fifty feet above the tree-line, flashed into Baz's mind, with the impression of what might have been Kitson in the canopy.

"I mean," said Baz, "has anyone fallen that far and survived? It'd be a one in a million chance."

"Well," said Jim, "he's got a family and right now they'd probably like to bury him, if nothing else. I'm not going to leave him there to be eaten by wild animals because no

174

one can be bothered to find his body."

Baz shook his head. "It's a fucking jungle out there, mate. You could be standing three feet away from his body and never know it was there. We can't even spot our drilling rigs from the air, bloody great lumps of metal they are, bigger than a fourteen-wheeler. Chances of finding a body are next to nothing. We tried, you know – we have a pretty good idea of where he went out of the chopper. I was sat right next to the bloody idiot. You've heard the expression 'impenetrable jungle'? Well, there it is,' he jabbed a finger at the map on the wall, "fucking miles of it."

Jim sighed. "At least I'll be able to say I did my best."

"Yeah," said Baz, "and I respect you for that, I really do, but you have to remember that this is Africa. Miracles don't happen here."

Man Bites Dog came in with a big dish of rice and vegetables, then disappeared and returned with a bowl of steaming stew and a pile of plates. He put the bowl to one side and spread out the plates then disappeared again. He came back this time with knives and forks.

To Jim the stew smelt tasty but unfamiliar, rather like a curry he had never come across before.

"Man Bites Dog, what is this?" asked Jim, as the boy brought three beers to the table.

"Stew."

"I guessed that, but what's in it?"

Man Bites Dog rolled his eyes. "Porcupine."

"Rat," said Higgins.

"Really?" Jim felt a little shaken.

"Porcupine," reiterated Man Bites Dog, his chin jutting forwards.

"Monkey," said Baz.

"Maybe," said Man Bites Dog. "Maybe Porcupine."

"Great. Ebola casserole again," said Higgins, spooning some on to his vegetable rice. "Bloody tasty, though, I bet," he said.

Jim forked up a small piece of meat and sniffed. It smelt hearty. He tasted it. "Pretty good rat," he said.

Baz had filled his plate. "Maybe it is porcupine."

Jim helped himself and began to eat.

"We'll take you up on to the kimberlite in the chopper – it's less than a mile to where Terry fell. If you don't find him in a couple of days, you never will. We'll come and pick you up when you're done or, failing that, MBD'll walk you out. Just head downhill and you'll come out somewhere you can get back to us."

"Uphill bad, downhill good," said Higgins, with his mouth full.

"I've got GPS," said Jim.

"You're sorted, then," said Baz. "We'll give you the co-ordinates of where we lost Terry. When you get there you'll see what we mean. And if you haven't had enough in a day or two you need your head examining." The chances were that, in roughly eight hours, Jim Evans would be so fucking sick they'd have to air-ambulance him out of Goma to the Hospital of Tropical Diseases in London. He and Higgins had had years of eating native grub that would kill a normal Brit stone dead. The next morning Jim would be able to do nothing, except shit and puke. He wouldn't be able to even stand, let alone go yomping around the jungle.

He snapped himself out of his thoughts. "We're pretty much fucked on the cobalt, so we'll have to do another money raise, probably about another ten mil – deeply discounted, of course – thirty or forty p. Now you've pushed the price up to a hundred and ten we've got to make the most of the panic. You good for your three or four million of it?"

Jim was chewing a stringy yet satisfying piece of meat. He swallowed before he spoke. "Sure," he said, "no problem."

Baz laughed. "You must have a lot of fucking money."

"Yeah," said Jim, "I do."

Baz fixed him with a cheeky stare. "How much?"

"Enough," said Jim.

"Well, hats off to you" said Baz. He smiled again. He had been selling short Barron stock hard into the ridiculous rally that Jim had fired off and would cover his short in the rights issue for a thumping profit – another few million into the fuck-off-permanently fund. It wasn't the way he'd planned it but a profit was a profit.

Jim helped himself to more of the flavoursome rice and stew. He hoped it wasn't a monkey he was eating – that would be really sad.

"This isn't monkey, it's pygmy," Baz declared. "Ker, ker, ker."

"Shut up, Baz," said Higgins.

Jim's fork had arrested in the air. "Pygmy?"

"They eat 'em here," said Baz, with a cold glint in his eyes.

"It's not pygmy," said Higgins, "but they do get eaten – well, they did. Or so they reckon."

"Fucking hell," said Jim. "I thought that kind of thing was a myth."

"Maybe it is," said Higgins, "but the militias have been said to kill and eat them because pygmies are magical people and by eating them you get their magic. They even

177

complained to the UN. Didn't read that one in your London newspapers, did you?"

Baz was laughing – Jim couldn't understand why. "That's horrible," he said.

"There have been plenty of horrible things around here," said Baz, suddenly serious.

"That's another thing about wandering around the jungle," said Higgins. "The pygmies don't take shit any more. If they get pissed off, they'll have you – and I don't blame them. There they are, happy chappies living in the Garden of Eden, and all these fuckers keep coming along to fuck them up. If it is not loggers, it's militias. If it's not militias, it's farmers burning their forest down. If it's not farmers its gorilla conservationists trying to boot them out because they might eat one occasionally."

Man Bites Dog was standing in the doorway and when Jim caught his eye he turned and vanished.

"That's why it's so hard to bring a mine into line here. The country's like a big bag of sharp rusty nails – you have to stick your hand in it and ferret around."

"So why are we here?" asked Jim.

"Well," said Baz, "there are three kimberlites jam-packed with diamonds out there – worth suffering a whole lot of shit for. Ker, ker, ker." That awful quacking noise was beginning to irritate Jim. "For diamonds you can put up with almost anything."

A hill packed full of diamonds and the future Barron stock chart he had imagined suddenly fused in Jim's mind. Suddenly it all made perfect sense. A diamond was just a piece of carbon crushed under a huge amount of pressure till it formed a clear crystal. Volcanoes did that and he was sitting next to the most amazing set of volcanoes imaginable. Diamonds were compressed wealth, tiny crystals of a valueless element that became the earth's ultimate treasure. And Baz Mycock must indeed have located a major diamond deposit. What a tragedy that Kitson had had to come out to prove what Jim had already known from looking at the chart. The chart said that the Barron mining claim was worth a fortune and so it would be. The charts never lied to him – he had all the money in the world to prove that – so why hadn't Kitson or Sebastian listened to him? Jim sighed. He was about to make a pile more money that he didn't need. He started on his second beer.

Man Bites Dog came in with a large plate of fruit. There was sliced pineapple, bananas, oranges, melon and, unexpectedly, two avocados. He trotted out with the dirty plates and came back with some clean ones.

"Now there's one good thing about this place," said Higgins. "The fruit's great."

"Yeah," sniggered Baz, "so long as you've got someone like MBD to get it for you."

Jim bit into the pineapple. It was like he had never eaten it before. It was so sweet and soft and wholesome. He wiped the juice from his chin with his shirt cuff for want of anything else. "Amazing," he said.

Man Bites Dog was watching them from a corner of the room. This time when Jim met the boy's gaze he didn't disappear.

"People always wonder why Africa's such a shit hole," Baz observed, "and you know why it is?"

"No idea," said Jim, now gnawing a slice of melon.

"It's classic mercantilism."

Jim shrugged. "I don't know what that is," he said.

"In a nutshell, industrial nations keep these guys in a vicious circle of poverty and war."

"I'm not an economist," said Jim.

"It's salt," said Higgins. "There's no fucking salt here. No salt, no civilisation, full stop."

What the hell had he got himself into? Jim wondered. He finished his beer. "Well, guys, I'm going to get some shut-eye. It's going to be a big one tomorrow."

"Yeah," said Baz.

The air was heavy and full of the sounds of night creatures. He felt a tinge of excitement, this place really was something. He walked into his bungalow.

There was a girl in his bed.

# 25

In his bedroom the mosquito net was open and she was asleep. She looked adult yet childlike. She had a boyish face and her curly hair was cut short, a beaded tuft poking out at one side. Her shoulders were those of an adult, sturdy and toned. He thought for a second, then closed the door behind him. He coughed, hoping to wake her. She didn't stir.

"Excuse me," he said. When there was no response he repeated it, louder this time.

The girl made no move.

He walked to the bed and touched her arm. "Excuse me."

She rolled over, wide awake now, and regarded him silently.

She seemed about the same age as Man Bites Dog and he knew exactly why she was lying naked in his bed. He stood back, shaking his head. "No," he said. "I think you'd better get dressed and leave."

She smiled at him pleadingly.

"No," he said. "You'd better go."

She said something in her own language, then lay back and turned on to her side.

This was Mycock's idea. Jim scratched his head. What to do? He could stalk into Mycock's bungalow and tell him to get the girl out of his room, but that might get her into some kind of trouble. He decided to strip down his rucksack and then, if she hadn't got the message, he'd ask her again to go away. It didn't seem like much of a plan but he was stumped for anything better.

He laid out the rucksack's contents on the floor and went through the inventory printout. All of a sudden everything seemed potentially useful. Forty cigarettes had struck him as unnecessary when he was on the plane but now, with his upcoming jungle adventure, he remembered that cigarettes were a kind of international currency that might come in useful. He thought about the ten days' worth of rations: might he need them, after all? He studied the packing diagram, which showed the order of things inside the pack. It made perfect sense – but would his body stand the weight? He looked at the list again. It would take him ages to break it down and he might end up with roughly the same stuff but in a different order.

What was he going to do with the girl?

He got up and went over to the bed. He tapped her arm. She rolled over. He pointed at the door. "You have to leave," he said. He waved his arm commandingly. "Go." He held her shoulder gently and pointed at the door.

She began to babble at him, looking scared.

"Christ," he muttered, stepping back. He looked at the bare chair. Sleeping in that would be hard. Sleeping on the floor would be hard too, but there was a bed roll in the rucksack and a blanket. She fell back on to the bed and turned away from him.

He could confront Mycock, but he could see the bastard's laughing face. "Don't you like girls?" he'd say, and Jim would want to punch his lights out. He could sleep on the floor and feel like crap in the morning when he had to be rested.

He walked out of the bungalow. In the distance a shadow stood up. It was Man Bites Dog. Jim went over to him. "Want anything?" said the boy.

"What are you doing there?" Jim muttered, aware that if he spoke any louder his voice might carry straight to Mycock and Higgins.

"Waiting for you."

"Why?"

"In case you need things." Man Bites Dog seemed to be staring at him as if he presented some kind of challenge.

"You speak really good English," said Jim, trying to be friendly.

"Yes," said Man Bites Dog.

"Where did you learn it?"

"When I was little," said the boy.

"OK," said Jim, "right." He looked over his shoulder. "I've got this problem, and maybe you can help me."

"I try."

"There's this girl in my room and I need to get some sleep. Can you get her to leave?"

"No," said Man Bites Dog.

"No?" said Jim.

"No," said Man Bites Dog.

"Why not?"

"Because she is a present from the army over there." He gestured to the dim lights of the barracks.

"Why would they give me a present?"

"Because Mr Baz will have paid them to give you a present."

"I don't want the present."

"She is better with you than with them. Maybe she can run away tomorrow."

"Run away where?"

"Home."

"Where would home be?"

"No home." He cocked his head. "You shouldn't turn down a virgin. That's special money." He looked Jim up and down. "You must be a big man."

Jim took a deep breath. "Let me ask you something. If I was the biggest man in the world, what would I do?"

Man Bites Dog squatted and picked at the earth. He looked up at Jim, the whites of his eyes glittering in the darkness. He stood up. "Send her to America."

That would be easy, Jim thought. It would cost him a grain of sand from the desert of his money. "OK," he said, "I'll do that, but you'll have to explain I don't want to have sex with her and what I'm going to do."

"You don't lie?"

"I don't lie."

"See," said Man Bites Dog, pointing to his right eye, "I look and I listen. I see everything, I know everything. Show weakness here, only once, and you will die." He stared right into Jim's soul. "You understand?"

Jim nodded. He held out his hand and the boy shook it. "What's your real name?" he asked.

"Dog Bites Man," said the boy.

Jim hesitated. "Right. I'll stick with Man Bites Dog for now."

"Let's talk with the girl."

"Wait," said Jim pulling out his sat phone. "Let me make a call." He went back to his bungalow and sat on the floor of the rough wooden veranda. The boy squatted down by him. He rang Stafford.

"Everything all right?" said Stafford, before Jim could say anything.

"Fine," said Jim. "Got a young girl here in a spot of bother. I want her taken care of."

"Very well, sir."

"I can get her to Goma, but we need someone to meet her at the airport early tomorrow morning and take her out of town somewhere."

"As it happens, I've managed to arrange an agent for us in Goma, in case you needed things done – a lawyer chap. I'll arrange for the jet to be there in the morning to pick her up. Failing that, our man will be waiting for her. I'll email details."

"Great."

"Does she have a passport?"

"I doubt it."

"May I suggest we fly her to Kinshasa and look after her there?"

"Sounds good."

"Apart from that, how are things?"

"Grim."

"And are you safe and well?"

"I'm not sure of the percentages. I'll keep you posted."

"Jolly good."

Jim hung up. "Man Bites Dog, this is what we're going to do. In the morning, I'm going to get Higgins to fly the girl to Goma in the helicopter. Someone will meet her at the airport and fly her to Kinshasa. We'll look after her there for a bit. I'll take care of the rest once I'm finished here."

"And you send her to America?"

He wanted to say something vague, like, "We'll see" or "It depends", but Man Bites Dog's comment about weakness was in the front of his mind. "Yes." He stood up. "Now you're going to have to explain to her what's going to happen and get her to agree to it."

"Yes," said Man Bites Dog.

"Tell her I don't want to sleep with her and that I'm going to look after her away from this place."

Man Bites Dog's head tilted back and he looked at the canopy of stars above as they appeared between the clouds. "She won't believe but I will make her," he said.

The girl was still lying in the bed but sat up clasping the blanket when they came into the room.

Man Bites Dog started shouting at her in a kind of speech-making way. Jim had no idea what he was saying. The boy was waving his arms, his words bubbling out in a deep, pounding rap.

The girl shouted back at him, clasping the sheet with one hand and waving her right arm to punctuate her sentences. She didn't seem that happy.

Jim sat down on the chair.

Man Bites Dog was being very adamant.

"What's she saying?" asked Jim

"She is scared."

"I can imagine."

"I'm trying to make her understand."

"What's her name?" said Jim.

"Hélène." Man Bites Dog pointed at Jim with one hand, at her with the other and broke into more protestations.

Suddenly the girl seemed happier. She gabbled incomprehensibly back at Man Bites Dog, who was underlining what she said with gestures and exclamations. He smiled. "I've lied something, "he said. "I told her you need a maid, and she likes that but she still thinks she has to sleep with you or she will be in big trouble." Then he twitched, as if an idea had flown through his head from left to right. He was shouting again. He seemed to quell the last embers of resistance in her. "I told her she would be in bigger trouble if she tried. I've told her to sleep on the floor."

"What did she say about that?"

Man Bites Dog looked at him as if he was a cretin. "Better the floor than with soldiers. If you like she can sleep in the toilet."

"No," said Jim, "in here's fine. I might need to go in there." He got up, fished in his trouser pocket and pulled out a bundle of money. He peeled off a couple of hundred-dollar bills and gave them to Man Bites Dog.

Man Bites Dog looked at the money and then at Jim. He gave a short high-pitched chuckle and stuffed the money into a small pocket on the arm of his shirt. "I'm going," he said, with a broad smile.

As soon as Man Bites Dog had loped out of the room, the girl got out of bed and went to get dressed. Jim had an idea. He went to his pack and pulled out the inventory with its map of contents. He unzipped the top, fished halfway down and retrieved a little orange plastic packet. He dropped it on to the floor and dug down for the all-weather blanket.

The girl was dressed now and stood like a statue, watching him. He took the pack, about the size of a paperback, opened it and shook out the inflatable mattress. Then he blew it up, closed the valve and laid it on the floor at the end of the bed. He pulled the blanket out of its pouch and laid it on top of the mattress.

He should sleep on the mattress, he thought, then imagined the confusion that would ensue. He pointed at her and it. The girl stripped off again, to her underwear this time, and climbed under the blanket. He turned off the main light, took off his trousers and socks and got under the sheet. The bed had an earthy perfume. He switched off the bedside light, the glow from outside illuminating the room.

There was a rustle from the foot of the bed and the girl stood up, outlined in the shadow. Oh dear – what now? He thought he knew.

She walked up to the side of the bed and reached forwards. He didn't move. She took the mosquito net and pulled it closed around the bed, then went back to her mattress.

With a bit of messing around he set his alarm for six on the sat phone. He wanted to be up at first light to download Stafford's arrangements. What a freaky day, he thought.

# 26

He sat on the veranda with his notebook. He was wearing linen combat pants, a linen shirt and a light combat jacket. All the pockets made sense now. He stuffed them with things he might need from the rucksack, like maps, a pocket knife, his GPS, an old-fashioned compass, painkillers, the fire-lighting kit, his phone and some money. He put a sweatband on his left wrist, where his Rolex Cosmonaut had been, for when the sweat on his forehead was running into his eyes.

He plugged the sat phone into his USB port. Windows 7 picked it up and opened a network connection. Jim's email would take fourteen hours to download at the speed his phone could talk to the Internet so he went into it via a web interface. His old bank had insisted on sending him huge document files filled with market news and analysis, which were furring up his email. He ignored it and went to Stafford's message.

The plane would land at nine a.m. and the lawyer, Mr Benoît Mbangu, would arrive beforehand to resolve any issues that arose. He replied to Stafford:

Her name is Hélène. I will call when she is on her way to the airport with more details. She is scared and confused and needs treating with kid gloves. As soon as this is

189

sorted, I'm going into the jungle to look for Terence. It's boiling here.

He added the lawyer's details.

There was an email from St George: Jim was the beneficial owner of 28.9 per cent of Barron. St George noted that if he bought any more he would have to mount a full bid for the company. Jim also noted that shortly after he had left London the company's price had shot up dramatically on the back of news that he had such a big holding. The markets loved rumours and his apparently wild buying spree had set off a blizzard of them.

Jim wrote back to St George: "No takeover, thanks."

He replied to an email from Tulip. He told her how nice it was in Congo and not to worry. Sitting outside in the heat was a nuisance but the phone wouldn't connect for the data in the bungalow.

Jim couldn't possibly log off without checking the markets so he logged on to his ed websites to find out what was going on. The pages loaded at a snail's pace, if not slower – it took a minute just to get a new screen up. Time was flying past so he logged off and closed down his notebook. The phone's batteries were more than half gone so he went inside to put it on charge.

Hélène had tidied the bedroom and was sitting in the chair. She watched him inscrutably as he got his cables out of his flight bag. There seemed to be just one socket by the bedside table. He bent down to inspect it. "Bugger." It was a strange semi-oval-shaped thing with three round holes. His adaptor wouldn't fit. Maybe Mycock had one. If not whatever charge was left in his phone would have to do. He put his computer away and stuck the phone into his pocket. It was seven thirty.

Jim walked to Mycock and Higgins's bungalow, and found them inside having breakfast. "Morning, *bwana*," said Mycock. He seemed disappointed to see Jim so early.

Higgins nodded.

"Thanks for the girl," said Jim.

"Liked that, did you?" said Baz.

Higgins looked at his boss – a flat expression Jim might have taken for contempt.

"Yeah," said Jim, "a lot. I want to fly her to the airport at Goma after breakfast. I'm going to add her to my collection."

"Collection?" asked Baz.

"Of little helpers," said Jim.

Higgins looked at his plate and seemed to be taking a long, deep breath.

"And you want us to fly her to the airport for you?" asked Baz

"Yes," said Jim, "after you've finished breakfast, of course. I own a third of the helicopter so I don't think that's too much to ask."

"All right, I'll get on to it," said Higgins.

"As soon as you get back you can drop me and Man Bites Dog off at the kimberlite."

"OK," said Baz, a smirk on his face. "How big is your collection of little helpers?"

"Very," said Jim.

"Nice," said Baz.

"If it flies, floats or fucks," said Jim, "make sure you own it."

Man Bites Dog had appeared in the rear doorway. "As soon as Mr Higgins has finished his breakfast," Jim said to him, "bring Hélène to the helicopter pad."

"Yes," said Man Bites Dog.

Jim took out of a pocket the piece of paper with the lawyer's details written on it. He turned to Higgins. "My plane should be waiting but if it isn't this man, Benoît Mbangu, will be there to take care of Hélène. Here's my phone number if you need to call me."

"How do you know Mbangu?" said Higgins, his brow furrowed.

Baz threw him a questioning look.

Jim yawned. "Do I look like a muppet?" he said.

Higgins didn't reply.

"Well, that's settled, then," said Baz. "Coffee, Jim?"

"Sure," said Jim, sitting down. "Black, no sugar. I hope it's strong."

"Oh, it's strong, all right – it'll put hairs on your tongue."

Jim's eyes flicked to Man Bites Dog, who was waiting to be called. He couldn't start to imagine the life the boy had led. His youthful voice repeated in Jim's head: "Show weakness here and you will die." The ferocious coffee hit his stomach and suddenly his insides were turning over. He finished it with a poker face, then stood up. "See you guys later." He sauntered out of the room. If the bottom wasn't going to fall out of his world, the world was certainly about to fall out of his bottom.

He walked casually, if somewhat stiffly, to his bungalow and as soon as he was through the door he sprinted for the bathroom where the porcupine wreaked its revenge.

By the time he emerged, the helicopter was taking off. He watched it appear above the rooftops and arc away. He had taken some Imodium from the medical kit and felt just about all right. There had been fifteen minutes of discomfort but the purge, he hoped, had done the trick Nature intended. Perhaps that would be the last of it. Having the trots in the jungle would be no fun at all.

In about an hour the helicopter would be back and he would be on his way into the hinterland. Man Bites Dog was standing by Baz's bungalow, a sack on one shoulder and a Kalashnikov on the other, slung low, ready to be brought to bear. He had a machete on his hip and an ammo belt strung across his chest. He looked perfectly comfortable, as if this was his natural dress.

He looked terrifying.

Jim went across to him. "Hi."

"Hello," said Man Bites Dog.

"So, we're off in a bit."

"Yes," said Man Bites Dog.

"I've got to see a man about a plug," said Jim.


"No, mate," said Baz, "there's not one spare in the whole fucking place."

"Shit," said Jim. "I'm down to, like, a third of my power on my phone."

"Too bad," said Baz. "You can use mine when you get back if you need it."

"Not much use while I'm in the bush," said Jim.

"It's a tough break," said Baz. "You should just keep it off until you need it."

"Sharp thinking," said Jim, in a bid to fit into his new tough-guy persona.

" We'll just jump on and get over to the Kimberlite. The

sooner you're in, the sooner you'll be coming back." Baz grinned.

"Agreed," said Jim. "Would you mind if I mount a takeover bid?"

Baz shrugged. "Yeah – at this stage anyway. When we've proved the diamonds are there you can go ahead, but we're way too cheap right now."

Jim nodded. "That was my thinking."

"But we're a public company so you're free to do what you like." Baz, of course, controlled Barron through a network of front companies, but he'd happily sell out to Jim for a big hike in the price: the young man was clearly loaded and full of shit, so why not take advantage of that?

"I wouldn't like to go against the founder," said Jim. "You know what you're doing."

"Yeah," said Baz, "but you're a clever fellow."

"I'll need the grid references of where Terence fell."

"Sure," said Baz. "I'll get 'em for you."

"See you later," said Jim.

"Jim," called Baz. "Something's been eating me since breakfast."

"What?" said Jim.

"How come you're hooked up with a Directorate guy like Mbangu?"

Jim had no idea what Baz was talking about. He put on his best teenage sneer. "You do think I'm a muppet, don't you?"

"No," said Baz, "just wondering how a guy like you happens to have connections with the French secret service."

Jim was flabbergasted, but he didn't show it. He'd have to ask Stafford...

He went back to his bungalow, switched on the GPS and

walked out into the rising heat. He waited for the yellow Garmin handset to synchronise with the navigational satellites above, then set the camp as a way point.

Man Bites Dog had come up behind him and was looking over his shoulder. "I can find you back," he said.

"Thanks," said Jim, "I'm sure you can, but we can't be too careful. We'll take this as back-up." He pulled out the sat phone and called Stafford. The phone was answered immediately. "She's on her way. Can't talk." The French secret service thing would have to wait. "Battery's low."

"Very well."

Jim hung up. He looked at the two battery bars. He really hated his mobile running down, even if he was only going for a short walk in London. Now he was about to go hoofing it in a jungle full of wild animals and angry pygmies, with the world's most dangerous volcano over his head, a belly full of dodgy monkey stew, three septic ulcers on his torso, and a boy with an assault rifle. "I must be fucking mad," he muttered.

Man Bites Dog let out a peal of laughter and clapped. "Yes, you are! Oh, yes, you are."

# 27

Baz sat in the front seat of the Huey, Jim and Man Bites Dog in the back. The boy was as excited as Jim was apprehensive. The visibility from the back was much less than it was from the cockpit and Jim could see why Kitson had perhaps been pressing himself against the door. Man Bites Dog was humming to himself quietly, jiggling his legs.

"You've been in this helicopter before?" asked Jim.

"Yes, no, maybe," said Man Bites Dog.

"Won't take long," shouted Baz. "Five minutes in this is a day on foot, or maybe more, depending."

The helicopter heaved up into the air amid a cloud of dust.

"Yes, yes, yes!" said Man Bites Dog.

Jim gazed out of the window as the chopper rose above the dust-cloud. He had seen Vesuvius but that was just a puppy compared to Nyiragongo and Nyamuragira. At four thousand feet it was barely a third of their height. Aeons ago the Nubian and Somalian tectonic plates had clashed here to form the Rift Valley to the east and giant volcanic mountain ranges to the west, separating the wet Congo basin from the dry plains of the East African savannah. The great collision had created the cradle of humanity itself, where perhaps as few as a hundred struggling apes had survived to become the forefathers of *Homo sapiens*.

Jim looked at the approaching Nyamuragira: a green nuke just resting between detonations.

Man Bites Dog was looking out of the other window as he bounced his Kalashnikov on his lap. His excitement was almost infectious. Jim went back to watching the jungle, which was probably unchanged since his great-granddad fifteen thousand generations back had swung out of a tree and decided to take his chances in the long grass. If human generations were scaled down from twenty-five years to one in a minute, then humanity had about ten days' worth of ancestors. That was the kind of thing Jim thought about when he was trapped in an uncomfortable situation, and he was no lover of helicopters.

The chopper was dropping down now, heading for somewhere in the jungle ahead.

Baz was holding up a thumb. A five-minute ride, Jim decided, was definitely better than a day's walk in the sweltering heat.

Man Bites Dog seemed oblivious to Jim's discomfort: he was a picture of happiness.

Then they were below the tree-line and they landed with a bump. Now Jim was smiling too.

He waited for Higgins to make his move, then opened the door and climbed out. He grabbed his rucksack and swung it to the ground. The rotor blades were still sweeping menacingly above his head. Crouching, he moved away from the helicopter, blown by the wind and the dust. Man Bites Dog jumped out behind him and ran past. The blades were slowing, the wind was dying and the dust settling.

When he was at a comfortable distance from the Huey he retrieved his GPS and fixed the kimberlite's grid reference.

Baz was fumbling in his bush jacket as he approached. He pulled out a scrap of paper. "These are those co-ordinates," he said.

"Read them out, will you?" Jim asked, and as Baz did so, he entered them into the Garmin. The point was west, about two miles. "So this is our kimberlite?" he said, when he'd finished.

"Yeah," said Baz. "One of three beauties."

Jim walked to the rim of the kimberlite and looked down into the valley. He could make out the camp on a plateau in the foothills, and beyond that the jungle rolled onwards. It was an amazing vista across an endless land, which seemed barely touched by man. There were roads and villages in there somewhere, farms, hamlets and people, but from the kimberlite, there was nothing but never-ending forest, stretching to the distant horizon.

His eyes caught something flashing in the ground about twenty feet away. He walked over to it, took his penknife out of his trouser pocket and opened the blade. He picked up what looked like a piece of smashed windscreen as big as his thumbnail, a transparent rhomboid. Jim stuck the blade into the crumbly cindery ground and prised it out. "Is this what we're looking for?" he said, holding it up. It looked like two glass pyramids stuck together.

"What you got?" said Baz, crunching over to him.

Jim passed him the stone.

Baz closed one eye. "Fuck me." He rolled it between his thumb and index finger.

"Baz?" said Higgins. "What is it?"

"A fifteen–," he shook his head, "twenty–, maybe even twenty-five carat diamond."

198

Jim spotted another flat surface glinting translucently in the sun. He knelt down and popped it out of the ground. It was smaller than the first but still much bigger than the cut stones he'd seen in engagement rings at jewellers'. As he stood up the whole oval surface of the kimberlite flashed and sparkled in the mid-morning sun. He took the first diamond back and handed the second to Baz, who examined the facets.

As he studied the stone, Jim got out his phone and dialled St George. "Bid for the company," said Jim. "Can't talk – low on batteries."

Baz was clearly horror-stricken. "You can't do that," he said. "That's insider trading."

"Don't think so," said Jim. "Kimberlites and diamonds at Barron is all over the Internet chat rooms. The bulletin boards have been singing the story for weeks."

Baz squeezed the diamond. "Oh, why not?" he said. "We'll announce as soon as we get back that we've got rocks."

Jim's phone rang. It was St George. "I really need a price, old chap."

"Two pounds fifty a share. Got to go." Jim hung up. He still had two bars of power. He switched off the phone.

Higgins had taken the stone from Baz. "Nice quality," he mused, "somewhere between white and blue."

"Now all you've got to do is find Terence alive and you're done," said Baz, with a grudging smile. "You're going to make a packet."

"Yes and yes." Jim strode back to his rucksack and stuck the GPS in his trouser pocket. He hauled the rucksack on carefully.

"Good luck," said Higgins, patting his shoulder lightly.

"Yeah, good luck," said Baz, punching the rucksack.

"Thanks," said Jim, tottering.

"This way," said Man Bites Dog.

Jim followed the boy to the lip of the kimberlite. He turned to see Baz and Higgins watching them go, almost as if they might wave.

Man Bites Dog stepped down from the kimberlite into the jungle and Jim followed.

"Fuck me!" exclaimed Baz, as they disappeared. "We've actually got a mine."

"That's funny."

"Funny?" said Baz. "It's not funny, it's bleedin' orgasmic. I can make an empty hole worth a hundred million dollars. Guess what I can do with a real diamond mine." He plucked the stone from Higgins's fingers.

Higgins was scanning the eroded surface of the kimberlite, his head down. "Here's one," he said.

"I'll go and get some tools," said Baz, and made for the chopper.

"And another," said Higgins, as Baz sprinted off, "and two more. That's a whopper."

Baz returned with a giant screwdriver. He whistled when he saw the large diamond Higgins was indicating, lying practically loose in the crumbly rock. "I've never had to dig the hole before," he said, sweat pouring down his face. "What a doozy," he marvelled, when he had it in his palm.

"Tell you what," said Higgins, "why don't I spend a few days here, bag up the top stuff? I'll split it with you."

"Sure," said Baz. "This goes down thousands of feet so I don't see why we shouldn't help ourselves to a bit on the top."

"Fifty-fifty," said Higgins.

"Mate, mate," said Baz, "that's robbery."

"Well, yeah, it is."

Baz stared at him. "OK, then, you . As it's robbery we'll go fifty – fifty."

# 28

The jungle was like a sauna with plants. The canopy was uneven, sometimes high and complete, emptying the ground below, sometimes patchy with thick undergrowth. Man Bites Dog seemed instinctively to know which apparently impenetrable vegetation could be easily pushed through and which was too dense to attempt.

The air was alive with insects, their hum counterpointed by chirrups and shrieks. They were progressing at less than a mile an hour, but Jim couldn't have cared less. The jungle was magical and touched something deep inside him.

Man Bites Dog pulled him up. He pointed forwards into the gloom where something was rustling. "Elephants," he said. "If I talk they will move away pretty quick." For a few moments they heard branches cracking. "Let's wait," said Man Bites Dog. "Give them time to move further away."

Jim took off his rucksack, sat down and pulled a water-bottle out of a side pocket. He drank some, then offered it to Man Bites Dog. The boy took a few gulps, wiped his mouth on the back of his hand and gave the bottle back to Jim. Then he took his own canteen off his hip, drank more and offered it to Jim. "Thanks," said Jim. He was studying the GPS screen. "We've got another hour and a bit of walking before we're at the spot Mycock reckons Terry fell out of the helicopter."

Man Bites Dog nodded. "We eat when we get there," he said.

Jim was as wet as if he had been thrown into a swimming-pool fully clothed, but the linen absorbed the moisture and didn't cling to his body. Stafford was a genius, he thought. He imagined how awful it would be if his clothes were sticky and chafing. He got up. "Time to go."

"Wait more," said Man Bites Dog. "No hurry here. Mustn't get tired. Not to start with."

Jim sat down again.

A quarter of an hour passed.

"OK," said Man Bites Dog, "let's go." He got up, slung on his bundle and hung the assault rifle on his shoulder. "The elephant trail will go our way, I hope. We move easy and slow and make plenty of noise."

"OK," said Jim.

"The animals don't like noise so they will keep away."

"What else is in this part of the forest?" said Jim easing on his rucksack.

"Depends," the boy replied. "Depends on where you is."

"Lions?"

"Maybe."

"Crocodiles?"

"Not up here."

"Hippo."

"Down further with the crocodiles."

"Elephants we know about."

"Pigs, monkey, antelope, lots of birds."

"Fish?"

"Stream fish."

"Gorillas?"

"Other side of the mountain. None this side, all gone – eaten during the war."

"That's sad," said Jim, wondering whether the forest creatures were being frightened away by their talking. With their sensitive ears, they'd be able to hear them coming from miles away. "Giraffe?"

"Sometimes."

"Snakes?"

"Plenty of snakes, big ones and little."

"Where did you learn your English?"

"Stripy horses."

"Zebra?"

"No not zebra, like zebra, but like antelope too."

Jim couldn't imagine what that might be. "I know I've said this before, but your English is very good, Where did you learn it?"

"A long time ago," said Man Bites Dog.

"Not when – where?"

"Small monkeys, big monkeys, lots of monkeys," said Man Bites Dog.

"You're not going to tell me?"

"Tasty monkeys, not so tasty monkeys." He stopped in his tracks and listened, concentrating. "OK," he said finally and started to walk again.

"What was it?" said Jim.

"Nothing," said Man Bites Dog.

Jim was starting to feel the weight of his pack. He was looking forward to arriving at their destination. The GPS told him they were eight miles from the mining camp and two from where they had left the Huey. They were nearly at the point where Kitson had fallen.

The jungle was very dark at the grid reference Baz had given him, a dense canopy of high trees blotting out the sun, but for shafts of light that streamed through the odd break in the foliage. It was a dappled, shady world of roots and leafless vines where they could step across the only impediments to the path, rills of shallow water. The air was heavy with the scent of rotting humus. "We're here," said Jim. "We've arrived."

"Look for butterflies," said Man Bites Dog. "They circle the dead. They like the sweetness."

"And flies?"

"Yes."

Jim took off his rucksack and put it in a direct beam of light, then set the GPS to record the spot. "Let's look for ten minutes, then eat."

"Let's eat," said Man Bites Dog. "Better to eat before finding than after."

There was a grim logic to that and Jim was hungry. "OK," he said. He burrowed in the rucksack and pulled out two packages about the size of a girl's clutch purse. They said "First Strike Ration" on them. Jim threw one to Man Bites Dog. "I don't know what's in here – maybe it's a picnic." He tore off the plastic packaging and opened the card pouch, which contained a selection of plastic bags. "Honey barbecue beef pocket sandwich," he read.

Man Bites Dog was rifling through his parcel. "Pepperoni pocket sandwich," he said.

"Two drinks." He opened one. "Water." Jim passed him a half-empty bottle. Man Bites Dog poured the water into the bag that contained the powdered Lifesaver drink and watched it inflate to the size of a balloon. He drank from it and a peculiar expression crossed his face. "Taste funny," he said, and handed it to Jim who sampled it.

"Gatorade," he said, "well, something like it." He took a couple more swigs and passed it back. "Pour it into the bottle."

Jim opened his sandwich and had a bite. Not bad, he thought. "Not as good as your monkey stew."

Man Bites Dog was devouring his sandwich with gusto.

Jim went through the rest of the food and put most of it into the ziplock bag that had come with the pack. He set aside the poppy-seed cake to one side and bagged up the tuna sandwich, tortillas, crackers and cheese. Then he bagged the drink packets and dithered about saving the dessert bar. He left it out with the beef jerky – what with all the sweating he could do with the salt. He stuffed the bag into the rucksack and dug down to the water purification bottle. "We'll fill up the water bottles here, then set up camp and go looking for Terence."

Down one side of the rucksack, Jim found a long nylon envelope and pulled it out. It was about the size of an old style broadsheet newspaper and weighed two or three pounds. "Tent," he said sceptically, to Man Bites Dog, and opened one end. He was still holding the remains of his sandwich so he slid the contents out a little way by pinning the whole thing under his arm and tugging the innards with his left hand. It was a collection of nylon sheets with bendy canes. He finished his sandwich and turned the envelope around to get a more comfortable grip on the contents. Another tug – and it exploded into his face knocking him backwards.

"Bloody hell!" cried Jim, through a mouthful of sandwich,

and shoved the fully expanded tent off him. It bounced away and Man Bites Dog grabbed it.

Jim stood up, picked up his water-bottle and drained the remnants. Then he returned to the tent's bag. He found six little stakes inside it, which he used to fasten the tent down. At a pinch they would both fit into it.

Now he remembered his cake and began to eat it. "What have you got?" he asked Man Bites Dog.

"Chicken sandwich," said the boy. "It's good."

Jim put the dessert bar and the jerky into his right trouser pocket. "We'll burn the rubbish later," he said, scrunching it into a ball. "Give me your canteen and I'll fill it up."

"I'll come with you."

They walked fifty yards to a rill that ran down from the steep gradient above. Jim unscrewed the base of the water purifier and dipped it into the shallow stream. "This inner core," he said, pointing to the ceramic structure in the centre of the plastic bottle, "is a filter. It cleans out all the nasty stuff, like bacteria, viruses, mud and shit, all the crap that pollutes water and makes you sick." He screwed the bottom back on and pulled out a plunger in the base, gave it a couple of pumps, took the nozzle off the top of the bottle and water poured through the filter jacket into an inner bottle. He poured the contents into Man Bites Dog's canteen, and repeated the process until it was full.

"That's magic," said Man Bites Dog. "Let me try please."

Jim handed him the bottle, which, following Jim's instructions, the boy filled. "Magic bottle," he said, each time he took the top off and water flooded into the inner bottle. Jim's pet bottle was full. Jim drank what was left in the Lifesaver.

Man Bites Dog drank some water from his canteen then cupped water from the stream in his hands and drank it. "Tastes the same." He topped up the canteen from the stream.

"That water would probably kill me," said Jim.

"No," said Man Bites Dog, "not mountain water. It's clean."

"Maybe," said Jim. "I'll make a quick call, and then we need to start searching."

He tapped in St George's number and got voicemail. "Blast." He tried Stafford.

"All sorted?"

"All sorted," came the reply.

A minute later he was through to St George. "How's it going?"

"Not getting much stock," said St George. "It shot up to nearly eight pounds at one stage."

"Leave the order in at two fifty," said Jim.

"We instructed lawyers on the bid, but chances of pulling it off don't look good."

"Leave it as is till I get back."

"Very good," said St George. "Any luck?"

"With Terence?" Jim felt a little guilty. "Not yet. I'm sitting approximately where he fell, but there's no sign of him."

"A good sign, I hope," said St George.

"Yes," said Jim. "I'll be back next week but now I've got to sign off."

The phone was on one battery bar when he hung up, but it flicked back to two. The bloody thing certainly sucked the juice. He turned it off. He turned to Man Bites Dog. "Where shall we go?"

Man Bites Dog rolled his eyes. "Don't know."

"Let's go across till we're just out of view of the camp, swing down in a circle, then come up the other side and back down again to the camp."

Man Bites Dog shrugged.

"He's meant to have fallen here, give or take. There's not much ground cover. He can't be far away."

"Don't think he's here," said Man Bites Dog. "Doesn't feel right."

"Come on."

They walked down the incline of the forest till the camp was just out of view. "You go a bit further," said Jim, "but keep me in sight and follow me around." It was now well into the afternoon and they had about four hours of sunlight left. The jungle crackled in his ears like dying embers. The undergrowth was sparse but still dense enough to act as cover for anything even a few metres ahead. It seemed like a pretty hopeless task – even if they successfully combed a few dozen acres of forest, there was still the probability that the location might be out by a quarter of a mile, which was more than enough to throw them hopelessly off target.

But he had come this far for his friend, Jim thought, so he'd give it his best shot. If they found Kitson's body, he would bury it as best he could and take a GPS fix. Someone else would have to come back and get it.

Half an hour later they saw an aerial display of butterflies circling in a shaft of sunlight ahead, fluttering and whirling in the brightness. Jim braced himself for an ugly scene, but when they reached it they found a giant pile of elephant dung, still steaming.

*

Jim sat quietly and watched the fire, which Man Bites Dog had lit with a book of matches from the fire-lighting kit. He was very tired, happy to sit in the dark and eat his tuna sandwich, cheese and biscuits, and dessert bar. He toyed with chewing a stick of caffeine gum to perk him up, but decided against it.

Jim was glad he hadn't found Kitson rotting in the undergrowth. While his body remained undiscovered he was, in a way, still alive. In a quantum mechanical way, Kitson was both alive and dead till observed by someone in either state. It was nice to think that somehow you could skip between life and death in the way that a photon passed through the "twin slit" in the quantum-physics experiment. Science seemed to suggest nothing was absolutely true and that miracles could spring from paradox. But people weren't massless particles of light. They were great lumps of atoms. When they were propelled by gravity into something hard, they didn't form waves. Instead they shattered and splashed.

"Where did you learn your English?" Jim asked, for the third time. His brain was shaking off its torpor and he was determined to get to the bottom of this.

"A long time ago," said Man Bites Dog, slowly.

"Who taught you?"

"An old man," said Man Bites Dog. "A priest."

"In your home town?"

"Yes."

Jim waited to see if Man Bites Dog would add some more information. He didn't, so he went on, "Why did you leave home?"

Man Bites Dog looked at Jim for a long moment. He tore

210

open a packet of beef jerky and bit off a chunk. He swallowed it. "I was taken," he said finally. He gazed up at the canopy, then hopped to his feet and jogged away into the dark.

# 29

Higgins woke at dawn, got up and dressed. He felt fore-boding, a sense that had served him only too well in his years of operating in some of the nastiest places on earth. He never, under any circumstances, ignored the nagging ache of uncertainty. He could be taking his kids to Disneyland Hong Kong or out shopping in London when it crept over him but, wherever he was, he would stop what he was doing and triple check for anything with the slightest chance of causing him trouble. Paranoia wasn't some kind of disease: it kept a man alive. He didn't need to imagine that everyone hated him to keep sniffing the air.

He went out on to the bungalow's veranda. Everything was quiet as the giant red sun began to rise over the horizon. There was nothing going on in the barracks, not that that surprised him – yet it seemed quieter than usual and he couldn't see any of the itinerant dogs that normally sloped around. He walked towards the compound. He couldn't hear any of the usual noises. Not a single snore or clatter came from the forty men in their barracks. He went to the door of the main blockhouse and opened it. The room was in a state, beds thrown aside and cupboard doors open. No one was there.

Higgins ran to the next block. It, too, was deserted.

He dashed up the hill to the bungalows and crashed into Baz's bedroom. "Get dressed and grab any stuff you can carry. You've got about three minutes."

Baz raised his head. "Wha'?"

"I'm out of here in three minutes. If you're not by the chopper in five you can talk to the rebels on your own."

"What?" Baz sat up with a start.

"It's the Christ Reunion – they're coming up the hill."

Baz vaulted out of the bed. "Shit," he said, naked and suddenly wide awake.

"I won't wait," shouted Higgins, and ran outside.

Baz could see distant figures in a disordered column about three hundred yards from the mine. He ran along the front of the bungalow and down the side towards the helipad. He was carrying the leather tote bag in which he kept everything important, but that was no guarantee he hadn't forgotten something vital. Too fucking late, he thought, as he sprinted to the gate, which was jammed open with an oil drum.

The prop on the helicopter was already turning over; Baz pulled the barrel out of the way and the gate swung closed. With the bag under his arm, he ran flat out to the Huey. He jumped into the front seat, panting, and slammed the door. His face was red, and sweat was bursting out across his forehead. The three Chinese support staff were sitting, fearful, in the back and he tossed his bag on to them. "You told those bastards first."

"Shut up – I'm busy," said Higgins, powering up the chopper. "We've got to be out of here pronto."

He pulled the yoke and the helicopter lifted off. He poured on the power and turned, swooping away low over the treetops.

"You told those bastards that the Christ Reunion army was coming before you told me!" Baz was livid.

"It was either rescue one evil bastard, or rescue three innocent guys and risk leaving the nasty sod behind," shouted Higgins, above the engine noise.

"I won't forget that," roared Baz.

"Good," shouted Higgins. He was smiling to himself. Evidently Baz had forgotten the pound of uncut stones in his luggage. As soon as they touched down in Goma, Higgins was going to be on the next plane to Kinshasa and then home. In about a day and a half he would be in the arms of the little lady he loved. He'd been away too long.

As Adash saw the distant helicopter take to the air, soar above the trees and head for Goma, he smiled. The slightest whiff of his presence and everyone fled. He took towns and villages like that. He told them he was coming, approached, and the enemy soldiers melted away, leaving only those who couldn't flee, normal people, women and children. Then he was free to do as he pleased. "The Christ Reunion army is the most feared band of men on earth," he whispered, to a soldier, who nodded respectfully.

The mine was supposedly worth a billion dollars and he had come to take possession of it for himself and his patron. He wondered whether anyone had been left behind for him to kill.

# 30

Jim was woken by someone rattling the tent from outside. "Time to wake up," said Man Bites Dog's voice. Jim clambered out. He went to the rucksack that was covered with rain from a downpour, opened it and took out a clean shirt, some pants and socks. He changed into them and stowed the old ones in a plastic bag. Then he took out a map from a side pocket and sat down to study it. Man Bites Dog was brewing coffee. It was eight thirty.

"Let's go west for a couple of miles," he said. "We'll look for Terry as best we can, then come back here for the night and go back to the kimberlite tomorrow afternoon so they can pick us up."

Man Bites Dog nodded. "We not find nothing," he said, with certainty.

"But I need to look."

"Sure," said Man Bites Dog, "we look. Maybe we find your friend." He handed Jim a dented tin mug. Jim took a mouthful of coffee. It was hot, sweet, and like any instant he would have drunk at home.

Man Bites Dog swigged his from the small billycan he'd brewed it in. "What happened to your side?" he said.

"I got blown up."

"Blown up!" echoed Man Bites Dog, clearly impressed.

"By a bomb?"

"A grenade."

Man Bites Dog's eyes lit up. "A grenade? So you are a soldier?"

Jim had run with soldiers. He'd helped them stop the catastrophic detonation of nuclear warheads. "Not really. I was just the right guy in the right place at the wrong time."

"So you are a warrior?"

"If you like," said Jim. "And now you know who I am, you can tell me who you are. What's your real name?"

Man Bites Dog looked at him. "Dog Bites Man," he said slowly.

"No," said Jim, "the name you were born with."

Man Bites Dog sat back. "What happened to the people that blew you up?"

"They died," said Jim.

"You killed them?"

"Not all of them." He fixed Man Bites Dog with a stern look. "So, I've told you my secrets, what about you?"

"My name is Pierre, but do not use it with others near."

"Pierre, I'm Jim. Nice to know you, Pierre." He offered him his hand.

Pierre shook it. "You in very big danger, Jim," he said. "Very big danger."

"What from?"

"From Dog Bites Man."

Why had he said his war name backwards? "What do you mean, Pierre?"

"In the camp I am Man Bites Dog, but with my boss I'm Dog Bites Man. Dog Bites Man and his boss are very dangerous, very dangerous to you and to everybody. He keeps me for my English and my eyes."

"Who is your boss?"

Pierre scanned the trees around him. "The prophet of Christ Reunion," he muttered.

"Who's he?" said Jim.

"I pray you will never find out," said Pierre. He suddenly smiled. "But now I am Pierre we can play in the forest and be happy." He jumped up. "Let's find your friend. He must be waiting for us somewhere."

Jim lifted up the map and drew a ring around a spot about two miles away. "Let's walk there and come back lower down."

Pierre looked doubtful. "OK…"

"What's wrong?"

"Just small men."

"Pygmies?"

"Around there, I think."

"How do you know?"

"I've hunted here," he said, tapping the map between the mine and the zone. Then he circled a whole area around the mountain to the east. "We have to be careful here. Pygmies hate everyone."

"Why?" Jim was mystified.

"Bush meat."

"People take their game?"

"Mai-Mai take them for bush meat." Pierre spat on the ground. "They eat them for black magic."

Jim was horrified. "No wonder they're hostile." Jim shook his head.

"If I suddenly run, run after me."

"OK," said Jim, "that's a promise."

"The further we go, the quieter we must be."

"Understood," said Jim. "You lead and I'll follow."

Jim had emptied the rucksack of everything he wouldn't need on the trek into the tent. He was carrying just two packs of rations, the medical kit and the water – he'd had enough of lugging thirty kilos on his back and now the pack felt as light as a feather. He fixed the GPS to his jacket by the strap and put the unit into his pocket. Unlike the sat phone, it didn't seem to use much battery.

"This way," said Pierre, and strode up the incline.

After about half a mile the canopy broke apart and they were in an area of low lush greenery. Pierre walked through it as if he knew exactly where he was going. The sun beat down and Jim thanked his stars he hadn't left his canvas hat in the tent with the rest of his clothes. This place, he thought, was like a proud bastion of a world without man, a final defiant gesture against the smart monkey that had conquered all before it. Not far ahead he could see another tree-line, and between the great trunks to the massive walls of the Nyamuragira volcano, which rose like a titanic chimney. Occasionally, further in the distance, he glimpsed the brooding Nyiragongo, with its plume of smoke spewing into the sky.

Jim kept drinking and refilling his bottle whenever he could. He was sweating as much as if he was in a steam bath. He actually enjoyed the heat, but it made the going tougher than the terrain warranted. Four miles hadn't seemed very far when he had planned the route, but now he realised it was an ambitious target.

218

Not surprisingly Pierre wasn't bothered by the stifling atmosphere, and Jim was thinking idly how strong the boy must be in comparison to himself, when Pierre caught his arm. Something whistled past his ear, and then Pierre was dragging him and he was running behind the boy.

Pierre was fast and Jim was having trouble keeping up, his wounds jarring as he stumbled over hidden tussocks.

Eventually Pierre pulled him behind a tree and, panting, started to rustle in his bag. He pulled out a pink piece of cloth, covered with large white and yellow flowers, and tugged it over his head. It was a dress. He grabbed bullets from his bandolier and started to thread them quickly through his tight curls. "Let's go," he said jumping up and grasping Jim's hand again.

They were running downhill as fast as Jim could manage until they burst through another bush and Pierre hauled him behind another tree.

"Pygmies," Pierre said. "They warned us off."

Jim was looking at Pierre, the dress and the shiny brass shells in his hair.

Pierre returned his stare defiantly. "This battle dress saved me many times," he said. "Now listen." He closed his eyes to concentrate on the jungle sounds. After a few minutes he said, "Let's go further away."

Jim was just getting his breath back. He took a look at the GPS and pointed in the general direction of the camp.

Pierre nodded. "I think so."

Dog Bites Man, child soldier, Congolese insurgent, hardened killer, was wearing a little pink dress. He was the most frightening thing Jim had ever seen.

An enemy would gun down a kid with a Kalashnikov, but

the second's hesitation that a girl with spangles in her hair caused was all the time Dog Bites Man needed to blow you away. This was real-time evolution, Jim thought, forced on souls clinging to the edge of an abyss.

His side was aching badly now. They were not going to find Kitson and the sooner he could get out of the jungle and back to civilisation the better.

"Pierre," he said on impulse.

Pierre stopped and turned.

"Thanks for saving me back there."

"No problem."

Jim shuffled in his pocket. "I've got a present for you," he said, and held out the giant uncut diamond. He handed it to him. "It's yours."

Pierre was mesmerised by the stone. "I don't think the little men wanted to hurt us," he said vaguely. "If they'd wanted to they could have hit us with their arrows for sure."

"It's yours anyway." Jim smiled.

"This is big money," said Pierre.

"Yes," said Jim, "and that's why I'm giving it to you. It's the Étoile Pierre – *étoile* is star in French, right?"

"Yes," said Pierre, holding it up to a ray of light that had punctured the canopy above them. "*Étoile* Pierre." He laughed. "You're crazy." He put it into his pocket. "Let's go, Jim, before the pygmies change their minds."

# 31

Jim switched on the sat phone and called Baz.

"Hi, Jim, have you found him?"

"No," said Jim.

"Shame," said Baz. "Didn't think you would, though."

"Can you come and pick us up tomorrow at about midday?"

"No, mate," said Baz. "The chopper's out of commission."

"Really?" Jim was appalled.

"Yeah, you'll have to come out on foot."

"That's about eight miles!"

"Shouldn't take you more than a day or so." Baz sounded as though he was grinning. "Just walk downhill and you'll pop out by the camp. You've got GPS so you won't get lost."

"Bloody hell," said Jim. " I've had about enough already."

"Yeah, it's pretty harsh in there, isn't it?" he said. There was a slurping noise. Jim guessed he was sipping a cold beer and was overcome by the desire to join him. "Don't worry there'll be a nice reception laid on for you when you get back."

Baz wanted to laugh. With luck the insurgents would hack Jim to pieces and a nice RNS to the market would crash the stock. Then he would pick up his lovely mine for pennies in the pound.

*

"I guess I'll see you in a couple of days," said Jim.

"Mind how you go."

He called Stafford. "I'll be stuck in the jungle for a couple of more days than expected. I'll call you when I'm out. Out of batteries."

"Ri–"

He hung up.

The sat-phone screen advised, "Low batteries." Fuck, he thought. "We're going to have to walk out," he said to Pierre.

"Easy. You going home straight?" asked Pierre.

"Yes," said Jim. His companion was so much less terrifying out of his battle dress. "You want to come away from here?"

"No," said Pierre, "I can't."

"Why not?" said Jim.

"This is my fate."

"But don't you want to go home too and be Pierre again?"

"I can't," said Pierre.

"You can't leave?"

Pierre looked down at the ground.

"Can't we change your fate together?"

"No," said Pierre, "not even a big man like you."

Pierre was out of the tent and making breakfast by the time Jim woke up and remembered with a jolt that he hadn't switched the phone off. He rummaged for it among his clothes and pulled it out. He switched it on and it went live. Thank God for that, he thought. He had switched it off after all. Then it flashed and switched off again. Jim moaned. He hadn't and now the battery was flat.

They ate breakfast and broke camp, Jim loading his rucksack with all the clobber. It would be a long walk, even though it was all downhill. They would finish the day about two miles from the mine and Jim calculated they should get back by about midday the next day. He was longing for the air-conditioned cool of a five-star hotel. Wherever Kitson had fallen, it was unlikely anyone would ever find him.

The terrain going down the mountainside seemed to change every few hundred metres. Even though he was weary of the jungle it was still a place of constant amazement to him. He saw a bird that looked like a vulture eating fruit from a tree while tiny birds flitted around him like flashing blue darts. All the time he could hear running water but, as they descended the mountain, the heat grew and the sun beat down through the canopy.

Pierre seemed almost part of the forest, always alert but happy and relaxed, sauntering through the undergrowth as if it was his own garden. Jim was happy enough, chewing salty snacks and topping himself up with water. The rucksack was a formidable weight but he pushed on behind Pierre as the hot day dragged by. When they reached the four-mile point, they stopped for a breather. Pierre brewed some coffee and Jim wondered about pitching camp there. If they did, he thought, they'd have gone four miles with four more to go the next day, which would put back the glorious moment of arrival by several hours. Five down with three to go would feel much better than four down with four ahead.

The distance ticked down slowly, a long stumbling ramble through increasingly challenging terrain. Pierre had no difficulty with it, but Jim's pack got heavier and heavier and even felt wider as they wove in and out of the undergrowth.

223

"Five miles," he called to Pierre.

"We camp over there." Pierre gestured forwards to a point Jim couldn't distinguish. He pressed on and followed Pierre to a tall, broad tree. It was a nice spot and Jim heaved off the pack, with a groan of relief, and slumped on to the ground. He drank some water and rubbed his forehead with his soaked sweatband.

"I'll put up the tent," said Pierre.

"Thanks," said Jim. "I'm going to rest my bones for a few minutes.' He checked his side with his hand. It was holding up fine. What an idiot he was coming out here with an injury, he thought. He'd got away with it, but only just.

The tent exploded in Pierre's hands and he shrieked with joy. It would be a tight smelly shelter, but welcome for all that.

Jim was on his last change of clothes and he stank, but by midday or thereabouts they'd be back at the camp and he could luxuriate under a shower, even if the water was warm. He examined the sores on his side. Remarkably they seemed to be healing faster. Maybe it was the heat – or maybe the months of antibiotics were finally finishing their work. Encouraged, he washed and dressed them.

A couple of hours, and he'd be back at the mine. From there, he'd get a chopper to fly in from Goma – or a jeep or any kind of transport – and soon he'd be back in London, looking at the river.

Once he'd got back to base he'd ask Pierre again if he wanted a hand out of his predicament. He had so much money and so little to do with it: why not try a few good deeds? In fact, helping just a few people seemed suddenly like a pretty pitiful gesture.

He would ask Davas about philanthropy. The old man was certain to know what to do and how to do it. Congo's poverty had shocked him; it was almost too terrible to contemplate.

The Garmin GPS was a magic piece of equipment. Its simple black LCD display told him where to go, and it had lasted on a couple of AA batteries the whole three days. Without Pierre or the GPS he would have been in terrible trouble. The screen said they had about three miles to go.

# 32

Jalbinyo sighed loudly down the telephone. "I'm sorry," he said.

"I'm sorry, too, Laurent. But I need you to get these people off my mine."

"If only," said Jalbinyo.

"You'll have to try," said Baz. "I don't need it to happen right away, but you have to fix it so that they leave when I say they must."

"It is out of my hands."

"Why?" said Baz.

"Because I didn't put them there."

"I'm not asking you to put them somewhere. I'm asking you to arrange for them to move on in a little while."

"I didn't put them there but my boss did."

"Your boss?"

"Yes."

"Your boss has invaded my mine?"

"Yes."

"Why?"

"Because it is now worth so much he wants to protect it."

"From what?"

"You, I should think."

"Fuck!" said Baz. "That's not on. What are you going to do about it?"

Jalbinyo sighed again. "What can I do?"

"For a start you can stop collecting the money I send you."

"I mean, what I can do for you?"

"Set up a meeting for me with your boss."

"That will be hard."

"Sorry, Laurent, I can't hear you – it must be the pain in my cheque-writing hand distracting me."

"It will be hard."

"Well, tell him to see me in a hurry or I walk and he can keep his bloody friends sitting in the jungle until hell freezes over. I'm not hanging around in this shithole to be fucked about over a worthless plot of jungle." Baz laughed. "You've got twenty-four hours and then I'm off back to London, where I'll make sure that that plot of land is blighted for the next century."

"Why would you walk from such a valuable mine?"

"Laurent, excuse me, but you know fuck-all about mining, right?"

"I am not an expert."

"What we've got here are deposits. Deposits like these need large-scale investment. You can't fucking dig it up with a spade, you need to invest hundreds of millions of dollars just to get the first load out. You need a power station, you need dams and you need equipment the size of the Empire State Building to dig. You can't build that kind of mine if every time you start digging a bunch of armed fuckers shows up and holds you to ransom. No one is going to put a dime into a project that has a whiff of those kinds of problems."

There was silence at the end of the phone.

"So if I can't talk to the top man, and quick, I'm walking and that's curtains for Barron."

"I will do all I can but I'm not sure he will see you so quick."

"Laurent, I've got the world to play with and I've had it up to my back teeth with this little corner of it." He stabbed his mobile off with his thumb.

He picked up his whisky and took a big mouthful. He should be selling out of the mine right now, rather than trying to resurrect the situation. He could make an enormous killing if he did – the price was hitting ten quid. Fuck it, he thought, fuck the diamonds, fuck everything.

He called Ralph. "Ralphy, close me out, close the lot."

"What?" said Ralph.

"Close me out of all the Barron – sell as many of my positions as you can into this buying."

"That's a hell of a lot of stock," Ralph quavered. He sounded as if he'd gone into shock.

"I know. Do it as best you can. Sell it down right to the bid offer price, but get as much as you can."

"What about the diamonds? Is that a red herring?"

"No, mate, they're there by the sackful, but I've had it."

"That's not like you."

"I've had bad news," said Baz, "and just when I've hit it big."

"What bad news?"

"I've got throat cancer."

"Oh, God…"

"I've been getting these bad throats for a few months now," he said. "Anyway, I've just got back from the American clinic here and they say it looks pretty clear cut."

"You need to head for the States – they've got the latest stuff."

"Yeah," said Baz. "So get me clean out as best you can. Let lucky Jim have the show."

"Are you sure?" said Ralph.

"I haven't got a lot of time to think about it."

"It'll take me maybe a week if we want to avoid crashing the stock."

"That's all right," said Baz. "Get as much as you can."

"When are you back?

"I'm on the next possible flight out," said Baz. "I'm going to check into Harley Street and get a load of tests and take it one day at a time."

"Baz, if there's anything I can do?"

"No," said Baz, "there's nothing. Thanks." He hung up. Claiming imminent death was as corny as cons came, but he'd never used that one, let alone on one of his trusted conspirators. With a bit of luck he'd pocket a hundred million and Ralph's no doubt handsome profits would add to his joy over his friend's swift recovery.

Baz was filled with a wave of relief. Pretty soon he'd be back on the beach shagging lovely young whores. He grabbed his hotel-room key and walked to the door. The sooner he booked his ticket the sooner he'd be gone.

# 33

They were out of the forest and into the grass of the plateau, the mine compound fifty yards ahead. "We did it," said Jim.

Pierre didn't respond. He was looking at the building and the two soldiers who were walking down towards them. Their combat pants bore light green patches. He turned to Jim. "Run! Run away!"

Jim started.

"If you want to live, run!"

As Jim turned the soldiers started to shout and Pierre was running towards them yelling and waving his arms. There was a burst of gunfire but Jim couldn't see what was going on because he was struggling up the hill and into the bushes. When he had reached cover, he spun round in time to see Pierre remonstrating with the soldiers. One knocked him down with the butt of his rifle. The other took his Kalashnikov and hauled him to his feet. Jim ran a little further along the trail but it wasn't taking him upwards. Instead every time he took a turning that he thought would lead him further into the jungle it twisted back on itself and he was heading towards the mine. He was exhausted, his legs trembling and uncoordinated. He jerked to a standstill when he almost ran out of the trees and saw the soldiers dragging Pierre towards the camp. The boy was limp and staggering.

Jim reversed himself into a stand of reedy plants that lay in front of a tall large-leafed bush. He crouched down, threw off the pack, pushed it into the bush's hollow centre and climbed into the dark alongside it. Through a tiny gap in the dense vegetation he could see pretty much the whole camp. He might as well hide there, he thought, as anywhere.

Pierre was groaning. His head was throbbing and his mind was only just coming back to him. He could see General Adash standing outside Mr Baz's bungalow.

"He let a miner get away," shouted the soldier who had hit him. "He's helping them."

Adash stepped off the veranda with two of his captains, who looked angry on their general's behalf.

"Dog Bites Man," said Adash, "what have you done? I thought you would be loyal to me, but I see I was wrong."

The soldier let go of Pierre and he fell to the ground. "He's a liar," said Pierre, struggling to his feet. There was a large lump on his temple, which was bleeding.

"Why would they lie?"

Pierre hesitated. Adash slapped him across the face and he fell.

Adash was pulling a machete from one of his captains' belts and smiling down on him.

"Kill me and kill my secret with me," spat Pierre, blood trickling from his mouth.

"I don't need your English 'secret' any more," said Adash, feeling the edge of the machete with his left thumb. "I have two other followers now who speak as well as you," he sneered, "perhaps better."

"My secret is in my pocket, so kill me like you killed my

231

family." He scrambled up and the two soldiers grabbed his arms and shoulders.

"I didn't kill your family." Adash pushed Pierre in the chest with the dull nose of the blade. "Now you have reminded me, I will."

"I don't believe you – you kill everybody. They were dead the day you took me."

"So, Dog Bites Man, what have you got in your pocket?"

"Let me go and I'll show you."

"Let him go."

The soldiers stepped back grudgingly.

Pierre reached into his top pocket and pulled out the diamond. "This is my secret, my star," he said, holding it up, like a challenge.

Adash put the machete into his left hand and snatched the diamond out of Pierre's grasp. "Where did you get this?"

"Why should I tell you? You are going to kill me."

"If you tell me perhaps I will let you go."

Pierre said nothing.

Adash slapped his face with the flat blade of the machete. Pierre yelped and fell to the ground. He had a thin gash across his face, which swelled with blood that began to run down his cheek. He lifted himself up on one arm. He was panting.

"If you don't change your mind by morning, I will kill you then." Adash held the diamond out at arm's length and watched it sparkle in the afternoon sun. "Tie the Dog up outside my villa and fetch him a bowl of water."

"What about the miner?"

"He will come to us when he is desperate enough, and that won't be long."

*

Jim had seen the gruesome scene enacted by tiny figures on the horizon through the almost useless pair of binoculars he'd had in the pack. He had practically howled when he saw the figure in white hit Pierre with what looked like a sword and had nearly cried with relief when the boy had kept moving. He watched the indistinct blobs tie up the boy and leash him to a beam that held up the veranda roof of Mycock and Higgins's bungalow. They would probably come for him next, he thought, but running didn't seem an option. If they hadn't caught him by nightfall, he'd have a try at freeing Pierre. If he was caught he could maybe buy them both out, but if he pulled it off, they'd make a run for it. It might be a week's march to Goma, but he'd worry about the practicalities of that later. He took the jungle knife from the pack and strapped it to his leg. It was an evil-looking piece and razor sharp. He imagined stabbing the man in white in the gut with it. It would do the job nicely.

Baz was checking in for his flight to Kinshasa. The selling had gone well – the market was insatiable, gobbling up his stock. Ralph was doing a good job; on the phone he'd seemed genuinely upset and worried about him. He'd do better to worry about Jim Evans, who was either hopelessly lost in the jungle or having tea with the nastiest people in Africa. Good riddance to him, and hello retirement. He watched a beautiful Congolese girl walk by in a bright green and white dress. Every step he took away from that hole, the better he felt. Leaving a scam usually made him feel a bit sad but not this time. This time nothing would bring him back to the game, however much he loved it.

# 34

Jim was examining his tiny Sony mobile phone. The battery was different from the sat phone's and would not replace it. He glanced up frequently but there was little going on in the mining camp, save the occasional arrival of small groups of soldiers who pitched tents near the barracks. Jim calculated there were perhaps around a hundred men and wondered if some would soon be heading his way. He reassembled the small phone and set the alarm to vibrate at three a.m. He hoped that would be the optimal time at which to rescue Pierre.

At least there were no dogs to wake and bark – or, at least, none that he could see. He wound his Rolex Cosmonaut and put it back on his wrist, shoved the phone in his top trouser pocket and settled down to watch the camp. The sun would set in an hour and then he'd be a lot safer. He would eat something and go to sleep. He examined the night-sight goggles, and was pleased to discover that their battery was full of life.

Thank God for Stafford, he thought. He looked at the inside of his all-weather blanket. It was lined with silver foiled material that would shine like a beacon in the dark with the night-sight goggles on. He would hang it on the bush when he left and its reflection would lead him back to the pack. That was all good in theory, but first he had to make it that far.

The night-sight goggles were almost as sinister as the hunting knife. There was something demonic about both articles. Black straps fitted eyepieces to his face and a snout poked out at the front above his nose like a stubby telescope. It could see ahead about half a mile and would run for ten hours. Thirty minutes after leaving his hideout, he would be back – or, more likely, captured or dead. He laid the goggles on their black nylon carrying pouch and put the pack down so he could use it as a pillow. The sun was setting fast and in six hours the alarm would go off and he would start his foolhardy rescue mission. His life must be like a pixel in one of Davas's crazy financial models. He was the single tiny chaotic element in a universe of data that flicked on and off at random and sent its neighbours cascading into waves of unpredictable turbulence. In other words he was totally fucked up. He was like a giant lightning conductor poking up into the sky as a black Kansas stormcloud rolled in.

He could practically feel the air filling to rupturing point with electricity.

Was his fabulous luck at calling the markets matched by a balancing curse? Was his meteoric rise about to be followed by a spectacular crash to earth? Stocks went up like a rocket and fell back like a stick. Maybe he was now the biggest short in history. Was he Icarus?

He tried to get comfortable. He drew the chart of his life, which went on and on. Yet one day he knew his predictions would be wrong and tonight he was more likely to be wrong than at any time before.

It was getting darker by the second, so he closed his eyes

and tried to drift off but he couldn't fall asleep. It was seven thirty. He was just going to have to stay awake all night.

Adash walked out on to the veranda, a jug in his hand. He came to stand over Pierre, who was bound hand and foot with cord. The metal chain leash around his neck had a leather handle, which had been threaded around a post, tethering him like a guard dog.

Adash poured water from the jug into an empty bowl set out for the boy. "Drink," he said.

Pierre looked at the bowl and then at Adash. His face was full of hate.

"Drink, little Dog, or you won't be strong enough to take me to the diamonds and then I will have to cut off your hands to make you sorry." He smiled. "And perhaps your nose and lips, too. You know I will do it, so drink and maybe if I am happy I will just send you away."

"You would never do that," said Pierre, trying to challenge him to do the opposite.

"And not let you return to tend your family's grave?" said Adash.

Pierre rolled on to his knees and elbows and started to drink from the bowl. Adash only spoke lies so maybe what he had said meant he would be killed soon, maybe it meant his family lived, maybe both.

Adash pushed him away with his foot and Pierre rolled awkwardly on to his back.

Adash laughed. "I have complete power over you," he said. "Worship me and you may live."

"God will smite you," said Pierre, wriggling on to his knees.

Adash laughed. "There are no gods to smite me." He lifted his boot to kick Pierre with his heel. The lights of the camp went out. Adash stopped mid-stride and his foot returned to the wooden boards. He looked into the dark of the night, then walked back into the bungalow muttering to himself.

# 35

Jim woke because something was buzzing in his pocket. His mind caught up. It was his semi-useless London phone, vibrating to wake him. He pulled it out. It was three a.m. He switched it off and struggled in the dark to stow it. He had fallen asleep and not even noticed. He grabbed the goggles, fitted them on to his head and switched them on. They gave off a little turbine-sounding whine and lit up green. He could see everything as if a giant green candle illuminated the world. He picked up the blanket and stepped out of his hiding-place, opened the blanket up, turned it inside out and hung it on the tall grassy reeds. Through the goggles, green light shone from it like an emerald lighthouse as the infrared bounced off the insulating foil and back down the optics and electronics to his retinas.

He looked through the few feet of cover at the walk downhill to the mine. He could just make out Pierre curled up on his side. A figure sat ten feet away from him in a chair, a rifle in his arms. The generator had gone off and wouldn't come on again until mid-morning.

He took a deep breath and strode forwards.

He could hear his every breath as he walked, the knife in his hand. There looked to be a deer to his far right grazing and bats flew above him. His feet were loud in the undergrowth as he picked his way forwards, his heart drumming in his chest. His eyes were watering and sweat was pouring off him. The compound was still, not a single light shining from anywhere but the sky. It was just a five-minute walk but each step felt like a minute passing. He reassured himself that if anyone came out they couldn't possibly see him but his nerves were on fire with anticipation. He was breathing deeply as, one foot at a time, he paced through the rough grass and tussocks that covered the uneven space between the bush and the mining camp. He moved on to the rough, dusty pathway that led from the jungle to the camp. A pair of eyes stared out at him from a spindly tree – some kind of bird, he thought. He was fifty yards from Pierre and maybe thirty from the guest bungalow he had slept in just a few days ago – it felt like years.

The ground in front of the bungalows was gravelled and made a loud grating noise as each step pressed down on it. The guard was asleep, his mouth open in a quiet snore. Pierre was asleep, too, and as Jim approached he saw how swollen and battered the boy's face was after the beating he'd received.

Jim's breathing was quickening and his heart racing. He was trying to stay calm but losing the battle. He was at the wooden pillar where Pierre's leash was fastened. If the boy woke with a start they were screwed. He lifted the leather handle, put his blade between it and the pillar and tried to slice through it. The leather was tough and wouldn't cut easily, the knife gnawing into it. The chain rattled a little. He glanced at Pierre, who had woken without Jim realising and was looking up at him, his eyes wide. He checked the guard, ready to rush him if he woke, but the man was motionless.

The handle was two-thirds cut through. He hauled on it with everything he had, holding his breath, and heard a tearing crunch as it gave.

Jim took the chain and lowered it carefully into Pierre's lap, knelt down quickly and cut the boy's ankle bonds as if they were paper. The knife was razor sharp, after all. Pierre didn't need his hands to run so they could make a break for it now if they had to, but Jim threaded the blade gently between Pierre's wrists and, with a quick careful movement, severed the rope. Pierre was standing and pointing at the soldier and his gun. He drew his hand over his throat.

Jim shook his head. He wasn't going to cut anyone's throat.

Pierre motioned to Jim to give him the knife.

Jim shook his head again.

Pierre clenched his fist in frustration but Jim grabbed his hand and pulled him in the direction of the jungle. Perhaps they were both going to live after all, he thought. The silver blanket shone like a beacon half a kilometre in front of them and every step was one step closer to a dangerous kind of safety.

Pierre looked at his saviour, who was just a faint outline in the moonless night, only inches in front of him. Like a leopard, Jim could see in the dark. Tomorrow Adash would be hunting them both: the Dog and the Leopard.

Jim pulled down the blanket and towed Pierre into the bush. "We must keep going," said Pierre. "In the morning they will come looking for us right away." He was undoing the neck collar.

"OK," said Jim, stuffing the blanket into the pack.

"I will carry that," said Pierre. "I can go faster than you weak people."

"Thanks," said Jim. "Be my guest. Where shall we head?"

"To the Pygmies."

"Pygmies? You sure?"

"Christ Reunion is more scared of them than we are. They are gentle people."

"OK," said Jim, "that's not what you said a couple of days ago."

"Compared to the Reunion they are gentle people."

They clambered out of the bush and Pierre threw the pack on with a grace that underlined his strength. He pushed ahead of Jim. "I can find the way," he said.

"How?" whispered Jim.

"My eyes and my feet," he said, "they follow the trail uphill. When we find a stream, we follow its course."

"Fine," said Jim, following as Pierre picked his way into the bush.


The soldier woke as the first light of day fell on to his eyelids. He looked down to where Dog Bites Man lay and jumped out of his chair. The boy was gone – and Adash would spill his guts, then hand them to him as he died. He leaped off the veranda and ran down the hill out of the camp. He could maybe get two miles away before anyone noticed he or the Dog was gone. He was running fast now, running for his life.


Adash stepped out of the shower and pulled on his long flowing robe. The diamond looked even better wet and he marvelled at its size. No wonder this mine was worth a billion. If they had found diamonds of this size and so many

241

of them that they were giving them to their servants it must be a mine of unlimited treasure.

Diamonds were power and these would buy him enough, perhaps, that he would again answer to no one. He stepped into worn brown sandals and sauntered to the door of the bungalow. He walked out. Dog was gone and so was his guard. He sat down on the chair and waited. Someone had rescued the boy and the guard had sensibly fled. Who would rescue Dog Bites Man? Surely not some miner. He went back into the bungalow and picked up the papers found in the next villa.

They were emails to a Jim Evans: he owned 10 per cent of the mine, or so Adash thought the English said. If it was him, he was brave. That was good, because the brave were much easier to trap and kill.

# 36

Jim was exhausted: they had gone five miles and he was ready to drop. They were eating some of the last of the rations he had with him, sitting by the huge trunk of a nameless mighty tree that rose two hundred feet into the air. Pierre had snagged some avocados but they were as hard as cannonballs. Hopefully they'd ripen in the heat.

By dark, if he could get a second wind, they'd just about make it to the area where the pygmies had scared the hell out of them. Pierre didn't seem bothered by the exertion even with the weight of the pack. His face was a mass of swelling and cuts, but he bore it as if that was its normal state. He just walked in silence, occasionally looking back at Jim to make sure he was OK.

They hadn't said anything since they'd started their trek back up the mountain; the overriding necessity was to move – fast.

Apart from his exhaustion, Jim was happy. He had done the right thing and got away with it. Now all they had to do was march through thirty miles of mountainous jungle. Suddenly he had an idea. He rifled through the rucksack and pulled out the sat phone.

"Light a fire, Pierre."

"Are you going to cook the phone?" asked Pierre.

"Yeah," said Jim. "You've got it in one."

"I know it's dead, but you still can't eat it," said Pierre.

"A little cooking will do it good," said Jim, pulling off the battery compartment.

Pierre put down the rucksack and went into the trees. A few moments later he returned with a branch covered with dead leaves and broke it into kindling. Then he whittled some of the wood into tiny feathers. He rubbed two matches hard against his trouser leg to dry out any damp and lit the little heap he had made. The fire was quickly alight and Pierre built it up to a blaze. "Nothing too wet," he said. "We don't want to send smoke above the trees."

Jim had stripped the battery out of the sat phone and carefully cut off the plastic cover leaving just the plain metal jacket. He stuck the jungle knife into the middle of the fire. It wouldn't be so sharp when he took it out, he thought. "I'm going to heat the blade and then warm the battery on it," he said. "With a bit of luck that'll give it some juice."

"Maybe it explodes," said Pierre.

"Probably," Jim agreed, "but it's worth a try."

Jim watched the knife in the fire and imagined it somehow red hot. A simple fire could never do that. The wooden handle was very hot and Jim slid the blade out of the glowing centre of the flames and laid it flat. He licked a finger and dabbed it on the metal. It hissed. "Too hot," he said, "I think." He counted a few seconds off and tried again. No hiss. "Here goes," he said, and dropped the battery on to it. He sat back a bit, expecting the case to pop open and start burning. It didn't. He counted a few seconds, then turned the battery over with a quick flip. It was hot but not so hot as to blister his fingers. The blade was losing its heat quickly and

Jim turned the battery again. It was as hot as if it had been in hard direct sunlight for a long time. He got ready with the sat phone in one hand and snatched up the battery with the other. He snapped the battery in. It was suddenly a very tight fit. He clipped the back on and pressed the on button. "Come on, baby," he said, "you know you can do it."

The screen came on, but it had last time, then gone out again after a few seconds. He selected normal transmit mode and held his breath. The phone was searching for a signal. He stood up and tried to find a stretch of ground with little canopy in the way. There was a single bar of power and signal, and they were both flashing.

He went to SMS.

"In deep shit," he typed, and sent it to Jane. He pulled the message up again and tried to send it to John and Stafford.

The phone rang. "Jane Brown," read the screen.

He pressed *answer* but the phone went dead and the screen was blank. He switched it on again and the phone started to boot, only to flip back into darkness.

He stuck the knife back into the fire. "Well, we got through," he said.

In a couple of minutes the embers had heated the knife again and he laid the battery on the blade. There was a crack, a bang, a fizz and the battery caught fire. Jim and Pierre jumped back as a small spitting white cloud spewed up. Jim grabbed the handle of the knife and spilled the battery on to the ground. It was burning hard, like a badly constructed firework, jumping about in little fits and starts.

"We'd better get going," said Pierre. "We need to keep far ahead of them."

# 37

Jane tried the number a couple of times before she gave up. Then she plugged her phone into her notebook and made a secure connection. She traced the call.

What the hell is he doing in Congo?

She booted up the satview. The globe spun and zoomed into an area of jungle in the DRC near the Rwandan border. There was a little flag on the mountainside. Why would Jim be in a place like that?

She selected the Situations, Issues, Threats icon and a window opened and loaded. The scroll bar shrank and shrank. The software wasn't loading a report: it was loading an encyclopedia of trouble. She scanned it. The tags said: Insurgency, Genocide, Civil War, Trafficking. Never mind deep shit, Jim had got himself into a major clusterfuck. The DRC was about as far away from her and America as you could get. It was in the middle of Africa and, as such, on the edge of the world.

She called Max Davas.

Max was waving his arm over the digital whiteboard. His room of Quants – like bank traders, but each with a PhD in maths – didn't seem to get his point. These guys were so smart that with the advanced physics of their derivatives they had nearly bankrupted the world only a few years ago by accidentally creating the equivalent of a financial black hole. Davas hired the best of the best.

The phone in his pocket was buzzing and he knew if it rang it was more important than a room full of his private army of brilliant but today pea-brained mathematicians.

"It's intuitively obvious," he said, in conclusion, and pulled out the phone. "Excuse me," he said, and made for the office door.

The mathematicians looked at the fluctuating surfaces on the whiteboard and then at each other. They liked to think their peers didn't understand and hoped they thought *they* did.

"Jane, an unexpected pleasure."

"Do you know why Jim is in deep shit?"

"No," said Davas, "only that he went to the Congo to try and find his broker."

"Funny place to go look for your broker."

"The man fell out of a helicopter over a mine Jim has an ownership in."

"OK," said Jane. "I just got a text from him saying he's in big trouble."

"What exactly did it say?"

"It said, 'In deep shit'."

"Just that?"

"Yes."

"So he must be in really deep shit," said Davas.

"Yes."

"That's very bad."

"Max, I'm going to need your help. Stand by."

She called John Smith. "Have you heard from Jim?"

"Why?" asked Smith.

"Is that, like, no?"

"It could be."

"He's in trouble."

"What kind of trouble?"

"Don't know. I just got a single text."

"What did it say?"

Jane sighed with irritation. "'In deep shit'."

"Nothing else?"

"No."

"He must have been pushed for time."

"Yeah, well, that's my thinking. The signal came from a sat phone smack in the middle of the African jungle."

"Need help?"

"I don't know."

"I can probably get backing," said John.

"In DRC?"

"DRC? That's a tricky one."

"Tell me about it. Look, stand by, OK?"

# 38

Jane went digging and pulled up the mine. Barron was some mad crazy London stock. Its price had been flying and it was all over the London financial pages.

Typical, thought Jane. She pulled it up on the satview. The compound looked like an army campsite with three, maybe four hundred soldiers on it. She parcelled the image out to analysis with an emergency priority on it and started probing for information on company staff.

The CEO was flying back to London from Kinshasa.

She forwarded his details to Smith. "Arrest at the airport. I'm coming over."

John was immediately on the phone. "What have you got?"

"The boss of this mine, Bartholomew Mycock, just left the area and is headed back to London. There's a small army parked on the property and the message came from five to ten miles away from it."

A newsflash from the analysts flashed across the bottom of her screen: "Targets Mai-Mai insurgents. The troops are insurgent."

"Possible candidates," said the ticker, "CRA ... FRDKI ... FNRA ... M40 ... MLA ..."

"Tagged target acquired," said the screen.

"Stand by," said Jane, hanging up.

A little green soldier sat alone in a box on the top right-hand corner of the screen. She right-mouse clicked it and selected *focus*. The map zoomed in; the view was blocked with cloud. She went to radar, which was dramatically lower resolution, but all she could see was jungle canopy. She switched back to visual view and put it on track. The point was jiggling as she'd expected, but was Jim moving or was it just noise?

They had tagged Jim's ass in the hospital in Venice – some bright person in Washington didn't want such a valuable piece of collateral to go missing. And during the operation on his ruptured torso, they'd put a transponder in one of his bust ribs that let them keep tabs on him, as if he was an expensive sports car. They had been so very right to do so.

She called Smith back: "Screw arresting Mycock. We've just got to get to Jim fast."

"OK," said Smith. "I'll do my best at my end."

"I've got a fix, I'll send you co-ordinators."

"That was quick," said Smith.

"We don't rely on the BBC for intel," she snapped.

"How close did the sat-phone signal get you?"

"I'm looking right at the spot." Trouble is, she thought, it's not moving. "Stand by."

She called Davas. "I've got to get into the DRC within hours," she said. "There's a small army of insurgents parked right on Jim's mine and he's up in the hills in the middle of the jungle. If we don't go get him quick, he'll be toast."

"Send a request to the President and copy it to me," said Davas. He looked at his smartest employees, each one a young genius. "I may be some time," he said, picking up his little netbook. "Please have this worked out by the time I return. I need you to understand it."

Davas walked quickly to his corner office in the black rhomboid building overlooking the Hirst-Brault Expressway in Hendon, Virginia. Jane's email was waiting for him. He forwarded it to the President and wrote below the header: "As you know, Jim is my planned successor. We have no credible replacement and in fairness I should have expired long since. If you would, please, kindly give this the highest priority." He sent the message and closed the netbook, then returned to the meeting room.

Only he understood the maths that let him model the world's markets. Only he could codify the insights necessary for the US government to stay one step ahead of the efficient market. When it finally caught up with the profligate US economy it would tear down its walls and smash its aqueducts like the Hun had destroyed Rome.

Yet Jim could see this future in his mind's eye. It was a unique skill and beyond price. Where Davas's army of computing slaves would take a day to render an outcome from Yottamips of calculations, the young guy could just glance at a chart and see everything.

When Davas was gone, only Jim would stand between the US – the world – and a collapse into barbarism and war because only Jim could replace him and his market simulations.

The man who could see even ten minutes into the future of the financial markets could, as Davas had done for twenty-five years, control the finances of the world.

A box flashed on Jane's mission screen. Approved. She opened the resources box. If priority was low she would be flying coach class on her own dime. If priority and resources were high enough she could move mountains.

"Wow," she said. "Ninety-nine/ninety-nine." She could go to war against France with that kind of clearance. The commanding officer was Acting Major General J. Brown.

The Jim situation had got her promoted a whole two jumps.

The bastard, she thought, shuddering with a flash of fury and clenching her fists. Then she smiled. This time she could repay him double by saving his ass, a debt that no amount of money could repay.

She stared at the map. Was the dot at the feet of the red-soldier icon now making a line? She zoomed in. The line made a jagged pattern but the range seemed to be expanding. It jumped about fifty yards to the right and continued to blip around, then jumped a few more yards. She tweaked the smoothing setting but it didn't help. The crazy line was moving east. Unless someone was carrying Jim's body, he was alive.

She forwarded the mission to Bill and Will at Special Ops. That would shit them up.

Will was first on the screen. "Holy cow," he said, by way of introduction.

"Holy cow," responded Jane.

"Better get you to Andrews Air Force Base."

"I'm coming from the office," said Jane. "It's about a hundred miles to you from Charlottesville. If you can keep the roads open I'll be less than an hour with my bike."

"I'll get on to it."

Bill came on line. "Hey."

"Got to run, Bill. Catch you at the base."

She called Smith. "I'm going straight in. Do anything you can." She closed down the computer and walked straight to the car park and her bike. Acting Major General Brown. She fired the bike up. She was going to have a fun forty-five minutes. She thought about the resource allocation and the priority: 99/99 was off the dial. She must be missing something. It was like Jim was an aircraft carrier that had gone missing with a hull full of nuclear Tomahawks.

If the Kawasaki Ninja ZX-14 had been a horse, she would have stuck her spurs into its flanks. The bike screamed down the road to the gatehouse. She swiped the pad and the gate opened. She would be driving at 120 m.p.h. in just over six and a half seconds.

# 39

It was dark and the fire was building. They had made it to within about a quarter of a mile from where Pierre thought the pygmies' territory began. They hadn't had any contact with the Christ Reunion which Jim found infinitely reassuring: with every step they took their chances of being captured reduced. Pierre didn't seem so sure. They shared the last of the rations; a French toast pocket, processed jalapeño cheese and crackers. Jim had some caffeinated chewing gum, tomato sauce, salt and pepper straggling in the last ziplock bag.

"They will track us," said Pierre. "They will come after me because I told them I knew where the star came from. That kept them from killing me."

"Don't blame yourself," said Jim.

"Tell me," said Pierre, "why you came for me?"

Jim looked embarrassed. "Was I supposed to leave you there?"

"Yes," said Pierre. "I would have left you."

"Really?"

"Yes."

"So why did you warn me to run away?"

Pierre squeezed his nose hard and looked into his lap. "That was stupid," he said.

"So I'm stupid too."

Pierre looked up. "I think my parents are alive."

"I didn't know you thought they were dead."

"When the Christ Reunion took my village they killed and killed. But they found me and I told them I could speak English. Adash came and he gave me a pistol and all the soldiers laughed. 'Kill your father now and your mother and sister will live and then you will follow me,' he said. My father was begging me to kill him. He was crying, 'Kill me, son. Please kill me.' But I was not crying I was filled with hate, blind red anger. So in a fury I took the pistol and I pushed it into Adash's throat and said, 'You will die first and then we all go see God.' He was smiling, smiling, laughing at me, with his death in my eyes and me with his gun in his throat. He didn't care and he said he would let my family live as long as he owned my soul. So that was how it was, but soon I knew my family were dead. Adash would kill all he came across. He butchered everybody. Why would he have not killed my family as soon as I couldn't see? But I hoped and I followed him, but my hope died in my heart and my heart became a stone." He clenched his fist. "Dead like the burnt rocks that fall from the mountain. But Adash told me they were dead yesterday, and I know that what he tells you is lies. Truth is poison in his mouth and twisting is everything. So I have hope. My family is far away. They must have made themselves safe. Once you meet Mai-Mai, if you do not flee you die."

"How are we going to handle the pygmies tomorrow?"

"We try to trade."

"And then?"

"We keep moving. Until we get to Goma or find a big UN

unit we will not be safe. Adash will stop at nothing to find the diamond mine, to find me."

Adash sat in the darkness of the bungalow. None of his men had been able to figure out the generator and the lights went out at midnight. He had called his commanders from all over the region. They were to converge on the mountain and find the boy and the owner Evans. Then they would share in the spoils of the mine.

Since the civil war had fallen into a violent kind of peace, his commanders had become increasingly hungry. Men were drifting homewards. War had brought power and money, but peace drained it away again. The mine would reignite the struggle and Christ Reunion would stand alone, a fluid horde that would sweep everything aside.

# 40

Heathrow wasn't Baz's favourite place, but compared to the DRC it was like walking through the gates of heaven to be serenaded by flapping angels with trumpets.

He was tired so he was pleased to zip through Immigration and Customs. He was going to flop at the Dorchester and count his winnings. Ralph had excelled himself, and for all his selling, the share price of Barron was still over four pounds. He had made a royal killing, more than all his other deals put together. He was back, he was made, he was done.

He sat in the empty first-class carriage of the Heathrow Express, watching the stupid news from the BBC. Why did they import this misery? What was more, why did it have to be piped into his happy little first-class bubble? They could fuck off with their depressing reports – how about some soothing music instead?

His mobile rang.

"Mr Mycock," said a deep cut–glass accent. It was a rich African voice.

"Yes," said Baz.

"I'm Julien Julius," said the voice.

It was the Congolese Minister for Interior Infrastructure.

"What can I do for you?" Baz almost added "mate" but stopped himself in time.

"I wondered if we could meet."

Too late, thought Baz.

"I was hoping in London," continued Julius, "if that's not too inconvenient, as I'm in England for a bit."

Baz grinned slyly and put his feet up on the seat in front of him. "Oh, I think I could manage that. How can I reach you when I arrive?"

"Call the embassy."

"Is it regarding anything in particular?"

"Oh," said Julius, "just a few ideas I've got. I thought we could have a chat."

"All right," said Baz. "I'll be with you as quickly as I can." His original plan was accidentally in play. He was going to have some fun with it.

Will was pushing the digital map around on the tabletop screen. "So you want to go right now – you won't even wait a day?"

"Not if I don't have to," said Jane.

"You want to just drop right in there, no back-up, no nothing?"

"Is that so unusual?"

"Without proper planning? Hell, yes."

"He may already be dead. His survivability is limited to hours."

"We can fly you in a B1 Lancer, refuel at Lajes Field in the Azores and drop you out the bomb bay into the jungle. You'll be hanging in a tree, dead, in about nine hours from now."

"I've done a jungle landing."

"At night?"

"Yes."

"Two," said Bill, "if I recall. But we can drop you on one of the lava flows. That's maybe a fifteen-kilometre hike to Jim."

"Sounds good," said Jane.

"All you have to do is find him, get him to a lava flow and we can chopper you out."

"Got to tell you," said Will, "that no one's ever jumped from a B1 before, it'll be a first for everyone."

"How do the crew get out?" asked Jane.

"The whole cockpit jettisons."

"We'll work it out," said Bill. "We've got about an hour because they're landing in about fifteen."

"B1 is designed for dropping nukes," said Will, "so it's just made for you."

"Why, thank you, Will," said Jane.

"With a bit of luck we can drop you in at dawn their time," said Bill.

"Kit me out," she said. "I don't want to waste another moment."

"Move very slowly now," said Pierre, "and call out like me. Yoyoyo!"

"Yoyoyo," hollered Jim.

"Look down at your feet like you are humble. Yoyoyo!"

Jim hunched up. "Yoyoyo."

"Yoyoyo," called Pierre.

They came to a clearing with tall grass.

"They are watching," he said. "Yoyoyo. Sit down here next to me. Yoyoyo. Slowly."

"Yoyoyo," called Jim, dropping to the ground, his legs crossed under him.

Pierre had the pack beside him and pulled out the blanket and the ziplock bag, which he had stuffed with oddments. He took out the cigarettes and lit two, giving one to Jim.

"Yoyoyo," he said, and took a drag.

Jim coughed as the smoke caught his lungs. "Yo-yo-yo," he spluttered. Pierre laid the cigarettes on the blanket with the oddments. "Yoyoyo."

"Yoyoyo," came back from the bush in front of him, then a yelp of surprise or perhaps joy. A little figure was shoved out of the cover.

"Yoyoyo," called Pierre.

The pygmy held a bow. He looked at them seriously but in a shy and wary way.

Pierre held up the pack of Marlboro Lights. He said something in a strange tongue and shook the packet. "Yoyoyo."

"Yoyoyo," said Jim.

Two more figures bundled out of the bush, bows in hand.

Jim was astonished: they had nine-year-old bodies and forty-year-old faces. Suddenly a dozen had lined up before them, bows at the ready.

Pierre was talking to them, preaching like he had to Hélène at the camp. He was smiling despite the bruising on his face. The oldest sat down and Pierre offered him his cigarette. The old pygmy smiled and toked on it. Jim held out his and the pygmy at his side took it, puffed and passed it to another. They were sitting down. Pierre pulled out a cigarette for each man from the pack and they all lit up.

Pierre was telling them a story, pointing down the mountain, touching Jim, showing the bruises on his face. The pygmies were riveted. Then he began to empty the bag, giving each piece reverently to the oldest pygmy, who especially liked the fishing line and hooks. He hugged the boy and pulled him to his feet. The second in command put all the pieces carefully back into the bag and put it under his arm. The cigarettes were smoked and Pierre gave the remnant of the pack to the leader, who took them out and pushed them behind his ears. He gave the pack to his adjutant.

"They will help us," said Pierre, tugging on the rucksack. "We are friends."

"Amazing," said Jim.

Pierre laughed. "They are taking us to your friend."

"Say that again." Jim couldn't believe his ears.

"They are taking us to your friend. They found him in a tree."

"He's dead, right?"

"No, no," laughed Pierre, "he's not dead, he's alive."

"How can that be possible?" Jim was stunned.

"Be happy," said Pierre.

"I am," said Jim. "That's brilliant." He wondered what kind of state Kitson could be in. "That's totally fucking brilliant."

# 41

Jane was breathing 100 per cent oxygen to drive out all the nitrogen from her blood.

A 'Haho' jump from eight kilometres up would mean no one would hear or see the B1 Lancer and no one would hear her coming. She would fly the chute to the landing spot and not a soul, should there be one on the lava flow, would see her coming. She stood in front of the bomb–bay doors, over which the bomb racks normally lay, and waited. She switched to her air supply.

"Doors opening. Will count you down from three."

The doors opened and there was a sudden rush of air.

The B1 was going at the lowest speed it could at that altitude, about 300 m.p.h.

"Three, two, one…"

She hopped forwards into the void.

From the pure fact that she still existed, she knew she had cleared the plane successfully. She pulled the ripcord at the count of twelve. The black chute opened. She would fly it perhaps twenty-five miles to the destination. She watched the GPS on her arms as she steered. Pretty soon the sun would be coming up and she would get one hell of a view. From five miles up she could see into the blazing caldera of Nyiragongo three miles below. She could see the lights of

Goma and the outline of Nyamuragira ahead. It was a ten-million-dollar joy-ride with a desperate mission at the end. The sun showed its blazing edge over the rim of the earth and she could see it rushing over the land. It would reach her as she touched down.

Acting Major General Brown had set another record along the way. Falling at sixty miles an hour, armed to the teeth and on a mission, she felt liberated. This was who she was: this was what she had made herself for.

She looked down at the east lava field of Nyamuragira. She would land at the north end just before the jungle started, near the foot of the volcano. There was about two miles to go. Light came from the lava field as if it was spotted with orange landing lights. The morning sun hadn't hit it yet.

"Shit!" She flared her parachute. "It's molten down there." She had to glide past it to land after the lava and before one of the huge trees. A landing in trees would be less bad than touching down on a flaming griddle, but it was non-optimal.

The smooth control of her planned landing had gone to hell: she was coming in slow and with little control. As her speed decreased so the chute became less a flying wing and more like an old-style parachute that just fell slowly. It was going to be a very close call. The black lava now didn't look black at all: it was like a 1,000-degree *crème brûlée*, black stuff covering a soft core. She lifted her legs up and gave a final haul on the control lines, the heat of the lava across her butt and neck. She was going to crash in the trees. It would be brutal but it was better than being barbecued. The chute lifted a little, stalled, then swung her into a high bush about ten feet off the ground. She let out a groan as she fell. The

263

chute caught hold and halted her fall some four feet from the ground. She grabbed the strap, tried to right herself and tumbled down, landing on her back, pack first. She struggled out of her harness.

"Safely landed," she typed into the GPS computer on her arm. No thanks to you or me.

The pygmy village seemed to have been made out of giant wilted cabbages. The inhabitants had built little huts covered with big heart-shaped leaves that acted like scales to deflect the periodic torrential rain.

Without having said a word to them, Jim had decided the pygmies were incredible, the most real people he had ever met, walking bollock-naked through the wild jungles, smiling and chatting with each other like the happiest guys in the world. These little people were the giants of the jungle. As the Americans had grown tall to conquer their wilderness, the pygmies were made small to coexist with theirs. Only they were strong enough to thrive in this environment. They were the masters here.

The leading pygmy showed them to the opening in one of the leaf huts.

Jim pushed his head inside. "Terry?"

"Who's that?"

"Jim."

"Jim?"

Jim's eyes adjusted to the gloom and he pushed into the cramped space. Kitson was lying on a mattress of grass. His chest was bare and his arm was in a makeshift sling constructed from what looked like pieces of his shirt. "Jim," he said, sitting up on his right arm. His face showed he was experiencing considerable pain. "Thank God – I'm rescued. I thought I was going to be lying here till I mended."

"Ah," said Jim, "well, I was here to rescue you but, like, I'm now in need of a bit of rescue myself."

Pierre pushed in beside Jim and Kitson looked at his bruised face, then snorted. "Well, I suppose I'm in less trouble than I was."

"I'm not sure about that," said Jim. "We're in big trouble ourselves." He smiled awkwardly. "But, hey, we've found you. How are you?"

"Shot," said Kitson. "I think I've smashed my pelvis. At least it's not my spine. Did you know I was a junior doctor once?"

"No," said Jim.

Kitson shifted awkwardly on his bed of grass with a grimace of pain. "The City was better pay and better hours."

"I've got painkillers and some antibiotics."

"I've not gone septic," said Kitson, "or I'd be already dead."

"Painkillers?"

"Love some," he said longingly, "but why waste a limited supply? I might need to take them all at once, if you follow me."

"Oh," said Jim, working out what he meant. "You're going to make it," he said. "We just need to get back to Goma and call someone to come for you." He took out his GPS. "I'm registering our location. You just need to lie here for a few more days."

"Are those swines from the mine after you?" said Kitson.

"No," said Jim. "Not Mycock at any rate."

"That blighter pushed me out of the helicopter."

"Mycock?"

"Yes – the bugger beat me round the head and booted me out into thin air." He winced. "It's nothing short of divine intervention that I'm alive."

"How did you survive?"

"I have no idea – well, not exactly." Kitson shifted on his elbow. He looked in a lot of pain. "I remember falling into a tree – or, rather, waking up in a tree. We were hovering over the treetops at the time. Maybe I fell fifty or sixty feet. However far it was, it was far enough." He looked very uncomfortable, propped up on his good arm. "Then Alan and his friends came and hauled me down." He smiled. "They are the most immensely strong, agile people and by far the kindest."

"Who's Alan?"

"The pygmy chief. I call him Alan because, for the life of me, I can't pronounce his name. He doesn't seem to mind. I must introduce you. Alan," he called, trying to sit up a bit more. "Alan."

The head pygmy strode in. He looked ancient but was probably barely forty, when you took into account the implied spread of ages among the tribesmen. The children resembled small teenagers and the teenagers hardened men. The adult men looked very old indeed, their faces gnarled busts fashioned by the rough hands of the forest.

"Alan," said Kitson, "these are my friends. I am very happy to see them."

Pierre rolled his eyes and translated.

Alan laughed, replied in a shout and went out.

"He says you are crazy," said Pierre.

"Quite right," said Kitson. "So would you be in my situation."

"He likes you," added Pierre.

Kitson shifted painfully. "So what is your spot of bother?"

"Militia have taken over the mine and they're after us because they know we know where there is a big deposit of diamonds."

"Diamonds?" said Kitson, grimacing. "There's nothing here."

"I've seen them," said Jim. "Dug one up the size of a sugar cube myself."

"Really?" said Kitson. He lay back, staring at the roof of the hut. "How ironic. I'm sure successful miners don't go throwing people out of their helicopters." He winced as pain shot through him again. "So what is the plan?"

"Well, the plan was to get into pygmy territory, stock up on some food and then try to use it as a buffer for the escape route."

"Head for Rwanda," said Kitson. "To get to Goma you have to go around both these volcanoes. If you head into Rwanda you can get quickly to Kigali and then go wherever you need to. I can sit it out here for a couple of weeks, and then, if you don't show and I haven't dropped dead, I'll be halfway to healed up. Then I think I can persuade Alan to stretcher me out."

"They would do that," said Pierre.

"Would they?" said Jim. "It's a hell of a long way."

"Pygmies are looking for protection. It would be good for their cause."

"Well, that's great," said Jim. "I've no idea about pygmy politics, though."

"It's just about guns and land and money," Pierre told him.

267

"Hear, hear," said Kitson. "Are you MBD from the mine?" he asked.

"Yes and no," said Pierre. "I am Pierre Nonda and I was from the mine."

"Make for Kigali," said Kitson.

Jim got the map and studied it. It was about thirty miles as the bird flew to Kigali. "What do you think, Pierre?"

"You got big dollars, right?"

"Yes," said Jim.

"Let's go Rwanda, I know routes."

Jane wasn't making the sort of headway she'd hoped for. The ground was rough and her pack made it hard to progress through the undergrowth. The terrain was very variable. One moment it would be easy-going and then she would be presented with an impassable wall of vegetation that she had to scout around. It was midday and she was still three and a half miles away from the beacon that was Jim. It was looking like she would make contact with him by nightfall. That was good enough.

Jim watched Kitson asleep. He wondered if his friend was going to die – he wondered if he was going to die too. Thirty miles across country was a hell of a trek after such a long haul already. He was tired out, dirty, bruised and battered. Pierre was playing some kind of game with the pygmy children that involved throwing twigs and stones. He looked a sight too, laughing beneath his injuries.

They'd be eating parrot that night – a hunting party had brought back three large colourful dead ones. He wondered how it would affect him – he hadn't forgotten the dramatic purging he'd experienced after his one and only locally prepared meal. Could he get thirty miles across country with dysentery?

He felt low. He had achieved the impossible in finding Kitson alive but now, rather than bringing him back triumphantly from the jungle, he was mired in a deadly trap.

Adash stood on the kimberlite and looked at the mining camp below. Fifteen hundred of his men, maybe his whole army of two thousand, were converging on it from all over Kiva and both sides of the Rwandan border. They would find the boy and mine the diamonds. From his vantage-point he could see for miles but, like all the visitors before him, except one, he could not see the ground he stood on. For just a moment each day, as the sun set, the earth would flash and twinkle.

# 42

To Jane, the jungle seemed quiet but the whole area was on the move, according to intel. It was all sketchy, but the satphones were jabbering about diamonds and Nyamuragira and the phones were on the move. They were converging on the volcano from a sixty-mile radius. It looked like the Christ Reunion army and fragments of Mai-Mai militias were on their way. Was Jim part of this shit storm? He wasn't moving, so he might already be dead or taken prisoner.

The biohazard alarm suddenly went off on her arm. Gas, it said.

She took out her mask and put it on, then peered at the device through the circular windows in the rubber mask: carbon dioxide. It seemed unlikely but you never disagreed with kit unless you wanted to end up dead. She walked forwards. There was a carcass ahead. A collapsed grey mound covered with what looked like white paint. There were dead birds, maybe half a dozen vultures, in various states of decomposition. There were the bones of another animal ahead, then more bones, a dead guy – all kinds of bones piled next to each other haphazardly as if the creatures had just fallen dead on the spot while gawking. The place was a graveyard, an open ossuary where everything died. She took a Zippo out of her right shoulder pocket and lit it. The flame was weak. She lowered it to the ground and the flame went out. She tried to relight it and failed. She held the Zippo high and tried again. It fired up, another weak flame. The volcanic activity was venting carbon dioxide and was carpeting the ground with a layer of lethal gas. The smell of carrion was attracting animals to it and they were dying as they came to the scene.

She picked up her pace. This place was a death-trap and, while the filters on her mask would block the gas for quite a time, she wasn't going to stick around marvelling at the savagery of nature.

A hundred yards ahead the warning on her arm went out. She kept the mask on. The stuffy contraption was just a little more welcome than a face full of lethal gas, and she wouldn't take it off for at least another couple of hundred yards.

Alan called to Pierre. "I will be back," he told Jim.

"OK," said Jim, "be careful."

Pierre waved a hand dismissively. He loped over to Alan and five pygmies with bows in hand. They were laughing and joking as they headed off into the forest.

"Yoyoyo."

Jane froze.

A green fruit fell with a dull thump about ten feet in front of her. It was an avocado.

"Yoyoyo," came the call.

She was holding the grip of her M4 carbine. She pulled off her mask.

An unarmed guy, silhouetted by the sun, was walking down the hill towards her.

271

"Yoyoyo," he called.

There was a rustle behind her.

She turned… and saw that she was ringed by four small guys – no, five – carrying bows and arrows. They weren't aiming at her but they could let off their arrows in a moment, not that they would puncture her armour. "Hello, boys," she said.

They looked at each other.

"Yoyoyo," said the young guy sauntering towards her.

"Yoyoyo," she replied.

"*Qui est vous?*" He seemed shocked and confused by the sight of a woman with a fabulous rifle.

"American."

"It's a good job you surrender or you would be dead," he said, one nervous eye on the obviously advanced weapon.

"Don't push your luck," she replied.

"What in hell's name are you doing here?"

"I'm looking for a friend."

The boy burst out laughing, "We are all looking for a friend here," he said. He suddenly snapped her an intense stare. "Who?"

The kid had a nasty cut across his cheek and the other side of his face looked like it had taken a thorough beating. "Jim Evans," she said. "Do you know him?"

"Sure we know him." He spoke to one of the little guys, and they began to laugh and joke to each other.

Now Jane was confused. "Can you take me to him?"

"Sure," said the kid.

"Is he far away?"

"No."

"Is he safe?" she asked.

272

The boy stiffened. "No," he said, craning his neck, eyes bulging. "Nobody's safe. We are in big trouble and," he clapped his hands, "so are you." He sneaked a look at the M4 carbine. "But not from us. Let's go before it's dark."

# 43

Baz had been waiting in the private room at the embassy for twenty-nine minutes exactly. He watched the second hand on his watch sweep around the dial. In twenty-five seconds he would get up and go. Sure enough, when the second hand hit twelve, he stood up and walked out. As he went past the inner reception desk a tall, strong-looking bald African guy in a blue suit, expensive white shirt and silk tie walked his way. He looked down on Baz and smiled.

"Baz?"

Baz recognized the fruity English accent. "Yes indeed."

"You're not leaving, are you?"

"I was," he said.

"It's Julien." He shook Baz's hand with both of his hands, a politician's smile wide on his face. "I'm so glad I caught you."

Baz put on a tired grin. "So am I, Julien."

"Shall we?" Julius said, gesturing with an open palm at the meeting-room door.

They went inside and sat down.

"What has happened to my mine?" said Julius. "The price has collapsed."

"Which mine is that?" said Baz.

"Barron, of course," said Julius, smiling, perhaps mischievously.

"I seem to recall it being my mine," said Baz, "or, in theory at least, my shareholders' mine."

"All mines in Congo are my mines, Baz," said Julius.

"Yeah, I imagine that could be true."

"So what's happened?"

"Well, someone's parked their fucking army on it, haven't they?"

"Was that wrong of me?"

"No, just stupid."

Julius took the comment like an unexpected splash of bird shit to the face.

"I see."

"What do you want, Julius? Some payola? You sit on fifty trillion dollars' worth of minerals and you look to me for a nice little bung? Is that the limit of your vision?"

Julius sat back, his nostrils flared.

"You've got it all wrong, mate. You're playing Russian roulette but at the small-stakes table." Baz grinned. "I've already made my hundred million from this and you can have my piece of jungle back and grow fucking pineapples on it. If you'd only learn not be so greedy you'd make yourself so much richer."

Julius looked down his nose at him. "Teach me, then," he said, tilting his head back angrily.

"OK," Baz said. "Look at the balance sheets of the big miners. They're billions and billions in debt, yet they own mines and when they dig the stuff out and sell it they get cash immediately. Why? Well, it's because they have to scrape around on shit prospects and squeeze the last gram of mineral out of their poxy crap mines. You've got mineral deposits so rich that people are mining them with kitchenware – not spades the size of office blocks. You have resources so rich you can spot them by looking for bald patches on the ground where the copper kills all the plants. You could borrow all the money in the world against those kinds of mineral deposits, if you have the right ideas and backing, and then," he chuckled, "once you've borrowed it, you could steal it." Baz grinned. "But you're not going to, are you? Because you don't know how to and everybody would be on to your game in a second. You haven't got the expertise, you haven't got the contacts and you haven't got the time. In short, you haven't got me." Baz was trying not to laugh but the sneer was all over his face.

"Think about it. I made forty square miles of coconuts worth a billion. Imagine what I could do with a mine as big as Europe." Baz stood up.

"Wait," said Julius, smiling again. "How do we go forwards?"

"First off, you can get those rebels off my mine and then I'll know you're serious."

"We will go there, you and I, and I will show you that these rebels are not only in my power but my servants too."

"OK," said Baz.

Julius shook his hand with a firm muscular grip. "Give me your card and a car will pick you up in the morning."

"I'm at the Dorchester."

"Even I can remember that address," laughed Julius. "I will see you tomorrow."

# 44

Jim thought he was seeing things. Pierre, Alan and his merry men had a soldier in black with them and it was Jane. He jumped up and ran to her. He would have thrown his arms around her but they wouldn't have reached around her pack, so he grabbed her shoulders and kissed her. She didn't respond. He stepped back. "That's not appropriate," she said.

"To hell with that," he said, and kissed her again. He was expecting some sharp ninja response, but suddenly she was kissing him too.

"Oh, a friend," shrieked Pierre, "quite a good friend." He was hopping up and down, laughing, and the pygmies were nodding to each other as if something was suddenly making sense.

"God, am I glad to see you! We're up Queer Street here. We've found Kitson and he's alive."

"Alive?" she said, "I thought he went skydiving without a chute."

"He did but he survived it."

"And you're going to give me some shit about not leaving without him, aren't you?"

"What's the correct answer?" said Jim.

"No," she said.

"Yes, I think I am," he said.

"Great," she said angrily, and almost stamped her foot.

"Look," said Jim, "there are two hundred soldiers down there after our blood and I have no idea how to get out of this fix, but I don't want to leave Terry here to die."

"Correction," said Jane. "There are two thousand soldiers out there heading this way."

"That's all right, then," said Jim. "We can slip off in all the confusion."

"Yeah, right, let's try that."

"Two thousand," said Pierre, clearly horrified. "That is the whole Christ Reunion."

"CRA, huh?" said Jane. "Oh, good, this is going to be *Dawn of the Dead Two*."

Jim heard a noise behind them and turned to see that Kitson had dragged himself out of his hut. "Is this our salvation, Jim?" he asked, as pathetically desperate as a man could be.

"Sure," said Jane, kneeling in front of him. "We'll find a way out of here." She stood up. "I've got to link in." She broke out a notebook and a sat dish and phoned home.

When Will and Bill were on the screen she updated them quickly.

"We're sending a squadron of Big Dog Doombahs," said Bill.

"Sixty-four to be precise."

"OK," said Jane. "Are they in Beta?"

"Nope," said Bill. "Halfway through Alpha, but they can be there tomorrow, whereas troopers will be three days and then of limited use, unless you can get yourself to somewhere we can dust you off."

278

"Apart from the fact I know you can't pick us up from that bunch of molten lava we landed me on, I've got no visibility on that."

"OK," said Will. "Since we have such a high-resource priority, we've formulated a plan. We're going to tungsten the Barron mine and drop in Big Dog Doombahs. Then you and the Doombahs fight your way to the mine and we dust you off there. The Doombahs can carry casualties so we can get your other friend out. Otherwise you're going to have to hole up till we can get a force big enough to fight a full-scale jungle war."

"How do you rate these 'Big Dogs'?"

"Awesome," said Bill and Will together.

"Just awesome," repeated Will. He was panting with some kind of lust. "It's the future."

"They have no fear," said Bill, "or anger, they don't seek revenge, they have no sympathy, remorse or shame and they absolutely do obey orders."

They were describing her, she thought. "Cool," she said. "We'll get along just fine. Promise me they don't crash or break down."

"We'll see about that," said Will.

"When do they get in?"

"In about four hours, and we'll try not to drop any on you," said Bill. "We've got other fall-back plans. If the tungsten doesn't work we'll go thermobaric. Whichever, keep well away from the camp."

"You're really going to drop the first HE for me?" said Jane.

"Oh, yeah," said Bill.

"Can't drop them anywhere but Africa," said Will. "Looks

too much like an ICBM – that's an intercontinental ballistic missile, Jim, if you're listening – which could be bad, heading anywhere else. This might make a few early-warning systems sit up but it clearly isn't going to look like it's heading any nuke-wielder's way. Mind you, we gotta hope the Russkies can actually tell."

Jane shuddered but managed a laugh.

"We thought," said Bill, "if we can cut the head off the command with a huge pyrotechnic, the rest of the force might go home. Just don't be within a one-mile radius."

"What about civilians?"

"The area's clear," said Will, "and anyway the civilians are fleeing the zone for twenty miles around. They think a war's going to start and I guess they're right."

"I'm relying on you," said Jane. "Don't make an oversight I'm going to regret."

"We'll keep evaluating," said Bill. "Until we let go, we can always switch to a Herc flambéing the spot. It'll just hold things up a day or two."

"OK, going dark till the morning."

"What was that about HE? Is that high explosive?" asked Jim.

"No," said Jane. "High energy."

"And what's that when it's at home?"

"They bust tanks these days with so-called HE rounds, sharp lumps of tungsten fired out of a tank barrel. Tungsten is heavier than gold and hard and sharp. When you fire it at a tank it cuts through it and vaporizes everyone inside with the heat of the energy on impact. If it didn't vaporize everything it would cut it to pieces with all the shrapnel. When it strikes, anyone in the tank is beamed straight to heaven. Now take

280

that idea a bit further. You put a rack of tungsten rods in high orbit, and when you don't like someone, you drop a rod of tungsten on their head from space and, *foop*, they and everything for about a mile around them simply aren't there any more. It's like the Big Dog Doombahs, all top-secret cutting-edge stuff."

"What are Big Dog Doombahs?"

"Doom dogs? You'll be meeting them tomorrow. I don't even know where to start explaining that one. You'll just have to wait and see."

# 45

All the magazines on the plane were in Chinese and the privately owned Airbus clearly belonged to someone extremely rich and important – and very unlikely to be Congolese. The Congolese flew in 1970s aircraft that were unfit to land anywhere outside Africa, so this was definitely on loan. The servants on the plane were also Chinese.

China was desperate for raw materials and was making big moves to secure them. Turning imported commodities into finished products for export was the strategy the country had chosen to drag itself out of poverty, even if that meant dragging everyone else into bankruptcy. The likelihood that China flooding the world with cheap goods might break the hungry consumers of the West might have seemed ludicrous a few years before but the recent disastrous credit crunch had its roots in the US trade deficit, which had ballooned and refused to deflate.

This was another reason China was in love with raw materials. As it hollowed out American wealth, it was slowly but surely destroying the dollar. It would move heaven and earth to get out of dollars, and it was literally doing so by taking America's currency and swapping it for commodities. They were denominated in dollars but a copper ingot could not be debased and therefore was better than a piece of paper, which could be devalued.

It seemed like a clever gamble but it didn't take into account that, at a certain price, an infinite amount of commodities would gush from the ground and miners would, in effect, do what the Chinese government was afraid the US authorities would do: devalue the wealth its treasury was hoarding. Dollars might prove better than gold in the long run, but that ran against the grain for a resource-strapped, cash-rich, command-and-control dictatorship.

Baz knew this was the flaw but, clearly, China was more scared of the US Treasury than a bunch of implacable miners. That was a mistake in its own right. People like him would stop at nothing to make a buck – they'd be wheeling and dealing long after bureaucrats were tucked up in bed. If they wanted to swap rocks for cash, they could step right up.

Because the People's Republic had made the decision to get out of the greenback, the Chinese were all over Africa, building roads, railways and ports to spend dollars to facilitate the extraction of resources. Unlike the old colonial powers, they didn't want gratitude or deference and kowtowing, they just wanted cheap unfettered access to raw materials. They didn't observe any rules of international transparency or bother with accountability: they just did a deal, did the work, carted off the result and cut a cheque. They didn't give away old clothes on the dock or dig village wells; they didn't spread the word of God or hand out condoms. They just asked to be left alone to ship ore on to waiting ships and carry it away with no strings attached.

It wasn't a charming strategy but it worked. The Western powers were not used to fighting for attention in Africa and weren't sure how to respond.

The old-boy networks of Europe and America were at a loss as to how to compete. The competitor had no colonial desires, just that voracious hunger for raw materials and was prepared to pay top dollar for them. The cosy zones of influence were dissolving under a new wave of macro-economics and the West was losing at its own game of beggaring the customer for their finished goods. In fact, China was doing to the West what the West had been doing to Africa for generations: playing to its vices and hollowing out its core. Baz thought it was funny, the biter bitten.

This was no colonial African "great game": it was bigger than that, driven by commerce, the world playing for global ascendancy – and China was winning.

Julius had clearly plugged into this new source of pragmatic deal-making. Was he dragging Baz into a complex and dangerous game of geopolitics? That was way out of his league but he was loving it.

He was eating macadamia nuts from a white porcelain bowl and drinking a beer. "So tell me, Baz, what is your big idea?"

Baz was trying to get a piece of nut out of a back tooth that had decided to welcome it as a permanent fixture. He gave up and picked up his whisky. "There are mines and then there's mining. Not the same thing," he said. "Mines are about hope but mining is about logistics." He drank. "Mining is like the brain-dead bit. You're digging and shipping and digging and filling. It's as boring as fuck. No one likes you, no one wants you. They'll take your profits and not even say thank you. It always has and always will be like that. A mine is a different thing all together. You know the saying, 'A woman is just a woman, but a good cigar is a smoke'?"

Julius was smiling politely. "Rudyard Kipling, I believe?"

"Oh," said Baz. "I thought it was Groucho Marx. Anyway, the real value of a mine is just the pure hope it can inspire. When a mine is proved, it's like a bond. You dig out some copper at so many dollars a tonne and make so much profit. It's a fixed yield, its worth is a simple calculation and it's boring and limited. By the time this is the value of a mine, the mine is finished. What is of real value in a mine is what else might be in it, because finding new resources can completely change its value. That's where the big bucks are. And that's what you have for millions of square miles." Baz was grinning.

"The American civil war was won because of one mine, the Comstock," he went on. "Half of South America was conquered because of El Dorado, a fantasy mine that never existed. The whole Middle East is based on one giant mineral complex. Everyone knows if you kick the right stone you can find billions right there under your foot. The money in mining is selling the sizzle, not the steak, selling the possibility not the reality. What you need is someone to sell the sizzle and make sure you get to keep the steak. Ker, ker, ker." He laughed his trademark cackle.

"How could that work?"

"Well," said Baz, "I could have just found a whole new region of copper."

"Have you?"

"No, but that's not the point. I could have, and I could raise five billion to exploit it with your government's backing. I could then have a lot of fun spending the money and making sure you were getting the bulk of the cash flow.

"Um," responded Julius, appreciatively.

"Halfway through spending the first lot of the money we

could do another couple before the first started to disappoint. You see, you have to sell hope backed by credibility, but know the outcome before you start. You raise the money and then you steal it – it's that simple."

"And you think you could pull this off."

"I've been doing just that for twenty-five years. The possibility here is the size of the opportunity. I've been doing eight- and nine-figure deals, but with you, it could be ten, eleven figures." Baz was thinking of Barron. "The funny thing is, we could actually end up with mines that work. There's so much potential out there that we can cheat and actually deliver something."

"That's very interesting," said Julius. "You see, I wish to build on my position in government and for that you need backers and money, but the sort of backing I need is not forthcoming – not on the scale I need it."

Baz sipped his whisky.

"This country needs to be turned upside-down and for that it needs a strong man to take control, and that kind of strength needs hundreds of millions, perhaps billions, of dollars. Now, mining is lucrative for us but there are limits to how much my plans can benefit. Most of the deposits are dangerous, disputed and therefore unattractive. Big companies are also unable, by law, to help me to help them. I'm attracted to your proposal but you must understand I need action and it must be fast and definite and money must flow quickly."

"Look, Julien, I'm in the same spot you are, only different. Look at me and you see someone who doesn't think he's going to live forever. I've got my dough. I don't need to go another round for a hundred million dollars – that's not exciting to me any more."

286

Julius was smiling, but underneath he was livid: why did these men always have the upper hand? A hundred million was a vast fortune, one that would fund an army for years.

"A billion or two, that's different," said Baz, "I'll get out of bed for that."

"So what are your terms?"

"Twenty per cent."

"I make a billion, you make four billion. I make two billion, and you make eight."

Julius's eyes lit up – he couldn't help himself. "Over how long a period?"

"Four or five years. After five I'm out of it anyway – I'm not putting off my happy retirement longer than that, not for all the copper in Congo." He smirked. "All you've got to do is show me the power, and if you can shoo those bleeding militia men off Barron, I'll know you're the man. Frankly, if you can do that, then you run the fucking place as far as I'm concerned and we can make a fortune together – a big country-sized fortune, an old-fashioned nineteenth-century one."

"I don't run Congo, but if you can keep your promise I will soon enough. You do understand what you are committing to do?"

"Yeah," said Baz. "I think I know what you're capable of, so let's leave it at that." He smiled. "You have to be nice to me. If you're nice to me, I'll make you the richest man in Africa, and if you're right, the fucking Emperor of Congo." He winked at Julius.

Julius laughed. "If I didn't know your mines' stock performance I would believe you were a conman, Baz. A big conman."

"I am," said Baz. "That's exactly what I am, and I'm going to be working for you on the biggest theft in history."

"I'll be nice to you, Baz, but you must be straight with me at all times. Such big money will make everyone nervous so I need to have everything clear between us. I need no voicemail, I need no excuses and I need no surprises. Money must come without asking."

"We'll be in this together, mate."

Julius caught the Chinese hostess, who was topping up his glass, around the waist and she squealed, half in shock and half in polite embarrassment. She ran away.

Julius shook his head. "These girls are no fun. Do you like girls, Baz?"

"Yeah," said Baz, "occasionally – but not more than three at a time."

Julius saluted him. "I'm glad," he said. "I like to work with real men."

# 46

Jane was alerted as soon as the drop was executed. She sat up sharply, which woke Jim in the next tent. He had been flitting in and out of sleep all night and he knew immediately that she was awake.

She was experiencing two emotions: excitement and guilt. The excitement came from the notification on her arm that the drop had happened, and the guilt from what she had said to Jim before turning in. "I'll join you in your tent when I smell as high as you do and that might never happen." The look on Jim's face as the zipper went down had made her instantly regretful of her quip. It was like a light slap to the face that resulted in a broken tooth. Not the outcome that had been meant, or the level of pain she had sought. She hated feeling sorry.

She pulled the night-sights out of her pack and strapped them on, then looked out of the tent into Jim's night-vision goggles. "Going somewhere?" she said.

"For a moonlight stroll with you."

"Can you keep up?"

"You in a big hurry?"

She waved her arm display. "I've only got a heading not a firm distance."

"That's primitive."

289

"OK, it's a mile from here."

"No hurry, then."

She stood up. "OK, let's go."

"Just let me change the batteries on these."

She almost said something hard but held herself in check.

A couple of minutes elapsed.

"Are you going to be much longer?" she said, with exasperation.

"Nearly got it," said Jim, having finally found the fresh batteries. "Two minutes."

Jane looked around to find Pierre behind her. "What are you doing?"

"Nothing," he said. "What are you doing?"

"I'm going for a walk."

"So am I."

"Can you see in the dark?"

"Sure," he said. "Can't you?"

"When I need to."

"Me too."

"This could be dangerous."

"My middle name is Dangereux," he said.

The night-sight was a definite barrier between Pierre and the deadly look she threw him.

"OK, Dangereux," she said, "you can come too."

Jim stuck his head out of the tent. "Ready," he said. "Oh, hold on." He ducked back. "Forgot the GPS."

"I've got one," said Jane.

"Don't need one," said Pierre.

Jim and Jane looked at him.

"Sheesh," said Jane, "it's an Eagle Scout outing." She looked at her arm display, which shone in the infrared.

"Follow me, guys, and don't fall behind or get lost. If you do, it's ninety minutes until sunrise, so stay put and I'll come get ya later. Whatever you do, don't go wandering about lost."

Jim looked at Pierre, who shrugged in the fluorescent green light of Jim's headset.

They set off. It was uphill but the going was lighter than usual so the two factors together made for a trip of about fifty minutes. A lot of things were moving around in the jungle at night. Creatures low to the ground were snuffling and animals in the trees were shuffling about. They would freeze as the party approached in the belief that the stillness and dark would shield them. That was before the human ape had become an infrared augmented Cyborg and before man melded with machine. This had made the rest of the animal kingdom obsolete and only useful for TV shows or snack food.

Fifteen thousand generations ago humanity had branched from the rest of life on earth, and barely one generation ago it had grown the next branch – it was no longer a solely carbon-based life-form like the rest of creation. Silicon let Jim and Jane see in the dark and made life possible in their world, and silicon was about to change it forever as it integrated itself into the wet carbon of flesh.

Jim saw a large black container, the size of a wardrobe, lying on the jungle floor.

Jane was looking at her display. "We're on top of it but that's not the one we want," she said.

"Yoyoyo," called Pierre behind them.

They turned. Pierre was sitting on another container, smaller, like a large steamer trunk.

Jane returned to her display. "That's it?"

"What is this stuff?" said Jim.

"It may shock you," said Jane, "terrify you, and it may save your life." She pressed a button on the arm-display control. There was a cluck and the lid of the steamer truck lifted, throwing Pierre into the bushes behind him. He was shouting something in a language Jim didn't recognise.

"Sorry," said Jane.

They went to the trunk.

Pierre was already there and peering in. There was a stack of four M4 carbines and boxes of ammunition. There were rations, grenades and a small bright yellow box that glowed with fluorescence. Pierre reached forwards for a carbine. Jane slapped his hand.

"No," she said, "that's not for you."

"Awww."

"He's handy with a Kalashnikov," said Jim.

"Just one goddamn moment," said Jane. "You need to see something." She tapped her panel and the top of the yellow box opened. She took out a set of controls from its padded socket and put it into her pocket. Then she took out a bag of plastic blobs. She opened it and removed what looked like a plastic lozenge.

"OK. Your life is going to depend on one of these so listen up. Snap off the end." She ripped something off the bottom of the fob, then ran the open end under her arm and down the side of her face. "The tab now has my DNA and my chemical signature." An LED was blinking green on the lozenge. She took off her night-sights. "You see this light flashing? With your thumb on the dimple, point the light at your face with a straight arm. Press the dimple hard for three seconds." There was a flash. "The fob now has my

292

face." She handed one each to Jim and Pierre.

Jim had trouble finding the bit to break off but Pierre was quickly dabbing his armpit and scratching his face. He held the fob up at arm's length and there was a flash.

"Got it," said Jim. He was giggling as he scratched his face with the fob, then smiled at the tiny camera as it took its picture. The sun was coming up.

"Now, whatever you do, wherever you go, do not be parted from this device. Put it in your safest pocket." Jane undid her dog-tag necklace and threaded the fob through it. "I'll show you why." She took the control from her pocket and switched it on. She aimed it roughly at the large container twenty metres away.

There was a mechanical clunk. The lid rose and three sides tried to fall away but the undergrowth stopped them. The front wall lodged on the trunk of a tree. A fluid, sticky and gelatinous, began to pour out and they heard a whining, chugging noise.

"Just wait and stay very still. Try not to make any noise or sudden movements. Got that, Pierre?" she said. "It applies to you too."

"Yes," said Pierre, as an erratic banging issued from the container. Someone or something was trying to get out. With every shudder, ooze poured out and ran down the hill in a slick.

Now a desperate thrashing noise came from within the crate and the container began to shake from side to side, the walls falling further away with each frantic blow. Suddenly another furious blow freed the front wall, which fell open with a gush of oily jelly flopping forwards into disintegration. A long, dark form, like a giant dog, black and dripping, jumped around on tiptoe and stepped menacingly out of its cave.

"What the fuck is that?" said Jim.

"It's a Doombah," said Jane, "and it's coming over to say hello. With a bit of luck, it won't kill us."

Pierre grabbed Jim's shoulder and Jim found he was holding Jane's hand. Without a doubt she was holding his too. The black machine was walking slowly towards them, liquid pouring from its body. After every two steps it would shiver and throw off more glutinous liquid. In Jim's headset he could see the two cameras on its head moving backwards and from side to side, in focus at one moment and out the next. He pulled off his night-sights to see it in the growing daylight. Its four spindly legs were like those of two cartoon men carrying a long box, one walking backwards, another forwards. It was nimble yet ungainly, robotic yet animal. He felt as though his gut was about to react violently to the parrot stew, but it was the evil-looking machine, not last night's dinner, that was threatening his dignity.

The Doombah looked at them one at a time, flashing lasers over them, rather like a supermarket checkout registering a barcode.

There was a buzz and a sudden high-pitched whirring.

"Damn," said Jane, as two Gatling guns rose from the body of the machine. Her hand was squeezing Jim's so tightly he almost cried out in pain. "Just don't move," she hissed.

The Doombah was fixating on the M4 by her side, the barrels of the Gatlings rotating in a blur. "Shit," she said, and pressed something on the control panel.

The Doombah started and the Gatlings slowed. There was

the buzz of servos and the guns disappeared into the body.

"What was that?" said Jim.

"Nothing," she said.

"Don't tell me it was nothing."

"Aaaah!" She groaned. "I had to upload our data. I just figured that out. I've got no training on this crap. It's not even in Alpha. It isn't meant to exist. I hate this goddamn tech."

"Thank God you…" began Jim.

The Doombah stepped forwards.

"What's it doing now?" Jim's voice held more than a shade of panic.

"Don't know," said Jane. "Just let it do its thing. If it doesn't like us we're probably toast."

The robot was up close to her, buzzing as if a model aeroplane was trapped in its body. It seemed to sniff her.

"Think it's verifying me." She held her hand out to it and it moved close to her palm, then jumped sideways, like a horse, to Jim, "Good boy," said Jim. "*Gooood* boy."

It didn't seem to need to get so close to him. "Is this thing sniffing me?" he asked.

"Probably," she said. "It runs heuristics. Gun, no tag, kill. No gun, no tag, deal with object with gun no tag. It's collecting data. It's probably taking time to get to know us, its three tagged friends."

The Doombah was sniffing Pierre now.

"That's good," said Jane. "I just gave us high priorities for defence."

The machine jumped back. "Jane, Jim, it's Bill. Can you hear me?" it said.

"Fuck me," said Jim.

Pierre had fallen over backwards.

"Good to hear you, Jim," said Bill. "This shit might just work. I'm not getting good pictures. In fact, to tell you the truth I'm not getting jack, only audio."

"Can you hear me crapping myself?" asked Jim.

"Don't worry, these boys are fully tactical. They can do a better job than us and do it in real time."

"Great," said Jane, "but this thing nearly just blew me away."

"Relax," said Bill, "you'll be fine. One of these has never gone blue on blue before. Admittedly that's because it's never been used in a real mission but, hey!"

Pierre was crouching down staring intently into what passed for eyes on the Doombah.

"I'm going to crack the cases now, and Will and I will set up the Doombahs," said Bill. "As soon as they're in position you can set off for the RV at the mine, whatever's left of it when we're done. We'll get you in position by night for the end run in the morning. I'm going to vaporize the camp at midday – don't want you anywhere near when we drop the rod. It should be cool and kind of peaceful by the time you get there. A chopper will come by and take you to Kigali and you'll be home for cocktails in thirty-six hours."

The Doombah jumped up and down on the spot. "Hah," came Bill's voice, from somewhere near what passed for its chest, "it does emoticons."

"Cool," said Jim, sarcastically.

Jane stripped off her night-sights – the sun was rising fast.

Pierre, the happiest boy alive, was riding the Doombah like a horse, a matt M4 carbine slung on his shoulder. It was a hybrid, driven by a small petrol engine that charged a battery that powered the system. When the battery was full it ran silently, only the sound of metal joints clacking to give it away. It could sit still, like a sentry, for two days and recharge itself with four hours of engine time. Petrol held far more energy than any battery and the Doombah could be refuelled with ease. "Big Dogs" were the cavalry of the future – cavalry without riders, except occasional grateful passengers.

There was no one in the camp when they returned except Kitson. He crawled from his hut as soon as he heard them, lay on his side and propped himself up on an elbow. He looked incredulously at the Doombah. "Good Lord," he said weakly.

"You're riding out on this," said Jane. "It can be rigged as a stretcher."

"If you say so," said Kitson, too frail to argue.

"I can fix you up with some diamorphine," said Jane, "and you won't feel a thing. You'll just lie back and sail home."

"I guess this is what's scared off Alan and the tribe," said Kitson, watching the beast stare at him.

"Hold still," said Jane, breaking the end off a fob. She ran the tab over his chest and the light went green. "Smile," she said, and snapped him, then pushed the fob into his tattered trouser pockets. "Don't lose that," she said. "I don't think it shoots people without metal weapons, but let's not test that out."

Jim heard a rustle and looked up. The pygmies were up in the trees, dozens of them, hanging from the branches. He waved. Some were climbing down, dropping like circus acrobats with an almost superhuman grace and poise. "How do they do that?" he muttered.

297

"Power to weight ratio," said Jane, "and I guess if you try and fail you never get to have little itsy-bitsy pygmy babies."

The whole village was coming down out of the trees. They were surrounding them, staring silently at the Doombah.

Alan was speaking and Pierre translated. "He says the forest is full of soldiers and demons so we must flee to the trees."

The Doombah looked like a demon to Jim, so he understood exactly where the pygmy chief was coming from.

"Tell them," said Jane. "Do not fight the demons and they will not hurt you." Pierre took it sentence by sentence. "Do not hold metal if they are near you. Do not throw anything at them. Do not try to scare them away. If you see them, walk away. Only if you attack will they attack. If they attack you, you will die."

"Jane," said a voice from the Doombah.

The pygmies gasped and jumped back.

Jim cursed: it had made him jump too.

"Come back in five," said Jane.

The Doombah sat down and lay flat.

The audience gasped again.

"There will be a war for three days between us and the soldiers and then we hope it will end," said Jane. "Thank you, friends."

"We go to the trees," said Alan. He shouted and the pygmies marched out of the village of giant wilting cabbages.

"Will, Bill, can receive now."

The Doombah got up. "Everything's in place. You're good to move."

There was a whine of a distant chain-gun.

"It's started," said Jane. "Will, can you put this Doombah into stretcher mode?"

"Sure."

It lay down again and there was a humming noise as the top morphed and a long black sheet rolled out of its side.

Jane took something from the pack. "Terence, I'm going to inject you now and you'll soon feel a whole lot better." She jabbed something into his neck. Kitson fell off his elbow face down on to the ground. "Help me get him on the Big Dog," she said.

Jim grabbed him and Jane turned him over. They laid him across the top of the Doombah and Jane put the rubber sheet over him, then threaded it back into the robot. She selected "secure casualty" from the menu. The sheet tightened and the base formed around Kitson. He was awake.

"Are you OK?" said Jim.

"Comfortable," said Kitson, dreamily.

"Let's roll," said Jane.

Jim picked up his M4. If he had to use it, there was likely to be an almighty fuck-up. Pierre, Jane and the Doombah looked like the meanest crew on the planet. It felt natural. He had crossed an invisible line and nothing could pull him back to his funny little world, where the weather or a parking ticket or a piece of litter could be a big deal.

He wasn't sure whether he was high on hunger, exhaustion, fear or perhaps the fragile beauty of his own life, but he was high on something. The humid air was pulsating through his lungs like a eucalyptus inhalation.

# 47

The lead soldier stopped in his tracks. A black animal was standing in front of him. It was a strange, frightening shape and made an unearthly buzzing noise. He lifted his Kalashnikov. There was a buzz and a burst of fire cut him in half. The soldier behind him fell dead as did the next. The two remaining soldiers in the column were bringing their arms to bear on the black monster. The Doombah hopped to the left and sprayed a short burst of caseless .22 into the kneeling figure and then blew apart the last soldier as he fired his first shot. The 7.6mm bullet struck the robot on what would have been its chest if it had been a dog, knocking the machine back with a sharp jolt. It left a dent in the armour and took the paint off around a shallow crater. The Doombah galloped down the hill to its new position.

Adash was pacing around the kimberlite. He could hear gunfire and a sound he had never encountered before: a harsh buzz like the short burst of a chainsaw. Something was going on and it was bad. He was calling his commanders, but either he got hold of them scared and ignorant of what was happening or he didn't get hold of them at all. He stood on the rim of the platform and looked down on the camp, shimmering in the blazing heat. There was shouting behind him and a soldier was running up to him, waving his arms. Guards intercepted him. He was frantic.

Adash looked to the horizon deep in thought, listening for the next round of fire. The terror-stricken soldier was being brought to him.

"There are devils," he was screaming, as the guards held him, "terrible devils."

"There are no devils." Adash slapped the man hard and he sagged. "Control yourself."

"Great leader, I swear there are devils in the jungle. One cut my comrades to pieces."

There was another strange burst of noise from below the kimberlite in the forest. The soldier was shaking.

Adash grabbed him by the shirt. "There are no devils. Tell me what you saw."

"A beast, a panther, a terrible animal. It looked at us and it killed us. I ran."

"There are no devils!" shouted Adash, pulling a machete from his belt.

The soldier fell to his knees, cowering.

Adash raised the blade. "What did you see?"

Suddenly a ball of fire erupted in the sky and everyone froze. Then came a shriek – as if a vast monster had opened its mouth and was screaming.

Adash spun around and watched the tongue of fire smash into the mining camp below. There was a flash, a shockwave punched the air, the ground shook and he was deafened by a tremendous roar. A hurricane struck and they were thrown off their feet. Adash crabbed away from the rim of the kimberlite. Dog Bites Man's words rang in his ears: "God will smite you." And his own reply: "There are no gods."

301

The wind died down and he stood up. He went back to the kimberlite rim and looked out on to the plateau. The huge area of ground around the camp was obliterated and on fire. His guards and the soldier were agog at the devastation.

Adash knew that if he ran now he would be finished. With his reputation broken, his army would evaporate and he would eventually be killed. Now, however overwhelming the vision before him, however terrifying the news from the jungle, he had to fight. He would search out a demon and see it for himself. He had to maintain his legend or perish in the attempt. He put his arm around the man's shoulders. "Take me to one of these monsters."

The soldier looked at him. It was twenty feet from the platform to the jungle below. He jumped.

Adash laughed. "You can jump too if you like or come with me," he said to his guards. "The choice is yours. Or you can stay here until you die of thirst. Come."

They looked at the devastation below and then at Adash. They were going to fight demons. Who better to fight them with than their own devil?

# 48

Jim, Jane, Pierre and Kitson were ringed by six Doombahs. An outer cordon of eighteen more was fifty yards out with twelve groups of three in a cordon still further away. The three remaining made a far perimeter. The formation would have looked good on a map or as a diagram but in the jungle, where the undergrowth went from skimpy to completely impassable, the plan was unrecognisable in action. The Doombahs were balked and had to backtrack or were forced to make large detours to find their way around an obstacle. They were in effect traversing a giant medieval maze made of shrubbery walls. A robot could be only feet away but cut off from them for hours and hundreds of metres of terrain.

Jane had a small headset in her ear and was constantly talking with Bill and Will back in Virginia.

The machines had coalesced around them as they marched slowly towards the mining camp and the end of the jungle. They had made contact with the militias as they headed to their masters and there had been a constant cracking of the militias' assault weapons and the chainsaw buzzing of the Doombahs' Gatlings.

There was a flash, the ground shook and a monstrous growl echoed through the forest. They stopped in their tracks. A high wind buffeted the trees and all manner of jetsam fell from the canopy to the ground in a shower of twigs, seeds, leaves, flowers and earthy detritus. Jim found himself crouching with his arms over his head. Pierre had crawled under the belly of a Doombah. Jane touched her earpiece. "That must have been the delivery," she said. She gave Jim the thumbs-up. "Right on target."

Pierre jumped out as the wind died away.

"That was one fuck of a big bang," said Jim, dusting leaves off his shoulders. He did the same for Kitson.

"That's what you get when you hit the ground with the force that costs the Space Shuttle a thousand tonnes of fuel to launch into space. It's Newton's third law of thermodynamics combined with his theory of gravity," Jane told him.

Kitson was glassy-eyed.

"You OK?" asked Jim.

"Fine," said Kitson. Clearly the diamorphine had done the trick.

They moved on.

Satellite phones were chattering all over the jungle. Jane asked Will and Bill to peel off two Doombahs and go shoot up the nearest signals. They agreed.

Adash peered at the black monster that was walking downhill. There were three in a loose formation stepping along at a measured pace. They weren't devils: they were machines. He let them fall out of sight and returned to his guard. "You are women," he said, grabbing an RPG from the captain. "I will kill one of these demons. Wait here for me to return."

Adash stalked off into the undergrowth, wondering whether they would still be there when he returned – if he returned. He turned. They were following him. "Stay far enough back that you can just see me." He jumped into a shallow stream and followed it downhill. Soon he could hear the occasional engine noise. He raced along until the sound was behind him, then crouched below the steep line of the stream's bank. He lay there, his head covered with humus, the RPG beside him. His small squad squatted fifty metres upstream. Two machines passed, plodding methodically along. He could hear the third coming. It passed about thirty feet in front of him and as it showed its rear he swung up the RPG, took aim and fired. He dropped below the rim of the bank. There was an explosion. The RPG struck the rear of the machine and detonated, severing its back end and throwing the front into the air.

Adash ran up the stream away from the heat and smoke the RPG had vented. He saw his squad jump to their feet and run upstream too. He leapt out of the stream into a bush and crawled into the heart of it.

The two machines galloped to their fallen comrade, then to the heat cloud hanging above the stream. They looked into the water. They listened. Within their radius of interest there was nothing. They jumped about and charged off.

Adash waited until everything was silent, then climbed out of the bush and back into the stream. He fixed a new grenade to the launcher. He could see the squad further up the river. His three loyal captains. He beckoned them to him, and when they arrived he crawled slowly up the bank and into the open ground. The sound of the machines was gone. He went to the smashed robot. The front end was still struggling to right itself, almost rising to its two remaining feet before it fell back to the ground, unable to balance.

"Machines," Adash said. "War machines." He grabbed the feet and began to drag it to the stream. Its cameras tried to focus on him, calling its broken Gatling guns to deploy and fire, but the system did not respond to its calls. He heaved it across the bank and into the stream. There was a hiss as water filled the exposed inside of the machine and a crackling noise as the broken chassis twisted and shook. Then, with a sputter, it was still. Adash took out his sat phone and went to switch it on, then had second thoughts. "These people and their army of machines must be very important. If we can ambush them and take them prisoner they will be worth millions and millions of dollars to us. We will be rich."

The captains kept silent.

"We will follow the machines downstream and see if an opportunity presents itself." They got up and went to the bank. The fourth soldier was waiting there sheepishly.

Adash smiled evilly at him. "Decided to be a man?"

The soldier said nothing. Silence was always the safest option around General Adash.

# 49

There was an explosion half a mile behind them. "What was that?" said Jim.

"Sounded like an RPG," said Jane. She listened to something in her ear. "We've lost our first Doombah. That leaves sixty-three intact, though I think some may be stuck in the undergrowth, but we've got plenty of cover on all sides. Pretty soon we'll be in the zone to set up camp. We don't want to be split up in the dark. The Doombahs will post sentry. We should start looking for a nice defendable area of cover."

In two hours it would be dark and at that pace Adash's targets would be near the jungle edge, wherever that had ended up after the titanic explosion at the mining camp. They walked along the shallow stream bed as the rain fell, keeping the buzzing engine sound of the trailing machine just in earshot.

Jim was imagining each step he took as a step closer to home. He fantasised about riding a Doombah the rest of the way but preferred its guns to be free to deploy if an attack struck, rather than to be locked down like the Gatlings on Kitson's mount. It had been another exhausting day of struggling through the unpredictable terrain of the forest.

Jane was chatting to Will and Bill in Virginia almost all the time in a low, muffled voice. Half of what she said was in some kind of military lingo that didn't mean much to him and he found himself concentrating on navigating the rough ground rather than trying to overhear the conversation. It seemed, however, that things were going well.

The sat-phone locations, which represented various militia commanders, were at bay and enemy contact had ceased. Since the RPG there had been nothing. The bad guys were melting away, terrified by the demonic horrors in the jungle. The fragmented army of two thousand men, welded together by greed, had disintegrated under the nauseating pressure of fear. The groups had decided it was best to fall back and fight another day. Their general was out of contact, perhaps dead, and unspeakable monsters were on the prowl. Even the promise of diamonds was not enough reason to stick around.

The air had an acrid, burnt smell; the charred rim of the forest was not far ahead. Dusk had fallen and within minutes it would be night. Between them and a stream there was a large clump of tall grass backed by a giant tree. It was like a giant nest. If they camped there, Jane thought, they would have cover and the Doombahs would encircle them. It looked kind of snug, which was the one thing she didn't like about it – but Jim, the kid and Kitson looked like they could use a little slack. "In here," she called.

She laid out the plan to Bill and Will and, taking her as the centre point, they planned the layout of the Doombah sentry picket. As soon as all the robots had fought through the bush and arrived at the campsite, a ring of sixty-three Gatling-armed machines would be standing guard. It was a formidable defensive force. The Doombahs would not sleep;

they would watch in the dark for the slightest danger. In the morning the team would be on its way home.

Adash looked out from the river. The machines had stopped and were forming a defensive ring around a large clump of tall grass, the kind favoured by the mountain gorillas. He smiled to himself. A corridor of that grass led from the stream to the giant tree at the rear of the camp. The machines treated it as an impenetrable wall and used it as a defensive structure. It wasn't a wall at all: it was a tunnel to Adash's prey. He and his men moved down the stream a little way. He crawled up the bank and into the tall grass. The others followed him. They would stay there till first light, then crawl through the bush. Using the cover of the tree they would enter the party's camp and take them. He might become the master of the machines too. He had known, even as the boy's voice had echoed in his mind, that there were no gods to strike him down. His will alone was enough to master all situations and all those around him. However steep the odds, however hard the battle, he would win. Nothing on earth could stop him.

"Not bad, boys," she said, then logged off from Virginia. The campsite was almost comfortable. She gave Kitson some water and injected him again in the neck. He fell asleep. After they had pitched her tent, Jim and Jane lifted the injured man down from the Doombah and bore him inside. Jim made a pillow by stuffing his dirty clothes into a pair of trousers.

Then Jane broke out her rations and they ate.

Pierre wolfed his calorie-packed sandwich and pulled out Jim's exploding tent from the backpack. He opened the contraption and crawled in without a word.

Jim looked at Jane. "Want to share my all-weather blanket?"

"I have my own."

"Oh, well."

"But I might let you cosy up," she said.

"That's very nice of you."

"I thought so," said Jane.

Jim pulled out the blanket-cum-all-weather-sleeping-bag and climbed in, arranging the pack so he could rest his head on it. He moved around to get comfortable and could feel himself drifting away. As he did so, Jane's arm went around him.

# 50

Baz was extremely irritated. They had landed at Kinshasa and had had to change planes. The Airbus was not allowed to fly to Goma: a landing there would apparently invalidate the airliner's insurance. They were to fly in the presidential Boeing 707 to Goma, a step down from the modern luxury and safety of the Airbus. On their way to the plane Julius had received a phone call: the President requested his and Baz's attendance.

The appointment was at two o'clock but by four thirty they were still waiting to see him. Julius sat impassively in silence. He had made it known that the reception area was likely to be bugged so nothing could be said.

Baz's frustration was increasing by the minute. He didn't wait more than thirty minutes for anyone, but this was a little bit special. This was the shot for the moon he had always dreamed of, the ultimate scam, the once-in-a-lifetime chance at an operation so large that no one could conceive it possible. For that he would wait.

There were only so many cups of coffee he could drink and they didn't make him any less agitated. He contemplated his plan. Of course he would give Julius 80 per cent of the money raised for the projects, but the real money was to be made from trading the news through front companies. There had been a time when all fortunes were made through insider trading, but in the last few decades that had been outlawed in its old crude format. In the modern era, shares had to be held through a series of fronts and controlled, like any secret organisation, with cleverness and precision. Well, that was how he did it. With 80 per cent of all takeovers showing obvious price action before the important news, it was clear to everyone, including the regulators, that insider trading was alive and well even at the crudest level. So, anything handled with a little more finesse went undetected. As he waited he consoled himself that the vast fortune he stood to make would more than compensate.

It was six o'clock when they were ushered in. The President was sitting behind a huge ebony desk, ten feet long and six deep. It was inlaid with ivory and gold and looked ancient. He was an old man, skinny, his sunken face skull-like, his eyes bloodshot and a rheumy yellow. "Julien, how are you?" he said, not getting up.

"I'm very well, Mr President, very well indeed." Julius laughed jovially.

"Good," said the President. "Keep me in touch, won't you?" He looked at Baz but didn't acknowledge him, then back at Julius. "Goodbye and have a safe flight."

"Thank you," said Julius, and bowed. He left the room, Baz following.

"What was that about?" said Baz, as the door of the ministerial limo was closed by Julius's driver.

"The application of power." Julius wiped his face with a handkerchief. "This is why we are working together, so that I am the man behind the desk and other people are left waiting at my door." He smiled at Baz. "Not for so long, of course."

312

Baz laughed quietly. It wasn't his normal hearty quack, but more subdued. Momentarily the millions in his bank seemed enough – more than enough – but then the idea for the biggest swindle of all time rushed back to him. His laugh regained its normal bark. "Don't do it to me, though, Julien," he said.

"Of course not, Baz. How could I?"

They headed to Julius's ministry: they would rest there till four a.m., then head out and arrive in Goma at eight. They would drive in convoy to the mine.

Julius made his excuses and had Baz shown to a room at the top of the fifties monstrosity that was the ministry. It was like so much of Africa, a building that time had forgotten. If an office block could be embalmed, that was what had happened. The whole construction was held in a kind of mouldering suspended animation, a product of sweat and a hopelessly forced determination. Where something should have been replaced it had been repaired; where it couldn't be repaired, it had been painted over or removed or tidied up as much as possible, then left. The building was in a kind of zombie state, somewhere just below operationally functional but above derelict. It was a pickled whale.

Baz's suite was as palatial as it was uncomfortable. The bed was on a dais and made to look like a horizontal throne. The other furniture was covered with lace and everything seemed slightly damp. He showered, got dressed again and lay on top of the sheets. He was going to have to lure Higgins back, he thought. A little convincing and a lot of money would do the trick. He'd give him some time with his wonderful missus and after a couple of weeks he'd be practically begging to work for him again. His eyes closed and he could see the

313

whole region in front of him, a mass of mining promotions, one huge complex of prospects offering the world a chance to get in on the ground floor of the new Saudi Arabia.

The Doombahs sat in their defensive rings staring out into the green-lit night. The controllers sat at their work-stations in Virginia and listened to the night sounds of the jungle. The contract engineers were working to get video, but the satellite above didn't want anything to do with the file format the Doombahs were sending. They were pulling their hair out. The system wasn't even out of Alpha test and they were being asked to perform technical miracles. It was an opportunity for the company to break into the big-time but this was not the way they would have liked to prove their concept. The Doombahs were little more than demo models designed to prove a concept – it was like taking synchronised swimmers and making them Navy Seals. A typical military situation: SNAFU – Situation Normal, All Fucked Up. Quite likely it would turn into FUBAR – Fucked Up Beyond All Recognition.

The Doombahs estimated forty-seven kills with one loss, but the interesting thing was how the robots had scared off nearly two thousand men. Forty-seven dead, 1,963 paralysed with fear made them almost a non-lethal-force weapon. That could be an additional selling point.

Deep below the mountain a huge ball of lava was slowly moving up from the depths of the earth. It had begun its journey from the core hundreds of years before as the currents of the earth's furnace had formed a sphere of almost immeasurable energy and sent it rolling towards the crust. It entered the root system of the volcano and began to effervesce where the core met the mantel. The volcano was like a huge boil swelling to burst. The Doombahs sensed the vibration, and as the data streamed back to Virginia the engineers wondered at the seismic readings flickering across the many control graphs. There was no sound in the jungle to indicate that tremors were pulsating through the ground, and earthquakes were not rare. Nyamuragira and Nyiragongo were in a constant state of activity, which meant plenty of quakes and a full-scale eruption every two years. A volcanologist would have recognised the cloud of steam coming from the Nyamuragira crater as different from the heavy raincloud above it but it would have been pretty pointless to wake Jim and Jane's party. A catastrophic eruption would be just that and a lesser one would require no wake-up call.

As the sun rose they were served notice.

A Doombah jumped up and Jim groaned. Why the fuck was someone shaking him?

He sat up. He heard a growl in the distance. The ground was juddering: it was an eruption.

Adash leapt to his feet. Now was the time. His men were awake and knew what to do. They crawled through the grass towards the tree. They couldn't see it but the machines were standing up, Gatlings rotating, jumping from side to side hunting an invisible enemy coming from far up the mountainside. Jane and Jim were lifting Kitson on to his Doombah and strapping him in. Pierre was stowing the kit. The volcano was legendary for its lava. It contained no silica and when it burst from the cone of the volcano it rushed down the sides at a hundred kilometres an hour. Nothing on the ground could outrun it, neither beast nor machine, and even birds could be knocked out of the air by the ash and gases.

Jane jammed in her earpiece. "What have you got?" she said.

"Minor eruption," said Control.

"Where are Will and Bill?"

"On their way."

"Is the pickup ready to fly?"

"Taking off as soon as you leave. They'll be waiting for you."

"As soon as we're packed we're on our way."

The Doombahs were skipping around in a frenzy.

"Get these things under control," she said. "They're losing the plot."

She heard a rustle behind her and turned as a tall soldier walked through the grass, his Kalashnikov pointing right at her. He was looking into her eyes, ready to shoot her down if she so much as went for her carbine. There were two more behind him.

Jim saw her look and followed it. "Shit," he muttered.

Pierre looked up: Adash was with four men. They were on top of them, their rifles aimed. Adash walked into the camp. Pierre had seen that look before. It was the wicked smirk of conquest and conquest meant that death would follow.

"Breach," said Jane.

"Copy," said an impassive voice.

The Doombah twitched, its camera eyes rolling about.

"Dog Bites Man, tell them to give me control of the machines."

316

Pierre relayed the message.

"No can do," said Jane.

There was a thunderous clap from the mountain and they all blanched, including the Doombah. The ground rolled and heaved and they were shaken from side to side. The Doombah kicked out with its legs like a dressage horse and felled two of the soldiers. Jane grabbed the barrel of Adash's Kalashnikov and tore it from his grasp. Adash ran forwards, grabbed Jim's M4 carbine and dashed through the wall of grass. Pierre pulled the knife from the sheath in Jim's belt and toppled into the third soldier, who gasped.

Jane opened up on the fourth. Instantly, he crumpled backwards.

Pierre was looking into the eyes of his victim, who was in the throes of death. He twisted the blade. The man buckled and fell. He whirled round to face another enemy but there was none. Jane was heading through the wall of grass. The Doombahs were sitting on their back legs aiming up at the mountain, preparing to fire on some massive computed foe created by the artificial intelligence wired into their silicon synapses. The ground was shaking and as she ran she toppled on to one knee. She could see Adash running into the gloom, thrown from side to side like a drunkard by the heaving ground. She let off a burst of fire, but it missed its target. Then, as she tried to aim, running on the rolling ground, he swerved behind the trunk of a tree and was gone.

"Damn it," she shouted. The mountain roared again and she saw a flame of red streak into the air.

"Erupting," she said into the mouthpiece. "We've closed the breach."

Jim was mesmerised by the bloodied blade in Pierre's hand.

Pierre saw his expression. "Sorry," he said. He wiped the knife on the grass, then cleaned his hand on the shirt of one of the soldiers. "I should cut their throats," he said, as if to prove his compassion.

"You'll do no such thing," said Jane, stalking back. "Disarm them quickly and then we have to hurry." The ground moved again. "This mountain could blow and give us a real hot shower."

Pierre picked up the assault rifles, pulled out the magazines and put them into Jim's pack. He jammed the barrels into the ground with all his might, then threw them into the long grass.

"Let's rock," said Jim.

"Let's roll," said Jane.

Pierre shouldered Jim's rucksack as the ground trembled. The Doombahs were completely confused, and when Virginia tried to control them they responded strangely, fixated by the huge enemy behind them that shook the ground as it approached. They were running around in a robot panic.

"Let's pick it up," said Jane. "The sooner we're out of the jungle the happier I'll be."

As she spoke, the tremors subsided and the ground was solid once more.

The forest stopped abruptly in a torn mass of charred and lacerated vegetation. It was the sort of thing that an eruption would do but the destruction had not come from the mountain: it had been caused by the rod of tungsten that had fallen twelve thousand miles from space, giving up all its energy as it touched the ground in a plume of earth. The

318

landscape was seared and black, a congealed mass of uneven ground, melted, thrown into the air and pulled back to earth.

Adash moved himself into position, embedded in the destruction like a maggot in the decomposing body of a fallen elephant. They would come his way and then he would shoot them, as they exposed themselves on the flat, featureless plain. He would leave the Dog alive and the Dog would take him to the diamonds. Then he would kill him and leave the mountain until it had stopped its eruptions. He would return to take the diamonds and once again he would be the master of an army. Nothing would stand in his way ever again. He looked up at the volcano. "The fire god is angry today," he said to himself mockingly. The mountain might pour lava but it would dump its flaming pus along the routes it had used before. Of that he was sure.

# 51

"There's a whole lot of helium coming out of the ground," said Virginia.

Jane laughed. "You've got helium in your goddamn mine," she said to Jim, as they hurried forwards.

"That's good?" said Jim.

"Sure – it's a strategic element. Only two helium mines in the world."

"OK," said Jim. "Like I need to get into the kids' balloon business."

Jane snorted. "Just think about the word 'strategic'," she said.

Jim didn't.

Pierre was lamenting his new Kalashnikov. He hadn't been the one to lose his M4 carbine, so why did he have to get the poorest weapon now?

The jungle was lightening: they were approaching the edge. Jim's spirits rose. He drew his personal chart and it went forward for years. He wasn't going to be wrong this time. He was only a few hundred metres from safety.

They pushed through a stand of grass, the thunder of the volcano in their ears.

"Oh, shit," he muttered. A giant wall of shredded, twisted jungle vegetation stood between them and the plateau. The

Doombahs were looking up at it, trying to work out how to get through.

"We'll find a way," he said.

"No problem," said Jane.

"Rock and roll?" said Pierre, ambiguously.

"We're going to see some fireworks." Julius laughed.

"OK," said Baz. He wasn't too happy at the prospect as he looked out over the Goma airfield at the erupting volcano on the far horizon. Nyiragongo looked bad enough, smoking away to itself; Nyamuragira looked more threatening, even though it was further away. Its smoky plume had a certain intensity about it that said, "Fuck off somewhere else."

Baz was happy to deal with explosive situations and volatile personalities. People he could handle, but a mountain was a different matter. It wasn't a fireworks display: a natural disaster was about to happen. His top lip was sweating, not because it was so humid but because fear was coursing through his veins. But there was no turning back.

The great force of the blast from the fallen tungsten had blown the jungle edge into a solid wall of tangled vegetation. They moved along the margin of the devastation. The Doombahs were trying to cross the tangle but their software didn't seem able to cope with the jigsaw of broken tree limbs. They were trying to scale it, but they hopped, stumbled and struggled in vain.

As the party moved along the wall, so the Doombahs backtracked from their ascents and kept the line.

"We're going to have to start climbing soon," said Jim, "if we can't find a break."

"Or burrowing," said Pierre.

"Let's find a spot the Doombahs can get across, or we'll be crossing the open space with no back-up. You stay here," said Jane. "I'm going up the log pile to see if I can find a way."

"Can't HQ see anything?" asked Jim.

"They've no field of depth. Ten feet high could look like fifty from space." She took off her pack and put on her carbine, then swung up on to a torn tree-trunk. "I won't be long." The view from the top was breathtaking. There was a large blasted area that took up the entire plateau, with a deep crater in the centre where the tungsten rod had impacted.

The area might have been struck by a meteor – which it had been, except that the meteor was not extra-terrestrial but man-made.

Jane looked to the north and along the concave wave of debris. A couple of hundred yards ahead a chunk of jungle had been blown further inwards than the rest. The pocket penetrated the semicircular wall of debris. Maybe they could climb over the thin side wall of the hollow and be in clear ground. That would be easier than trying to struggle over anywhere else. Lugging Kitson over the high barrier was at the bottom of the list of things she wanted to do, and leaving the Doombahs behind would be extremely risky.

She was smiling as she picked her way elegantly down the giant climbing frame. "OK," she said. "We're going that way for a half a klick. We can see if the Doombahs can get Terence over, and if they can do that we'll follow."

They moved carefully along between the jungle and the tangled wall. Flying debris had thinned the jungle on the margin, but everywhere wicked splinters were aligned against them. Jim found his right forearm was bleeding a little. A

splinter the size of a toothpick was sticking out of his arm.
He pulled it out and threw it away.

"You OK?" asked Jane.

"Just a scratch."

She went over to the breach. It was manageable for
humans, but not necessarily for the Doombahs.

"Come on," said Jim, "Let's get Terry off the robot and
carry him."

"I'll be OK," said Kitson. "Don't mind me."

Jane was about to agree with Jim but the Doombah
crouched and sprang on to the jungle wreckage. It balanced
and swayed, inspecting its surroundings with whizzing
rotating eyes. It tapped its forefeet on the surface, adjusting
its rear in a half-clumsy, half-delicate way. It resembled a
pantomime horse being driven by two blindfolded ballerinas.
It jumped up again and scrabbled. Jane followed it, hoping
she could stop it falling as it balanced precariously. The
Doombah seemed to stare ahead, and then, with four steps,
climbed a few more feet up. It collected itself and sprang like
a deer on to a spiky severed log. Then it clambered another
nerve-racking few feet till it was poised on top of the breach.
It hopped off and fell on to the branches below. Jane followed
it. She could still hear the engine buzzing and revving. At the
top she looked down. Below she saw a mass of spears pointing
up, like an elephant trap, at anyone who would dare to climb
down the other side.

The Doombah had fallen on to them but had smashed the
many jagged splinters with its armoured belly, its thin metal
feet threading through the gaps and finding a footing.
Precision guidance or luck? It was snaking its hips, reading
the ground below. It trembled and shook to realign itself,

then sprang down again. It was halfway to safety.

"Are you getting all this data?"

"Sure," said Will in her earpiece. "If this one makes it, we'll network it to the others. It's marking the trail as it goes."

Jane couldn't see anything – but, then, she didn't see in infrared or ultra-violet unlike the Doombahs, which could follow the trail using their acute machine vision.

Jim was looking back at the volcano and she turned briefly, curious to know what had captured his interest. The column of white ash was impressive, blown south by the winds at fifteen thousand feet.

When she turned back, the Doombah was feeling the way ahead. It crabbed down on to another trunk. Two more bounds and it would be on *terra firma*. It dropped its forefeet on to a branch three feet below, balanced, then sprang forwards on to the ground.

Amazing, Jane thought. "Come on up," she called to Jim and Pierre. "We should be able to get down from here. Kitson's made it."

Pierre jumped up and Jim followed. He was extremely glad he wasn't carrying his pack. He felt grateful to Pierre but absolutely no shame in letting the boy take it. Even without it he was at almost his physical limit.

Pierre bounded up the debris wall, Jim toiling behind. The boy disappeared over the other side while Jane waited for Jim to reach the summit. She looked at his drawn face, covered with filth. He was breathing hard. "You OK, buddy?"

"Perfect," he said. He peered at the chaos below. "Nearly there," he panted, smiling. Pierre was picking his way along the path, made easier by the Doombah's splinter-crushing progress. "You go ahead," said Jim. "I'm going to need to take this really slow."

"Go ahead," said Jane. "I'll stand guard here."

The Doombahs behind were starting their assent now. Without passengers they seemed recklessly keen to conquer the wall.

Pierre watched Jim climbing tentatively down: he was kind of weak and shaky. Jane was picking her way down behind him, scanning the forward ground for problems. She had one eye on Jim: a fall now and he would be impaled on any number of spears. He sat down on a branch and studied the short route ahead. "You OK?" she asked.

"My legs have gone to jelly. I think I'm dehydrated or something."

She passed her canteen down to him and he drank. "I'll be OK," he said. He swung the bottle up without letting go of the strap. Jane caught it and he let go. She dropped down beside him and they looked at the wicked puzzle below.

"Tricky," she said.

"How did the Doombah do it?" he asked.

"It just dropped ten feet from up there," she said.

"Good idea," said Jim. He slapped his legs. "OK – I'm going." He took a nearby branch in his hand and slipped forwards, his foot out to catch the edge of a fractured stump. It didn't land where he'd meant it to and he slid forward. His shirt caught something and yanked him under the arms. Buttons flew. He struggled, his foot pushing away from the spears, and fell on to a branch below, feet first. He tilted forwards, his knees buckled and he fell backwards. He grunted. There was the sound of branches cracking and a thud. Jane traipsed down the wall.

"I'm OK," came a muffled voice, and she saw that he was lying on the ground ten feet below her, his legs and arms in the air.

Pierre was burrowing through the branches to him as Jane lowered herself down.

Jim's hair had blood in it. "I'm OK," he said, "but I'm stuck."

"Move your feet," said Jane.

Jim stared at her, dazed.

"Just move them for me, will you?" she persisted.

He did so.

"Good. You haven't broken your neck," she said.

He held out his arm and she hauled him out of the wedge of branches. "Thanks," he said.

Jane thought he seemed a little concussed. "No problem," she said. "Take it slowly."

"Come through here," said Pierre, from his burrow. Jim followed him on all fours while Jane climbed out and down.

Jim sat on the ravaged ground and drank more water. Jane had given him a salt tablet. The Doombahs were scampering down the other side of the breach. It was like a crazy circus show. He watched them as his sight cleared.

"OK, guys, the RV is on the other side of this plateau, about fifteen hundred metres."

"Can't they come here?" asked Jim, hopefully.

"It's too close to cover for an RPG attack on the chopper. The Doombahs will defend for us on the walk, and by the time we're across the plateau our ride will be there. As soon as ten Doombahs make it across the wall, we start walking."

"Deal," said Jim. "It's not far, after all."

He got up, feeling almost normal, apart from the big bump on the back of his head.

Jane was programming a Doombah. "Ride on this."

"I'm OK," said Jim.

"No," said Jane, "you're not. Ride the friggin' Big Dog." She smiled. "Please."

Jim gave in, swung his leg over it and jumped on to its back. "Let's rock," he said.

"Let's roll," said Pierre.

"Let's rock and roll," said Jane. They moved off.

# 52

Adash had picked his way into the wall of jungle debris, snaking and burrowing through the tangle. At times he thought it stupid of him but at others he was convinced of his genius. The machines could not go into the heart of the splintered tangle so he was safe from them, and if he could make the other side he would have a bunker from which to fire as his quarry crossed the blasted plateau. The occasional tremor from the ground filled him with fear. Perhaps a quake would entomb him. He emerged on the other side halfway up the mountain of vegetation, some thirty feet above the plateau below. It was a vantage-point that any sniper would have been proud of. He got himself comfortable and waited. At some point, he was sure, they would cross the plateau, and when they were far enough into no man's land, he would shoot the woman and the man, then hunt down Dog Bites Man.

He would win a great victory single-handed. The diamond mine would be his and his alone. He would buy the allegiance of the army's other commanders and then, one by one, he would kill them. As he waited he began to plan each murder. It was an amusing challenge that wiled away the time. In the distance he began to hear the buzzing of the machines' engines. He was correct: they were coming his way. They would never clear the hurdle.

*

The Doombahs on the wrong side of the breach waited their turn to begin the climb. Twenty had crossed and there were forty or more to come.

As they walked across the seared ground Jim looked to the far horizon and the crater in the middle of the plain where the camp had been. I should have backed up my notebook, he thought absently. The rolling motion of the Doombah was quite relaxing and he could see the finishing line ahead.

There were now twelve guardian robots in a perimeter, some facing the jungle, walking backwards, guns ready.

Adash saw a machine three hundred metres to his right, then another. They were the vanguard of a defensive ring around his target. He would pick them off as soon as they were too far from cover to escape his marksmanship. A few yards more and he would open fire. He cocked the carbine and took it off safety. He pulled out the telescoping stock and locked it. He looked through the stubby sight and turned the rear. There was a click and a laser dot appeared on the ground where the carbine aimed.

Excellent.

If he had not been squinting through the sights he would have seen the Doombahs stutter. Jane did: she cocked her own M4 and crouched as the Doombahs freaked.

Adash brought the sight to aim at the party, and as he did so, he saw the machines staring at him, their Gatling guns raised. His targets were only a fraction of a second's aim away but the machines were set to fire on him. He let off a shot and pulled himself into cover. The machines let rip and the Gatlings hammered the tree-trunk in front of him.

Jim jumped off the Doombah, which lay flat on the ground offering him cover. Jane lay down behind another, while a third masked Kitson, lashed into his stretcher. Pierre jumped up and ran for the jungle. He knew who had fired on them: Adash lay in the twisted pile of trees and would try to pick them off.

"No!" shouted Jim. "Wait!" But even if Pierre had heard him over the cacophony of the Doombahs' barrage, it would have made no difference.

Adash stuck his head up. There was no firing. He realised that unless the laser in the rifle's sight was trained on the machines they could not see him. He forced the sight off and held the gun up over the line of the trunk. There was no reply. He held the rifle, sat up and aimed, using the aperture sights, at the party lying prone behind their metal guards. He fired and ducked down. A hail of gunfire came from the machines and ripped into the tree-trunk behind which he hid. The firing continued for a few more seconds, then ended.

His enemies were effectively pinned down. He could inter-mittently fire on them and they could not move for fear of being hit. He looked out from his hide at the protecting machines. They stood confounded. He took careful aim and fired.

Jim heard the twang of a bullet on the side of his protecting Doombah.

The others replied.

One more shot and he would move, Adash decided. When the firing subsided he sat up again. He took aim and fired.

*

Jane heard the shot whistle off the top of her Doombah. "Nothing," Will was saying. "We've got nothing but the Doombahs to cover you."

"We'll wait until nightfall," she said, "but I'm not sure Kitson and Jim are going to be in much shape after baking in this sun for six hours."

"We can lay down a barrage of covering fire for maybe five minutes from the Doombahs, but we need to get them all across the wall and we need to be sure of a fix on the shooter. Five minutes should get you out of range."

"OK," said Jane, "but the kid's gone AWOL."

"That's tough," said Will. "He's nice to have, but not a mission objective."

"Roger," said Jane. Stupid kid, she thought. Brave but stupid. He was lucky to have made it to the wall. If he had any sense he'd keep running and not try to get the shooter, which she knew was exactly what Pierre was planning to do.

There was another shot and the Doombahs fired back.

The trunk in front of Adash was smouldering. It was time for him to pull out and move closer.

Pierre was walking carefully down the denuded zone inside the wall of smashed jungle. The Doombahs were struggling like a collection of giant ants to scale it and one by one they were traipsing to the other side. From the sound of the gunfire, Adash was some way ahead. Pierre knew he would move, because snipers had to or they were killed. This would be Adash's undoing because as he moved he would show himself, and when he did, it would be the end for him.

331

# 53

Ash was falling from the sky on to the windscreen of the large black Cadillac Escalade. Baz was cursing his luck. Why the fuck had he agreed to come on this trip? Pigs get fed and hogs get slaughtered, he thought. His whole life was about not being so greedy as to get himself slaughtered, and here he was, suddenly the greediest man alive, going to make a meeting with terrorists under the smoke and ash of an erupting volcano.

He had made a big mistake and he knew it. Death was running his cold index finger down Baz's spine. It wasn't far to the mine but the convoy of bodyguards in their flash black American SUVs made slow progress over what could hardly be called roads. They wouldn't reach the camp till three.

They could have choppered in but none of the local pilots was prepared to fly into the Barron mine with the mountain erupting. He didn't blame them. Rumour had it that the volcano had spewed a huge fireball out into the jungle, and as he looked at the two blazing volcanoes, that seemed totally credible. Julien Julius obviously thought he was a man of destiny, he mused, sourly. He was not afraid of two erupting mountains. He had clearly made a bargain with the devil to ensure that he wasn't burnt to a crisp like half of the surrounding countryside. Baz wanted to hit the bottle but that wouldn't get the job done. He sat in the plush leather of the Escalade, looking like a man with agonising toothache.

Julius was enjoying his companion's discomfort. Militia were far more dangerous than volcanoes. Volcanoes, in comparison, were more predictable and far less likely to take your life. He had been dealing with the Mai-Mai for fifteen years, so no routine eruption was going to scare him.

Adash was peering down on the party. There were now thirty machines defending them. Could he see the cowering figures below or was he imagining it? The black machines stood sentry, staring ahead, but none seemed to be training their weapons on him. He had found a new vantage-point to shoot from and he had twenty rounds, so he had to be careful not to waste them.

He felt a sharp pain in his cheek. He saw the barrel of a gun.

"I have complete power over you," said a voice. "Drop the gun and you may live." The Dog had vengeance in his eyes.

Adash let the carbine fall and it rattled down into the tangle below. "Why didn't you kill me?"

"I didn't want you to fall like your rifle. Give me my diamond and I will let you go."

Adash put his hand into his top pocket.

"No tricks or I will blow your face off."

Adash's fingers touched the diamond and he plucked it out.

The boy pressed the gun barrel harder into his face. "Pass it back," he said, hate and rage in his voice. "Drop it and it will be your last action."

Adash held his arm backwards, the diamond pincered in three fingers.

"Stay very, very still," Dog Bites Man hissed. He reached forwards and took the stone with his free hand. Then he stepped back and down. "I keep my promises," he said.

Adash reached for the dagger in his boot, but just as he pulled it out the boy snapped back, the Kalashnikov aimed at his chest. He saw the knife in Adash's hand. "I knew you would do that," he said, looking Adash straight in the eyes. "Did you know I would do this?" He shot Adash in the chest. Adash grabbed the right side of his torso and blood bubbled through his fingers. "You die now," said the boy, and squeezed the trigger again.

"What have you got?" said Jane, as the second shot rang out.

"Don't know," said Will, "but the tag's moving."

Pierre climbed into view at the top of the pile of vegetation. He was waving his rifle in an all-clear signal. Jane waved back and he started to descend. "Maybe he's fragged the sniper," she said.

Jim sat up: if Pierre was climbing down that wall it seemed unlikely that anyone was going to shoot at him. "Get down," shouted Jane, and he did so.

Pierre picked his way over the twisted trunks and branches, his head low. He walked slowly towards them, swaying like a slow dancer. He seemed contented. "You can get up," he called. "I got Adash – I finished him."

"We're on our way," Jane said, into her mouthpiece.

"Pierre, you're a bloody hero," said Jim.

Pierre offered him a little smile. "We are kind of even now," he said.

"Even Stevens," said Jim.

"Let's rock," said Pierre.

"Let's roll," said Jim.

"Let's ride," said Jane, straddling a Doombah.

Pierre picked up Jim's rucksack and jumped enthusiastically on to one. It reared up and threw him off. Jane pulled out the control unit. "Let's try that again," she said.

Pierre got up. "Maybe I walk." He laughed. "OK, one more time." He climbed on and this time the Doombah obliged.

"Hi ho, Silver, away," said Jim, and off they rode.

# 54

Forty Doombahs surrounded them as they rode across the blackened plain, the mountain belching steam and ash behind them.

"The chopper's going to be here in minutes. We're nearly home, boys," said Jane.

They skirted around the deep crater where the tungsten rod had struck. It was hundreds of feet deep, and from where they rode they couldn't see the bottom. Jim wondered whether the shock had set off the mountain but then he decided that, however immense the explosion had been on the plateau, it was a tiny spark in comparison to the power of the molten magma in the belly of the volcano. How much energy did it take to turn a whole mountain into liquid rock? An unimaginable amount.

They could hear the chopper blades humming in the distance. They'd arrived at the RV. Jim sighed with joy as the sound grew louder. He climbed off the robot and looked towards where the throbbing noise was coming from.

"Over there," shouted Jane, pointing north as a chopper appeared above the tree-line.

The Doombahs freaked out. The two lead robots turned on the helicopter and opened up on it. They shot at the rotors in a focused burst of fire. Shards of metal flew everywhere, and Jane knocked Jim and Pierre to the ground, winding them. The helicopter tried to turn to avoid the fire but the blades disintegrated in a hail of metal and it spun out of control. Moments later, it crashed to the ground.

"Holy crap!" yelled Jane, and sprinted for the wreckage. Jim ran after her, with Pierre overtaking him, and the Doombahs galloped behind.

The chopper was smouldering but there was movement in the cockpit. Jane leapt in and hauled out the pilot. While Jim and Pierre led him away, she climbed in to release the co-pilot's harness, then reappeared with him on her shoulders. She dropped him on to the ground as Jim and Pierre rushed back to pull him clear. He was breathing.

Jane jumped down. "Let's get away from here in case it blows." Jim and Pierre dragged the co-pilot away as fast as they could and put him down forty yards away from the helicopter beside the pilot.

Ash fell from the skies like grubby snowflakes.

"Any ideas?" asked Jane, into her mouthpiece.

"We can send another chopper and disable the Doombahs," said Will.

"Might be tricky to know if we've succeeded," said Bill. "The system has lots of autonomy."

Jim turned: he could hear a cranky old diesel engine coming up the hill from the valley below. "Christ," he muttered. It sounded like a bus. There was the scrape of struggling gears and a desperate engine fighting its way up the incline.

"It's a bus," said Pierre.

"I hope the Doombahs don't mind buses," said Jim, "or the driver's in for a nasty shock."

"It might be full of soldiers," said Jane.

"Soldiers come in trucks not buses," said Pierre, with certainty.

"What the fuck would a bus be doing up here?" said Jim. "Not that I'd be too proud to take a bus to Goma right now."

A sky blue bus with a yellow roof appeared on the lip of the plateau. The Doombahs turned towards it and formed a defensive ring around them. The vehicle was struggling towards them, slowing as it approached. The Doombahs watched it quizzically as it ground to a halt.

The shadow of the driver moved behind the windscreen and a squeaky door swung open. John Smith stepped down, grinning. "What have we got here?" he asked. "Oh!" he exclaimed, as ash fell on to his head. "You all look a bit rough, if you don't mind me saying."

"What are you doing here?" said Jim.

"I've been on my way ever since you texted your lady-friend, but this is a tough place to get to on a peace-time budget."

"Thank God you've come," said Jane. "The sooner we get out of here the better."

"I agree," said Smith. "All aboard."

The chopper pilot stood up unsteadily and tried to haul his co-pilot to his feet. Jim helped him.

"What the hell are these machines?" asked John.

"Later," she said. "Are you packing heat?"

"Yes," he said. "Is that a problem?"

"Just don't move." She pulled a fob from her pack, swabbed and snapped him. "Put this in your pocket and they won't cut you in half."

"All right," said Smith.

338

"Let's get Kitson."

"Kitson!" Smith looked astounded. "You mean he's not dead?"

"Follow me."

They walked to the stretcher Doombah.

"Wonders will never cease," observed Smith.

Jane unstrapped Kitson. "You haven't got any more medicine, have you?" he wondered.

"Yes," she said, pulled out a syringe and stuck the needle into him. "Let's get out of here."

Jane was the last into the bus. "Stay," she called to the Doombahs. "There's good boys."

"We got it," said Will in Virginia.

"Let's rock," said Jim, who had found a bottle of beer and was prising the top off with his jungle knife.

"Let's roll," said Jane.

"Let's ride," said Pierre, from where he was nursing Kitson.

"You're all stark staring bonkers," said Smith, crashing the gears and lurching off. "There's a rough old road ahead but if you can stand the shaking we'll get there."

Jim called Stafford on Jane's sat phone. "Send the plane to Goma," he said.

"Are you all right?" his butler enquired.

"Not really," said Jim, "but we've got Kitson and he's alive. We need to evacuate him as he's all smashed up."

"I've arranged that," said Jane. "Way back."

"Forget that, Stafford," said Jim. "I'll call you later."

The bus lurched violently to one side.

"Bastards," roared Smith, as a convoy of Cadillac Escalades passed.

*

"Fuck me," said Baz, getting out on the plateau. It was like a scene from hell. Barron was gone, replaced by a huge crater and a crashed helicopter. The ash had fallen hard and lay a couple of inches deep on the ground.

"I don't understand," said Julius. "What has happened here?"

"Don't look at me, Julien. I'm not a volcanologist."

Ash-coloured rocks stood in a ring a couple of hundred yards away, strange yet organic shapes, rather like tombstones. "What are those?" Julius walked towards them, his retinue of guards following.

Baz stared at the closest one. It was weird. He didn't like it at all. "Where are your people?" he asked, preparing to suggest that they left.

"I don't know. Something must have happened. Maybe the eruption has made them leave. It is very strange."

One of Julius's guards pushed the rock with his foot.

It sprang to life, the ash falling off it – a great black beast. The bodyguard drew his gun and went to shoot. There was a burst of flaming gunfire and he was blown to pieces.

Baz threw himself to the ground, as did Julius. Now all of the stones rose, and as the bodyguards drew their weapons they were torn to shreds in a hailstorm of fire. Within seconds the twelve men were dead. The weapons on the monstrous machines sank back into their flanks.

Julius got to his feet. They didn't seem interested in him so Baz stood up too – he had very nearly messed his pants. The sight of the carnage made him gag: all that remained of the bodyguards was unidentifiable red pulp. "Let's get out of here now," he said desperately.

The machines were looking up at the sky. Julius and Baz followed their gaze.

A fireball was heading swiftly across the heavens, coming directly towards them. Baz had no time to wonder what it was before he was vaporized by the blast. There was no evidence now that he, Julien Julius and his men or the Doombahs had ever been there. In the distance the jungle debris began to burn as the fire god of the volcano exhaled smoke into the sky.

# 55

Mbangu had got them straight into the airport, no questions asked. He was a powerful untouchable so that even though they were armed to the teeth they drove in the battered bus straight on to the runway and up to the Gulfstream. He shook Jim's hand as the young man staggered last into the plane. Mbangu's face wore a knowing look. The Presidential 707 sat parked by the terminal and the G5, a far more expensive plane, was leaving with its interesting crew.

An Englishman had been loaded into an air ambulance, yet another rarity, and two injured pilots had been taken away by a CIA man in a black limo. He had seen the fireball fall to earth. They said it was the second from Nyamuragira but it looked to him to have come from elsewhere. He would, no doubt, be asked to work out what had happened but, meanwhile, when the jet had taken off, he would cross the border into Gisenyi. The lava flowed into Goma, not the town on the other side of the lake. Once the volcanoes had settled he would begin his evaluation, but not until then. He stood back as the steps were pulled away, then strode to the terminal to watch the jet head on its way.

"I hope there's a shower on this flying gin palace," said Smith. "Frankly, you two are as ripe as vintage Stilton."

"There is," said Jim.

Pierre was running up and down the jet. "This is big," he said emphatically. "Whose is it?"

"Mine," said Jim, and collapsed into his seat, exhausted.

"This is big, Jim," said Pierre again, as if he hadn't already made himself clear.

"Thanks," said Jim.

"Buckle up," said Jane.

Jim did as he was told, then tilted the chair back. "Wake me when we level out." He fell straight to sleep.

Smith looked at Jane. "Close call?"

"Very," she said.

Pierre bounced up and down in his luxurious leather seat. Then he stopped and looked at Jane. "Are we going to America?"

"England," she said.

"Great Britain," corrected Smith. "London."

"That's fine," said Pierre. He was beaming as the plane lifted off.

"Let's rock," said Smith, sarcastically.

"Let's roll," said Jane, putting her seat back with a sigh.

"Let's fly," said Pierre.


The rear compartment of the plane was like a small hotel room, with a toilet and shower. Jim stripped off and Jane examined him. "You've healed up," she said. "You're covered in cuts, bruises and bites but the wounds are healed. No leeches, but it looks like you've had a few."

Jim touched the side of her face. "You were incredible. You *are* incredible."

"You're not too bad yourself."

343

He kissed her.

"In that shower, soldier," she said, "before I puke."

The hot water was heavenly, if not plentiful. Black filth ran from his head and torso and formed slurry in the shower tray. He piled on the shower gel – it would take a lot to get him clean. He could have stood there for hours but Jane was next so he sluiced the mud and grime away with the spray, turned off the water and stepped out. He dried himself, put on a robe and staggered into the cabin.

"That's better," she said, sniffing him.

"And you stink."

She laughed and went into the shower room. The door closed.

Jim sighed as he sat down. He might not be able to stand up again, he thought.

A moment later the shower door opened and Jane emerged. "What is it with you?" she said, slapping something on to the table. She was smiling ironically. "Gold nuggets in your shower tray."

"Maybe you've some in your pants too," he offered.

She grinned. "I'm not answering that," she said, and went back for her shower.


Pierre was teaching Smith how to play Congo poker. He appeared to make up the rules as he went along. Smith didn't mind – the kid clearly had the right idea about life and Smith enjoyed his explanations of how exactly he had won. The kid made him laugh.

From time to time Pierre looked out of the window. He had never flown in a plane before. "You aren't very good at this game," he said.

"Clearly," said Smith.

Jane came into the main cabin. She was wearing a pair of Jim's jeans – with the bottoms turned up about four inches and anchored at the hips with her belt – and one of his white T-shirts. He was following her. "Your turn," he called to Pierre. "The shower's waiting."

"I don't need a shower," Pierre assured him.

"Trust me, mate," said Smith, "you do."

Pierre threw down his poker hand and got up.

"Check for gold," said Jane, pouring a sprinkle of tiny nuggets on to the table.

Smith pushed them around with a fingertip. "Curious," he said.

Jim sat down and picked up Pierre's cards. "What are we playing?"

"Blackjack," said Smith.

"I'm bust." Jim threw down the five cards.

"So I win at last," observed Smith.

# 56

Stafford opened the door. "Hello, sir. Good to have you back."

"Thanks," said Jim. He, Jane and Pierre trooped in. "And thanks for all the organising," he added.

Stafford and Jane exchanged a funny look. Odd, Jim thought. They seemed to recognise each other.

"Drop your bags in the hallway," Stafford said. "I'll deal with them. Will Madam be staying?"

"Yes," said Jim.

"Very good."

Pierre was staring at the butler. "Are you his father?" he asked Stafford.

"Good Lord, no," said Stafford. "I'm Mr Evans's retainer."

"What do you retain?" Pierre asked.

Stafford smiled. "I'm his butler."

"Butler?" said Pierre.

"Through here, Pierre," called Jim.

"Servant," said Stafford, quietly. He looked a little uncomfortable now.

"OK," Pierre said. He ran to the window. "Oh, big river," he said. "Big, ugly grey river."

"I think it's cute," said Jane.

"Cold-looking river."

"Well, I wouldn't go swimming in it," said Jim.

Stafford came into the room. Pierre ran over to him. "Take a photo of me with your servant," he told Jim, and grabbed Stafford's arm.

"Good idea," said Jane, smiling mysteriously. She took out her iPhone and photographed the pair.

The iPhone faked a camera snapping sound. "Got it," she said. She highlighted Stafford's face and sent it to Virginia. "Look," she said, resizing the image. She showed Pierre, who took the iPhone and passed it to Stafford.

"Very good," he said, as Jane reclaimed it.

Jim was booting his trading screen while he talked to St George. "I know – it's a miracle … Nothing, really – the least I could do."

Jane's phone went "bing". "Just a Coke Lite for me," she said to Stafford, in reply to his question.

"Beer," said Pierre.

"We're out of beer, young man," said Stafford, "Coke, tea, coffee?"

"Bad news," said Jim into the phone. "What bad news?" He made a T-shape with his fingers at Stafford, who nodded.

"Coke," said Pierre.

"I own Barron?" Jim threw a look to Jane. "That's all right – I think the place has got a future. If the volcano doesn't rub it out, that is. I'm sure Terence's friend Alan will be pleased. Look, I've got to go."

Jane was smirking at her iPhone. She stuck it under Jim's nose. There was a picture of Stafford. It was captioned "Bertie Lees. MI1/MI10 retired".

Jim had heard of MI5 and MI6 but not MI1, let alone MI10 "I know," he fibbed.

"OK, OK," she said.

"Do you think I'm a muppet?" he asked, smiling.

Jane pulled a face. "Well, no, of course not."

"I don't mind if you think I'm a muppet." He laughed.

She thought he was laughing because he'd scored a point, but he was laughing because he was a muppet.

It was six thirty. Jim was dead to the world, head buried in his pillow, mouth slightly open. She laid the back of her hand on his cheek and instinctively he rolled his head around. She kissed him on the lips and he kissed her back.

She sent a text, then left.

When he woke he read it.

Had to go. See you soon. Love Jane.

Stafford was looking at the screen of his netbook. Jim's paramour, who had taken his photo, was none other than Acting Major General Jane Brown of the DIA and US Marines. His pager buzzed as he considered the consequences.

Jim was staring out of the window at a pile driver as it hammered the rusty braces of the copper dam into the foreshore forty feet in front of the window. He was dreaming of the coming excavation. What amazing artefacts were buried deep under the mud and rubble of the London dockside? If he could find such bizarre and interesting bits on the surface, how much more might be encased in the morass below? Every minute, at random intervals, there was a loud clang as a heavy weight on a vertical track lifted and fell from above on to the iron casing. It was whacking the wall section into the banks of the Thames, like a hammer driving a giant flat nail.

Bonk!

Jim sensed Stafford entering the room. "Come and sit down," he said.

Bonk! The pile driver crashed, and a ratcheting noise followed as the hammer was lifted.

"Dreadful racket," said Stafford, parking himself opposite.

Bonk! There was the chug of a primitive engine doing its jerky work.

"I've got some bad news and some good news," said Jim, absently.

"What is the bad news?" asked Stafford.

"I don't know how to say this, but your goddaughter, Tulip, is a call-girl – well, let's say a courtesan – working for dark forces." Jim studied Stafford closely for his reaction. "I'm afraid I got acquainted with her a bit too well."

Stafford knew he'd been rumbled. "I'm flabbergasted," he said, his face expressing cartoon shock. He leant forwards earnestly. "What is the good news?" His eyes narrowed intently.

"Well, I'm going to need a chairman for Barron. You're used to working in large secretive organisations so you'll know what to do."

"Large secretive organisations?" Stafford queried.

"You know," said Jim, "the Royal Household."

"Right you are," said Stafford, sitting back uncomfortably. "Of course."

"It'll be good money if you fancy it – a quarter of a million a year or something like that."

Stafford folded his arms. "I've never been particularly motivated by personal gain," he said, in a slow, measured voice.

"Well, you'll be like me and paying most of it to the government in tax, so I shouldn't let that hold you back." Jim smiled. "Think about it."

Stafford stood up. "I will," he said. He left the room and went to his quarters, where he took his suitcase from the built-in wardrobe. His target was going to compromise him. He put the suitcase down. He was retired: he could walk away from the mission and into the twilight there and then. Nobody would say anything but "Thank you".

He took his gold hunter from his pocket and flipped the lid open. It was one thirty p.m. A gentleman never retires before tea, he thought, and a player never retires full stop. He shut it and put it back into his pocket. He would remain in the crease and bat on.

Pierre stood by the entrance to the headmaster's wing. It had a stone portico that was somewhat weathered after two hundred years. From where he stood he could see the headmaster writing at his desk. England was a cold damp place. Even with the sun out and the sky blue, it was chilly. He felt utterly isolated in the school. The children were babies, soft and weak, like infants. They were friendly to him and he tried to be friendly back, but they were princes and children of rich, famous people: he had no understanding of their minds as they had none of his.

On the sports fields he could laugh and play with them but

he could be too rough for them. Compared even to the teachers, he had the soul of an old man. He was a veteran of a horrific world that was as far away and unfathomable to them as the one he now lived in was to him. He missed his homeland; he was a hostage and a prisoner of it. He was trying very hard not to let himself and Jim down.

He pulled at his shirt collar. Every morning when he saw himself reflected in the mirror while he did his hair he thought he looked like a Kinshasa politician in his school uniform – and perhaps one day that was what he would become. Meanwhile the collar chafed his neck. The children in the town from the other schools opened their collars and slipped their ties low as a mark of rebellion but not his school friends. They wore bow ties and upheld the uniform. Pierre understood uniform: it defined who you were and who were your allies and enemies. He shared this knowledge with his new friends.

A black Mercedes pulled into the car park and Pierre jumped up and down with delight. Jim got out of the front passenger seat and then the back doors opened. An African couple got out. They were both smartly attired, but the woman wore Congolese national dress.

Jim was smiling but Pierre was looking past him. His mouth fell open and he ran forwards. His parents threw their hands into the air and rushed to meet him.

"Maman! Papa!" he cried, throwing himself into his mother's embrace. He turned and grabbed his father. They were all crying.

"I'm sorry I didn't tell you," said Jim, "but I wanted to see the look on your face."

Pierre and his parents were delirious with joy.

Jim turned away, his eyes burning. The headmaster had come out to join them and was now watching the scene. Jim walked up to him. "Wonderful," said the headmaster. "truly wonderful."

"How's he getting on?" asked Jim.

"Surprisingly well," said the headmaster, "considering all he's been through."

"I'd like to help the scholarship programme a bit more," Jim told him.

"That would be most kind."

Pierre and his parents were talking and hugging. It was the happiest scene in the world.

Jim looked down at the cheque. It read: "One billion pounds only" and had his signature at the bottom. Stafford held out his bowler hat, which contained a series of folded paper slips in it. "I wonder which charity is going to be the lucky winner," said Jim, dipping his hand in and rootling about. He took one out and opened it. "And the winning charity is …" He looked up at Stafford. "Why does this have your name on it in your handwriting?"

Stafford affected a pained grin. "Very amusing, sir. Will that be all?"

"That's a very good question," said Jim.

## THE END

Here follows a short extract from
Clem Chambers' next book

*The Excalibur Trade*

which will be published in 2011

# 1

*April 2010*

Jim Evans sat forlornly at the end of the examination table. The doctor had been gone for thirty minutes and he had put his shirt back on. He was pretty surprised that, considering the stupendous amounts of money these private clinics charged, he had been left to sit semi-naked for so long without even a nurse poking her nose in to see if he was still there. What the hell was keeping the doctor?

Being rich and seeing doctors seemed to go hand in hand. Before he had made any money, his life had been a bit of squalor and a lot of health. Since wealth had entered his life through the front door, mayhem and destruction had come in through the back. He got off the table, put his shoes on and sat on the high leather armchair beside the doctor's desk.

He waited.

At last the door opened and the old doctor walked in. He didn't look very happy. He sat down by his desk, a folder in his hand, and looked at Jim. "I'm really sorry, but I can't help you."

The colour drained from Jim's face. "What is it?"

Now the doctor looked very unhappy indeed. He opened the folder and took out a sheet of paper with an image on it.

"This is not something I can deal with." He pointed at the picture.

"Is that me?" said Jim, peering at a ribcage with what looked like a large battery pack embedded in it.

"Yes."

"What is that?" he asked.

The doctor held his eyes. "Well, Mr Evans, you tell me."

"I don't know," he said, rubbing his face with both hands.

"Well, whatever it is, I'm not qualified to deal with it. What's more, whoever put it there clearly has a mandate."

"A mandate?" said Jim.

The doctor didn't reply.

"Can you take it out?"

"That would require replacing a large part of your ribcage," said the doctor. "In any case, whatever it is, it's probably doing a better job than anything I could replace it with."

Jim touched the area on his ribs where he felt the periodic twinge and where the scan showed a plate across three ribs. His fingertips couldn't detect the device.

"I'm sorry I can't help you," said the doctor, standing up. "I won't charge you for this consultation."

"Why?" said Jim, getting up.

"I'd prefer it if you didn't mention you'd seen me," the doctor said. He sounded as if he was trying not to plead.

"Don't worry," said Jim. "My friends did this to me."

"Really?" The doctor stiffened.

"Not the grenade injuries, you understand," said Jim, apologetically.

"Please don't tell me any more," said the doctor, and hurried to open the door.

# 2

*Tokyo, March 1970*

Akira Nakabashi was looking up at the cherry tree, trying to stare at the blossoms with the same blank concentration as his father. The pink flowers were pretty but, at six years old, he was soon bored with them. His father stood perfectly still, gazing up as the wind dislodged the fragile petals and blew them away.

"Father, what do you see that is so interesting?" Akira asked eventually.

"The cherry blossom is an ideal beauty," said his father. "It shows us a perfect existence. Its life is so joyous."

"But it falls so quickly."

"Is that not also beautiful?"

Akira looked down at the petals on the pavement. They seemed to melt into the oily black surface. Unlike most other people, Akira had no right arm. Instead his wrist was attached directly to his shoulder. His hand was uncomfortably hot beneath the layers of clothing that covered the awful family embarrassment.

He pulled his right hand up inside the sleeve of his coat and flapped it from side to side. "I'm glad I'm not a cherry blossom," he said. His father closed his eyes and sighed.

A passer-by noticed the flapping sleeve and Akira caught his eye. He brought his hand up from his armpit and let the sleeve hang at an impossible angle. The stranger gaped, then glanced away in shock. Akira's father peered down at him, an eyebrow raised. Akira dropped his hand and the sleeve fell into place. He had upset the passer-by and his father. He felt shame. Now his father looked angry.

Suddenly a gust of cold spring air blew straight into his father's face and lifted off his brown hat. He twisted around and ran back up the road to catch it. Another gust sent petals tumbling about Akira in a dense cloud. He swiped at them with his left arm as if they were a swarm of bees, laughing as they fluttered around him.

His father was watching him thrash at the petals. As they fell to the ground and eddied, he walked over to Akira and picked him up. "So, young Samurai," he said, tugging at the empty sleeve, "shall we cut these off all your clothes so your little arm can be free?"

"Yes," said Akira, happy in his father's embrace. "Yes."

"Fate has a purpose," his father said, and Akira nodded although he didn't understand what he'd meant.

"Let's get some *tako yaki* octopus balls," said his father.

The walk was long, but Akira didn't mind. To be alone with his father and to walk to the palace was a great event. His father worked there, in the royal bodyguard, as had his grandfather and his great-grandfather. He imagined himself marching like a soldier beside him.

"How much further?" he asked.

"Just around this corner."

The palace was set inside a giant moat with ramparts. The walls were made of flat-sided dark grey-green boulders, like a huge vertical jigsaw. Treetops towered above them from a mysterious garden, whose delights were shielded from view.

Akira's father stopped and lifted him onto a crude fence made of what appeared to be scaffolding posts. He looked down the sloping face of the wall into the dark waters below, then across to the impregnable walls. "Let me tell you about your great-grandfather."

Akira leant forwards in his father's grasp until he was almost hovering over the water.

"It is 1900 . . ."

# 3

*February 1975*

James Dean Yamamoto was driving as fast as his Harley Davidson would go, heading towards the meeting point for that night's unofficial Tokyo road race. His bike was far too slow to win, but winning wasn't the purpose of the Saturday race – or, for that matter, any other that he and the others took part in through the city. The purpose was ritual and spectacle.

Outlaws had their place in society, just as politicians and businessmen did, and racing was part of it. They made as much noise as they could as they tore along the city's roads. Rebellion and crime were part of everyday life, like sewers and rubbish tips, and on Saturday nights the garbage drove through the city, reminding sleepers that it was there and, in a strange way, kind of friendly. The bikers, the junkies, the crazy rebels, the mobsters — all were represented on their bikes, be they home-grown souped-up racers or fat, unreliable Harley hogs from America.

James Dean Yamamoto's Harley couldn't have been fatter or louder, its black paint spotless, its chrome shining in the late-night city lights. Locally made bikes — the Hondas, Kawasakis, Yamahas and Suzukis  had seats — but his machine had a saddle. His black leathers and peaked cap were a tribute to his other hero, Marlon Brando in *The Wild One*, but when he took his cap off he would comb his greaser quiff back in imitation of James Dean or Elvis, yet another of his American heroes. To the Western eye he was a crazy figure, a small Japanese guy who aped an American pose that even ten years ago, in the early sixties, had seemed dated. Yet to the citizens of Tokyo he looked dangerous and, as a member of the Yakuza crew, however peripheral, he was.

The hog suddenly began to misfire in a series of bangs and clunks. He tried to nurse it with the throttle but it rattled, coughed and was silent. He cruised into the kerb on a hill to the south of the Imperial Palace. He grimaced, resigned to missing the race. He tried to resuscitate the engine, turning it over with a series of kick-starts, but the Harley wasn't having it. The hog was dead.

He climbed off and took out a soft pack of Lucky Strike. The Harley would probably start again if he tightened the plugs. He'd wait for the engine to cool. He lit up with his Zippo, staring at the inert bike. Something caught his eye beside the fence that separated the pavement from the palace moat. It was a pile of clothes, neatly folded.

He took the cigarette from his mouth and walked over to it. Had someone jumped into the water? He looked over the rusty old barrier down the sloping side of the moat. A few feet below a child was clinging to the wall. Yamamoto looked away, took a drag of his cigarette then looked back.

The child, about eleven, was gazing up at him.

"What are you doing down there?" Yamamoto asked.

The child said nothing.

There was something funny about the boy. "Do you need help?"

"I don't know," said the child.

Yamamoto was peering at his right shoulder. The boy's hand seemed to come straight out of his armpit as if he had no arm. His wrist was plugged into this chest. "What are you doing down there?" he asked again.

"I was planning to swim the moat, but I'm stuck."

Yamamoto let out a short laugh. "That's brave," he puffed at the cigarette, "but pretty stupid." He looked down at the boy. His hand really did come out of his shoulder. He must be one of those drug-crippled kids. "If you fall you'll die."

"Yes."

"Do you want that?"

"It might be best."

"Let me pull you up," said Yamamoto. "You can always throw yourself into the moat another time."

"Please."

Yamamoto flicked his cigarette over the boy's head and into the moat. He lay flat out on the pavement, then crawled on his elbows under the barrier. Holding it with one hand, he leant down to the child below. His prized twelve-inch flick-knife slipped out of his top pocket and fell towards the boy, who caught it in his flipper-like right hand. The kid studied the illicit weapon with interest.

"Can I have that back?" asked Yamamoto, reaching down for it.

The boy lifted it the couple of inches he could manage and Yamamoto took it. He stuffed it into the back pocket of his jeans and leant forwards again. He grabbed the boy's forearm in a fierce grip. "Let go of the wall and take my arm." The kid grasped his wrist. "Now I'm going to pull you up and you have to do the best you can not to fall. Ready?"

The boy nodded.

"*Ichi, ni, san.*" He pulled, and the boy scrambled and slipped on the wall.

It was a very awkward lift, lying under the barrier, heaving the kid upwards. Yamamoto's shoulder struck the rusty metal — painful. Then the kid was above the lip of the wall and, with a lunge, rolled forwards and caught the barrier with his stunted hand.

The boy's face was beside Yamamoto's. "Have you got a good grip on the fence?" Yamamoto asked.

"Yes."

"I'm going to let you go, OK?"

"Yes."

He let go and the kid grabbed the barrier with his other hand. Yamamoto crawled out from under the barrier and stood up. The kid wriggled through. Yamamoto brushed himself down. The boy was naked but for his underpants. "You OK?" he asked.

"Yes," said the child, and went to his clothes. He picked up his shorts and put them on.

Yamamoto lit another Lucky Strike with a clink of his Zippo. The boy picked up his vest.

"A vest!" exclaimed Yamamoto. "What do you need that for? Men who would scale the walls of the Emperor's Palace don't wear vests."

He dropped the vest, picked up his socks and sat down to put them on. "They do wear shirts and jumpers, though, don't they?" he asked.

"Sure," said Yamamoto. He walked to his bike and examined the engine, then took his tool-kit from a saddlebag and tightened the plugs.

362

He looked up — the boy was watching him. "I owe you my life," he said, bowing low. "My name is Akira."

"James Dean Yamamoto," said Yamamoto, offering his hand.

Akira shook it. "How can I repay you?"

"That's a good question," said Yamamoto. He didn't want to embarrass the kid by laughing at the idea. "Tell you what — I'll run you home. Then, when I need you, I can come and call in my marker."

Akira made a little bow in agreement.

Yamamoto combed his quiff carefully, put on his cap and mounted the Harley. He wrestled it upright and kicked it into life. "Jump on, kid."

Akira thought perhaps he had fallen asleep – he was rushing through the sodium-lit streets of Tokyo on the back of a noisy black beast. He was dreaming surely – either that, or he'd died and gone to heaven  Yamamoto didn't seem to obey the lights at junctions or the speed limits. He simply flew down the streets with heroic skill and determination. They wove in and out of the late-night drivers and past police booths as if they weren't there. The minutes seemed like a lifetime to Akira, a lifetime that encompassed the seconds it took a butterfly to climb from its chrysalis or one fish to be bitten in half by another.

Yamamoto stopped at the end of his street and Akira got off.

"Thank you," said Akira.

Yamamoto pushed his hat back. With a grumble of rolling consonants, he said, "Remember, kid, don't be a little prick."

Akira nodded. "I won't."

*

Akira's father looked into the boy's room. It was empty. There was a folded piece of paper on the pillow. He switched on the light, unfolded it and read, "Father I have gone to swim the moat like our grandfather. Then perhaps I will be worthy. If you read this tonight please do not come for me. If you read this in the morning do not be sad. Your loving son, Akira."

He stood up, his mouth distorted. He was angry and he was proud. A host of conflicting emotions boiled in his heart. He left the room. His wife was standing at their bedroom door. "I'll deal with this," he said quietly.

He parked on the road that led up around the east ramparts of the palace near to the spot he had taken his son all those years ago to see where his own grandfather had swum the moat and scaled the walls into the palace garden. His grandfather had been a street urchin, whose father was dead and whose mother was bedridden. Several times he had invaded the gardens in search of little trinkets, such as the golden bells that hung in the trees, to bring back and sell. No one saw him, except the Meji Emperor, who watched him from behind the shutters, flitting from bush to bush. It was a little delight to the melancholy old man.

Then one day the child was discovered and the Emperor intervened. He ordered that the urchin be taken under the protection of the Imperial Household. In time he had joined the imperial retinue, a bodyguard to the family. Then his son had followed him. The family had enjoyed three generations as royal retainers — but Akira could not continue the tradition.

Now his only male child had sought to prove himself or perish trying. It was right and proper that he should be proud but that was not how he felt. He felt as if his guts were being wrenched out.

He spotted something white by the barrier and went over to it. He recognized Akira's string vest, clenched it in his fist and gazed down into the dark waters below. "Akira," he called. He waited. "Akira," he called again, at the top of his voice this time. The road behind him was empty and the buildings around looked down on his desolation. "Akira," he called, a third time. He would not call again.

As he walked towards his front door, it opened and his wife stood there, smiling. His heart jumped. "Our son is back," she whispered.

He went straight to Akira's bedroom and slid open the door. "Are you awake, son?"

Akira sat up. "Yes, Father."

"Where have you been?"

"I went for a swim across the moat."

He knelt down by the bedroll. "And how was it?"

"I could not climb far enough down the wall."

For a moment his father was silent. Then he asked, "What did your adventure teach you?"

"Not to be a little prick."

Where had his son picked up those words and that pronunciation? He stood up, confused, and looked down at his child. "I'm very glad you came back." He turned away.

Akira trudged homewards, his satchel on his back. His face was grazed and his blazer dirty down the right side. The bullies had roughed him up again — a daily humiliation. His eyes widened. There was a black Harley at the end of the street and James Dean Yamamoto was astride it, smoking. Akira couldn't help but run towards him.

"Hey, kid," said Yamamoto. "I've got a job for you."

"Great," said Akira. "Anything. What is it?"

"I need you to take a package to someone."

"Yes," said Akira.

"Now."

"OK."

"It will be dangerous."

"I don't mind."

Yamamoto reached into one of his saddlebags and pulled out a small brown-paper parcel. "Take this to this address." He pulled out a piece of paper. Akira put the parcel in his satchel and examined the directions. Getting there would be an adventure.

Yamamoto took out five 1000-yen notes from his pocket and gave them to him. "This is for you too. I'll run you close, then you make the drop-off and find your way home."

"Yes."

"Hey, kid, don't say yes," he waved his cigarette, "say, 'Sure.'"

"Sure," said Akira.

Akira waited nervously at the door. It slid open and a pretty woman in a dressing-gown was looking down at him. "Are you Miss Mai?"

"Yes," she said, smiling.

"I have a package for you." He swung his satchel off his back and took it out.

"Thank you," she said. She ruffled his hair, went inside and closed the door.

He put his satchel on again and ran down the steps to the street.

Akira took his favourite *Manga* comic from its position on the end of the bookshelf and put the four 1000-yen notes between the pages. The change from the taxi ride was in his pockets and he would think about spending some of it tomorrow on his way home. He might buy his mother some flowers, perhaps some sweets for his sisters. He wondered whether he would see James Dean Yamamoto again. Surely he had not repaid his debt so easily. He hoped not.

"Are you John Wayne?" he asked the tall, fat American, who stood on the corner of the street.

The American practically jumped into the air. "Yes, I am," he said, flushing red.

"Do you have something for James Dean?" read Akira from the note he had been given.

John Wayne glanced around furtively. "Yes."

Akira took the heavy package from his satchel and gave it to the American, who pulled a fat envelope from his back pocket and handed it to him. "You're a bit young for this kind of thing, aren't you?" said the American, uneasily, looking at Akira's short arm.

While Akira didn't understand a word of the English the man had spoken, he recognized the look. It was one of horror.

As he put the envelope in his satchel and bowed, the American was walking away.

James Dean Yamamoto was sitting on his Harley at the end of the road. He gave Akira a 10,000-yen note on receipt of his package.

"Why so much?" asked Akira, putting the money in his pocket.

"It was a heavy package," said Yamamoto. He pulled out a piece of paper and gave it to Akira. "Come to my place tomorrow. I need to talk with you about some stuff."

"Sure," said Akira.

His mother was waiting in the hallway. "Why are you coming home so late?" she asked gently. "And why are you always so scratched and battered?"

"I fall over a lot," he said.

She knelt in front of him and looked at the arm of his jacket, which was scuffed. It had a new tear in it. She examined it closely, then noticed the new cuts on his knees. "You must be more careful."

"Sure," he said.

She frowned at him sternly, then vigorously brushed the dust from his arm.

"Don't just stand there," said Yamamoto. "Come in."

Akira walked into the small flat. The curtains were drawn and it was in deep shadow. "Come into the kitchen," said Yamamoto. They went through the living room, and Akira sat down at a low breakfast table as Yamamoto took a beer from the fridge. "Want one?" he asked, looking closely at Akira, a cigarette hanging precariously from his mouth.

"No, thank you."

Yamamoto sat down at the table, the chair back to front.

"You know, Akira, what you've been doing for me is kind of illegal."

"How can delivering a package be illegal?"

"Well, it depends what's in the package." Yamamoto stubbed out his cigarette and lit another.

"Can I have one?" asked Akira.

Yamamoto looked at his cigarette as if to say, "One of these?"

Akira waited.

Yamamoto offered him the packet. Akira took one and Yamamoto lit it for him. He sucked the smoke into his mouth and blew it out in a long jet. "Well, I don't care," said Akira. "I want to work for you."

"That's fine, but I want you to know you can stop anytime you like."

"You're my only friend," said Akira.

"Surely not."

"Yes." He felt suddenly very sad. "Every day, after school, three little pricks trip me up and roll me on the ground and every day nobody does anything." He held the smoking cigarette in his armless hand and turned his head to drag on it. "A friend would help me."

"Wait a second." Yamamoto got up and left the room.

Akira tried to flick the ash from his cigarette like an experienced smoker. He failed.

Yamamoto came back. He turned his chair the right way around and put a roll of coins on the table. "Hold these in your fist."

Akira stubbed out his cigarette and took the object. It was a stack of 100-yen coins held together by nut and bolt. It poked out at either side of his fist. It felt heavy.

"If you're going to work for me, you've got to be able to handle yourself."

Akira looked at the bar in his fist and then at Yamamoto.

Yamamoto held up his palm. "See my hand. Imagine it's the face of your worst enemy. You need to punch that face straight on the nose."

Akira pushed his fist out slowly to Yamamoto's palm and touched it where the imaginary nose would be.

"Next time you see one of those arseholes, just walk up to him and punch him on the nose, then walk away. Never walk with your knees when you can talk with your fists."

"Sure," said Akira.

# 4

Akira walked through the school gate into the playground, his three torturers were standing near the front door, talking. His heartbeat quickened as he looked at them. Then he remembered standing naked against the wall, high above the black moat water, shivering on the warm summer night. In time his legs would have given out and he would have fallen down the wall into the water below. Only the miracle appearance of James Dean Yamamoto had saved him from a horrid death. Yet he hadn't been scared of that and he was proud to know it. If he could brave death he could brave attacking his enemies.

He held the coins tightly in his hand and walked up to the boys. Yasuda, the chief bully, watched him approach. "What do you want, Mr Cripple?"

Akira waved his shoulder hand by way of decoy and struck Yasuda with a blow he aimed as instructed at the boy's nose. Yasuda bent double, blood suddenly pouring out of him in long red streams. Akira turned and walked away, the sound of his breath and his pounding heart drowning the cries of his victim.

A bell rang, the school door opened and the children walked towards it obediently, staring in surprise and shock at Yasuda, bent and bleeding on the threshold.

Akira filed past him as a teacher ran to the injured Yasuda's aid.

Yasuda wasn't in class that morning, or in the afternoon, and the usual reception party was not there to greet Akira after school. His hand hurt, but it was a good pain.

The next morning he arrived as the school door was unlocked. Across the playground his three tormentors waited, Yasuda with plasters over his nose. Should he go over and punch him again? That seemed too much. Akira stood on the other side of the playground, his face blank. They were throwing evil looks in his direction but they were not coming his way. The bell went and the children filed in.

All day long he sensed the venomous cloud emanating from the three bullies. As the day drew on their stares became threatening. Then classes were over. Akira made straight for the door. He could tell they were after him — he could feel their presence looming behind him as he had so many times before. They would catch him by the school gate or soon thereafter and, as the other children passed him, they would rough him up.

As he saw the playground gate and the road beyond, he imagined Yamamoto sitting on his Harley by the kerb, challenging him to act. He took the coin bar from his pocket and turned. They were only a few feet behind him. Yasuda seemed surprised to see him ready to confront them. Akira punched him in that instant, exactly on the nose. Yasuda folded in half as he had buckled before — but this time he let out a howl, as if he had been mortally wounded. Akira moved to punch Umebayashi but the boy jumped back. Akira turned and walked to the gate.

He heard the roar of an engine and James Dean Yamamoto pulled up. "Jump on, kid," he said, surveying the scene. The children looked on in shock and awe as Akira climbed onto the back of the Yakuza man's motorbike. The Harley grunted away.

Akira's father sat down at the low dinner table. His mother and sisters got up and left the room. His father sipped his tea. "Show me your hand."

Akira held out his arm across the table. His hand was bruised and swollen, the knuckles heavily grazed. His father moved the fingers. "Nothing broken," he said, letting go. "The school has complained that you struck one of the other children. Is this how you injured your hand?"

Akira remembered James Dean Yamamoto's words. "I was tired of falling on my knees, so I spoke with my fist," he replied, in a mangled version of his mentor's advice.

His father stiffened and gave Akira a long look. Then he smiled. "Let me see that hand again."

Akira held it out. His father examined the swollen knuckles. "No wonder the child is not returning to your school." He called to his wife and the family returned to the table.

Akira wondered whether the huge fat guy in his dressing-gown was a Sumo wrestler. The man gave him a thick envelope in exchange for the package he had handed over and slammed the door in his face.

That didn't seem right to him. When he met people at their addresses they were normally happy to see him, and kind. He looked carefully about the street as he turned away.

There were a couple of men across the road in the sort of raincoats his father wore. His stomach lurched and his heart began to pound. He walked quickly along the pavement, trying to keep his eye on them. He could feel them coming after him just as he had felt the bullies behind him at school.

He walked down into the subway and began to run as soon as he thought he was out of sight. He followed the signs for the platforms and picked up another route to another exit. He came out on the other side of the road and as he did so he spotted another man in a raincoat fifty yards away. Akira walked into a department store. He raced through the rows of merchandise and out through another door, ran in front of a cab, waving, and jumped in. He gave the driver Yamamoto's address and slumped in the back seat as low as he could. The driver pulled away. Akira couldn't look out of the window for fear of being seen. He counted the seconds as the cab moved slowly with the traffic. He would sit up once he reached three hundred.

"Policemen, huh?" said Yamamoto. "Well done for giving them the slip." He slapped a 10,000-yen note on the kitchen table and picked up his beer glass. "That's for you. For surviving your first chase."

Akira flicked the ash from the cigarette in his short hand into the ashtray a foot away. He took the note and pushed it into the top pocket of his blazer. "What does it mean?"

"Time for you to lie low."

Akira's heart sank. "For long?"

"I don't know." He swigged his beer. "We have to be careful. You're too good to waste on a stupid deal."

Akira smiled. "OK."

*

Akira sat by the concrete flyover pillar and looked down into the green canal water. It had become a daily ritual to go there on his way home and smoke two cigarettes. It was a private place to wait and think. His days without a mission were passing slowly. He longed for James Dean Yamamoto to be parked at the end of the road, waiting for him, engine running. Yet the days had rolled into weeks and he felt that the gates to his magical world of excitement and adventure had slammed shut.

Someone was approaching. He looked up and saw a grey-brown figure in a raincoat. It was his father. Akira stood up smartly from his crouch.

"Quiet smoke?" his father enquired.

Akira relaxed a little. He was not furious with him for smoking, it seemed.

A moment later Akira had his Zippo out and was offering to light his father's cigarette.

"I thought I should seek you out," his father said, after he'd had his first puff. "Your mother is worried about you."

"Worried?"

"Yes."

"She didn't worry when I came home every day beaten."

"Certain hardships she expects. She wonders why you often come home so late."

Akira swapped his cigarette into his short arm, took a drag and said nothing.

"So this is where you come?"

"Sometimes."

"Friends?"

Akira turned his head to his right hand and puffed. "I

don't have friends. Other kids think they will catch something from me."

"That is their loss."

Akira flicked his cigarette into the canal. "Shall we go home?"

"Yes — your mother is waiting and worrying."

# 5

Akira glanced out of the schoolroom window as the bell rang. James Dean Yamamoto was parked on the road. He jumped up from his desk. The other children were heading for the next class, but he went through the empty corridors to the floor below, out to the yard and sprinted into the street. He stepped in front of a tree that covered the view from the school and Yamamoto rolled his bike to him. His face was cut and bruised. "Jump on, kid."

Akira loved the little coffee shop. The owner welcomed him and Yamamoto as if they were brothers and didn't question why Yamamoto was with a crippled child in school uniform. Akira ordered coffee like any adult would and was served as such. They sat in the wooden shack like the real outlaws of his comic books.

"What happened?" he asked finally.

"Trouble," said Yamamoto.

"No kidding," said Akira, in Yamamoto's style.

"I need to ask you a big favour."

"Sure."

"I need you to go to my place and get some things for me."

"Sure."

"It will be dangerous."

"OK."

Yamamoto gripped his right hand and squeezed it. "Very dangerous, Akira."

No one ever touched his short hand. No one dared. He squeezed his friend's hand as hard as he could. "OK. What do you need?"

"My gun. My money. A black book." He showed the diary's size with his forefingers and thumbs. "In the kitchen in the top drawer by the sink."

"You in big trouble?"

"Nothing I can't fix with my money, my gun and my little black book."

"Easy," said Akira.

"But people might be waiting for me outside. They mustn't get the book."

"OK."

"I'll drop you two streets away. Go in, get the stuff. Come straight out and back to me."

"OK."

The street outside the small, rundown apartment building was empty. His heart was racing as he entered and went up the stairs to Yamamoto's flat on the second floor. Nothing stirred. He put the key into the lock and turned it slowly, then pushed the door open. He looked inside. The light was out in the living room and through the gloom he could see it was empty. He went in and closed the door. It felt safer now he was inside, unnoticed. He moved towards the kitchen and opened the door slowly. It was empty too. The table was covered with beer bottles and the ashtray was full, as if Yamamoto had been entertaining friends.

Akira moved to the sink and opened the drawer

immediately to the right. There was a pile of tea-towels but no gun or money — until he lifted the folded linen. Bundles of cash lay on the right side of the drawer, with a pistol and a black book, held closed with an elastic band. Akira picked up the gun. It was a shiny, stubby chrome revolver with a black rubber handle and no hammer, heavy in his hand. He stuffed it into his blazer pocket. He put the book into his inside pocket, then loaded the cash into his satchel. Yamamoto's stash had to add up to millions and millions of yen. To Akira, it was a fortune of neatly bundled notes. It was in fact around four million, a good proportion of James Dean Yamamoto's life's earnings. The satchel felt as if it had books in it.

He went to the living-room window and tried to look out. There was nothing to be seen from its highly restricted view. He put his ear to the front door and listened. He heard nothing. He opened the door slowly. The landing was empty. He closed the door and walked down the stairs.

On the ground floor, two figures were slouched in the hallway, dressed in leathers, smoking and talking gangster. At the front door, space was tight — the mailboxes left barely enough room for two people to pass. Akira put his hand into his jacket pocket and took the pistol by the handle.

One of the figures glanced at him. He scuttled past them to the door, twisted the handle and went outside. The air felt good as he trotted into the street. He ran up the lane and back through the alleys to James Dean Yamamoto, who kick-started his engine as soon as he saw him.

"Did you get the stuff?"

"Sure."

"All of it?"

"Sure."

"Was the coast clear?"

"No."

The bike surged off.

Akira was in his history class. No one had noticed he had been gone for nearly three hours. Truancy didn't exist so the school was not equipped for it. If he had left the building, it must have been for a good reason, such as a trip to the optician. There were no guards in the prison camp, no tripwires to snare transgressors. He had slipped between the sunlit world of children to his dark adventure land unnoticed, like a student between a lecture and a daydream.

On the first Wednesday of every month Akira would travel to the coffee shop in Roppongi and from five until six he would drink, smoke and wait. He had visited James Dean Yamamoto's flat on several occasions but it had been empty. Until the last time: then a woman had answered the door and he had glimpsed new furniture and family life, which meant this was no longer Yamamoto's home.

Akira's fourteenth birthday had come and gone. He passed the cigarette from his short hand to his long hand and stubbed it out. He would leave soon and not return for another month. Perhaps his friend was in prison . . . dead, even.

A figure came through the door, a salary man, out of the rain of a dark blustery Tokyo evening. Akira started. If the man had had a quiff, sideburns and a little less weight, he could almost have been Yamamoto. The man was coming towards him. Akira tried to focus in the dim brown light of the coffee-shop shack. He found himself standing up.

"Sit down, kid," said Yamamoto, plonking himself on the bench across from him.

"James Dean — at last."

"I've been busy," he said, lighting a Lucky Strike. A pot of coffee, with a porcelain cup and saucer, was delivered to the table without reference to an order. Yamamoto acknowledged the café owner with a nod. "I've been busy lying low."

"I'm glad you came. Have you a job for me?"

"Yes — but first I have to tell you I'm going to disappear. Maybe for good."

"Why?"

"It's right for me and it will be right for you." He looked around as someone came in, then turned back to Akira. "Look, kid, I've got this idea and it could be big. I've got to cut myself free of the past and take a shot at the moon. This town is going to go crazy and I'm going to ride the madness. But first the old James Dean Yamamoto has to die so that the new one can be born." He pushed his little black book across the table. "I want you to keep this safe for me."

Akira took it. "Sure."

"And I've got you a present." Yamamoto took out his flick-knife and gave it to him. "This is for you."

Akira picked it up and passed it to his short hand. He pressed the silver button halfway down the handle and the blade clicked open. "Thank you," he said. He twisted the lock with his thumb and folded the blade shut.

"Well, this is it, kid," said James Dean Yamamoto, getting up. "Remember, don't be a little prick."

"Will I ever see you again?"

Yamamoto smiled and patted his own head, as if the quiff was still there. "You never know, kid."

# 6

Akira looked from the palace rampart to the far wall of the moat. He squinted, imagining that if he could focus his eyes just so he would see himself thirty years before, clinging to the far wall.

"And what of the mirror, Sensei Nakabashi?"

Akira snapped out of his daydream. "The mirror? Oh, that's very difficult — not even the Emperor can see the sacred mirror."

"So does it – or, for that matter, any of the imperial regalia — actually exist? After all, as curator of the imperial treasure you must be one of the few who know for sure."

"Yes, yes," he said, "of course it all exists. It has been at every coronation, as you surely know, since the beginning of history."

The two American professors were looking smugly at him. The tall stork-like woman from the New York Metropolitan Museum tilted forwards as if she was going to peck the top of his head. "Do you think you might be able to arrange for me to see the sword Kusanagi-no-Tsuragi?"

"Very difficult," said Akira. "The priests at Atsuta only

382

allow access to it for a coronation."

"And what of the Yasakani no Magatama?" asked the relaxed, informally dressed young man from the Getty in California.

"Very beautiful — and very difficult to see. The priests at Kashikodokoro cannot bear it to be placed at any risk. They guard it with every sinew. But I can tell you a secret about it. It is not *a* jewel, but many pieces of the most exquisite jade, a necklace held together by a golden chain."

"And you've seen it," said the improperly dressed Californian curator.

Professor Akira Nakabashi, keeper of the Sacred Imperial Treasures, waved his short hand at the honoured guests. "Please let me show you the view further along."

The two Americans smirked.

"I am very sorry to disappoint you," said Akira, looking up at them. "The imperial regalia are sacred items, drawn from the dawn of our history. They represent the very soul of the Japanese nation. They encapsulate imperial rights and status, the throne's authority, continuity and legitimacy. They are not items to be examined and tested. Not even by the Emperor himself." He smiled. "Please come this way — there is so much else to see."

**Clem Chambers** is CEO of ADVFN (www.advfn.com), Europe and South America's leading financial market website. Established in the last quarter of 1999, Chambers floated the company in 2000. The ADVFN website now has over 1,700,000 registered users. ADVFN is the number one destination for UK private investors, who log on to view global market data and use the site's leading edge trading tools.

A broadcast and print media regular, Clem Chambers is a familiar face and frequent co-presenter on CNBC and CNBC Europe. He is a seasoned guest and market commentator on BBC News 24, *Newsnight*, BBC 1, CNN, SKY News, TF1, *Working Lunch*, China's *Phoenix TV*, Canada's *Business News Network* and US radio. Clem is renowned for calling the markets and predicted the end of the bull market back in January 2007 and the following crash. He's appeared on ITV's *News at Ten* and *Evening News* discussing failures in the banking system and featured in the *Money Programme's Credit Crash Britain: HBOS – Breaking the Bank* and the BBC's *City Uncovered: When Markets Go Mad*.

Chambers has written investment columns for *Wired Magazine*, *The Daily Telegraph* and *The Daily Express* and currently writes for *The Scotsman* and *Forbes*. He was The Alchemist – stock tipster – in *The Business* for over three years and has been published in titles including: *CityAM*, *Investors Chronicle*, *Traders Magazine*, *Stocks and Commodities*, the Channel 4 website, *SFO* and *Accountancy Age*. He is a regular market commentator across all the main UK national press.

His first novel *The Armageddon Trade* was published by No Exit Press in 2009.

mailto: clemcham@advfn.com
http://twitter.com/clemchambers
http://en.wikipedia.org/wiki/Clem_Chambers
http://en.wikipedia.org/wiki/The_Twain_Maxim